DEAD END

Recent Titles by Brian Freemantle from Severn House

Sherlock Holmes

THE HOLMES INHERITANCE

Charlie Muffin

DEAD MEN LIVING
KINGS OF MANY CASTLES

AT ANY PRICE
BETRAYALS
DEAD END
DIRTY WHITE
GOLD
HELL'S PARADISE
ICE AGE
THE IRON CAGE
THE KREMLIN CONSPIRACY
THE MARY CELESTE
O'FARRELL'S LAW
TARGET
TWO WOMEN

DEAD END

Brian Freemantle

This first world edition published in Great Britain 2004 by
SEVERN HOUSE PUBLISHERS LTD of
9–15 High Street, Sutton, Surrey SM1 1DF.
This first world edition published in the USA 2005 by
SEVERN HOUSE PUBLISHERS INC of
595 Madison Avenue, New York, N.Y. 10022.

British Library Cataloguing in Publication Data

Freemantle, Brian, 1936-
    Dead end
    1. Human experimentation in medicine - Fiction
    2. Genetics - Research - Fiction
    3. Corporations - Corrupt practices - Fiction
    4. Suspense fiction
    I. Title
    823.9'14 [F]

    ISBN 0-7278-6106-9

To Victoria, the first who could never be last.

One

In such an internationally established, acclaimed and aggressive pharmaceutical conglomerate, there were obviously laboratories in every overseas division of Dubette Inc., but each was effectively a subsidiary of the North Virginia headquarters at McLean's Priority Park, just off the 495 Beltway. That laboratory was designed to a rigid structure that provided the name by which it was universally referred to: never Research and Development but always the Spider's Web, which was apposite. The office of the fittingly spindle-limbed, bespectacled vice president, Dwight Newton, was at the very centre of a concentric series of specialized research departments and divisions. Included here, because their cure or prevention was the Holy Grail of commercial medical research, were a variety of cancers, AIDS and its human immunodeficiency virus precursor, HIV, both A and B strains of hepatitis, the common cold and a variety of frequently mutating fatal influenza viruses. The final, outer circle was devoted to what was, with surprising unprofessionalism, suspiciously regarded as the new and unproven science of genetics and its engineering for medical benefit.

It was here that Richard Parnell had been allocated his laboratories.

Parnell liked America. He liked its can-do ethos and same-day deliveries of whatever he'd wanted to furnish the new, easily arranged apartment rented on the first day, and day-one car purchase – and most of all he liked the more than trebled salary that made everything affordable. And still left him with more money than he'd earned – apart, of course, from the international recognition that had resulted in his being head-hunted from Cambridge – as a leading participant in Britain's

1

considerable contribution to the global genome project codifying human DNA.

It was a reputation Parnell was determined to increase, which made his relegation to the outer circle an absurd and irritating dismissal he was about to rectify.

Like the spider's web after which it was nicknamed, the expanding circles were each linked by connected, threading corridors, all glassed and therefore all visible to everyone along his route to the vice president's inner sanctum. As he walked the gauntlet, Parnell was aware of the attention and recognition of people on either side, and recognized the point to the pretentious, outer-space laboratory design. No one could approach the spider-like man *without* being seen, to initiate the paranoia. *Is he being promoted over me? Have I made a dismissable mistake? Am I being reprimanded? Am I going to be fired?*

It was a good feeling, not to be afraid: to be sure enough of himself and his international reputation to do what he was about to do.

Professor Dwight Newton was thin to the point of being emaciated, a cadaverous face dominated – almost overwhelmed – by overly heavy, black-framed spectacles, stick-thin arms protruding from the sleeves of a white laboratory coat. Forewarned by his outside secretariat, Newton was standing, a tall man although still shorter than the broad-shouldered, athletically bodied Parnell.

'Good to see you again, Dick! Good to see you! Sorry it hasn't been sooner. Must say, though, I don't understand your memo . . .' There was a helpless sweeping gesture towards the empire beyond. 'So much to keep a handle on . . . never a moment . . .'

'It's a big operation,' acknowledged Parnell.

'The biggest, worldwide,' said Newton. 'And you're part of it now.'

Parnell said: 'That's what I very much want to be, part of it. But a proper part.'

Newton's affability went out like a switched-off light. He picked up and let drop Parnell's meeting request and said: 'So what's all this about keeping all your equipment on hold and not advertising for staff?'

2

'I've nowhere to put equipment. Or staff,' declared Parnell.

Newton gave an uncertain laugh. 'You've got your own internal laboratories! What . . . two separate working spaces, offices, secretarial space? Everything you could want . . . ?'

'In the wrong place. I've been appointed Dubette's professor of pharmacogenomics, applying what I did in England to drug development here. To do that, I need to be alongside the laboratories and the people developing those drugs. Not isolated as I have been.'

Newton frowned. 'Everything radiates out from what has to be the most tightly and securely controlled working area.'

'I didn't accept the offer here in order to be a totem, just a recognizable name on a staff list,' said Parnell. 'If I'm going to make any contribution to Dubette's research and development, I need to be at the centre of things. If I'm not, it makes quite pointless my being here, as part of the Dubette empire.'

Pinpricks of anger began colouring Newton's face. 'I don't believe Archimedes' principle came to him when he overflowed the bath water. Research here is programmed, according to a strict schedule of antibiotic exploration. Which is the business we're in.'

'I don't believe the Archimedes legend either. Nor see how it's supposed to fit what we're talking about,' rejected Parnell. 'It's now been recognized that the majority of what pharmaceutical industries produce does nothing to alleviate, help or – by the very worst analysis – save the lives of people they're supposed to help with the drugs they're offering. If I can create the proper research team, working in proper, liaising research with medical expertise, Dubette could revolutionize diagnostic approach. It's an approach already being tried in Europe, and one upon which I'm well advanced, from my work on the genome project.' Parnell, resigned to the thought that his job was over before it had begun, supposed he could always stay in Washington for an extended holiday, to minimize the loss on the apartment lease, and whatever else was non-refundable, before moving on. He was probably still within his relocation budget in any case.

There was another edge of uncertainty in Newton's laugh. 'You're talking as if you can walk away if you don't like the housing arrangements.'

3

'That's exactly how I'm talking.' Parnell was glad he hadn't advertised vacancies in his new department and given people false hopes.

'You forgotten you've got a legally enforceable contract, studied and agreed not just by Dubette's lawyers but your independent attorney as well?'

'It very specifically sets out in that contract that I shall have every research facility I might need. Which I don't have. I don't intend any ridiculous breach-of-contract litigation against Dubette. I'll just resign and we'll both put it down to experience.'

'*You* don't intend any litigation!' exploded the research director, incredulous. 'You think this organization lets people walk away just because they don't have a desk by the window!'

'I'm not complaining about not having a desk by the window,' retorted Parnell. 'I'm saying I do not have my contracted working conditions and facilities. Now tell me what you're saying. Are you telling me that if I resign, Dubette will take me to court?'

'You're damned right I am.'

'OK,' said Parnell, rising. 'I'll see the lawyer who negotiated for me, and get my resignation letter in to you in the next day or two.'

'Sit down,' ordered Newton, sharply. 'You've scarcely been here long enough to find the washroom. Let's not get off to a wrong start, the two of us. You want a change of location, I'll see what I can do. But if we're going to work together, there's something you've got to understand very clearly . . . I don't like – won't have – confrontations.'

'I don't want any wrong starts or confrontations, either,' said Parnell, easily. 'I accepted Dubette's approach precisely *because* I recognized the opportunity to extend genetic science through an international organization with huge research resources. That's all I'm asking for, that chance to do the work I came here to do. But can't.'

'Leave me to work it out.'

'So, I'll get the laboratory I want, where I want it?' persisted Parnell.

'That's confrontational!' accused the spindly man.

'That's honest,' contradicted Parnell.

'I said leave it with me,' insisted the American.

If he pushed any further – any harder – they'd both fall off the edge, Parnell accepted. 'I'm glad we've had this conversation.'

'So am I.'

Liar, Parnell thought. It was a trait he'd have to remember.

'I'm grateful for your staying late,' thanked Newton, who'd spent the afternoon with Dubette's in-house lawyers and didn't like what he'd been told.

'There's obviously a reason for your asking,' said Russell Benn. He was the large, black, rumbling-voiced scientific director of the predominant antibacterial research sections of the laboratory.

'We're going to have to move things around a little. Make some space,' announced the vice president.

Benn frowned. 'Space for what?'

'The English guy, Parnell, who's opening up the genetics section.'

'For what?' repeated the other man.

'He has to be part of the inner core, able to liaise with you.'

'I need all the space I've got,' protested Benn.

'This is how it's got to be, Russ: how I want it to be.' Newton enjoyed the power, knowing that people were actually frightened of him, as he, in turn, was frightened of Edward C. Grant. Newton promised himself he'd manipulate Parnell as he would a piece of modelling clay, until Parnell was as pliably obedient as he'd made everyone else in the research and development division.

Benn, who was trying to put three of his five sons through private school and had a mortgage lapping up to his chin, shrugged and said: 'It's going to upset things. My guys like their routines: knowing where they are.'

'It's what I want,' insisted Newton.

'If it causes problems, I'll need to talk to you about it,' said Benn, anxious to pretend he was not as intimidated as everyone else enmeshed in the Spider's Web.

'Do that!' urged the director, sincerely. 'The moment there's a problem, a conflict, I want to know about it.' That afternoon

5

the legal opinion had been that professional disruption affecting major research nullified Parnell's breach-of-contract claim and provided Dubette with a matching pressure to keep him in line: an outer, not an inner line.

Two

Richard Parnell's reassigned research area was directly in line with the vice president's office, which Parnell supposed was intended to be intimidating but wasn't. He was far more interested in the newly arrived equipment, everything he'd requested without a single budgetary challenge. Which was what he told Russell Benn at their first meeting after his transfer.

'Glad you're satisfied,' said the other man, the voice seeming to come from deep within him.

Parnell at once discerned the resentment. 'I'd like to think we're going to get on together.'

'So would I.'

'Why don't we establish our parameters right now?'

'Why don't we?' echoed Benn.

He was pushing against a closed door, thought Parnell. 'I'm here to head up a new pharmacogenomics division, right?'

The black scientist nodded.

'That involves me – or the people who are going to join me – employing what was discovered during the genome project to drug development. Which is your division, so we're going to have to work pretty closely together, wouldn't you agree?'

'You really think you can make a contribution genetically to what we do here?' demanded Benn.

'You accept that more than ninety per cent of the drugs produced – drugs *we* produce – are only effective upon between thirty to fifty per cent of the people for whom they're prescribed!'

'I've heard the figures. I think they're debatable.'

'And you've heard of single-nucleotide polymorphisms?'

6

'Genetically matching a person to the most efficacious drug? Sure I've heard of it.'

'But aren't impressed by it?' challenged Parnell.

'I'm waiting to be convinced.'

'*Abacavir,*' threw back Parnell, at once.

'OK,' conceded the other man. 'So, genetically it has been established that abacavir is a drug that could, potentially, be fatal to about five per cent of HIV sufferers in AIDS treatment.'

'And brings out violent skin reaction, rashes, in those to whom it isn't fatal?' persisted Parnell.

'I've read the findings and the stats.'

'Scientifically accepted findings and statistics,' insisted Parnell. 'Like there's general scientific acceptance that single nucleotide polymorphisms could not only test people's vulnerability to a particular drug's side effects but also whether or not it will work at all.'

'You want coffee?' the other man invited suddenly, making a vague movement to a percolator on a side table upon which several mugs, all loyally marked with the Dubette logo, were laid out in readiness.

Parnell recognized it as a gesture. 'Coffee would be good.'

'You know your stuff,' said Benn, as he poured.

'You were testing me!' accused Parnell.

'Wasn't that what you were doing with me?'

'No!' denied Parnell. 'I was trying to build a bridge for both of us to cross.'

'Seems to me you're arguing against superbug resistance?'

The awkward bastard was still testing, Parnell decided. 'I think – and intend to prove – that pharmacogenomics could become successful enough to reduce antibiotic resistance or rejection.'

The other scientist fixed him with a direct stare, unspeaking for several moments. Then he said: 'Am I hearing what you're saying?'

'It's a self-defeating ladder, developing stronger antibiotics when resistance makes useless those that already exist. Making cocktails of drugs, a lot of the constituents of which are totally ineffective and can even be harmful, is bad medicine. The logic can only be the build-up of even greater resistance which in turn needs even greater – stronger – antibiotics. It's happened worldwide with methicillin-resistant *staphylococcus aureus*. We're breeding our own superbugs from superbugs, not eradicating anything.'

'Eradicating?' picked out Benn, at once.

'Isn't eventual eradication the focus of medical science?' frowned Parnell.

'*Medical science*,' heavily qualified Benn. 'Our focus is pharmaceutical research and developing and improving drugs to combat known diseases.'

'Aren't they allied?'

'I suppose that's a point of view,' allowed the section director, doubtfully.

'It's always been mine.'

'You haven't yet been to a company seminar, have you?' asked Russell Benn.

'Not yet,' said Parnell.

'There's one soon. You'll find it interesting.'

'I am finding this conversation interesting,' said Parnell, directly. 'Interesting as well as confusing.'

'Did you know that years ago tyre manufacturers perfected a tyre that never wears out: if they were fitted to cars and trucks they'd last the lifetime of the vehicle.'

'No, I didn't know that,' encouraged Parnell, who did, but wanted the analogy expanded.

'Planned obsolescence,' declared Benn.

'Yes,' said Parnell.

'I think you're right,' declared Benn, on another tangent. 'I think there could be work we could do together.'

'There can't be any doubt: we're virtually the left and right hand, each having to know what the other's doing and how we can each realistically decide how to complement the other, towards a successful development.' He'd gone straight from Cambridge University into the rarefied atmosphere of pure medical research, Parnell reminded himself. But he wasn't in any rarefied atmosphere any longer. He was in the real, hard-headed commercial world now. How difficult would the adjustment be?

*   *   *

8

'Hi!'

Parnell looked up from *Science Today*, beside his unseen, stabbed-at lunch, to the dark-haired girl smiling down upon him. 'Hi.'

'This seat taken?'

'Help yourself.' He stood politely, taking her tray as she unloaded the sandwich and a pickle, the same choice he'd made. He saw there were several alternative empty tables throughout the commissary.

'My name's Rebecca.'

'I know,' said Parnell. The ID tag hanging from her neck chain matched the nameplate on her white laboratory coat, both reading 'Rebecca Lang.'

'And I know that you're Richard Parnell,' she said, reading his identification.

'Name badges, one of the great American innovations,' acknowledged Parnell. He closed the journal.

'You don't have to do that – stop reading, I mean.'

'Of course I do.' He sliced his sandwich, salt beef on rye, more easily to eat.

'Now I feel uncomfortable.' She bit into her sandwich without cutting it.

'No, you don't.'

She smiled again, her teeth a tribute to attentive dentistry and teenage torture. Confident that she didn't need any more facial help, Rebecca wore only a light lipstick, pale pink like her nail colouring. 'All right, so I don't. Want to know a secret?'

'Sure.' Parnell heard his own word and thought it sounded American. An early resolution was that he wouldn't let himself relapse into any idiom. It was one of several preconceptions.

She nodded generally around the restaurant. 'It was a bet, who got to talk to you first.'

'Talk to me first!'

'The mysterious and famous foreigner publicly known for his work on the genome project!'

'And you won?'

'I'm here talking to you, so I guess I did.'

'I'm English, which is hardly mysterious. And a lot of people

9

are known for what they did on the genome project. It was an international effort, involving many people.'

Rebecca nodded to the closed magazine. 'It's you everyone wrote about.'

'What's your prize?' Parnell wished he could go back to *Science Today*.

'Who knows?' It wasn't a coquettish remark.

'What section are you in?' If he had to talk, it might as well be professional.

'Back of the bus stuff, co-ordinating and cross-referencing overseas research with what we're doing here, where it's applicable. Flagging up stuff that might be worthwhile our pursuing further, concentrating upon.'

'I'd say that makes you a pretty important person, too.'

She sniggered. 'There are a lot of units. I don't do it all by myself!'

'Any breakthroughs?'

The girl hesitated. 'Not yet. Ever hopeful.'

'Still quite a responsibility for someone who considers themself at the back of the bus.'

'There's a line manager checking me and a section head checking him. It's all very structured. Haven't you appreciated everything's run here to a tightly ordered and controlled set of rules?'

'I'm beginning to get the idea.'

'I told you my secret. Now tell me yours.'

Parnell looked blankly at her. 'I don't know what you're asking.'

'How come you got shifted so quickly from the back of the bus?'

Parnell no longer regretted putting his magazine aside, trying to separate the discordant echoes of this exchange from the earlier one with Russell Benn. 'How can you imagine there's something secret about it, just like that?' He snapped his fingers.

'Everything's very structured,' she emphasized again. 'You were given your space but you moved it.'

'It was temporary,' avoided Parnell.

Rebecca regarded him doubtfully over her coffee mug, her sandwich abandoned half eaten. 'You're at the heart of the Spider's Web now. That's where the real research is.'

10

'And where I want – and need – to be to fulfil my appointment and justify the creation of the new department,' said Parnell.

'*You* want to be,' she isolated, at once.

'Where I have to be,' Parnell reiterated.

'You really think genetics could bring about miracles?'

'No,' Parnell immediately answered. 'I think it's an avenue with medical benefits that has to be explored, to discover what its engineering can achieve.' And I'm going to be among the first to achieve it, he promised himself.

'I don't think he's our sort of team player,' judged Russell Benn.

'It'll take time,' predicted Dwight Newton. 'In time he'll learn – or come to accept – the way things work here.'

'I'm not so sure.'

'Keep a tight handle on things, Russ. On him the tightest of all. You think there's anything I've missed, you come tell me right away. I don't want any disruption to the smooth way things always work here.'

'I know you don't,' said the black scientist. 'But he's got a proven track record. I've got an odd feeling, an instinct, that professionally he'll be useful.'

'Sufficiently useful to put up with his attitude problem?'

'Arrogance is an irritation, not a cause for censure,' said Benn. 'I'm suggesting we let things run their way for a while, to discover for ourselves how good he really is.'

'That's what we've got to decide,' agreed Newton. 'Just how good he is.'

'And how amenable he can be made to commercial reality,' came in Benn, on a familiar cue.

Three

It was Richard Parnell's first ever commercial-firm seminar and even though he was not looped into the internal machinations of Dubette Inc., he was conscious of a frisson ruffling the faint strands of the Spider's Web. It was, however, peripheral to his establishing himself in his new, inner-circle surroundings, which, coincidentally, on the day of the seminar, he finally completed. To achieve his self-imposed deadline, Parnell got to his section by six to supervise the technicians' last installations, and was fully set up, with time for an unhurried breakfast of an egg-topped corned beef hash. He saw Rebecca Lang's approach from some way off. The nameplated laboratory coat was replaced by a dark grey business suit which, by the severity of its cut, showed off an even more attractive figure than he'd imagined. There was more make-up, too, mascara and eye shadow: Parnell preferred her without either.

He smiled and said: 'Hi again. What did you win?'

She didn't reply, stopping to look down at him, as she had the day of the supposed bet. 'No one told you? Bastards!'

'Told me what?'

'Grant's addressing us. He always does.'

'I was told.'

'There's a dress code. He likes formality.'

Parnell looked down at his sweatshirt, jeans and loafers before coming back up to her. 'You are joking, aren't you – about it being important how we're dressed?'

'No.'

'I think it's funny, even if you don't. Anything that stupid has got to be funny.'

'I don't think it's funny.'

'I'll hide myself in the crowd,' promised Parnell.

But he couldn't. The seats were designated and his was in the second row, directly in front of an already emplaced podium on a higher dais. Behind the podium were seats for the parent-company directors and the chief executives from Dubette's overseas divisions. Parnell was aware of the attention and the frowns of those around him as he edged along his reserved line to his assigned place.

Parnell sensed the stir and rose with everyone else at the entry of the governing directors on to the raised area, led by Edward C. Grant. The president was a small, bull-chested man, the whiteness of his hair heightened by a deep tan. The man made his way across the stage with the confidence of someone who knew seas would part if he demanded it. He wore a dark blue suit that Parnell realized had been copied by virtually everyone surrounding him. Parnell's sweatshirt was yellow and he accepted that he stood out like a beacon. Being 6'2" made him even more of a lighthouse among his smaller neighbours. When the president came to the podium for his keynote address, Parnell at once became Grant's unremitting focus. Parnell stared back unperturbed. He'd heard of commercial companies ruled like medieval fiefdoms, but always imagined the stories exaggerated by those in pure research, to reassure themselves they were right to remain aloof in cosseted scientific academia.

The past year had been more successful than that preceding it, opened Grant. There had been a 20 per cent increase in after-tax profits, which he was later that month going to announce to the stockholders, with a recommendation for an overall salary increase. The excellence of the research division gave every expectation of new or improved drugs being introduced into the marketplace: medical breakthroughs even. They could not, however, relax. Competition was intense and would remain so: increase even. Turning to acknowledge one of the men assembled behind him, Grant said there had been, from their French subsidiary, a suggestion how to thwart reverse-analyses of their more successful drugs. It was essential to guard against that, from their competitors, as it was against their products being pirated by such analyses, particularly by Third World countries pleading poverty as an excuse for manufacturing their own cheaper versions from published formulae, denying companies like themselves the profits essential to recover their huge and continuing research expenditure. During the past year Dubette had initiated twenty-three patent and copyright infringement actions in ten countries, and so far had succeeded in fifteen, with every confidence of the remaining eight being adjudged in their favour. Although too large and too diverse properly to fit the description, Grant nevertheless considered Dubette a family structure, people working together, pulling together, according to a strictly observed set of understandings, like a united, cohesive household. Parnell went through the motions of clapping, along with everyone else, and thought that the individual presentations from chief executives of Dubette's foreign-based divisions that followed sounded exactly like an end-of-term report to the headmaster.

They funnelled into a lounge of easy chairs and potted plants that adjoined the commissary. Today the furniture had been rearranged to create an open communal space. Premixed drinks were already laid out on a bartended table that ran the full length of the glassed wall overlooking the grassed park and its artificial lake. Parnell noted the concentration of people helping themselves was around the mineral-water selection. He saved himself the search by asking one of the barmen for gin and tonic.

He'd separated from Rebecca Lang at the entrance to the conference room and not seen where she'd sat. He saw her now, though, among the mineral-water group. She saw him when she turned, hesitated and then made her way towards him.

Parnell said: 'We got a cure for leprosy among what we make?'

She smiled and said: 'That bad?'

He grinned back. 'You're risking infection, just talking to me.'

'I'll check our stock list, see what there is that I can take.' She had to tilt her head to look up at him. 'You sure grew up big when you were small.'

'I worked out and ate up all my greens.'

'Dubette should patent the formula.'

'You didn't tell me what you won.'

'You don't want to know.'

There was a shift throughout the room at the arrival of the president with a retinue of division and overseas directors, a general turning in their direction. Parnell said: 'It's your last chance to escape.'

From where he stood, and with his height, Parnell could see better than Rebecca the approaching dignitaries in their carefully stage-managed procession through the room. He said: 'They're getting closer. Time for you to distance yourself.'

'Don't mock me. You wanna bet upon their picking on us?'

'You'd have lost,' said Parnell, at the group's arrival.

'We haven't met,' announced the Dubette president. 'I'm Edward C. Grant.'

14

'I'm . . .' started Parnell, but the burly, white-haired man said: 'I know who you are, Richard. And you, Rebecca.' To the woman, he gave an odd, head-jerking bow. Coming back to Parnell he said: 'Welcome to the Dubette family.'

'Thank you,' said Parnell. Dwight Newton was amidst the retinue, which explained how he had been identified, and the Christian-name familiarity was an Americanism he was already used to.

'Think you're going to like it here?' demanded Grant. He had a short, staccato delivery that made everything he said sound urgent. There was no offered hand.

'Too early to tell yet.' Rebecca had slightly withdrawn and Parnell was conscious of the concentration from everyone in the room upon him and the smaller man, who had to strain up even more than Rebecca to look at him, which Parnell guessed would be an annoyance.

'Got everything you want?'

'I think I have, now.' Parnell was aware of Newton's features tightening behind the president.

'When are you going to start recruitment?'

Parnell wondered what excuse had been made for the delay, about which Grant obviously knew. 'Virtually at once.'

'We're expecting great things from you, Richard.'

'I'm expecting great things from myself.'

There was an over-the-shoulder head jerk. 'I've asked Dwight to keep me up to speed. Like to be able to talk about something at the next seminar.'

But he hadn't mentioned the creation of the new division in his keynote speech at this one, Parnell thought. 'I've got some ideas but I don't expect things to move that fast.'

'I'd be disappointed if you didn't have ideas,' said Grant, positive sharpness in his voice. 'That's why we made you our offer. Why we're setting up the division and have given you the budget we have.'

'And that's why I accepted it, expecting to be able to develop them through a company as large and extensive as this.'

'So, we're both rowing in the same direction.'

Was that a casual remark or a very direct reference to how close he'd been to getting a rowing blue at Cambridge

University, before his graduation? Parnell said: 'Let's hope we don't miss a stroke.'

'Let's both of us very much hope you don't miss a stroke,' echoed the other man.

'Am I also expected to apologize?'

'For what?' frowned Grant.

'Being improperly dressed.'

The smile was as tight as the manner in which the man spoke. 'You'll know next time.'

Parnell was tempted to respond but didn't. It wasn't, after all, a verbal contest.

As he led the group away, Grant said: 'Don't forget my expectations.'

Parnell decided not to reply to that, either.

Rebecca waited until the presidential party was beyond hearing before closing the gap between them. Parnell said: 'I warned you to go under the wire when you still had a chance.'

'At least he knows my name now.'

'Maybe not for the right reason.'

'I've thought about our stock list,' Rebecca shrugged. 'We don't do a leprosy treatment.'

'We wouldn't, would we?' invited Parnell, refusing to pick up on their earlier lightness. 'It's largely eradicated except in underdeveloped countries. And we've just been lectured that there's no profit trying to sell to the Third World.'

'Ouch!' grimaced Rebecca.

'You want to risk having dinner?'

'What time?'

Rebecca chose the restaurant, Italian just up Wisconsin Avenue from M Street, and said she'd meet him there instead of his going all the way out to Bethesda to pick her up. Parnell arrived intentionally early, which gave him time to study the menu, which looked good, and get through most of a martini before she arrived.

She laughed the moment she saw him and said: 'We've got to start getting this dress code right!' She wore jeans and a suede shirt: he'd changed into a blazer – with the Cambridge University breast-pocket motif – and grey trousers.

Parnell said: 'Let's keep surprising each other.'

Rebecca nodded to a matching martini and Parnell ordered a second. He offered the menu but she said: 'I know what I'm going to have. I worked through college as a waitress here. I get special treatment.'

She did. The owner, Giorgio Falcone, genuinely Italian-born, personally returned with the drinks and kissed her and shook Parnell's hand effusively and recommended the veal, which Parnell accepted. Rebecca and the owner conversed in Italian and the moustached chef, who was introduced only as Ciro, was brought from the kitchen to be introduced as well.

When they were finally alone Parnell said: 'I'm impressed!'

'You're supposed to be. I'm showing off.'

'Why?'

'Just because,' she said.

'Fluent in Italian?'

'Difficult not to be. Mom was Italian . . .' She nodded to the departing owner. 'He's my uncle: looks after me. You do me wrong, you get a contract put out on you.'

Parnell laughed with her, liking the atmosphere. 'So, a local girl with connections?'

'Georgetown University, reserve intern at Johns Hopkins for a year, then Dubette for fame and fortune,' listed Rebecca. 'Short on the fame at the moment but the money's good and there was a promise of more this morning, remember?'

Was this the moment to put the questions? he asked himself. It might puncture the mood and he didn't want to risk that, not yet. Edging towards it though, he said: 'Quite a lot to remember from this morning.'

'What do you think?'

'I told you what I think. I think the place is knee-deep in bullshit and posturing.'

'And you don't like bullshit and posturing?'

They paused for their first courses and for Parnell to taste the Barollo, another owner recommendation. 'It's not going to affect me. Or what I've taken the job to do.'

'You always been this confident?'

'I've always known what I wanted to do, from the day of my first science lesson. Specialization came at university.'

17

'How?'

Parnell hesitated. 'Genetics was comparatively new. A lot of opportunities.'

'Quickly to become known in the field,' she finished. She raised her glass and said: 'Here's to ambition.'

'You have a degree in psychology?'

'Native intuition. I've told you about me. Tell me about you.'

'Brought up by my grandmother while my abandoned, unmarried mother qualified as a solicitor. Grammar school . . . I don't know what the equivalent is here, in America . . . scholarship to Cambridge University, graduated in time to become involved in the genome project. Worked with a lot of very qualified and clever guys. Learned everything I could from them . . .'

'And achieved the fame?' she quickly finished, again.

'I finished off what a lot of those very qualified and clever guys began. Which I said at the time.'

'I read it. You were very generous.'

'Honest,' he insisted.

'I think that's been noticed.'

Their plates were changed, more wine poured. Deciding the remark made the timing right, Parnell said: 'Am I missing something?'

'I certainly am, with that question,' protested Rebecca.

'About Dubette. It's as if there's a second meaning behind everything that's said or done. All this dress code and understood rules and family crap . . . crap because there's an atmosphere, an impression, that people are insecure. Frightened almost, which is me compounding the nonsense . . .'

'Dubette are big payers . . . the best in the business. People with commitments, kids, don't want to lose big-paying jobs.' Rebecca began twirling her glass between her fingers, her meal forgotten, looking down into the wine.

'Why should they lose their big-paying jobs, unless they screw up? You get a good job, you do it properly, do it well, *not* to lose it.'

'Dubette expect the biggest commitment to be to them. Total loyalty. You signed the confidentiality contract, didn't you?'

'Of course I did. It's pretty standard commercial practice, according to the lawyer who negotiated for me. I don't see how it alters my argument. Or affects yours.'

'I think you might have given the impression that you're too independent ... that you're ... oh I don't know, not respectful enough.' A flush came briefly to her face, showing up freckles around her nose.

'Because I got my laboratory where it should have been in the first place and didn't wear a jacket and tie to Edward C. Grant's party! Come on, Rebecca!'

'I was just offering a thought. What about the laboratory? You get included in this afternoon's tour?'

Parnell shook his head. 'Passed me by.'

'How do you read that?'

'I don't. And won't,' said Parnell. 'But who were the bastards you kept on about this morning?'

'You were set up, to go into the seminar like you did. Newton should have told you. Or Benn. Or someone.'

'Someone like you.'

'Someone like me,' she accepted. 'Only I didn't think I'd have to.'

'I already told you, I'm not going to become part of it.' He had asked enough questions to indicate otherwise, Parnell conceded.

'Don't you think we've talked enough shop?' she suddenly demanded.

'More than enough,' agreed Parnell.

Rebecca had used her own car to get in from Bethesda, so she drove him home, refusing to start the car until he had fastened his seat belt. 'That's how Mom and Dad died, driving without their belts done up.'

He didn't suggest she come up to his apartment for a final nightcap, which she didn't appear to expect. She kept the engine running and said she'd probably see him the following day – in a voice from which he inferred she wouldn't be particularly concerned if she didn't.

When he did arrive that following day at the office he'd allocated to himself, adjoining the main, general research area, there were four responses to his genetics specialists advertisements and three for the secretarial vacancy.

There was also an email from the personnel director, saying that a psychological assessment appointment had been made for him for three o'clock that afternoon at Dubette's fully staffed medical centre.

Four

'What psychological assessment?' demanded Parnell.
'It's a provision, under the employment contract,' reminded the personnel director. His name was Wayne Denny. From their one previous encounter, when the man had been one of the selection panel, Parnell remembered a small, almost diminutive man who blinked a lot through thick-lensed glasses and found it necessary to consult papers and documents he never appeared able to locate.

Parnell knew such assessments were contractual provisions from the earlier guidance given by his lawyer when he'd seriously considered terminating his appointment before it had even begun. 'Psychological assessments come *before* employment, not after. If I flunk it – although not having transgressed any company policy – you going to pay me off with a two-year salary compensation? That's the severance term, isn't it?'

'Is there something medical – or mental – you haven't been totally forthcoming about?' asked the man from the other end of the telephone.

'What's the real question behind that question?' refused Parnell.

'You seem very uptight: resistant.'

'I've got a job to do, a department to set up. I want to get on with it.'

'So, there's nothing you have withheld?'

'Honesty is a legal requirement in the contract,' said Parnell, a reminder of his own.

'Yes it is,' agreed the man.

Surely they weren't, for whatever reason, legally seeking cause to get rid of him! Paranoia, he thought at once. 'Why not invoke it?'

'Why oppose the assessment?'

'I'm not opposing any assessment. Just any further unnecessary time-wasting.'

'I should have talked to you about your diary convenience. I'm sorry. But things have been moving slowly, haven't they? You want a postponement?'

He'd be conforming, becoming one of the unprotesting herd, if he agreed. But making an equally meaningless gesture if he demanded a rescheduling. 'I'll be there as close to three as I can manage. Better warn him I could be late, if he's got other appointments.'

'She,' corrected Denny.

'What?'

'She,' repeated the man. 'The psychologist is a woman, Barbara Spacey. And it'll be OK if you're late. She's blocked out her diary for the whole afternoon.'

Parnell remained unmoving for a long time after replacing – gently, holding back from slamming down – the receiver. It would be very easy to become paranoid: do something – behave somehow – to draw more attention to himself than he appeared already to have done. Maybe he was expected to, he thought, and at once recognized that that *was* paranoid. But *why*? Why in God's name was all this idiocy happening? Could it actually be psychological, trying to fit him into a convenient mental mould, another in the obedient flock? Why not go with the flow – very definitely not join the herd, but just as definitely not emerge the maverick – until he worked out the silly process in which he'd become embroiled, exasperating though the distraction was.

Parnell asked for and immediately got a temporary secretary, a matronly, grey-haired woman from the pool, and replied to all the applications so far, staggering his interviews over the following week, which gave him the intervening weekend fully to go through the geneticists' submissions, all of which looked impressive. While his responses were being typed, he referenced the three applicants on the Internet and discovered two had submitted papers to scientific journals. He printed off both. One was on the possible application of genetics to the treatment of hepatitis B, the other to the prevalence of genetic inheritance of Down's Syndrome. He judged both to be sound – certainly indicating a strong basic genetic knowledge – but lacking any substantive rethinking.

Both the secretarial replies, one from a medical secretary at Johns Hopkins, the other from the George Washington Hospital, listed DC addresses, and Parnell arranged appointments for the following day.

Parnell considered calling Rebecca on her internal extension but decided against it. He decided, too, against eating in the commissary, going instead for the first time to the staff health centre. The gymnasium had every piece of equipment he'd ever seen, anywhere, and some weight-training apparatus he hadn't. There was a bank of rowing machines, three in use, far superior to any upon which he'd ever trained. Parnell counted five logo-identified personal trainers, all working with individual clients. The sauna and steam room matched the Olympic-proportioned swimming pool and Parnell thought it would be easy – and good – getting back to the rowing fitness he'd once known but let lapse for far too long. When he returned to his office all his mail was immaculately prepared for signature and there was an email from Rebecca thanking him for the previous evening. It was still only two thirty but Parnell set out to be early, not late, wondering how Barbara Spacey would assess that psychologically.

She was a large, neglected woman who could have shed at least 20 lb in the sports centre he'd just left without it even showing. The straggly hair had deposited a snowfall of dandruff over a hand-knitted cardigan with odd buttons, two of which were missing, and the ashtray on her desk was mountained with butts, although she wasn't smoking when he entered. She sat in front of, not behind, her desk, so there would be no separation between them. His positioned chair was just a little over a metre from hers, in a direct line.

She smiled briefly, showing nicotine-yellowed teeth. 'I was warned you might be late.' She had a hoarse smoker's voice, too.

'I got through earlier than I expected.'

'You think this is going to be a waste of time, just bull-shit?'

Parnell didn't think he showed surprise at the abruptness of the question. 'Isn't that for you to decide?'

'Isn't that your avoiding the question?'

'I understand it's a common employment process, although, as I am already employed, it seems a little out of sequence. I haven't undergone the process before, so I've no criteria to judge if it's worthwhile or not. So, it really is for you to decide.'

'You smoke?'

'No.'

'Do you mind if I do?'

'No.'

'I shouldn't, of course. There's a strict non-smoking policy within the building' She lit her cigarette from a battered Zippo.

Parnell shrugged, unsure if there was a point to the admission.

'What about you, Richard?'

'What about me?' He frowned.

'You buck the system? Get impatient with rules and regulations you can't see the purpose of?'

So there was a point. 'Sometimes.'

'What about here? You found things you don't see the purpose of here?'

Parnell wished he wasn't so close to the cigarette smoke. 'I haven't been here long enough.' It was becoming an escape cliché, he recognized.

'You were quite a presence at the seminar.'

There was very definitely an intention behind this belated interview. Uncaring of the impatience, he said: 'It wasn't intended as any sort of statement. I simply didn't know.'

'You'd have conformed if you had known?'

'Certainly to have avoided all the nonsense that's followed.'

'No one told you?'

Parnell sighed. 'No, no one told me.'

'You resent that?'

'I think it was childish and therefore totally irrelevant.'

'So, you did resent it?'

'Something else for you to judge.' It seemed more like-cross-examination from a courtroom soap opera than what he'd expected a psychological assessment to be.

'How you liking America?'

'Very much.'

'No homesickness, adjustment difficulties?'

Parnell snorted a laugh. 'No homesickness, no adjustment difficulties.'

'No overhanging relationships then?'

'No.'

'You're not married?'

'No.' He nodded sideways to her desk. 'It says I'm not on my personnel file there.'

Barbara Spacey gave no response. 'Divorced?'

'No. It says that on the personnel file, too.'

'Children?'

'No. Also in the file.'

'Parents alive?'

'My mother.'

'What about your father?'

'I never knew a father. Whoever he was, he left my mother unmarried when she became pregnant.'

'You hate him for doing that, walking out on her?'

'No.'

The psychologist used the act of stubbing out her cigarette to cover the doubtful pause. 'I find that hard to believe. Makes her pregnant and then turns his back on his responsibility?'

'Wasn't that better than doing his duty and spending the rest of their lives unhappy or later going through the trauma of a divorce?'

'They might have become happy, in time.'

'That's hypothetical.'

'What about your mother? You despise her for becoming pregnant?'

'That's an absurd question!' erupted Parnell, discarding the determination not to lose his temper. '*She* didn't abandon *me*. She worked her way through college, qualified as a lawyer, took me through school and college. I love her. Admire her. She's a fantastic woman.'

'So, you despise me for asking an absurd question?'

'Yes,' answered Parnell. Fuck you, he thought.

'How would you feel about a word-association test? You know, day–night, black–white? The first word that enters your head . . .' She clicked her stained fingers. 'Quick as that.'

'I've never played one before. But if you want to, let's do it.'

'To get it over with?'

She was very definitely goading him. 'You've allocated all afternoon to me. So, we're in no hurry, are we?'

'Night?' she suddenly demanded.

'Black,' he said at once, not caught out.

'Sea?'

'Boat.'

'Woman?'

'Mother.'

'God?'

'Philosophy.'

'War?'

'Death.'

'Medicine?'

'Cure.'

'Disease?'

'Pestilence.'

'King?'

'Exalted.'

'President?'

Parnell hesitated. 'America.'

'Tyranny?'

'Overthrow.'

'Sermon?'

'Speech.'

'Church?'

'House.'

'Choir?'

'Song.'

'Failure?'

'Mistake.'

Barbara Spacey sat back in her chair, a fresh cigarette adding to the room's fug. 'I expected you to cheat. Reply with a word you thought I'd want to hear.'

'How do you know I didn't?'

'It's my job to know. On your application and CV you put yourself down as a Protestant. But you don't believe in God, do you?'

Parnell shifted, uncomfortable with the analysis. 'A lot of scientists don't.'

'Why didn't you say so, on your personal application?'

'I thought Protestant would look better than agnostic or atheist. America's a pretty religious country, isn't it?'

'Honest now but not then?'

'I've got the job now. I didn't have it then.'

'Which is it?'

'Agnostic, I suppose.'

'You did cheat once in the test, didn't you?'

Parnell accepted that Barbara Spacey was unsettling him more with her analysis than she had done by provocation. Perhaps one was a professional precursor of the other. 'Yes.'

'So what was the word you really thought of when I said "President"?'

'Exalted.'

'Why didn't you say it?'

'I had, once already.'

'You could have used it again.'

'Wouldn't it have meant the same?'

'Not necessarily.'

'I'll remember next time.'

'You expect there to be a next time?'

'Something else for you to decide.'

'You have any problem with authority?' she said.

'I don't understand the question.'

'Accepting it.'

'I don't think so.'

'How do you feel about exercising it?'

'I'm not sure I understand that question, either.'

'You ever been in a position of authority before, have power over a bunch of people?'

'No.'

'It frighten you?'

'I haven't thought about it.'

26

'Think about it now. You take on someone with an impressive CV but he turns out not to be so good: makes mistakes, affects your whole division. What do you do?'

'Tell him he's screwing up. That if he doesn't shape up his job's on the line.'

'He makes an effort but it isn't any good.'

'I give him the mandatory warnings and then tell him he's got to go.'

'He's got a kid with a permanent illness that needs the medical cover that comes with his job here. That's why he's screwing up. He's distracted.'

'It would have been on his personnel file.'

Barbara Spacey frowned, off-balanced by the reply. 'So?'

'I would have asked early on to look at the kid's case notes. Tried to find out if there'd been any genetic exploration.'

'Personal involvement like that would be against company policy.'

'So's smoking on the premises. If our distracted father was willing and the case notes indicated the slightest benefit from genetic exploration, I'd say we'd have a situation everyone should take advantage of . . .' Parnell saw the woman was about to speak. 'But everything would be legally consensual, with signed documents and agreements. Nothing that would lay myself or Dubette open to any legal or ethical challenges.'

The psychologist didn't try to speak after all, seemingly thinking. Then she said: 'You do your genetics exploration. It doesn't help. The guy's work doesn't improve.'

'Then he has to go.'

'You think you could do that?'

'If the department was being continually undermined, yes.'

'And you? If you were being continually undermined?'

'I'm going to be its director. The department's failures and weaknesses will be my failures and weaknesses.'

Barbara Spacey finally moved her head towards the personnel file on her desk. 'You haven't failed much so far, have you, Richard? It's been a pretty uninterrupted upwards climb.'

'I've worked hard to make it so.'

'So, you deserve it?'

Parnell considered his answer. 'Yes, I think I've deserved it.'

27

The Zippo flared again. 'We've used all our afternoon up.'

'How'd I do?'

'Interesting.'

'That's what scientists say when they're confronted by some-thing they don't recognize or understand.'

The woman dutifully laughed. 'As do a lot of other confused people as well. I'm intrigued by your word responses. They didn't fit a pattern.'

'Were they supposed to?'

Barbara Spacey shook her head, positively. 'That's what's intriguing.'

'Do I get a copy of the assessment?'

'It's a legal requirement.'

'I'll look forward to it.'

'Try to avoid being too independent,' advised the psychol-ogist. 'People need people. It's what's called human nature.'

'I thought it was called tribal instinct.'

'It's warm in the winter,' said the woman. 'Or when there's more of them than you.'

Richard Parnell preferred the second secretarial applicant, a middle-aged woman named Kathy Richardson who currently worked at the George Washington Hospital, but he deferred any decision because by the following afternoon, when he met her, there were two more enquiries, one from Baltimore and the other from New York. There were also four more approaches from doctorate-qualified research assistants – one a woman – listing genetics experience. Parnell got the same pool secretary as the previous day and scheduled confirmed meetings with each, accepting as he did that, with the possibility of postponements and rearrangements, a full fortnight, if not longer, was going to be taken up with job interviews. He sent an advisory memo-randum to Dwight Newton, who replied that it was essential to get the selection right the first time and that he should take as much time as he considered necessary. The final paragraph asked for three days advanced warning of the selection process.

Parnell kept to his intention to spend the early part of Saturday rereading those CVs so far submitted, and which he had taken home with him from McLean, but still arrived at the Tidal Basin before Rebecca. She wore no make-up and had followed his advice, with the bill cap, thick sweater and jeans.

'So, we're going on the river?' she guessed.

'Don't you like the water?'

'Let's find out.'

There were only tourist skiffs available, thick-bodied and cumbersome compared to the racing sculls to which he was accustomed, and Rebecca hindered more than helped by trying too enthusiastically to steer, too often taking the boat across instead of into the current once they got out on to the Potomac. He went upriver, past the canoe club by the Key Bridge, disappointed that he began so quickly to feel the strain across his back and shoulders, and resolved yet again to use the sports facilities in the Dubette building. Despite his slowly recited instructions, she brought the boat about too sharply for the turn, actually shipping water. It was easier going downstream, but Parnell was still relieved to get back into the basin.

They snacked off hot dogs from a stall and at the stand-up table Rebecca announced: 'I'm impressed.'

'You're supposed to be,' said Parnell, uncomfortable now at the posturing he so easily criticized in others. Because of the sudden embarrassment, he cut short the account of coming as close as he had to representing Cambridge in the traditional annual boat race.

'But you didn't make it?'

'No.'

'Pissed off?'

'Very.'

'Never the loser?'

'Never if I can help it.'

They walked without any positive direction across Constitution Gardens but decided against going to the Smithsonian. When he suggested a movie, she said: 'Or we could food shop and I could cook dinner at your place.'

They shopped in the supermarket in the basement of the Watergate building and Parnell bought cooking wine and drinking wine from an adjoining liquor store. He'd anticipated spaghetti. Instead Rebecca cooked beef and shallots in her chosen wine, with a garlicky vegetable stew, followed by a soft goats' cheese he'd never tasted before.

There wasn't a lot of conversation clearing away, and afterwards they settled together on the couch, although she was distanced from him by how she curled her legs beneath her, creating a barrier between them. Their small talk became smaller and smaller. After a long pause he said: 'You don't want to go out to a movie?'

'Absolutely not.'

'Anything?'

'Just staying here is good.'

'I think it's good, too.'

'I told you I brought some clothes . . . things . . .'

'I thought you just said . . .' he began, but she stopped him.

'I mean, I don't have to go all the way back to Bethesda tonight.'

'What about your Mafia connections?'

Rebecca sniggered, welcoming the lightness. 'I was trying to impress you, like you tried earlier, breaking your back rowing up and down the river.'

'So, we're quits.'

'Not quite. I told you a lie, about the bet. There never was one. I just wanted to speak to you.'

'I'm glad.'

'I want this to be right.'

'So do I.'

'So, this isn't any big deal. Not unless it becomes one. OK?'

'OK.'

'You think you can manage, after all that rowing.'

'We won't know, until we try.'

They tried – twice – and afterwards, wetly pressed against him, Rebecca said: 'I'm not sure I'll be able to manage once you get in shape.'

'I'll be gentle.'

'Don't be.'

Five

The eventual establishment of Dubette's pharmacogenomics unit took a further month and a half. The secretarial choice remained Parnell's but, having gone through a similar process himself, he should objectively have known the choice would be decided not by him alone but by a filleting committee composed of himself, Dwight Newton, Russell Benn, Wayne Denny, company lawyer Peter Baldwin and the deputy head of the budgetary division.

Parnell's budget was sufficient for a scientific staff of six, with a review after a year. His rejection of five candidates as underqualified was supported by the selection panel. The strongest argument against his choice of the one woman applicant came from Russell Benn, who insisted she was too inexperienced, having only graduated from medical school three years earlier. It took Parnell an hour to win a majority decision in Beverley Jackson's favour, arguing her graduation pass was the highest of any applicant, that she'd already risen to joint deputy of the genetics research department at Johns Hopkins and published two respected scientific journal papers on the genetics links with drug research. Two of the other applicants, one from Los Angeles' Cedars of Lebanon hospital, the other from the research department at Harvard Medical School, had also published impressively on the genome project. Ted Lapidus, a fourth applicant and the oldest candidate, with specialized experience in his native Athens before moving from Greece to the George Washington Hospital in DC, actually questioned one of Parnell's own published opinions.

'Which is a pretty good way of talking yourself *out* of a job,' opened Newton, in the after-interview analysis.

'I want a man with that sort of confidence,' contradicted Parnell.

'He probably sees himself taking over your job,' warned Benn.

'Then he's going to work like hell, isn't he?' replied Parnell. 'I want that, too.'

Parnell's longest theoretical scientific discussion about applying genetics to drug development came with Deke Pulbrow, another Johns Hopkins University candidate. For almost forty-five minutes the two men conducted a debate that more than proved to Parnell's satisfaction that Pulbrow had a much broader and deeper understanding of pharmacogenomics than had been obvious in the journal publication that Parnell had found disappointing. Not once did Newton or Benn intrude a comment or offer an opinion.

Parnell was surprised at Newton's luncheon invitation to a log-framed inn in the North Virginia countryside, not the Dubette commissary, the day after they made their final selection.

'I want us to get along,' declared the research and development director, at the bar. The thin man was drinking mineral water. Parnell chose gin.

'So do I,' said Parnell. He was already getting a déjà vu echo from this conversation – déjà vu upon déjà vu, in fact.

'You really believe you can map a genetically matched responder to a genetically acceptable drug, cutting out all the rejection?'

'Not all,' acknowledged Parnell, realistically. 'A lot, hopefully.'

'How much is a lot?'

'I can't give an estimate, not yet.'

'Ball-park figure?' pressed Newton.

'I'd be satisfied with fifty per cent.'

'Matching fifty per cent of effective drugs to responsive patients?' persisted Newton.

Parnell didn't hurry his reply. Matching responsive drugs to responsive patients was the very science of pharmacogenomics. Which Newton – which none of them – should have needed explaining. So why was Newton demanding just that? 'I don't think I could aim higher. Who knows?'

'So, you fit an acceptable drug to a genetically accepting patient, you knock two or three – four maybe – other drugs from a cocktail administration . . .' Newton paused as if seeking an example. 'AIDS or hepatitis, for instance?'

When the waiter came with the menu, Parnell ordered another gin and tonic and chose scrod. Newton took the same, impatient with the interruption.

'AIDS or hepatitis,' prompted the research director, when the waiter left.

'If we get the match right, we won't need the two or three or four others,' stated Parnell, flatly.

'So, we lose fifty per cent of the sale of two or three or four other drugs!'

'I said it was an estimate. Maybe I won't get that high.' There was an obvious direction to this conversation, Parnell recognized.

'Let's use it,' urged Newton. 'You start reducing drug multiplication by fifty per cent, you're talking of a lot less drugs being prescribed for a hell of a lot of conditions. You understand what I'm saying?'

'I understand that it's your business . . .' Parnell stopped, to correct himself. 'My business now . . . Dubette's business . . . to sell drugs. That it's a commercial operation. But I don't believe there'd be a dramatic financial fall if I'm anywhere near successful. Which I stress I've no guarantee of being, in either the short or long term. My specialized science is still very experimental. What, for instance, if we slot one of the unnecessary cocktail medicines into a condition where it's properly effective? You get an increase, not a decrease, in sales. To the commercial benefit of Dubette and the medical benefit of the patients taking it. Everyone's a winner.'

'You can't guarantee that.'

Parnell felt the irritation rising. 'I can't guarantee *anything*. Except, by a compensatory measure, an increase in the sales of one matched drug more than making up for any loss from the reduced sales of another.'

'What did you think of Barbara Spacey's psychological assessment?'

The profile had come in the middle of the first of the interminable selection weeks. The psychologist described him as independently minded, verging upon overconfidence, with a predilection to decide upon – and follow – his own opinions and judgements over those of others. It was, she'd judged, a tendency that could, in fact, lead to misjudgements. Her conclusion was that he should be encouraged to share and discuss his work throughout the research division.

Parnell said: 'Seemed to jar a few chords.'

'That's what worries me,' conceded Newton.

'You've lost me,' complained Parnell.

'You're not here to jar things,' said Newton, throwing Parnell's word back at him. 'You start a programme you think has got potential but which might detrimentally affect one of our existing products, I want to know about it. In fact I want to be kept fully up to speed on everything you do, on every programme you and your new staff embark on. No independent-mindedness, OK?'

'Of course you'll know what I'm doing,' said Parnell, which wasn't the undertaking Newton had demanded.

The waiter told them their table was ready and as they made their way towards it Newton said: 'A guy can live very comfortably at Dubette. You remember the president's salary-review promise at the seminar?'

'Yes?' said Parnell, questioningly.

'It's going to be ten per cent. You haven't even started to work properly yet and your salary has already gone up ten per cent.'

Parnell dismissed what had clearly been a conformity warning from Dwight Newton, just as he'd dismissed the much earlier but virtually identical conversation with Russell Benn. But not contemptuously. Both job-dependent men were overlooking how long it might take – years, potentially – genetically to refine a drug cocktail to a single constituent dosage. Until that happened it wasn't a personal consideration, if indeed it would ever become one. He was concerned with his science and its beneficial use, not the price on the label.

Parnell had had time on his hands during the appointments hiatus and, partially to fill it, established a rigid fitness schedule at the health centre. By the end of the month he'd dropped almost 10 lb, most of it, he was sure, excess stomach flab. When he ate lunch with Rebecca he swapped salt-beef sandwiches for salads and after three days she started to do the same and complained that she'd picked him out for sex, not healthy eating. In the comparable period she lost 3 lb.

Their relationship settled to both their satisfaction, although it was Rebecca who occasionally insisted that it remained *only* a relationship, with no binding commitments. They spent most weekends together, more often at his more central apartment than at Bethesda, where she rented a small clapboard house with a garden, which turned out to be her hobby. Parnell helped on the occasions they did stay there, but strictly under her direction after killing a long-established honeysuckle climber he believed himself to be pruning.

The honeysuckle mistake occurred on the final sixth week, and he took her withdrawal as annoyance at his gardening stupidity. Finally he said: 'If you want me to say it again, I'm sorry I cut your flowering thing down. I'll buy you another to replace it.'

'What?' asked Rebecca. They were in the lounge of the Bethesda cottage, littered with the fallout of the Sunday newspapers.

'You haven't said more than four words since I cut the honeysuckle down.'

'It's not the fucking honeysuckle!'

The vehemence startled him. He came forward towards her and said: 'Hey! What's the problem here?'

'There's something odd happening.'

'At Dubette?' They couldn't dodge it all the time – when he'd told her of the psychological assessment, she'd mocked that it was totally right, that he was an arrogant son of a bitch – but most of the time they avoided talking about the firm.

She nodded, saying nothing.

'What, for Christ's sake!'

'I told you I don't know!'

'Rebecca, you're not making a lot of sense! You want to talk about it, I want to listen. But talk in words I can understand.'

Rebecca straightened in her chair, forcing herself out of her reverie. 'There's some stuff coming in . . . stuff I'm not being allowed to assess and pass on up the line.'

'You're being sidelined?'

Rebecca shook her head. 'It's bypassing my line manager,

too. It's divisional director to Dwight Newton . . . we wouldn't have known it was even happening except for a misdirected email, asking for confirmation that it had arrived. Which didn't tell us anything but sent Newton into apeshitting cartwheels.'

'So, it's not personal?' persisted Parnell.

'It's never happened before: not since I've been in the division.'

'Relax. There's got to be a hundred reasons why things go between sub-director to God himself, without going the normal route.'

'It's never happened before!' Rebecca insisted.

'I heard you the first time.'

'The email came from Paris.'

'So?' said Parnell.

'Haven't you wondered what our ultimate God, Edward C. Grant himself, meant at the seminar about a way to prevent our products being reverse-analysed, for cheaper manufacture?'

'I am now,' said Parnell.

Six

Richard Parnell looked around his finally assembled staff and said: 'There were times I never thought we'd get here!'

'That bad?' smiled Beverley Jackson, sympathetically.

'That long,' complained Parnell. It seemed far longer than just a month and a half and, now that everything – and everyone – was in place, there was a hesitating moment of anticlimax. Parnell said: 'But at last we're here. Now we've got to prove ourselves and that ours is not a jungle science.'

'A what?' challenged Mark Easton, at once. He was one of the two original geneticist applicants, a languid, blond-haired, clipped-voiced Bostonian who'd worked at John Hopkins.

Parnell smiled, hoping to cover the thoughtless, too-glib expression. 'Pharmacogenonomics is new: we're new. There's got to be a coming together with everyone else here.' Which he singularly hadn't bothered to do since his arrival, he acknowledged.

36

'We're surely among qualified people . . . sufficiently qualified, at least, to know about the *existence* of genes and their potential application!' took up Ted Lapidus. There was little trace of an accent. The Greek had a very full, drooping moustache that made him look permanently doleful: even the smile, which accompanied the overstressed cynicism, was mournful.

'I misspoke,' Parnell apologized. This was sliding downhill into an awkward opening day. 'Let's just not forget our newness and human nature. Dubette go in for rules, although they're mostly understood rather than official. Within Dubette the recurring theme is that it's one big happy family. We're not an accepted part of that family, not yet . . .' Oh Christ, he thought, hearing his own voice and seeing the expressions of those facing him. 'I was trained that science builds upon the free exchange of ideas and theories. That's how I want us to operate. Any of you get – or already have – an hypothesis, you follow it. And talk about it, to each and every one of us. If, in the end, it doesn't pan out, it doesn't pan out. More experiments and research fails than succeeds, as you all know. At least we'll have taken a possibility as far as we can . . .' He paused, as an idea came to him, but decided against proposing it until he'd more fully thought it through, supposing that it was something he should mention first to Dwight Newton.

Before he could go on, Deke Pulbrow said: 'You mean there isn't going to be a formulated schedule, integrated with what other sections are working on?'

Parnell decided that Pulbrow would definitely need advice about the dress code for the next seminar: beneath the regulation, nameplated laboratory coat, the man wore bib-and-braces overalls and a denim work shirt. Parnell said: 'No, I don't mean that at all. I very definitely expect – and intend – to work in tandem with the rest of this division. And to get channelled through to us, via the ongoing research here, anything that comes in from overseas. It's our contribution that's got to be innovative. The most obvious is nucleotide polymorphism of Dubette products. We've been set up genetically to research and develop treatments and drugs, in conjunction, if necessary, with the traditional chemical experimentation that until now has been Dubette's established route.' Parnell accepted that he was preaching to the converted but he hoped at least he was making better sense than the careless way in which he'd begun.

'Bacteria are genetic,' declared Lapidus. 'Already there's been complete genetic sequencing of *Streptococcus aureus*, *Streptococcus pneumoniae*, *Mycobacterium tuberculosis*, *Helicobacter pylori*, *Pseudomonas aeruginosa* and *Vibrio cholerae*. Genetics – and its engineering – in the drug development for treatment of such conditions has already been scientifically accepted. Are you seriously telling us that there's a resistance here?'

Parnell acknowledged that he was very obviously, before an audience, being tested – by the man whom Dwight Newton had judged to be a potential challenger for his job. 'You missed off your list the genome of a prototypic streptomycete, *Streptomyces coelicolor*,' reminded Parnell, confronting professional knowledge with professional knowledge. 'And yes, that's exactly what I'm seriously telling you. And that is my battle to fight, as head of this department.' No one broke into the pause this time. Smiling at the Greek geneticist, determined to come out the winner of the exchange, Parnell said: 'I'm grateful for your listing, although I know none of us needed reminding of it. Any more than any of us needed reminding of the potential of genome exploration in combating disease.'

'Precisely what disease?' demanded Peter Battey, the second of the original Washington-based applicants, a balding, pebble-spectacled man.

'I've already told you I haven't worked out a specific tandem schedule; I won't until I've had detailed discussions with Russell Benn across the corridor. But there are obvious targets and I think we should shoot for as many as we can.'

'So, we're going for the top prizes: AIDS, hepatitis B, cancers, influenza variants, common cold?' enumerated Beverley Jackson.

It wasn't a sardonic, professionally combative list like that of the Greek geneticist, needing a matching confrontation. His unspoken idea came again into Parnell's mind as he said: 'Why not? I don't expect – won't have – any of you backing off from a project that's taken everyone else into a cul-de-sac. It's *because* they've ended in dead ends that we've got to try something different, something newer and better.'

'If we can think of something newer and better,' said Lapidus, doubtfully.

'The only way to find out is to try,' said Sean Sato. The Japanese-American had the deeply black hair of his Asian ancestry but was taller, almost 6'. He was immaculately and fastidiously dressed beneath the laboratory uniform, the club-patterned tie tight behind a pin-collared shirt, the trousers of his muted check suit razor-creased above mirror-polished brogues.

It wasn't a sycophantic remark, Parnell immediately guessed. 'You're arriving with some already-formed ideas?'

The man's smile was apologetic. 'Not so much pre-formed. Projects that could be added to the list.'

'Such as?' This first, getting-to-know-each-other meeting was evolving far differently from how he'd expected but it was better than he'd imagined. Certainly there'd been some professional posturing but already they were scratching the surface into which he wanted them more deeply to dig.

'I could be accused of personal interest,' announced Sato.

'I won't accuse you until I hear what it is,' promised Parnell.

'There's a lot of concentration upon AIDS. Rightly so,' said the man, eagerly. His gesture towards Beverley was a polite bow. 'There's a lot of concentration upon hepatitis B. Rightly so again: seventy-five per cent of the thirty-five million suffering from it are in the Western Pacific and South East Asia region, which very much includes Japan. But in less than five years – with little if any reduction in that figure – it will be overtaken by hepatitis C, an obviously genetically linked but wholly different strain of the same disease. At the moment the only antiviral agent that suppresses hepatitis B is lamivudine, which is also effective in treating HIV. Already there are some indications of superbug resistance to lamivudine. If that resistance becomes established, it will reduce any fight against not only hepatitis B, but C as well. And AIDS.'

'Which conveniently rounds the square to drug resistance . . .' began Parnell.

'Not quite,' refused Lapidus. 'Interferon is a very successful treatment for hepatitis C.'

39

'If the disease is identified sufficiently early,' accepted Sato. 'The problem is that it's usually without symptoms until it's too late, by which time liver disease and cancer are already established. The last paper I read estimated in five years from now, ten at the most, more people will be dying of the C strain than from AIDS.'

Far better than he'd expected, Parnell thought again: it could scarcely even be acknowledged as the first step but this was exactly how he wanted them to work, arguing not to prove him or herself more knowledgeable or qualified, but properly, expertly, bouncing ideas and theories off each other.

'That's a chicken-and-egg situation,' said Beverley. 'If disease is already generally established before there are any noticeable symptoms, the answer must be in much earlier screening of risk groups. And you've already identified them demographically.'

'Perhaps I haven't explained myself sufficiently,' said Sato. 'Earlier screening is obviously a factor and when the seriousness of hepatitis C is globally recognized, governments will have to devise a better and quicker diagnostic system: some, indeed, have already started to move in that direction. What I'm talking about is a new drug or treatment when chronic liver inflammation or cirrhosis or cancer is already there.'

'Let's start our list with it,' decided Parnell, unwilling for a specific discussion to become too protracted this soon. He decided, too, against remarking upon their seemingly unconscious adoption of his operating plan: to do so would have sounded schoolmasterly and he considered he'd already suffered too much from that himself. Instead he said: 'I think things have started well. I do want drug rejection and resistance to be on our agenda. That is where we might make our most obvious, hopefully even quick, contribution . . .' He nodded towards Lapidus. 'We're all familiar with the diseases that have already been genetically coded. I want our work to identify others high on our agenda, even before we start properly liaising with the people next door . . .' He hesitated, nodding now towards his side office. 'On the subject of doors, mine isn't ever going to be closed. Any problems, difficulties, anything at all upsetting anyone, I want to know about it and I want them solved, not gestating out of their proper proportions. Thank you for coming to work with me. I think it's going to turn out just fine.' Did he really think that? First an anticlimax. Now uncertainty about something he couldn't identify . . . unless, that is, it was not about his international acclaim as a genetic explorer, but self-doubt at his personal competence to control, administrate, financially supervise and lead, as he was determined to lead along the forever-God's-gifted upward spiral. Parnell was as unaccustomed to self-doubt as he was to commercial science. He wasn't sure he liked either.

Parnell was surprised at the same-day response from Dwight Newton, promptly although not prematurely on time for the agreed meeting, the earlier uncertainties boxed away, hopefully forever. Neither was to be ashamed of: each was understandable, acceptable.

There was no avuncular, standing-in-readiness greeting this time from the research and development vice president. Instead the stick-thin man remained behind his desk, gazing up from between humped shoulders, spider's-leg fingers at momentary rest before him.

Easily remembering the upbeat, reach-for-the-sky presentations at the seminar, Parnell enthused about his opening encounter with his staff, unembarrassed at the hypocrisy of intentional phrases like 'team players' and 'pulling together' as he recounted that morning's gathering.

The scuttle-ready hands remained unmoving. Newton said: 'I told you I always wanted to know what was going on.'

'I've just told you!'

'I would have liked to have sat in on it.'

'It was a getting-together of a team. Nothing formal. Nothing formative.'

'I would still have liked to have been there.'

'I've found where the washrooms are now,' retorted Parnell. 'And can go there all by myself and I wash my hands afterwards.'

'I don't understand that remark,' protested Newton.

'You asked to be fully informed of everything that happens in my section. You just have been. *Fully* informed. I don't expect everything I say or do or initiate to be monitored. I've been given the responsibility of a department, which I intend to fulfil according to the terms of my employment.'

'I've made it perfectly clear to you that I want to know every intended genetic research project *before* it is initiated, not after. There could be conflict with other, parallel research . . .'

'Not if it's carried out as it should be, with total co-ordinated exchanges between every section,' broke in Parnell.

'I am the ultimate co-ordinator,' said Newton. 'I'll decide if there's a conflict or unnecessary duplication.'

'What appears to be parallel duplication can't be avoided if my section genetically compares and cross-references matching although alternative experimentation: that's the whole purpose of pharmacogenomics being set up here, forming a part of what becomes a whole.'

'I will co-ordinate and decide upon everything that is conducted in the research and development division of this organization,' pedantically insisted Newton, the fingers at last scrabbling back and forth in exasperation. 'I'll make that clear in a written memorandum, which perhaps I should have done earlier. There seems to have been some verbal misunderstanding.'

There was no benefit in any longer revolving on this argumentative carousel, Parnell recognized. Just as he recognized the weak threat of putting this latest disagreement on written record. 'I came here to talk about something else.'

'What?' demanded the research vice president, the peculiar fingers drumming out his impatience at the dispute ending on Parnell's terms, not his.

'Science – all sciences – benefit from exchange, from the cross-fertilization of ideas.'

'Are you lecturing consciously to irritate or aren't you aware how you sound!'

'I want to set up a dedicated website,' announced Parnell.

The hands stopped. Newton became quite still, his rising colour the only indication of his incredulity, heightened when he finally spoke by the way in which he spaced the words. 'You-want-to-do-what?'

'Set up a website dedicated to my section,' repeated the more controlled Parnell. 'Upon which . . .'

'. . . Every competitor can log on and work out not just what you but every other Dubette research section might be working on and anticipate every patent and licence before we even apply for it! Are you actually expecting me to take you seriously!'

He hadn't properly balanced the counter-argument, conceded Parnell. 'I think that's a minimal danger, dependent entirely upon how the research is set out. What I propose . . .'

'Let's hypothesize, just to amuse ourselves and show this up as the insane, absurd idea it is,' persisted Newton, relentlessly. 'Let's say someone outside the company suggests something you incorporate. Whose copyright – exclusive patent or licence – will it be? How many civil courts in how many countries do you imagine we'd keep in business for the next millennium arguing infringement or plagiarism actions?'

'Let me tell you . . .' Parnell tried, yet again.

'No!' refused the other man, loudly. 'You're not going to tell me anything. *I* am going to tell *you*. You will not set up any dedicated website, now or in the foreseeable future . . . if, indeed, the future for you here at Dubette is foreseeable. I will put my refusal – and my reasons for it – in writing, too. And attach to it the legally binding and agreed confidentiality agreement signed by you, as a condition of your employment. To which I want a written response from you that you've read that agreement and fully understand it. Let's start right now. You understand everything, every single thing, I've just told you?'

Parnell burned with the humiliation, accepting that he'd not only been out-argued but that the defeat was entirely of his own making. Shortly he said: 'Yes, I understand.'

'The next time we talk I want common sense, not nonsense,' said Newton, warmed by the conviction that he'd irreparably punctured all the previous insufferable arrogance. He couldn't remember enjoying himself so much for a long time.

'It sounds like a one-victim massacre, if there is such a thing,' sympathized Rebecca.

'It was,' admitted Parnell. 'God knows what Kathy imagined I'd done when I dictated the reply Newton insisted upon.' Kathy Richardson was the greying, middle-aged divorcee whom he'd finally engaged as his secretary, the only position

Dwight Newton hadn't insisted be considered by the appointments committee.

'Hardly a day to celebrate,' said Rebecca. They were eating in her uncle's restaurant, accustomed now to the food and wine choice being made for them and to Ciro sometimes talking them through special dishes he'd created, always 'just for you two'.

'I wanted a change from eating crow,' said Parnell. 'And it was a good day until the Newton episode. I think they're all going to come together very well.'

'Shouldn't you give it more than a first-day impression, like you should have given the website idea more thought?' cautioned the woman.

'I am only talking first-day impression,' said Parnell. 'And I've already admitted to the other mistake. I still don't believe it represented more than a one or two per cent danger. Five tops.'

'Darling! To a company like Dubette the one or two per cent possibility of a competitor getting into its research is a major drama. Five per cent registers ten on the Richter scale. You're not involved in pure science any more. You've got to remember that.'

'I will, in future. Believe me!' Parnell didn't like losing, certainly not to someone like Newton, whom he judged to be a bully. But it *had* been an ill-considered mistake and he was determined not to make another.

'I asked outright,' suddenly blurted Rebecca.

'What?' frowned Parnell, totally confused.

'My section head, Burt Showcross. I asked him outright what all the secrecy was about between France and us.'

'What did he say?' His mind blocked by the humiliating confrontation with Newton, Parnell had forgotten his earlier conversation with Rebecca about back-channelled secrecy from Dubette's French division.

'That he didn't know either but that it sometimes happened and that I wasn't to concern myself with it – any of it – again.'

Parnell was about to say that she should let it go at that but was halted by a sudden thought. Instead he said: 'If Paris has come up with something they're excited about – something to which they're attaching such a degree of priority and secrecy – it could be something which has an application to pharmacogenomics?'

Rebecca shrugged. 'Who knows? But guess what?'

Parnell wished Rebecca didn't so often conduct conversations like a quiz game. 'What?'

'There was a mistyped report from Paris, a good enough excuse to telephone them direct. While I was chatting to the girl I normally deal with, I was told the chief executive had been recalled to New York . . . along with the research-division head who misdirected that one message that no one, not even Showcross, was supposed to see.'

'I think you should do what Showcross told you. Forget about it.'

'Maybe it's been a bad day for both of us.'

'Forget about it,' repeated Parnell. He wasn't sure he would, though.

Seven

Edward C. Grant said: 'I needed to speak to you like this, just the two of us. Discreetly.'

'Of course,' agreed Dwight Newton, who had caught the first shuttle from Washington that morning, wanting to be at the Dubette corporate building before the president. He'd failed. He'd been careful to wear his seminar suit, which matched the dark grey of Grant's. And to enter, as instructed in the summons, by the special penthouse-only elevator.

'We're talking risk assessment,' announced the Dubette president.

'I understand.' Newton thought the football-pitch size of Grant's desk accentuated the man's bantam-cock shortness.

'It was a good idea to have security check everything out as thoroughly as they did.' It was a safeguard to let the other man imagine he'd initiated the precaution, which he hadn't.

45

After what Grant regarded as the one and only mistake of his life – relegating that in his mind to a lapse more than a mistake – he now took no risks.

That amounted to praise, Newton decided. 'I thought so.'

'I had the same done in Paris. That was useful, too.'

'You've seen everything I sent up, about the website proposal?'

Grant nodded, tapping a folder on the left of his desk. 'You did good there, too, Dwight. I wish others had.'

Newton was quite relaxed, which he rarely was in Grant's presence, certainly on a one-to-one basis. But he'd calculated the situation from every which way and concluded that he was probably the only person who couldn't be accused of mistake or misjudgement. It certainly seemed that way from the conversation so far. Guessing the other man's reference, he said: 'What's the take from Paris?'

'Buck-passing,' replied Grant, at once. 'I hauled Saby back, for a personal explanation. And Mendaille, obviously.'

Newton was surprised, properly realizing how seriously the president was treating the misdirected communication. Henri Saby was the chief executive of the French subsidiary. Georges Mendaille was head of research in Paris and the man personally responsible for the mistake. 'What do they say?'

'Saby entirely blames Mendaille. Mendaille says it was a simple but understandable mistake, that out of habit he mishit the automatically logged email address, sending it to Washington in the normal way instead of personally to you, which was the specific instruction.'

'If it was the specific instruction, Mendaille shouldn't have been hitting keys from habit,' said Newton. 'He should have been concentrating.'

'Exactly!'

Toadying bastard, thought Grant. But hadn't he made everyone with whom he had to deal a toadying bastard?

'You firing him?'

Grant shook his head. 'Dismissed, he'd be resentful, wanting to hit back, a potential whistle-blower. I want him where I can see him, know what he's doing all the time . . .' The man paused. 'Mendaille's our hostage, we're not ever going to be his. That's the way it always works.' There was another pause. 'Which brings us back to your problems.'

Newton shifted uncomfortably at it being described as his problem, recognizing that no blame or culpability for anything would ever be traceable to Edward C. Grant. There'd be no record, not even a diary entry, of this meeting. Newton accepted, too, that despite everything being already set out in the file upon Grant's desk, it all had to be talked through.

'Rebecca Lang's in a relationship with Parnell,' he began. 'Sometimes she stays at his place, sometimes – usually weekends – he stays over with her in Bethesda . . .'

'We got photographs?' cut in Grant, who already knew the answer from his direct contact with Harry Johnson, the head of Dubette security. The question was to bind Newton into any future action that might be necessary.

'Coming and going from both places,' confirmed Newton. That wasn't in the file, so perhaps there was after all a purpose in talking it through. 'She asked Showcross outright what was going on. He told her it was beyond her clearance and nothing to do with her . . .'

'But then she rang Paris?' cut in Grant, again.

'On a cockamamie excuse about a transmission screw-up that could have been sorted out in a second by email.'

'We know who she spoke to in Paris? What was said?'

Newton humped his thin shoulders. 'Just the phone log, recording the outgoing call. It lasted six and a half minutes.'

'Long time to sort out a simple transmission misprint,' judged Grant.

'Too long,' agreed Newton. 'You think we should get Saby or Mendaille to find out who she spoke to – what was discussed?'

'We need to know,' said Grant. 'But I don't want any more curiosity in Paris than might already have been aroused by my bringing Saby and Mendaille back.'

Not my problem or my decision, thought Newton, thankfully. 'I think we've got to assume Rebecca will have told Parnell.'

'Told him *what*?' seized Grant, at once. 'Is there any way she could have seen anything other than that one misdirected message?'

Newton didn't answer at once, trying to assess the commitment being forced from him. Then he said: 'No. No, I'm sure she couldn't.'

'And what could she infer from what she *did* see?'

'Only that there was an out-of-the-ordinary exchange going on at the highest level between Paris and Washington.' You were the guy who mentioned France publicly at the seminar, thought Newton.

Grant pulled a sheet of paper from another folder, gazing down at it for several moments before reading aloud: '*Welcome your assessment of our detailed security proposal.* And it's signed Mendaille.' He didn't speak for several more moments, and Newton remained silent, too. 'No,' the bulky, white-haired man abruptly decided. 'By itself it wouldn't mean anything.'

'I think I'll keep security on to things – ensure that she does as she's been told. Warn Showcross that I want to be told if she shows any more curiosity.'

'Do that!' agreed Grant, who'd already given the order to the security chief. 'What about Showcross? He likely to become too curious?'

Newton shook his head, positively. 'Showcross knows where his salary cheque comes from.'

'Keep the security check on Parnell, too. Let's watch for any interest there shouldn't be from him.' There was another pat on the Washington dossier. 'I really do think you handled that website business very well, too. What I find unbelievable is that the son of a bitch actually suggested it in the first place.'

'He's got a lot of adjustments still to make to living in the commercial world. But I'm knocking him into shape. I've set up some other things,' openly boasted Newton.

'Keep on the job, Dwight.'

'I always do.'

'And I'm always grateful.' There was a too obvious look at his watch. 'Sorry I can't offer you lunch . . .' Grant put a hand tight beneath his chin. 'I'm up to here.'

It would have risked his New York visit becoming too publicly known, acknowledged Newton. 'I need to get back anyway.'

'We'll keep in close touch – the closest,' insisted the president. 'I don't want to lose control of this.' Control, of everything and every one and every cent, was Edward C. Grant's watchword.

'I'm not clear on one thing,' said Newton, briefly refusing the dismissal. 'Are we going to go ahead with the French idea?'

Grant gave himself time to compose the reply. 'Commercially it makes very good sense. But the medical decision has got to be yours, Dwight. If it is medically safe, as the French insist, there's no reason why we shouldn't do it. But we can't, obviously, risk being caught out.' Which is why you're being given the total responsibility, thought Grant.

It put his name very firmly – and provably – on the proposal, Newton realized. So he couldn't relax – the very opposite, in fact. 'If I decide there's a chemical danger, we don't go ahead?'

'We can't chance anything unethical. But at the same time we've got every right to protect our products, intellectual and otherwise,' smiled Grant. 'It would certainly be commercially good for the company. I want you to keep that in mind.'

That was the closest he'd get to a positive order, accepted Newton. 'We'll put it through every test.'

'I know you will. That's why you are where you are, Dwight. I'd trust you with my life . . . and those of everyone else whose lives are made better by the drugs and treatments we devise.'

'Thank you. That's good to hear.' It was almost as if they were working from a script now. He wished it wasn't a script written entirely by the other man.

'And Dwight,' added Grant, as Newton was almost at the door to the suite.

'What?' frowned Newton, turning back into the room.

'Not that way. The private elevator. Don't forget the security.'

Or the culpability, thought Newton.

'So, you're finally set up?'

'And ready to go,' agreed Parnell. Today there was no obvious resentment and the coffee had been freshly brewed and waiting when he reached Russell Benn's office. Parnell had considered inviting the head of chemical and medical

49

research across to the newly established pharmacogenomics wing, only changing his mind during the two-day delay in this intended work-planning meeting: inter-office protocol decreed he still go to the other man.

'Sorry I couldn't make it earlier,' apologized Benn. 'The way I understood our earlier meeting was, quite simply, that you'd like to be involved in everything we're currently doing?'

'Become an integral – extra – part of it, yes,' said Parnell. 'And run simple nucleotide polymorphism tests on what Dubette are already producing, to make them more effective.' The change in Benn's attitude was encouraging.

The other professor nodded. 'That, as of an hour ago, involves something like three hundred and sixty different experiments covering new possibilities with existing drugs, treatments and therapies currently under phase one evaluation between oral, blood or muscle injection. Additionally there are fifty-three other quite new investigations still at animal-level testing, which, obviously, are at the moment open-ended.'

'That's a hell of a schedule!' exclaimed Parnell. He hadn't anticipated half that number.

'We're a hell of a cutting-edge company,' said Benn. 'And I haven't included competitor analyses.'

'What's the extent of your total programme?'

'Stick a pin anywhere into an infectious-diseases dictionary and we're doing it, the most obvious and current at the top of the list.'

It was all very forthcoming, prepared almost. 'Looks like quite a challenge.'

'You really want it all?' frowned Benn.

'I want to go through the entire schedule,' qualified Parnell. 'Until I study it all, I won't be able to decide how applicable it is to my discipline. There'll have to be prioritizing.'

'Why? Of what?' challenged Benn.

The sharpness of the demand was Parnell's second surprise. 'I would have thought our liaising would initially be better begun with your newer experiments than looking for possible improvements to remedies already tried and proven.'

'You said you wanted everything?'

50

'In a proper, workable order.'

'How's that to be decided?'

'Between the two of us. Between others in our departments, maybe: with the workload you've just outlined, it'll make practical sense to delegate, don't you think?'

'You want details of *everything*!' persisted Benn.

'Unless you've got a more effective way of our co-operation getting off the ground.'

'You think you've got sufficient people?'

'No,' admitted Parnell at once. 'That's why it's necessary to prioritize from the very beginning.'

'So, you start – we start – with a long list!'

'And the research notes of that list, all of which I guess is computerized and easily downloaded without causing any of your people any extra work. We'll simply create our genetic order of priority, where we think we can make the best contribution, share it with you and arrange to the convenience of us both the inclusion of my people in the ongoing physical experiments. Which won't mean anything more than the exchange of slides and cultures and specimens, surely?' Parnell was glad he was talking now as if he'd had everything ready in advance, which he hadn't. There were only a few things, one specifically, that he wanted to introduce when he considered the time to be right.

'OK,' said Benn, not trying to conceal the doubt. 'Let's try it your way.'

'And if it doesn't work my way, we'll devise another,' said Parnell, easily. He nodded acceptance to the offered coffee refill.

'What about your people?' asked Benn. 'Any of those arrive with anything interesting from what they did before?'

'Sato's interested in hepatitis C. He's got a good argument, going beyond interferon, that I'll let him follow. You doing anything on that?'

'Tokyo is. Canberra, too.'

This could be the route he was seeking, Parnell realized. 'That fits the demographics. But you'd have everything copied here, right?'

'It'll be on the list.'

'What about Asia and severe acute respiratory syndrome?'

'SARS is being worked out of Tokyo again.' He hesitated,

forced into a concession. 'You know, of course, that the National Institute of Allergy and Infectious Diseases is experimenting with a vaccine containing the DNA from the virus?'

'Yes, I do know,' said Parnell, who had intentionally manoeuvred the conversation. 'Cross-species infection, from animals to humans, is a field we could successfully explore,' suggested Parnell. 'It's virus mutation, which is genetic, and it's a carrier-borne condition, so it isn't demographically limited. It just starts in China and Hong Kong from their live-animal trade but then spreads globally.'

'That's why it's on the list,' said Benn.

Parnell wasn't sure whether the other man's patience was forced. 'Working genetically on hepatitis C will obviously lead on to tumours, restricted perhaps to liver cancer.'

'Cancer's on every list, here and throughout all the subsidiaries.'

The door was creaking open, Parnell decided. 'Generally? Or defined, region to region?'

Benn frowned at the specific question. 'Rome and Canberra are concentrating on sun-generated melanomas, because of the predominant climate. Delhi and Manila on lung cancer, because of the combination of heavy nicotine use and uncontrolled air pollution in their countries.'

'What about France?'

'What about France?' echoed the black professor.

'Diet,' said Parnell, rehearsed. 'Japan, with its very particular diet, a lot of fish and much of it raw, has the lowest cancer incidence in the world. You probably couldn't find more polarized eating than the fat, oil and rich sauce preparations of France. Any subsidiary – or us, here – working on a dietary connection to cancer – bowel or stomach maybe?'

'Part of a general investigation,' said Benn.

'In France?'

'No,' said Benn. 'Here.'

He'd taken it as far as he could and wasted his time, Parnell decided. It had probably been stupid hoping Benn would disclose whatever the restricted French communications were about. And after the website debacle, he'd determined against stupid approaches. 'I look forward to getting the list.'

52

'I'm looking forward to your showing us how you can improve it.'

'There's no possibility of any complaint,' assured Russell Benn. 'I followed every lead you suggested. The pharmacogenomics division will have enough research material for months, if not years. Which is what Parnell wanted.'

'What did he say about the volume?' asked Dwight Newton.

The other man smiled. 'That it was a lot and that he didn't have sufficient staff to whom to delegate it. So that a priority schedule will have to be created.'

'We have to know what that is,' insisted Newton.

'We agreed that I'll have his itemized working schedule.'

'So, we've got a check on everything they're doing, quite separate from what he's under strict orders to tell me?' pressed Newton. It created a double-check system, the best he believed he could evolve.

'That's how you wanted it, wasn't it?'

'Anything out of the ordinary, anything you didn't expect, from the conversation?'

'He got a bit ahead of himself, began itemizing things. I told him to wait until he got the complete schedule to see what we were covering.'

'Itemizing what, particularly?' demanded Newton.

'Hepatitis, cancers, all the obvious stuff. Wanted to know if some of the subsidiaries were specializing.'

'He mention a particular subsidiary?'

'He's got some idea of a comparison between Japan and France that might show up a dietary connection with tumours.'

'What did he say about France?' demanded Newton.

Benn gave an uncertain gesture. 'Nothing particular.'

Newton let some silence into the conversation. Then he said: 'Would you say he explicitly manoeuvred the conversation to include France?'

'Maybe that could be an impression. It wasn't mine until now, when we're talking about it. Is it important?'

'We've worked together for a long time, Russ,' said Newton, ignoring the question.

'Yes?' agreed Benn, asking one in return.

53

'Dubette appreciates you. And your loyalty.'

'You know it doesn't have to be questioned.'

'That's exactly what we do know. Appreciate most of all. And what we want you to understand.'

'I'm not sure I do, not at the moment.' said Benn, doubtfully.

'I want you to carry out some tests. You, personally. No one else. Not delegated to anyone, not discussed with or known about by anyone.'

Benn straightened in his seat, his concentration suddenly absolute. 'What?'

'France is traditionally Africa's colonial power. French, or a patois of it, is the first language throughout a lot of African countries. It's our French subsidiary drugs and treatments that are predominantly copied.'

'The president's seminar remark,' remembered Benn.

'The idea is to cheat the cheats,' revealed Newton, at last. 'Introduce into the printed formulae of our most often pirated research, placebos or non-active constituents to make them more expensive – and less cost-effective – to replicate than our competitors.'

'That's not ethical,' protested Benn.

'Placebos and non-active constituents,' repeated Newton. 'Colour alteration, more palatable taste. There's nothing non-ethical in our doing that.'

'I'm not sure,' said Benn, doubtfully.

'How's the new house? And the kids?'

'OK,' said Benn, uncomfortably. 'Thanks for asking.'

'I want you to understand how much we appreciate the way you run your operation. In addition to the across-the-board ten per cent increase, I'm approving an additional salary increase for you of fifteen thousand dollars.'

'That's very generous.' Benn was beyond surprise, practically in shock.

'Very much deserved.'

'Who's got these formulae changes?'

'I have.'

'What if there are adverse reactions?'

'The idea's scrapped.'

'I'm to do this totally alone?'

'No. I'm your check. You initiate and confirm. I repeat the experiment and doubly confirm.'

'I've your word the idea will be abandoned if there is the remotest risk?'

'I am not going to put you at risk, myself at risk or the company at risk,' guaranteed Newton.

'And I'd see the results of your separate analyses and tests?'

'Of course.'

'Thank you, for the salary increase.'

'It's nothing you don't deserve.'

Eight

The Dubette computer printers were predictably the fastest state-of-the-art available but it still took almost five hours completely to download the full development schedules and each set of individually attached research procedures, in addition to the separate material covering the original production of those listed that were in the course of improvement or refinement. Ted Lapidus, finally facing Parnell over battlements of piled paper, said: 'It'll take five years, optimistically, to examine it all. We've just been avalanched.'

That awareness had come to Parnell halfway through the print run. He said: 'I got what I asked for. Now we've got to dig ourselves out.' He was conscious of looks quickly exchanged between Lapidus and Deke Pulbrow. Identifying both he said: 'OK, you two . . .' He turned to Easton. '. . . And you, Mark. Work from the provided dates and from what's identified as the most current research. At the moment you're speed reading. I want you to create a priority agenda with which we can potentially and most productively get involved, the research that's being giving the most time and attention, with no obvious financial constraints. Relegate anything you're unsure of to secondary or third lists . . .' He went to the Japanese. 'Let's go with your original instinct, Sean. Stay with hepatology . . .' Parnell encompassed the stacked paper. 'Sort out from all this anything genetically applicable to hepatitis B or C. Again, you're speed reading, flagging up where we could go forward. Log and cross-reference separately liver carcinoma . . .' He looked around them all. 'That's a general instruction. We're going to create our own dedicated cancer programme: in time we'll subdivide and specify, but before we even do that we'll take on board everything that Rome and Canberra have already done and are maybe currently doing, because according to Benn, both Italy and Australia are actively working on melanoma research . . .'

'And then there were three?' broke in Beverley Jackson.

Her smile took away any impatience in the remark. It was an easy smile and for the first time Parnell realized its slight unevenness lacked the sculpted dentistry of Rebecca's. The realization that he was consciously comparing the two women surprised him, although Rebecca had virtually invited it when he'd told her of Beverley coming into the department, demanding with feigned jealousy a detailed description and claiming the day after they were supposed to begin work that she'd lingered in the commissary, to see the woman for herself, and declaring Beverley to be very sexy. Properly and fully concentrating upon the other geneticist for the first time, Parnell acknowledged that she was extremely attractive, fuller-breasted but smaller featured than Rebecca and maybe taller by an inch or two. He thought the darkness of their matching, deeply auburn hair was about the same, but Beverley wore hers practicably short. Concentrating even more, he saw Beverley didn't have any freckles, either. From her application CV, Parnell knew that Beverley Jackson was divorced, although she'd kept her married name and still wore what he presumed to be her wedding ring. Looking between the woman and Peter Battey, he said: 'And we're the three. We'll work dates again. We won't initially go back further than two years into the improvement and re-evaluation of what Dubette already manufacture. We can work on what went before as and when. I won't have a schedule imposed upon us. We'll work at our speed, no one else's . . .' He smiled apologetically at Kathy Richardson. 'The bulk of the recording work is going to fall upon you, I'm afraid. You'll be the person creating the files.'

'That's what I came here expecting to do,' smiled the woman.

'You actually think we were avalanched!' frowned Lapidus.

'I got what I asked for,' repeated Parnell. 'And I was warned of the volume.'

'And as you've already made clear, we're going to have to work for our acceptance,' reminded Beverley.

'If we're working nucleotide polymorphism acceptances, we're going to need a lot of animals,' said Peter Battey.

'Something else for you, Kathy, when we establish a schedule,' said Parnell.

'I'm going to be a real busy person,' accepted the secretary.

Which is what they all set out to be, impressing Parnell by how quickly they came together as a cohesive unit. Unasked and unprompted, everyone worked late and frequently missed lunch or ate sandwiches at their benches. Parnell's fitness regime flagged and he put on 2 lbs in three weeks, even though he was missing lunch too. There were two consecutive weekends when he didn't stay over at Bethesda with Rebecca, and she didn't stay in his apartment at all during the second week. She didn't once complain, insisting she knew how important it was to him.

Parnell adhered strictly to Dwight Newton's demands and sent detailed memoranda to the research and development vice president, with copies to Russell Benn, satisfied that he was avalanching them in return and passingly curious at the lack of response from either scientist. During the second week he actually crossed into Benn's section but was told the man could not be disturbed in the secure laboratory in which he was working. All Parnell's exchanges, each identified by number and content, were acknowledged the following day. Newton's replies came the day after that.

Parnell insisted everyone take the third full weekend off and was glad when Rebecca announced she'd prefer to cook in at Bethesda on the Saturday night. They had drinks on the deck and he fell asleep in the colonial wicker chair when she went into the kitchen to prepare the meal. She woke him in mock protest that if he was as tired as that he wasn't going to be much use to a girl as denied as she had been.

'I was just recovering my strength.'

'How much longer do you think you're going to have to work like this?'

Parnell shrugged. 'A long time.'

'You won't be able to keep up the pace. The other guys are going to get pissed off.'

'They're working their asses off at the moment.'

'You've got to cut some them some slack.'

'I'll watch it.' He paused. 'I'm surprised at Newton – Benn too, for that matter – by his apparent lack of interest after all the bullshit about knowing everything I'm doing.'

'They're too busy,' said Rebecca. She grinned, conspiratorially. 'And I think I know why.'

'You promised to back off!'

'I don't think I did!'

'I think you did.' She'd cooked pot roast and Parnell realized that in his annoyance he was facing her across the table with his knife and fork held upright, like weapons. He put them down, pouring wine for them both.

'I didn't go around asking any more questions,' said Rebecca, defensively.

'What then?'

'I had coffee in the commissary with the filing clerk in Benn's section: she's the girl I deal with all the time. And she said Benn's locked himself away in a laboratory and no one knows what he's doing.'

'And you're surmising it's the great French mystery!'

'It all fits, doesn't it?'

'No,' refused Parnell. 'You're making it fit. And I want you to let it go. It's becoming an obsession.'

'It's not an obsession! I'm just curious.'

Parnell looked at her suspiciously. 'You spoken to Paris again?'

'Not about this.'

'So you *have* spoken to Paris!'

'A regular samples shipment went missing. I had to confirm the waybill number.'

'By phone!'

'Why not?' The defensiveness was back.

'When? Before or after coffee in the commissary with the file clerk?'

'The day after. But it *was* a coincidence, believe me.'

Parnell didn't. 'And all you talked about was a missing samples shipment and a waybill number?'

'There's a lot of curiosity in Paris, too. Their top guy wouldn't have been called to New York if it wasn't important, would he?'

'You said anything more to Showcross?'

'He knew I called Paris. And why. By reconfirming the waybill number, I was able to track down the samples.'

'I want a solemn promise that you'll keep to this time. I want you to stop.'

'Why's it such a big thing with you?' Rebecca demanded, showing her own irritation.

'Because I think it *is* approaching an obsession. Whatever the French thing is, it's something they're keeping under wraps. Which is entirely logical and understandable in a pharmaceutical company whose whole existence and future is based on exactly that, keeping as totally controlled and secret as possible what might be an advance. The way you're behaving you could far too easily become suspected of being a competitor informant. And if that happens, you're out.'

'So?'

'Where do you think you're going to work next, with that albatross around your neck? You'd be an untouchable pariah, never trusted. Nor in pure science, even if you could get a place.'

Rebecca remained looking at him for several moments, her barely eaten meal abandoned, her wine glass untouched. Finally she said: 'You really meant all that, didn't you? About protecting me . . . and stuff . . . ?'

'Yes, I really mean it!'

She went back to her wine glass like a clairvoyant studying a crystal ball. 'Does that mean we're moving on, into a commitment?'

'You're the resident judge of that – it's your chosen word.'

Rebecca remained engrossed in her glass for several more moments. Then she said, crack-voiced: 'It sounds like it is.'

'You're the judge,' repeated Parnell. Was that what he was offering, a commitment? He didn't think the conversation had started out in that direction. He pushed aside his own, now cold, pot roast, which wasn't anyway an American speciality he liked.

'I just delivered the judgement.'

'You don't sound very sure about it.'

'It wasn't supposed to come out that way . . . like . . . oh shit . . . !' she stumbled.

'You any idea where we're going with this?'

'No.' Rebecca's voice was now mouse-like.

Parnell wasn't sure about anything: about how they'd stumbled into this quicksand in the first place. 'Now we've got this far, beyond the refusal, why don't we wait a while, decide what we both want?'

'OK,' accepted Rebecca, mouse-voiced still.

'That was quite a loop.'

She smiled, uncertainly. 'I guess it was.'

'And now we're back at the beginning.'

'I've almost forgotten what that was.'

'No you haven't. No more spy games, OK?'

'I keep saying that.'

'Say it again.'

'OK.'

'Mean it. Don't commit professional suicide over some stupid non-mystery.'

Rebecca opened her mouth to speak but stopped. 'I won't say OK one more time. I promise. But this time I really, *really* mean it. I'll forget about France.'

'Good.'

'I know I shouldn't be, but I feel . . . I don't know . . . embarrassed, I guess . . . now that we've . . .' She floundered to a halt. 'What do you feel?'

Parnell only just stopped himself from saying OK, which wouldn't have been right in any context. 'I feel you and I have got to talk a lot and laugh a lot and, in our own time, without any hurry or pressure, decide a lot.'

'You don't like pot roast, do you?'

'It's not my favourite.'

'We're deciding already.'

Parnell supposed taking pot roast off the menu was a start.

Irrationally Parnell felt uncomfortable taking the weekend off, and compensated by getting to McLean around six every morning the following week, and on the Wednesday ran for the elevator that was taking Russell Benn to their shared floor.

'Sorry. Didn't mean to frighten you,' apologized Parnell, surprised at the medical research director's startled reaction to his door-thrusting arrival. 'I had to wait more than five minutes for a car to come back yesterday.'

'Not used to people this early,' said the black professor, recovering.

'This your usual time?' asked Parnell.

'Varies,' said the man. 'Usually try to make an early start.'

'Came across the other day. But you were busy.'

'I'm still going through your stuff. Look forward to talking about it.'

'You on to something new?' asked Parnell.

'What?'

'What you're working on. I was told you couldn't be interrupted. Which I understood.'

Benn made an awkward, arm-lifting gesture. 'Seemed a possibility. Doesn't appear to be working out.'

'What?' demanded Parnell, directly.

There was a hesitation. 'It's a respiratory thing: a chest-muscle relaxant. Like I said, doesn't seem to be working out on mice trials.'

'We going to get a look at it on our side of the fence?'

'I'm not getting anywhere, so it looks like a no-no. I would have thought you've got enough with what we've given you.'

'Always room for more.' The man was lying, Parnell knew.

Nine

Dwight Newton observed the previous protocol, catching the first New-York-bound flight from Washington and entering the corporate building on Wall Street using the unobserved, code-controlled penthouse elevator intentionally shielded from CCTV range. As before, Edward C. Grant was there ahead of him, waiting on the other side of the overpowering desk.

'You've finished the tests?' demanded the hunched, diminutive man, not bothering with any formal politeness.

'That's for you to decide,' said Newton. Knowing there was no possibility of lunch, he'd got up in time for the maple-syruped waffles that never added weight to his skeletal frame, but he had hoped for coffee. There wasn't any.

'And?'

'We added all the French-recommended colouring and flavouring to a slew of their products: linctus, cough medicines, bronchitis and asthma treatments, analgesics – most of their range. Tests on mice and monkeys showed no adverse reaction whatsoever.'

'You telling me we can go ahead?' smiled Grant.

'The French also experimented with liulousine, so we did too. It would add a good twenty per cent on to any pirating cost. Again, nothing adverse in any animal trial. Because it's in the same classification, we went further and introduced our beneuflous: that would hike the copying cost up to thirty per cent: there's no indigenous source, so both liulousine and beneuflous would have to be imported . . .'

'They'd be buying beneuflous – our drug – to pirate us!' sniggered Grant.

'It would be more cost-effective to copy other manufacturers, which I thought was the strategy we're trying to set up,' said Newton. 'But if they chose to use our formulae, then yes, they'd have to buy our drugs to manufacture their copies of our drugs!'

'I like it. I like it very much. No bad reactions at all?' There was always a near-orgasmic feeling at the thought of making money.

'None.'

'What are liulousine and beneuflous?'

'Expectorants.'

'So, you're signing the whole thing off as safe! We can go ahead?'

'Paris hasn't tested on humans. Neither have we.'

'I thought mice were comparable and compatible enough?' questioned the non-medical president.

'There could be minimal variations. We – or France – should test on human volunteers to be one hundred per cent sure.'

'We're talking Africa, not civilization.'

Dwight Newton, who'd believed himself beyond any reaction to anything Grant might say or do, was momentarily shocked into silence. 'You know the three-phase testings,' he managed.

'Every preparation we're talking about has gone through the French testing schedule and conforms to their licensing regulations,' insisted Grant.

'What about these additions?'

'Georges Mendaille doesn't anticipate any difficulty. Neither does Saby, providing none of it is sold on the domestic market.'

Once again Newton had to pause before speaking. 'How can that be explained to the licensing authorities?'

'Rifofludine,' said Grant, shortly, having rehearsed the moment.

'The French-recommended flavouring?' queried Newton.

'Saby described it as a preservative in hot climates.'

'It would have helped if I'd spoken to Saby when he was here! I didn't test for that!' It was the nearest Newton had ever come to confronting the president, and his stomach lurched as he spoke.

'You can test now, can't you?' said Grant, sharply.

'What else did Saby claim?'

'That the colouring agent is a total placebo.'

'But very practicable among people who have difficulty reading or comprehending, but who can understand differences in colours?' anticipated Newton. He felt physically nauseous.

'Exactly!' agreed Grant, enthusiastically. 'We could even get some public health recognition for this.'

He'd sold his soul to a man who was beyond imagination or parody, Newton realized. At once he wondered why it had taken him this long *to* realize it. 'I need to make the heat test on rifofludine.'

'Saby says it's OK.'

'I'm signing it off, right?'

'Right.'

'Then I should confirm the experiment and its result. As I should test upon human volunteers.'

'We got a sudden problem here, Dwight?' asked Grant.

Newton's stomach dipped again. 'We need to consider the company and its global reputation, don't we?'

'Always,' said Grant, at once.

'That's what I'm doing.'

'Of course you are,' said Grant, the smile as tight as the bitten-off words. 'How about this? It'll take a while to get French licensing approval. You finish off what you feel you have to do in the laboratory while Paris goes through the formalities. That way we're on the block ready to take off the moment we get the go ahead.'

He was a puppet in a responsibility-clearing performance, accepted the research vice president: the decision had already been made to go ahead with manufacture for Africa. 'What happens if I don't confirm Saby's insistence on the preservative?'

'I've already given you my word, Dwight. We scrap every-thing.'

'That's what I have, your word?'

'That's what you have: what you've always had.'

'OK,' agreed Newton, as he'd known he would agree from the beginning.

'We've got other things to talk about,' announced Grant, hand on the familiar, although expanded, file to the left of his desk.

'Security put a trace on Rebecca Lang's office phone,' started Newton, knowing what Grant expected. 'Got the full transcript of a conversation with the girl she talks to in Paris, Stephanie Paruch . . .'

Grant pulled the extract from the file, flicking the edge of the paper with an irritated finger. '*Your great mystery*,' he paraphrased. '*I'm going to keep on until I find out . . . known here as a smoking gun . . .* You know the trouble with guns, Dwight? They go off and hurt people. That's when they smoke.'

Newton hesitated, briefly unsure how to respond. He took his own copy of the transcript from his briefcase and, reading from it, quoted: '*It's the talk of the division here. Benn and Newton have locked themselves away: haven't been seen for days. It's got to be something big . . .*' He looked up. 'I don't like that, my name being on the record. I don't like that at all.'

'What about Parnell?' Grant hurried on.

'Caught Benn in the elevator a day or two back. Asked him outright what was going on.'

'What did Russell say?'

'That it was an experiment that wasn't working out.'

'Parnell accept that?'

'Asked if pharmacogenomics were going to get a look at it. Russ said there wasn't any point.'

Grant sat silently for a long time, the only sound the increasingly rapid click of his irritated flicking against the paper edge. Finally he said: 'Is it true, what she said? That it's the talk of the division?' There was an unquestionable benefit, repeating the questions he'd already put to Harry Johnson, the security director with whom he was talking, personally and only ever one-to-one, with increasing frequency . . .

'It's not my reading. Or Benn's. Security – Harry, personally – are tapping all outgoing calls from the floor. I've told them we suspect a competitor informer. Rebecca Lang's the only person who's shown any interest in France – spoken to Paris, even.'

'Not Parnell?'

'No. But they've got to be talking, haven't they? They can't just screw all the time.'

'She's a goddamned nuisance!' angrily declared the Dubette president, who'd had a contradictory conversation with Harry Johnson, whose professional experience and opinion he trusted more than an amateur like Newton.

'You think I should officially warn her off?'

'No!' refused Grant, still angry. 'That'll just make her more curious.' She certainly had to be stopped. It was not something to discuss with Newton. Not even, he thought, with Johnson. There were special people he employed for special things.

'What then?'

'Just finish off what you've got to . . .' Grant brightened. 'Looks like France came up with a good one. Had the figures calculated. We stop the piracy, reduce it even, in Africa and Asia, we could save as much as ten million dollars in a full year. And that could even translate into a matching loss to our opposition, if they become the alternative targets. That's a damned good day's work . . .' There was an abrupt reflective darkening. 'And why it isn't going to be jeopardized . . .'

'You want security to go on watching her?'

'Keep the telephone taps on, throughout the department. Hers particularly. And obviously keep an eye on Parnell. Leave me to worry about everything else. And Dwight . . . ?'

'Yes?'

'You're doing a hell of a good job.'

That morning Newton didn't make the mistake of trying to leave through the wrong door.

'Sorry I haven't got back to you before now,' apologized Newton.

'Not a lot for us to discuss so far,' accepted Parnell.

'Enough,' said the vice president. 'You seem to have every-thing parcelled up pretty efficiently.' Newton hadn't set out intending this meeting. His mind hadn't gone beyond the New York encounter and what there was to discuss with Edward C. Grant. It was only afterwards, on the return Washington shuttle, when he was still very much thinking of that discus-sion and Grant's numbing cynicism during it – and of his openly being named on the security eavesdrop – that the idea came of personally speaking to Parnell. And trying to assess what suspicion or curiosity the Englishman might disclose.

'Still a long way to go.' Why the sudden summons, after playing the invisible man?

'Looks to me like you're working to an agenda.'

'Trying to create one that's practical,' qualified Parnell. 'I thought the best initial contribution we might try was on some of the most current research, to complete an entire package.'

Was that a veiled reference to Paris? 'Sounds a sensible approach. How many have you got in mind?'

Parnell was sure he prevented the frown. 'Those that I've already memoed you about.'

'Sure,' said Newton, awkwardly, gesturing to a disordered pile of paper on his desk. 'You think there's anything likely?'

'Nothing that's leapt out of the petrie dish at us, but then we neither of us expect Archimedes-style discoveries, do we?'

Newton forced the smile, sure the other man was mocking him. 'Still be nice.'

'The exchange system appears to be working well, between Russell's section and mine.'

That *had* to be a reference to France. 'Sure you won't be overwhelmed?'

'No,' answered Parnell, honestly. 'That's why we're working to an agenda, trying to keep up to speed with what's ongoing, allowing space to go back to earlier stuff when we're able.'

He had to force it along, Newton decided. 'I'm afraid Russ has been a little preoccupied lately. Me, too.'

'He told me.' The quick halt was intentional, to lure Newton into saying more.

'Turned out to be a waste of time. It's all being scrapped,' insisted Newton.

Parnell didn't believe Newton any more than he'd believed Russell Benn. 'Gastrointestinal is where pharmacogenomics might have a real place.'

The son of a bitch was trying to trick him! 'It was respiratory. A decongestant.'

'Of course! Russell told me. My mistake.'

'You think of any way things could be improved for you?'

'I don't think so,' said Parnell. 'Might suggest closer contact between Russell and myself in the future. But not yet. The backlog's too big. You sure there's no purpose in my having a different look at the respiratory experiments?'

'None,' said Newton, positively. 'That's a principle I work from here, Dick. We don't waste time with failed ideas. It doesn't work, we scrap it, move on.'

'I'll remember that,' said Parnell. What *was* the point of all this?

'Maybe we should have lunch together again soon.'

'Good idea now that you can raise your head from the microscope. I look forward to it.'

Another reference, isolated Newton. 'We'll do it real soon.' There very definitely had to be another early-morning trip to New York – arranged from a public kiosk, he reminded himself. Every phone on the research floor was being security monitored.

From the way the Toyota was parked, Parnell saw the damage when he was still some yards away, despite the twilight. The damage began at the passenger door but was worse on the nearside wing, the dents deep enough to have broken a lot of paint. He looked for a culprit's note under the windscreen wipers. There wasn't one.

'Shit,' he said. He yanked at the nearside wheel, which felt secure enough. He drove slowly through the near-empty car park, satisfying himself there was no wheel damage before he reached the highway.

In the apartment, he made the single evening drink he allowed himself, a strong gin and tonic, briefly undecided but finally ringing Rebecca.

'You coming to the house?' she asked at once.

'Just wanted to talk.'

'What about?'

'Some bastard drove into my car, in the car park.'

'Did they leave a note?'

'No such luck.'

'How bad?'

'Passenger door and wing. The damage kind of goes around to the front, which is slightly buckled.'

'You told security?'

'Not yet.'

'You should,' she insisted.

'I will,' emptily promised Parnell.

'Don't put it off.'

'I won't.'

'I'm looking forward to the weekend.'

'So am I.'

'You really mean that?' she asked.

'I really mean it.'

'I love you.'

'I love you too,' said Parnell, once again wishing he didn't have so much difficulty saying the words.

Ten

Rebecca insisted it was her decision how they spent the weekend, although it was limited to Sunday. She arrived early at Washington Circle and told Parnell to dress in jeans and a work shirt. She refused coffee, which she'd already delayed herself by making in Bethesda. As usual she refused to start the engine until he fastened his seat belt.

'Now I'm strapped in, tell me where we're going.'

'Out into the great big country that you've never seen,' said Rebecca.

'What if I don't like it?'

'Too bad. You're being kidnapped.'

She drove him, in fact, to Chesapeake Bay to eat the in-season, bite-sized soft-shelled crabs with a pitcher of beer. Despite the jeans and work shirt, Parnell got glued and dirty from the shakers of glutinous salt and herb flavourings and couldn't properly clean himself up, even in the washroom.

Rebecca said: 'You think any clean-living, respectable girl would get into bed with someone looking like you do?'

'No,' said Parnell. 'But the food would be worth the absti-nence. And you've got grunge all around your face, too. I'll try to develop a treatment for it.'

'I've beaten you!' Rebecca declared, triumphantly.

'I'm getting accustomed to it,' acknowledged Parnell, in weak protest. 'Beaten me to what, exactly?'

'The guided tour. You know your way from Washington DC to McLean, North Virginia, and from Washington Circle to Georgetown, and that's it. Until today. Congratulations! You pushed the covered wagon out beyond the stockade, and hostile Indians aren't firing arrows.'

'They didn't three hundred years ago. Our settlers fired on them first.'

'Book learning!' she refused. 'This is your first great step for mankind.'

Parnell scrubbed his face with a gritty, crumpled paper towel, but didn't feel any improvement. 'So, I'm not much fun, eh?'

'Severely limited.'

'Why'd you stay?' He felt safe with the question because the conversation was light, unendangering, although embarrassingly he recognized that Rebecca was making a deserved complaint.

'We crossed the boundary. Made the commitment we always held back from. Which we still seem to be holding back from.'

'I could blame work. But I won't.'

'Good. You changed your mind?'

'No. I wasn't sure if you might have done.' That wasn't entirely true, he admitted to himself.

'You could have asked.'

'You keep nagging and I will blame work.'

'You do that and I'll know you've changed your mind.'

'You ever think of studying law rather than science? You'd have made a great prosecuting attorney.'

'That how it sounds to you, a prosecution?'

The lightness was going, as he'd feared it would. 'No, that's not how it sounds at all. I'm sorry and I'm wrong and I *have* put work before anything else, before you, and that's badly wrong, too.' It was at Rebecca's urging that he'd imposed a permanent Sunday-off edict and a seven-at-night finish, despite which people still often remained later at their benches, Parnell the latest stayer of all.

Silence encompassed them in a restaurant that was no more than a bare, trestle-tabled shack with a pier that thrust out into the bay and in which they sat with hands and faces tightening with the glue of the flavouring salt. They laughed, unprompted but simultaneously, reached out sticky fingers and Parnell said: 'How the hell did that build up!'

Rebecca said: 'I planned it. Angry at me?'

'No.'

'You've got to go on now. I don't have any words.'

Parnell wasn't sure he had, either. 'Are we talking marriage . . . ?'

'No!' The quickness – and vehemence – of the rejection visibly startled him and Rebecca said: 'This really isn't the place to have this sort of conversation.'

Parnell wasn't sure what sort of conversation they were having. 'Your choice. You take it.'

Rebecca slid her hand away from his, holding both of hers tightly before her, staring down at them as if they held some message. 'Yes. It is my choice.'

Aware of her tension, he said: 'I don't want to go on with this, not here, not now. Not if you don't want to.'

She said: 'This was supposed to be a day out! How the fuck did it get to this?'

'Let's stop,' he said.

'No!' Rebecca refused again, still vehement, but just as abruptly stopped.

Parnell waited.

'You want to go on: us, I mean?' she said finally.

'Yes.'

'You can't decide that yet.'

Parnell saw that Rebecca's knuckles were whitening, so hard was she gripping one hand against the other, and there were shudders rippling through her. 'Don't, darling. Whatever it is, don't.'

Rebecca's words came out in spurts. 'I have to. Everything has to be clear, out in the open. I had a relationship. Two years ago. Got pregnant. He wasn't sure, so I had a termination. That's why I have to be sure now. I've done all the pushing and I wish I hadn't now and today is a total fucking mess and I'm sorry I ever started it and I . . .'

'. . . wish you'd shut up,' interrupted Parnell.

Rebecca did.

He stretched across the table and took her clenched hands once more, prising them open, stroking them. 'Don't be frightened.'

'I wanted you to know.'

'Now I do.'

'And?'

'And nothing.' Now he was talking child-talk.

'Say something! Anything!'

'I've been selfish about us. I'm sorry. There's life beyond – far beyond – Dubette. I'm angry at myself for getting ensnared in their system.'

'It's insidious.'

'I was the guy determined not to get caught up in the spider's web, remember?'

'So you forgot for a moment.'

'Do I get out of the stockade every weekend?'

'You haven't said anything about . . . ?' she started but trailed off, unable to finish.

'I'm sorry to say it if you loved him, but I think he was an idiot. But I'm glad because I met you.'

'You sure?'

'I'm sure.'

Parnell did his best to fill the silences on the drive back to Washington, falling back upon exaggerated anecdotes from Cambridge and England, intentionally avoiding any references to Dubette but recognizing as he did so how blinkered he had become in his total absorption with work. They finally washed away the salt residue at his apartment and decided they didn't want to eat again. Parnell suggested a movie but Rebecca said she didn't feel like it, and when Parnell asked if she was staying, looked down at her stained shirt and said she hadn't brought a change of clothes for the morning.

'As it seems to have been a day for decisions, perhaps another one should be where we're going to live,' he declared.

She remained looking at him unspeaking for what seemed a long time. Then, almost in a whisper, she said: 'You asking me to move in?'

Parnell supposed he was, although he hadn't intended the

words to come out quite as they had. 'They say you don't properly get to know a person until you live with them.'

'Bethesda's bigger than here. And there's the garden. The commute's about the same.'

Parnell wasn't sure he wanted to move away from the convenience of the city. 'Why don't we try both places, see which we prefer?'

'Starting when?'

'Whenever.'

'OK,' she agreed. 'Here first? Maybe Bethesda at the weekends, to keep the place lived in.'

'Fine.'

'Help me move my stuff in tomorrow, right after work? With two cars we could probably manage it in one trip.'

He really had made a commitment, Parnell realized. 'Let's do that.'

Rebecca left Washington Circle promising to start packing that night, and Parnell was glad to be alone, wanting to think, although he didn't exactly know about what. At last he told himself to stop being stupid, because he knew exactly what it was. It was being permanently with, living with, sharing with, Rebecca. Which came down, quite simply and logically, to loving her. So, did he? He didn't know. Or wasn't sure. That was better. He wasn't sure. He enjoyed being with her and wasn't attracted to anyone else, and he actually liked the idea of their living together. But did that amount to being *in* love: was it sufficient for them to be together? It *was* a commitment. But it wasn't irrevocable. In fact, what they were doing was probably the best thing, the sensible thing. It would give them both the time and the opportunity properly to decide if there was enough between them to make it permanent. To marry. Perhaps he should change the way he was thinking, selfishly rather than objectively. What about how Rebecca felt? Or would feel? Among a lot of other things today, there had been some long overdue self-awareness.

If he hadn't already become a work-obsessed bore, he was certainly running the risk of doing so. Rebecca might easily tire of him. He had adjustments to make, Parnell accepted: positive changes, even. Starting the following day by leaving

McLean at a sensible time to help Rebecca ferry her stuff into the apartment. Not just a sensible time, he determined – early, so that after she'd moved in they could go to Giorgio's restaurant, to celebrate.

With everything firmly planned in his mind – assuring himself it wasn't work-obsession to compensate for leaving early – Parnell got to work before seven the following morning and had been at his bench for four hours when the secretary at Rebecca's section came hesitantly into the pharmacogenomics department.

'Burt Showcross says can you come,' the girl said.

Eleven

Richard Parnell was the last to arrive at the outer-ring section, and Burt Showcross's personal office was already overcrowded. Showcross had surrendered his desk to Dwight Newton, who sat at it white-faced, gazing unseeing at its empty top. Showcross, a haphazardly haired man with a distracted manner, was supportively at the vice president's shoulder, although appearing more distracted than normal. There were two uniform-identified officers from Metro DC police department, a man who introduced himself as Peter Bellamy and a woman whose ID named her as Helen Montgomery. The fifth person was the logo-labelled Harry Johnson, head of Dubette security, a balding, bespectacled man whose expansive stomach melted over a too tightly drawn belt, from which hung a variety of law-enforcement weaponry – the most obvious a pistol – and equipment.

It was Johnson, whom Parnell had never properly met but whom Rebecca had pointed out to him weeks before, who encouraged Parnell further into the cramped office. Johnson said: 'Hope you may be able to help us a little here, Dick.'

'What's happened?' demanded Parnell. From where he stood he could see Rebecca's bench space. She wasn't at it.

74

'Rebecca,' said Johnson. 'There's been an accident.'

'Where is she?'

'I'm sorry,' said the female officer. 'It's bad. As bad as it gets. She's dead.'

Everyone in the room, except Newton, looked sharply at Helen Montgomery, critical at the bluntness. She stared back at them, shrugging, unrepentant. Parnell waited – wanting – to feel something. But didn't. All the clichés snowed in, like it had to be a mistake and it wasn't true and what were they talking about, but he didn't utter any of them, either. He said: 'Tell me.'

Peter Bellamy pedantically took out a notebook, although he didn't seem to need its reminders. 'Seems she was going through Rock Creek Park a little too fast in the dark. Overshot a right-hander, went over the edge into a canyon. Took a while this morning before anyone realized the barrier had been busted: the car wasn't visible from the road. So, it took us even longer to find the vehicle, under a rock overhang.'

'What . . . ?' started Parnell but the forthright Helen Montgomery stopped him.

'The autopsy's going on now. There wasn't a lot in her purse but there was the Dubette ID. We're looking for next of kin. An address, in fact . . .' She nodded towards Johnson. 'From Hank we understood . . .'

'There's an uncle, runs a restaurant in Georgetown . . . Italian . . . Her parents are dead . . . Rebecca had a house in Bethesda . . . Do you go through Rock Creek Park to get to Bethesda . . . ?'

Instead of answering, Bellamy said: 'Were you with Ms Lang yesterday?'

Parnell nodded, trying to get himself – his thoughts – into some sort of comprehensible sequence, some sort of order. He didn't think it was necessary to talk about crab fests and salt glue and Rebecca moving in. Of positive commitments. No one else's business. Only theirs, his and Rebecca's. 'She took me up to Chesapeake. We ate crab . . . It was . . .' He stopped himself from saying fun, realizing that he was talking about crab fests and he wasn't thinking straight. Rebecca had driven away . . . crashed . . . why hadn't she stayed? Why hadn't he gone back with her? Wouldn't have happened if he'd gone back with her. Looked after her. Looked after her instead of staying by himself, thinking of himself.

'We need to ask you something, Mr Parnell,' said the woman. 'You been drinking, you and Ms Lang?'

Parnell wished they'd stop being politically correct or whatever it was, and pronouncing Ms as 'Miz', which sounded like a nickname. 'We had just one pitcher of beer. I drank most of it, because she was driving. Rebecca wasn't drunk.'

'You didn't stop, on the way back?'

'At my apartment . . . we got dirty, eating the crabs. Washed up there . . .' Parnell was suddenly caught by Dwight Newton's stillness. The man didn't appear to have moved since he'd come into the office, the usual twitching hands clasped tightly in his lap.

'You do . . . get dirty,' said Johnson, as if there were a need for confirmation.

'You have a drink back at your apartment?' persisted Helen Montgomery.

'No.'

'So, the day ended early?' questioned Bellamy. 'How early would you say, Mr Parnell?'

'I don't know,' shrugged Parnell, emptily. 'Eight-ish, nine-ish. I don't know.'

'The car clock's busted at eight fifty,' said Bellamy.

'Like I said, eight-ish, nine-ish,' said Parnell, numbly

'You have an argument, Mr Parnell?' demanded the woman, hard-voiced.

'No!' protested Parnell. 'Why ask me that?'

'Where she crashed. It's a bad spot. Lots of warnings to slow down. Be careful. To have gone through the barrier . . . *over* the barrier . . . like she did, she was going a lot too fast . . .'

'Speedo's broke, too,' came in Bellamy. 'Stuck at sixty-five. That's an illegal speed in Rock Creek Park.'

'Rebecca didn't drive fast,' insisted Parnell, defensively. 'She didn't drive fast and she wasn't drunk and we hadn't had a fight.' *Hadn't had a fight* echoed in his mind. But it hadn't been an easy day. The contradiction came at once. Yes, it had. Ended good, at least. They'd decided to live together, for

Christ's sake! She was happy, going home to pack. Could that have been it, the opposite of what they were thinking? Going home too quickly, to pack?

'So, she was a good driver?' persisted the woman.

'Very good.'

'What about seat belts?'

'What about seat belts?' echoed Parnell.

'She wasn't wearing hers,' said Bellamy, flatly.

'No!' refused Parnell. 'She always wore a seat belt. It was a routine. *Always*. That's how her parents died, not wearing their seat belts.'

'She wasn't wearing one last night,' said Bellamy, just as insistent. 'It might have helped if she had been.'

'You sure things were OK between you?' asked Helen Montgomery.

'Couldn't have been better . . .' Why not, he thought. 'We decided yesterday to move in together.'

The admission deflated some of the woman's belligerence but not by a lot. 'I'm not trying to be offensive,' she began.

'Maybe not trying hard enough,' said Parnell, angrily.

Helen Montgomery ignored the outburst. 'Did Ms Lang have other friends?'

Ms cut into his head like a buzz saw. 'What's that question mean?'

'Other men friends? Boyfriends?'

Parnell bit back the instinctive rejection. He didn't know, he conceded. She'd never introduced him to anyone else, male or female. Or talked about anyone else, until yesterday, the walk-away lover who'd made her pregnant. And he didn't know who he was. 'What's the point of that question?'

'What car do you drive?' avoided Bellamy, once more.

'A Toyota. Why?'

'What colour?' demanded the woman.

'You answer my question first,' said Parnell, still angrily.

'No,' she refused. 'You answer mine.'

'Grey. Now, why?'

The two police officers looked at one another. The woman smiled. The man may have nodded, Parnell wasn't sure. The man said: 'The barrier Ms Lang went into . . . and over. It's white. Fluorescent, to reflect light, like these things do. The offside of Ms Lang's car is all stove in . . . we found a lot of another car's paint. It's grey . . .'

A cohesive thought wouldn't form. The impressions, his reactions, were jumbled, one or two words at a time. 'You think . . . you mean . . . there was another car . . . ?'

'We need to understand a lot of things, Mr Parnell. A lot – too much – we haven't worked out at the moment.'

'Wait!' demanded Parnell, raising both hands towards the tightly packed group. 'You believe Rebecca crashed into another car – got thrown over the edge of a ravine . . . ?'

'Maybe *forced* over the edge,' said Helen Montgomery.

'Or sideswiped,' added Bellamy.

'But didn't stop?' stumbled Parnell.

'Why do you think she was going so fast?' said the woman. 'How about trying to get away from someone? In too much of a hurry even to fasten up her seat belt?'

'Maybe,' accepted Parnell. 'But she would have definitely fastened her seat belt.'

'You sure you didn't have a fight?' demanded the woman.

'We decided yesterday to move in together!' protested Parnell.

'You said,' nodded Bellamy.

'You actually think I drove Rebecca off the road! I loved her, for Christ's sake! We were . . .'

'. . . going to live together,' finished Helen Montgomery, flatly. 'Tell us some more about last night. Rebecca left around eight-ish, nine-ish?'

Parnell was holding himself rigidly under control, hands and arms stiff beside him, exasperated and impotent. Tightly he said: 'Rebecca left, like I said. I sat around, thinking. We'd already decided we didn't want anything to eat. I didn't want a drink, either. I went through some papers I'd taken home – work things. Research. Then I went to bed.'

'You'd decided that day to live together?' pressed the woman.

'Yes.'

'You didn't celebrate?'

'We were going to, tonight. At her uncle's restaurant. It was going to be a surprise.'

'You didn't call her, see she got home safely?'

'No.' Why not? Parnell thought, agonized.

'You didn't call anyone? Speak to anyone?'

'No.'

'Watch television? Remember a programme you saw?'

'No.'

'Listen to the radio?'

'No.'

'Your car outside in the lot?' demanded Bellamy.

A sweep of sickening awareness engulfed Parnell. 'It's damaged.'

The two officers looked at each other again. The man said: 'How did that happen, Mr Parnell?'

'Hit in the car park. This car park.'

'When was that?'

'Last week.'

'Guy who did it leave a note? Inform security?'

'No.' Parnell wished his voice hadn't wavered.

'Did you inform security?' said Bellamy.

'No.'

'Get an estimate from a repair shop?'

'No.'

'Make an insurer's report?'

'No.'

'Tell anyone?'

'Rebecca.'

'No one else?'

'No. No one else.'

Helen Montgomery said: 'I think we'd better take a look.'

Parnell was conscious of the attention of everyone in Rebecca's unit as he emerged into it from Showcross's office: aware, too, of the two officers forming up either side of him. They stayed that way even as they threaded their way through the lined-up cars. Parnell guessed there would be people watching from the windows behind him. As they approached the vehicle, he said: 'There! There it is.'

Bellamy, to Parnell's left, said: 'Quite a lot of damage, Mr Parnell. Just the sort of damage that would have been caused by your driving Ms Lang off the road.'

79

'You're making a mistake,' said Parnell, the cliché echoing in his head.

'People tell us that all the time,' said the woman.

They'd known about the damage before they'd even begun to question him, Parnell thought.

They arrested him there and handcuffed him and as they led him towards their Metro police marked car, Parnell saw there were people lined up at Dubette's windows. Dwight Newton, walking with them, told Parnell he'd talk to the company's legal department. Johnson said something Parnell didn't hear. He didn't hear a remark from Helen Montgomery, either, but didn't ask her to repeat it, withdrawing into himself, forcing himself to think logically, coherently. He needed a lawyer, obviously: not the one who'd negotiated his contracts, a lawyer accustomed to courts. America was a law-orientated country. It would be a formality, one he'd enjoy, humiliating the two assholes in front of him into a demanded – and necessary – apology. Science would be the answer, as it was to so much. He didn't know how long it would take, an unwelcome day, two at the most, forensically to establish that the crash-paint residue on Rebecca's car didn't match that of his Toyota. Which was hardly the problem, merely an inconvenience. Who *had* made her crash? Who had forced Rebecca to drive at sixty-five miles an hour, inevitably to crash. Why? An attack. That's what it had to be. She'd been running, fleeing, to escape from an attacker. Someone who *had* attacked her. Smashed into her car and forced her over the edge of a canyon or ravine or whatever they called it. Without a seat belt. That didn't make sense, Parnell decided, his mind back to Showcross's office and the knowing questioning from the two in front of him in the car. Rebecca never, ever, drove without a seat belt. Never drove off without buckling up, nagging him to do the same. So, hers would have been fastened outside the apartment at Washington Circle, long before she got to Rock Creek Park. What panic, aberration, had made her unfasten it? To jump out of the car – to escape? Not at sixty-five miles an hour. Why then? So many questions. Too many questions. Would – could – the two officers relaxing ahead of him ever answer them? He would, Parnell determined. When his own release had been secured – with apologies – he'd demand a proper investigation, not one already decided before it began. Which prompted another question. Had they known about the earlier damage to his Toyota? How? He hadn't reported the car-park accident to security: hadn't told anyone except Rebecca. So why had the two police officers behaved as aggressively, as disbelievingly, as they had in Showcross's office. And smirked and nodded when he'd shown them the damage to the Toyota? He was guessing, Parnell reminded himself. Shouldn't guess, like they'd guessed. If he was going to get this right – make them get this right and find the man or woman who'd caused Rebecca's death – he had to get everything right. Not guess. Be sure. He'd do it, Parnell promised himself. He'd make enough fuss, do whatever it took, to ensure there was a proper investigation. That the bastard was caught and tried and jailed. That would surely be the sentence on someone who'd chased a terrified woman through a forest, driven her to her death. That was murder. How terrified Rebecca must have been! All alone, fleeing an unknown pursuer, lights blazing in her mirror, knowing . . . knowing what? That she was going to be raped. Not a woman then. Had to be a man. A man depraved enough – insane enough – to kill her, if he couldn't have her sexually. The imagery, the horror, physically welled up inside Parnell and he choked and coughed against it, doubling up.

'No good crying, English boy,' said Bellamy from the passenger seat. 'We got you, fair and square. You're going to have all the time in the world for tears and regret.'

'You think . . . ?' started Parnell but stopped, intentionally, deciding it was pointless arguing with either of them. Instead he said: 'Don't call me boy. You're going to be made to look very stupid. Don't make it worse for yourselves, when I bring a case for wrongful arrest and blatant dereliction of duty and we discuss all this in a court with you in a dock.'

There was a long, unsettled silence. Then Helen Montgomery said: 'You quite sure we got those charges here on the statute book . . .' Bellamy filled the silence with an anticipatory snigger. '. . . English boy?' the woman finished, even exaggerating a southern accent.

'I hope not,' said Parnell, recovered and totally in control. 'I hope my lawyers can find something far worse than that.

You're giving more time for a killer to get away, by being stupid. That's what I'm going to hang around both your necks, a label saying *Stupid*.'

'You ever wonder what it feels like, getting a Billy club around *your* neck, English boy?' threatened Bellamy.

He'd picked the wrong fight at the wrong time, Parnell realized. There were a dozen witnesses to his docile detention but there would be two against one testimony to his later attempting to resist arrest.

'You lost your tongue, English boy?' said the woman, when Parnell didn't speak.

'There's a good English boy, learning respect,' mocked Bellamy, after a further silence. 'You're going to have to learn that well, proper respect, in an American jail. You could even be a prize. Now, wouldn't that be something, a big hunky English boy like you being a prison prize! You know what a prison prize is, English boy?'

'I don't think I want to,' said Parnell, forcing the humility.

'You bet your very sweet ass you don't want to,' guffawed Bellamy, a clearly rehearsed joke. 'But I got money that says you're going to find out in a very big way.' He and Helen Montgomery were still laughing when they pulled up in front of the police headquarters

Parnell had difficulty getting out of the car with his hands locked behind him, but managed it without coming into awkward contact with the two officers, who stood too close to the rear door. The manacles were only released inside the building. There they went through the property handover formality, bagging his belongings. In the interview room, all the recording apparatus on, Parnell was formally read his right against self-incrimination before being charged with causing death by dangerous driving, leaving the scene of an accident, failing to report an accident and driving in such a way as to endanger life.

'Those are holding charges,' finished Bellamy. 'Just the start.'

'Now you want to tell us what really happened?' demanded Helen Montgomery.

'I have a right to a lawyer, don't I?'

She sighed. Sticking to the necessary, recorded formality, she said: 'You have such a right.'

82

'I want to exercise it.'

'It's being done for you,' reminded Bellamy. 'Dwight Newton said he was talking to Dubette's legal people.'

'Then we'll wait until they arrive,' said Parnell. Seeing the immediate expression on Bellamy's face, Parnell decided he was lucky not to have arrived at the station without being beaten for supposedly resisted arrest. Perhaps – although only just perhaps – there was an advantage in being an English boy after all.

Both escorted Parnell to the detention cell, a narrow, tiled room equipped with a single bed and a lidless toilet bowl.

The woman said: 'I want your trouser belt and shoelaces. Your handkerchief, too. Had a bastard choke himself on his handkerchief once. Don't want you cheating yourself out of what's yours.'

'Or cheating a lot of other guys out of their pleasure,' added Bellamy.

Without a watch, it was difficult for Parnell to judge time, but there was still daylight through the barred window when the door opened again. The detention officer said: 'The canteen's got pot roast. You want pot roast?'

Parnell winced at the memory. 'No, thank you.'

'I thought you'd want that. I didn't ask about anything else.'

'I don't want anything else. I'm supposed to be getting a lawyer?'

'You called for one?'

'It was being arranged for me.'

'Don't know anything about a lawyer.'

'It's being done.'

'You wanna call again?'

'No.'

'You sure?'

Parnell nodded. 'What time is it?'

'Four thirty. You won't get another chance to eat.'

'I'm not hungry, thank you,' Parnell refused again.

He estimated it to be another hour before the door opened again to the detention officer, who jerked his head and said: 'Your lawyers are here.'

It wasn't until he was out in the corridor that Parnell properly realized how claustrophobically small the detention cell was. The man said: 'The pot roast was great. You missed a treat.'

Peter Baldwin, the head of Dubette's legal department, was already in the interview room into which Parnell had initially been taken. There were no flickering recording lights on the still-in-place apparatus. With Baldwin was another man, who was fat, balding and corseted in a tight, waistcoated striped suit. Baldwin said: 'This is Gerry Fletcher, your court attorney. Dwight wants you to know right away that Dubette's handling everything. Costs, I mean. I explained already to Gerry. He's in the picture.'

Fletcher's handshake, like the hand itself, was soft. The man said: 'Sorry it's taken so long, but maybe it's done us a favour.'

'What favour?' asked Parnell.

'They took your car, obviously,' said Fletcher. 'Part of the evidence – *the* evidence. And they recovered Rebecca's car from the canyon. They've done a paint match . . .'

'Thank God . . .' tried Parnell, but the attorney raised a podgy, halting hand.

'There *is* a positive match, Dick. They got forensic proof it was your car – you – that pushed Rebecca over.'

'*No!*'

'Of course, I'll go for independent forensic tests, but we've got to work a mitigating strategy.'

'*No!*' refused Parnell again, as loud as before.

'Dick, I can't defend you unless you're straight with me!'

'I did not run Rebecca's car off the road . . . kill her . . . that's being straight with you.'

'Dick!' said Baldwin. 'You're in bad shape. We're into limitation here.'

'No, we're not,' said Parnell, quieter, more controlled.

'Dubette are backing you . . . going out on a limb . . . don't make things any more difficult than they already are.'

Coming forward towards Fletcher across the table, Parnell said: 'You want me to plead guilty, to whatever the final charges are?'

'You're a scientist! You understand what I'm saying. They've got irrefutable scientific proof that it was your car that hit hers! And she's dead, at the bottom of a gorge. What other strategy do we have?'

Parnell turned to the company lawyer. 'Thank you . . . thank Dubette . . . for the offer. But no.'

Baldwin shook his head, uncertainly. 'What are you talking about, Dick?'

'Another lawyer. Another strategy. The right strategy.' Parnell stood. 'There isn't anything else for us to talk about.'

'Sit down!' said Baldwin, and at once Parnell remembered the same snapped instruction from Dwight Newton.

This time he didn't do as he was told, walking instead to the door and pressing the summons bell.

From behind him Baldwin said: 'You're insane. Perhaps that's it! You're insane.'

Fletcher said: 'You're making one hell of a mistake.'

'One of the officers who arrested me . . . who'd made her mind up that I was guilty, just like you . . . told me everyone keeps telling them that.'

'In your case she was right,' said the fat man.

'You through alrcady?' demanded the detention officer, from the corridor.

'Yes,' said Parnell.

'Don't expect any help from Dubette,' warned Baldwin, at the door.

'I don't. And won't,' said Parnell.

It took Parnell a further hour to convincc the desk sergeant that Fletcher and Baldwin had not been his choice of attorneys and that therefore he still had the legal right to a representative telephone call, part of his mind reeling with the awareness that he didn't have – or know – a lawyer to call, apart from the contract attorney. He'd already decided on his only approach, hollowed by the desperation of it, when he was finally shown in to an unsupervised inner office. So anxious, shaking, was he that he misdialled at the first attempt, jabbing at the button to disconnect, actually mentally praying – *Please God, let somebody be there!* – for a reply.

'Yes?' said Beverley Jackson's clipped voice.

'I'm in trouble,' said Parnell.

'We know.'

'Get me a trial lawyer. Please!'

Twelve

B arry Jackson was a heavily built, blond-haired man with a deep, half-moon scar on his left cheek. He wore a sports shirt, jeans and a sports jacket and apologized as he entered the detention cell. 'I was at home when I got the call.'

Reading the other man's watch as the lawyer handed him his card, Parnell saw it was nearly midnight. Frowning down at the introduction, Parnell said: 'Jackson?'

'Beverley and I are still good friends. Just not good at being married – she never can bring herself to admit I'm always right. She thought you knew I was a lawyer – that that was why you called her.'

'No,' said Parnell. 'Maybe it's my first piece of luck.'

'All I've got from the night sergeant are the charges. And I won't be able to make a bail application until the morning. In between times, why don't you tell me the story?'

His story was all that Parnell had thought about for so long it seemed forever, until his mind blocked and he didn't feel he could think about it from any other direction. 'You're not going to believe it.'

'You better hope I do.'

Parnell told it – hoped he told it – chronologically, from the moment Rebecca had picked him up from Washington Circle. And didn't leave anything out, not even Rebecca's admission of her pregnancy termination, his belief that the Metro DC officers had known in advance of the damage to his Toyota or the English-boy mockery on his manacled way to the station house.

'This guy, Fletcher? He told you there's forensic evidence that it was your car that hit Rebecca's?'

'Yes.'

'Did you?'

'No!'

'I can hear you well enough.'

'No,' repeated Parnell, more softly. He ached with exhaustion.

'I find you're lying, I relinquish the case, OK?'

'I'm not lying. And OK.'

'You make a formal statement?'

'No.'

Jackson sighed, relieved. 'You tell them about Rebecca's abortion?'

'No.'

There was another relieved sigh. 'So, they don't have an obvious motive.'

'Who's side are you on?'

'Mine, Dick. And yours. But I don't take on losers. That's what I meant about lying. The two officers threatened you? You threaten them back?'

'Yes.'

'Shit!'

'I told you what they were like – what they said.'

'Maybe we can turn it. It's not the major concern: I'm just worried about Rebecca's car.'

'I don't understand.'

'You don't have to. Beverley says I've got to do this pro bono.'

'I didn't ask for that!'

The lawyer sat looking at him, unspeaking. Realizing, Parnell said: 'No! There's nothing between Beverley and me! On my life!'

'Your life's not worth much at the moment but I'll believe you about Beverley, for the moment. It takes away another motive, you caught between two women.'

'I fired Fletcher because he'd already decided I was guilty – said that's how I had to plead and that we had to try for mitigation.'

'I haven't decided that or talked about guilty pleas or mitigation. But if you want to fire me, go ahead. It'll cost you three hundred bucks for the consultation. There was a Perry Mason rerun on television tonight. I didn't want to miss it.'

'I want you to believe I'm innocent!'

'I want to believe it, too. But I'm already way ahead of

you, wondering how many cans of how many worms I'm
going to have to open up to prove it.'

'Please help me,' pleaded Parnell. 'I've thought about it
every which way. I know how it looks.'

'You good for a personal bail bond?'

'Depends how much it is.'

'Perhaps we'll need a bondsman. You're a good enough
risk, with the Dubette position.'

'If I keep the Dubette position,' said Parnell.

'They fire you ahead of a formal verdict, I'll strip their skin
off, layer by layer, until they bleed to death.'

'What about Beverley?'

Jackson smiled, for the first time. 'You just impressed me!
They go for her while I'm going at them, her compensation
would match yours.'

'*You* just impressed *me*,' said Parnell.

'You don't say anything to anyone about anything, OK?
Just yes, please and thank you. The two officers are out of it
now, until a court hearing. But no more threats against them.
Or anyone else, no matter what they do or say.'

'OK.'

'Anything you want to ask me? Tell me?'

'I don't want this no win, no fee.'

'Neither do I. So it isn't.'

It was more of a collapse into exhaustion than sleep and
Parnell was awake long before the same detention officer,
yawning away the effect of his own rumpled night, came into
the cell with the offer of a bristle-matted electric razor, corned-
beef hash and coffee. Parnell refused everything except the
coffee, which came in a much stained, unbreakable tin mug
that retained so much heat it was uncomfortable to drink.
There were four other officers in the shower-equipped washroom to which the warder escorted him, but Peter Bellamy
wasn't among them. They all regarded him contemptuously.
Parnell, accustomed to communal sports-room bathing,
stripped without embarrassment. One of the watching officers
said something to the others when Parnell came out of the
shower cubicle and on their way back to the holding cell the

88

detention officer said: 'They think you're shit, for what you did.'

Obedient to the midnight instructions, Parnell said nothing. He estimated it to be another hour before the door opened again to the smirking Peter Bellamy, flanked by Helen Montgomery.

The woman said: 'Hear you got yourself a hot-shot lawyer.'

Parnell didn't reply.

'Got Judge Wilson out of bed this morning to put the cars under court jurisdiction. Cranky son of a bitch, old Davey Wilson. Won't like that one bit.'

Parnell guessed neither of the officers did, either.

'You got nothing to say, English boy?' said the woman.

'Are we going to court?' He'd expected Barry Jackson to come back to the police station.

'Bet that sweet ass we are,' said Bellamy. 'Gonna have you tucked up nice and safe in a proper jail with a lot of new and loving friends by tonight.'

Parnell hesitated directly outside the cell door, half moving his hands to be manacled again, but Helen Montgomery said: 'That smart lawyer of yours got an order against restraint.'

'Which doesn't prevent us from cuffing you, you do something we don't like,' warned Bellamy. 'You be very, very careful, English boy.'

It was bravado, Parnell guessed. He didn't think they were worried yet but there was an uncertainty. The impression remained as he walked between them out into the receiving hall, where three of the officers from the washroom were standing. The expressions were still contemptuous but there were no sniggering remarks. There weren't on the short drive to the courthouse, either. The car stopped directly in front of the building but it wasn't until he started to get out, the two deputies already posed, that Parnell saw the cameras, television as well as presumably newspaper photographers. There was a babble of questions, which Parnell ignored. He tried to hurry through the pack but felt Bellamy's hand upon his arm, slowing him, although at the same time he heard the man demanding that they be let through, which they finally were.

Jackson was waiting outside their assigned court, in a subdued suit and muted tie. The lawyer said: 'How you feeling?'

'Like shit.'

'That's just how you look. Those photographs aren't going to flatter you, either. You already got today's headlines, in the *Washington Post* even. Lot of background about your scientific work. Let's get out of here, somewhere quieter.' Jackson led the way into an anteroom equipped with a table, chairs and a closed, glass-fronted cabinet of neatly ordered legal books. As he sat where Jackson indicated, Parnell said: 'Gather you started early?'

'Earlier than you'd believe,' said Jackson. 'Did Bellamy or Montgomery question you about the contents of Rebecca's purse?'

'No.'

'What does AF209 mean to you?'

Parnell stared back uncomprehendingly at the lawyer. 'Nothing.'

'You sure?'

'If I tell you it means nothing it means nothing.'

'It's a flight number. An Air France flight number.'

'Of course,' understood Parnell. 'It just didn't seem to fit.' Or did it?

'What were Rebecca's political views?'

Parnell's breath came out in a laugh. 'We never discussed her political views. I don't believe she had any, not seriously.'

'What about you?'

'What's this got to do with Rebecca's murder?'

'It could have a lot to do with it. Answer the question.' There was a hardness to the man's questioning there hadn't been before.

'If you're looking for an American near equivalent I guess it's Democrat. But I don't know what the hell you're talking about.'

'You ever belonged to a radical political organization? At university, maybe, when everybody does.'

'I wasn't one of the everybodies.'

'Does that mean you never belonged or subscribed in any way whatsoever to a radical political organization?'

'That's very precisely what it means,' said Parnell. 'You going to make it any easier for either of us, because at the moment I don't know what the hell you're talking about.'

Jackson studied him across the table for several moments before saying: 'I find you lied to me, I'll throw you in the snake pit myself.'

'Oh, for fuck's sake!' said Parnell. 'What's the difference between a snake pit and the madhouse I'm in already?'

'You might find out in a very short time,' said Jackson. 'Something else you should know is that getting the cars under the court's jurisdiction gets them away from Metro DC police. I'm trying to fix independent forensic tests, as early as this afternoon if possible. Maybe, if you're telling me the truth, it will be by someone more independent than we could hope for. Prosecution are going for a remand in custody, which I'm going to oppose, obviously. This is scheduled as an initial formality, a bail hearing . . . All that stuff in the papers about your professional career and integrity could help, as well as the rabbit I might have in my hat. And there might even be another edge.'

'What?' demanded Parnell.

The man hesitated. 'Don't want to build up false hopes.' There was another pause. 'We've got the preliminary autopsy report. Rebecca's neck was broken and there were extensive crush injuries to the chest. And there was no finding of excessive alcohol.'

Parnell winced, coughing, at the listed injuries. 'They said, the officers, she wasn't wearing a seat belt. That can't be. She always wore a seat belt.'

'You told me last night,' remembered Jackson. 'She wasn't in the car when she was found. She'd been thrown clear.'

'What about crawling out . . . releasing herself and crawling out?'

The lawyer shook his head. 'Not with those injuries.'

'It's not right,' insisted Parnell. 'Something's definitely not right.'

'Let's not get ahead of ourselves,' cautioned Jackson. 'You're the immediate priority. They got an argument for a custodial remand, hit and run, leaving the scene of a fatal accident. I'm going to have to call you. Now don't get mad but I'm going to ask you one more time. Did you pursue Rebecca Lang into Rock Creek Park?'

'No.'

'Crash into her car and force her off the road?'

'No.'

'So how do you account for your car's paint being on Rebecca's vehicle?'

'I can't.'

'You ever been in a court before? Under cross-examination?'

'No.'

'The prosecution is going to roll all over you,' warned the lawyer. 'They've already guaranteed the publicity. Headlines. It's the sort of stuff they go for.'

'You think it was the prosecution who got all the stuff in the papers?'

'Yes. They think it's a big case from which they're going to emerge looking good.'

'I guess it is,' accepted Parnell.

'No you don't,' contradicted Jackson. 'You can't guess what it's like until it happens to you. Don't lose your temper, no matter how much they try to make you. Don't rush an answer until you've thought about it. Don't volunteer anything you're not asked. You think you can remember all that?'

'I hope so.'

'Don't hope so. Know so. Baldwin and Fletcher are going to be in court, by the way.'

'I said I didn't want them! Fired Fletcher.'

'They're not representing you. After all today's publicity, they applied for – and got – a watching brief on behalf of Dubette.'

'How are Dubette involved?'

'You work for them. Rebecca worked for them. It's an obvious precaution for Dubette. For their reputation.'

'Against what?'

'Against whatever.'

Rebecca hadn't been the only child-speaker, Parnell thought. 'I don't think I've properly understood things yet.'

'I *know* you haven't properly understood things yet. I don't think I have, either. Until I do, we go with the flow. There's something else you should understand. If there's a conviction on any of what they've already charged you with or charge you with later – most certainly if there's a prison term – it's virtually inevitable your preferential work visa will be revoked. You'll be deported, after serving whatever sentence is imposed.'

'I'm frightened,' blurted Parnell, wishing at once that he hadn't spoken. He couldn't remember ever admitting that before: not meaning it, as he meant it now. But then he'd never been caught up in such a nightmare before.

'Do the best you can. And try to remember what I said about what to do and what not to do in court.'

'I'll . . .' started Parnell, but quickly corrected himself. 'I will. I promised I will.'

'One more time,' insisted Jackson. 'A flight number, AF209, means nothing to you?'

'Absolutely not! Why's it so important?'

'I wish to Christ I knew. Knew, too, whether I was doing the right thing.'

The prosecuting attorney, Vernon Hanson, was a man whose thinness at once reminded Parnell of Dwight Newton, although the prosecutor was dressed better to conceal it, the suit tailored and waistcoated, the spectacles rimless and minimal. He had, too, the demeanour of belonging, of being sure of himself in familiar surroundings. Baldwin and Fletcher were in the row behind. Both had yellow legal pads before them. Baldwin smiled and nodded. Fletcher remained expressionless. To their right the press gallery was crowded, several reporters overflowing on to the extra seats provided. Everyone stood, to the usher's order, at the entry of the white-haired, jowl-wobbling Judge David Wilson, who pointedly remained standing for several moments, peering accusingly at Parnell over half-rimmed spectacles before taking his seat. At Jackson's halting hand, Parnell remained standing with the lawyer, formally to be charged, after everyone else sat. It was Jackson, just as formally, who entered the not-guilty plea to each charge on Parnell's behalf.

Hanson came up from his bench like a toy from a sprung box, his voice surprisingly resonant from such a slightly statured man. The charges were sample accusations, the prosecutor said at once. Others, more serious, might subsequently be proffered. The allegations were that the accused had knowingly pursued a terrified woman, with whom there had been an existing relationship, through a darkened park area at illegal speeds and forced her off the road into a 40' canyon, causing her death. There was already substantial and irrefutable forensic evidence of contact between the two vehicles. He was applying for Parnell to be remanded to a place of detention to enable the investigation to proceed and for further, possibly more serious, charges to be considered.

Peter Bellamy was the first officer to be called by the prosecution for formal evidence of arrest. Parnell was surprised by the close-to-verbatim accuracy of the man's account of the encounter in Showcross's office, curious what there could be for Jackson to contest when his lawyer was given the right to question.

'When did you come into possession of Ms Lang's purse?' began Jackson.

'At the station house,' replied the officer.

'Who had recovered it?'

'I understood it to have been found in the car, by the engineers who raised it from the gorge in Rock Creek Park.'

'Had it been opened, prior to being handed to you?'

'There had been a preliminary examination. That's how the Dubette ID had been discovered. It was closed again when it was given to us. The ID was inside.'

'To whom was it given, exactly? Yourself? Or officer Montgomery?'

'Officer Montgomery personally accepted it.'

'What happened then . . . ?'

'Are we working towards something here, Mr Jackson?' intruded the judge.

'I very much believe that we are,' assured Jackson.

'I hope we reach it soon,' said the raven-gowned man.

'I am sure we will,' said Jackson. To Bellamy he said: 'You were about to tell the court the procedure for an item such as Ms Lang's purse.'

'Its contents were examined. Listed.'

'Ah!' exclaimed Jackson, as if it were an important revelation. 'Could you read every item of that list to the court.'

'I must protest . . .' started Hanson, rising with hands outstretched.

'You promised we would reach the point of this questioning very soon,' came in the judge, supportively.

'A promise I intend to keep,' said Jackson. 'The list, please, officer Bellamy.'

The man went through a litany of cosmetics, a pen, credit cards, the Dubette ID, a tampon, a First City Bank cheque book and cash card, $52.23 in cash and finally a piece of paper upon which was written AF209.

'What significance did you draw from that piece of paper, with AF209 written on it?'

'I didn't,' said the man. 'We haven't begun a proper enquiry yet. It will probably be taken from us – go over to detectives.'

'You and Officer Montgomery were the first people to list the contents of Ms Lang's purse?'

'Yes,' confirmed the man.

'Thank you,' said the lawyer, plumping down beside Parnell.

'Mr Jackson!' demanded the judge, warningly.

'May I approach the bench?'

'If you hadn't asked, I was going to demand it,' said the judge.

It was a huddled unheard discussion between the judge, Jackson and Vernon Hanson, with several bursts of gesticulating from the prosecuting attorney. When they returned to the body of the court, Hanson said to the judge: 'Upon your instruction, I will say nothing that indicates the content of our conversation but I wish that restraint to be recorded, as well as the possibility of a complaint to another body for lack of prior disclosure.'

'This is a remand hearing, Mr Hanson,' said the judge. 'Prior disclosure is not a requirement, although I will concede there might have been a courtesy extended.'

Jackson was immediately upon his feet. 'If I have offended the court – or the prosecution – then I apologize. I would also like that entered into the record.'

Helen Montgomery's evidence of arrest was an echo of her partner's, as was her account of their receiving Rebecca Lang's handbag upon their return to the police building.

Jackson took her through that as meticulously as he had Peter Bellamy, towards the end insisting: 'Who did what, in the listing of the contents? Who wrote the list, who extracted the items, one by one?'

The woman shifted, uncomfortably. 'I think I took them out, Pete wrote them down.'

'What's AF209 mean to you?'

'Nothing. A flight number, I guess.'

'Which you would have pursued, to discover the significance?'

'If the investigation were left to us, yes. But I don't expect it will be, now that it's a homicide.'

Not once was there any intervention from Hanson, who spent the questioning bent over a yellow legal pad, hurriedly writing.

The forensic scientist was a small, elderly, thinning-haired man who very positively stressed his professorship and whose hand shook as he took the oath to be sworn in as Jacob Meadows. The man, who needed constantly to clear his throat, testified to being shown two cars the previous afternoon in the police-department garage. He was also shown substantial paint debris collected from the scene of a fatal accident involving a 2003 registered blue Ford. Grey paint adhering to the Ford, and in places wedged into that extensively damaged bodywork, together with more that had been among the dislodged blue paint, unquestionably matched that of the grey Toyota he had been asked to examine and compare.

Jackson was quickly on his feet again. 'Professor, where were the two vehicles when you examined them?'

'I have already told you, in the police-department garage,' replied the coughing man, testily.

'And the separate paint debris?'

'I don't understand the question.'

'Where did you find that?'

'It was handed to me.'

'By whom?'

'One of the recovery engineers?'

'In an evidence bag?'

'Yes.'

'So, you did not yourself examine the scene? Collect the samples?'

'I collected those samples adhering to the Ford in the garage. And I saw how the preventative barrier had been damaged: there was blue paint residue there, where it mounted the barrier to go into the canyon. The Ford, in the garage, was also marked by paint from the barrier.'

'But you yourself did not descend into the canyon, to carry out any investigation there?'

'It's a forty-foot drop. Recovery engineers had to be lowered by hoists. I understand the Ford was recovered by crane.'

'You weren't there for that recovery?'

'No.'

'And did not go down, on a hoist, into the canyon?'

'I have already told you I did not.'

'But you have carefully examined both cars in the garage?'

'Yes.'

'Tell me, professor, at the speed that these two vehicles are thought to have collided, causing the damage you've indicated, would you have expected a substantial amount of blue paint from Ms Lang's car to have marked Mr Parnell's grey Toyota?'

There was no immediate reply from Jacob Meadows, but there was shuffling in the court, particularly from the press bench. Finally the forensic scientist said, shortly: 'Yes.'

'Were there any such blue paint markings?'

'My examination was provisional, for this hearing.'

'Were there any blue paint markings?' persisted Jackson.

The man took a notebook from his pocket, flicking through the pages with a shaking hand for several moments. 'I haven't recorded any.'

'Is the direction of this questioning connected with our earlier discussion at the bench, Mr Jackson?' intervened the judge.

'Yes, your honour,' confirmed the lawyer. To Meadows he said: 'Were you shown the contents of the deceased's handbag?'

'No.'

'Was there any discussion between you and officers at the police station about any handbag?'

'No. My examination was cursory, for the benefit of this hearing.'

'Cursory!' seized Jackson. 'You conducted a cursory examination, for the benefit of this hearing, the purpose of which is to decide whether or not Richard Parnell should be remanded in custody.'

'I did what I was asked to do, at that stage.'

'Asked to do by whom?'

'I'm not sure I remember. Someone at the station.'

Neither Bellamy nor Helen Montgomery were smirking any more.

'I've concluded this initial questioning of this witness,' said Jackson. 'I call Richard Parnell to the stand.'

Parnell felt a vague unreality as he walked across the well of the court, and he fought against it, nervously aware that the last thing he could afford was light-headedness or lack of concentration. He recited the oath to the usher's dictation, glad his voice strengthened when he answered Jackson's first question, that he fully understood what it meant to tell the truth. Despite knowing the questioning was necessary to establish a good character, Parnell regretted having to list his academic and scientific qualifications, background and acclaim to the journalists' hurried scribbling, wondering if his arrest and arraignment would appear in British newspapers. He hoped it wouldn't cause any embarrassment or harassment of English colleagues if it did. Or, he abruptly thought, his mother. He had to call her, just in case. Jackson took him, in just as much detail, through his employment by Dubette and even into a detailed explanation of pharmacogenomics. The media note-taking increased when Jackson led the questioning on to Parnell's relationship with Rebecca Lang, generalizing at first before coming specifically to the Sunday at Chesapeake Bay and their return to the Washington Circle apartment. Parnell's tension tightened when he began talking about the decision he and Rebecca had made, to live together, frightened that Jackson would introduce Rebecca's admission of pregnancy, but the lawyer didn't.

'What was Rebecca Lang's demeanour when she left your apartment to return to Bethesda?'

'She was happy. We both were, about living together.'

'You didn't have an argument?'

'Absolutely not.'

'Fall out?'

'Absolutely not.'

'What did you do after Rebecca left your apartment?'

'Sat around. Did some work I'd brought home with me. Went to bed.'

'You didn't call her?'

'No.'

'Why not? You'd just made a romantic commitment. A lot of people might have expected you to call to make sure she got home safely.'

'I know. I just didn't. I wish I had. I could have started a search, earlier. Maybe . . .' Parnell swallowed, not finishing. He supposed Jackson was anticipating some of the questioning he had to expect from the prosecutor.

'Now tell the court about the damage to your car,' insisted Jackson.

'It happened last Thursday. It had been all day in the Dubette car park. There was no damage when I left it there, just after seven in the morning. When I came out, around seven thirty, nine o'clock, someone had hit it.'

'Describe the damage.'

'A wing and door were badly dented. The bumper – the fender – was bent in.'

'The paint was broken?'

'Yes.'

'Was there much paint around on the ground?'

'I don't remember there being any.'

'What about paint from the car that hit you?'

'No. I don't remember there being any trace of that, either.'

'Mr Hanson,' stopped the judge, addressing the prosecutor. 'Isn't that something that the court might have found useful to have been told?'

'As Professor Meadows has testified, his was a preliminary examination,' said Hanson, not as quick to his feet as before.

'Told the court under cross-examination,' reminded the judge. 'And used the word cursory, not preliminary. During a hearing to determine whether the accused is granted bail or remanded into custody, to decide which, the court wishes to know *all* facts available at the time of such consideration. Do you have witnesses, either available or who can be called, to help the court?'

Hanson turned questioningly to the two arresting officers. Bellamy shook his head. Turning back to the judge, Hanson said: 'Not at this moment.'

'Mr Jackson?' invited the judge.

'Mr Parnell,' resumed his lawyer. 'You've heard evidence of the contents of Rebecca's handbag, including a piece of paper with AF209 written upon it. Have you any idea why that was there?'

'Part of Rebecca's job was to liaise with Dubette's foreign subsidiaries and receive shipments from them, for analysis and testing at McLean. I can only assume it had something to do with that.'

'Assume?' picked out Jackson. 'You and she did not discuss it on Sunday?'

'No.'

'You had no idea it was in her purse.'

'None whatsoever.'

'I have an application to make, which you might have already anticipated,' Jackson told the judge. 'But at this moment I have no further questions for my client.'

'Mr Hanson?' came the second invitation.

It was jack-in-the-box abruptness again but Parnell had already inferred what Jackson had referred to as an edge – guessing that a lot of other people in the court were at least suspecting an inference, as well – and the sting was taken out of the attack. But it was still an attack. Hanson took Parnell through every question that had been put to him by Jackson, repeating them, rewording them, hectoring for replies, but Parnell remained quite controlled, relaxed almost, telling himself he hadn't really needed Jackson's warnings, although at once conceding that that was probably overconfidence.

There was a palpable desperation in Hanson's repetitive conclusion, culminating with: 'You killed her, didn't you?'

'No.'

'Chased her, in the dark?'

'No.'

'Rammed her off the road?'

'Why should I have done that, to the woman I loved and decided I wanted to set up home with?' It was not instinctive. It was a reaction that had been growing in Parnell's mind throughout the rephrasing and repetition but the timing was devastating.

Hanson had been bent over his legal pad, intent on his listed, hopefully hammer-blow questions. He came up startled by a question in return, not a denying response. Hurriedly he said: 'That's what I'm asking you to tell me.'

'As I have repeatedly tried to explain, there is nothing *to* tell,' retorted Parnell. 'Except to repeat, as many times as you have repeated yourself, that I did not chase by car, crash into, try to kill or successfully kill Rebecca Lang.'

'Points and denials that I believe already to be well established, Mr Hanson,' said the judge. 'I think it's time to get to submissions. I would like to hear yours.'

The confidence had gone from the prosecutor. He spoke coherently, prepared – prepared, clearly, before the courtroom reversals – but his argument lacked conviction or belief. He stressed the seriousness of the accusations and insisted even more serious charges were to follow, and demanded that the remand be in custody for the investigation to proceed to enable those additional charges to be formulated.

Barry Jackson's rebuttal was as forceful as Vernon Hanson's had been falteringly weak. The prosecution's grounds for a remand in custody had not been proved by a failed, premature and inadequately conducted investigation upon which he might at some later stage invite the court's comment. Richard Parnell was a man of unquestioned rectitude and integrity. He totally and utterly refuted all the current and any subsequent charges and was prepared to offer in his own recognisance whatever bail the court might demand. Parnell was further prepared to surrender his passport to the court and report daily to any police authority, although Jackson invited the judge to rule that that authority be other than the one involved in the ongoing investigation.

Throughout the submission, Hanson, the two officers and Professor Jacob Meadows sat stone-faced, not looking at anyone. The Dubette lawyers Peter Baldwin and Gerald Fletcher also remained expressionless.

'I want counsel to approach the bench again,' insisted the judge.

This time it was Jackson who did most of the gesticulating, but when they returned to their places Hanson said: 'I would once more like my strongest objection to any bail application to be placed on record, in view of our discussions.'

Judge David Wilson said: 'Let it be so recorded, but it is in view of that discussion and, at the moment unsubstantiated, observations of defence counsel Barry Jackson that I am minded to take an unusual course. I have concerns about several aspects of this custody application. I do not consider it is one upon which I can, or will, give an immediate decision from the bench, until matters raised by Mr Jackson have been resolved. I fully recognize, however, that this court is considering a person's freedom or detention, albeit how brief of either. Mr Jackson, where is your client's passport?'

Before his lawyer fully bent towards him, Parnell said: 'The apartment,' loud enough for the judge to hear.

'So,' nodded the black-robed man, without waiting for the relay. 'I am putting the accused into the temporary custody of a court official and yourself, Mr Jackson, for the passport to be retrieved and returned here, at two o'clock today, to be placed in the custody of this court, should it be my decision to grant the bail application. During that adjournment I shall properly and fully consider both submissions made to me this morning, hope to get guidance upon the matter that has so far not been disclosed in open court, and rule accordingly. Until then . . .'

Everyone rose, to the usher's order.

It was the same usher whom Wilson appointed their court escort, with the admonishment that any overheard conversation between Jackson and Parnell was wholly governed and protected by client confidentiality. Despite that instruction, Parnell waited for Jackson's lead in the car taking the three of them to the apartment, the usher driving. Almost before they cleared the court precincts, Jackson said, ebulliently: 'We got our breaks!'

Parnell said: 'I still need to know what the hell that is! Or was! Or perhaps still is! This really is Perry Mason!'

'I know,' grinned Jackson. 'Tomorrow's headlines are going to be twice as big as today's.'

'Please?' implored Parnell. He ached with the strain of the concentration with which he'd had to hold himself in court. 'What in Christ's name is the importance of AF209?'

'I haven't confirmed that yet,' said Jackson. 'Until I do, it remains a matter for the closed court.'

'So, how come I got released like this?'

'Professor Jacob Meadows,' announced Jackson. 'His expert evidence has been discredited on three appeals. One, two years ago, overturned a judgment of Judge Wilson. I couldn't believe Hanson's court list when I saw it this morning. That's why I so easily got the court protection order with the cars. I just busked the questioning in court, believing even less that I'd get the admissions that I did from him.'

'There's still a lot I don't understand, about what's being claimed,' protested Parnell.

'Me, too,' conceded Jackson, soberly now. 'I didn't know how right I was last night, about opening up cans of worms. There could be some we don't want to see.'

The usher was lucky with a meter very close to Parnell's apartment, outside of which there was already a waiting phalanx of cameramen. The usher said: 'I suppose I've got to come in with you. This is a first for me as well.'

'Come and get your moment of fame,' said Jackson.

They endured the flashlights and strobes and Parnell was conscious of faces at windows, as there had been when he'd left the Dubette building. Inside the apartment, he went directly to the bureau and retrieved the passport. As he turned away, offering it to the usher, Jackson nodded towards the telephone and said: 'Your light's flashing. You've got a message.'

All three men stood looking down at the apparatus while the message rewound. Then a bright voice said: 'This is the Acme Toyota garage, 9 a.m. Monday, responding to Ms Lang's message of Saturday. Sorry we haven't been able to get back to you sooner, Mr Parnell. You want to call us on 202-534-9928, we'll fix a time either in DC or McLean to sort a repair estimate for your Toyota. Like we told Ms Lang, our estimates are free and we are the authorized Toyota repair shop in the DC area. Look forward to hearing from you.'

Jackson extracted the tape from the machine with a surgeon's delicacy and said: 'This has gone beyond luck. We're now into I don't know what . . .' He looked Parnell up and down, disdainfully. 'I've got calls to make. And while I'm doing that, you got time to clean yourself up and put on something you haven't slept in. You got to start making yourself look good for the cameras, because there's going to be a lot more of those around before the day's out.'

Thirteen

Richard Parnell showered for a second time to wash off the imagined smell of detention and chose a collar and tie to go with the discreetly patterned sports jacket to match Jackson's conservatism. The lawyer nodded at his reappearance and said: 'That'll do fine for whatever the hell else is going to come today. I've lit a lot of fuses and there could be a very big bang.'

'I don't understand a word you've just said and I need to know when I'm going to,' protested Parnell. He felt like a specimen under one of his own microscopes, an essentially alive but inanimate object blindly writhing and twisting.

'You'll know when I know,' promised Jackson. 'For the moment, we're going an inch at a time, starting from when we leave here. If we get ambushed again you say nothing. I do all the talking. But we don't hurry. Guilty people hurry and, sure as hell, Richard my friend, we ain't guilty. But other people are, exactly of what I'm not at this moment quite sure. So we're lighting as many more fuses as we can.'

There was the expected media encirclement outside the apartment, and Jackson murmured it was just what he'd wanted, and waited patiently for them all to get into position with their cameras focused before announcing that there had been a sensational development which he was unable to disclose until it had been brought before Judge Wilson, with whom he had been in telephone contact and who had delayed for one hour the original court resumption for this new evidence to be produced. That new evidence had elevated the investigation into the tragic death of Rebecca Lang to a federal level, the circumstances of which would become clear later that day. In the car, the usher once more at the wheel, Parnell demanded: 'What federal level?'

'Flight AF209,' said Jackson. 'It rang a distant bell. I had my office check it out while you were cleaning up. And then spoke to guys I know at the J. Edgar Hoover building. It's a Paris to Washington DC flight that was cancelled four times about three months ago after intelligence electronic eavesdropping picked up a reference to a terrorism attack.'

'It was in Rebecca's bag!' said Parnell, disbelievingly.

'You heard what Bellamy and the Montgomery woman said in court.'

Had it anything to do with the mystery French consignment? wondered Parnell, at once. 'Why this one number?'

'That's a question you're going to be asked a lot of times over the next few days,' predicted Jackson. 'Like I said, I'm not sure we're going to be happy with all the cans of worms we've opened. This is now an FBI and Homeland Security investigation.'

'You're not suggesting Rebecca could have been involved . . . no, that's too absurd even to think about . . .'

'I'm afraid you're going to have to think about it a lot,' said Jackson.

'There was some stuff from Paris that didn't arrive in the usual way,' disclosed Parnell, at last. 'Rebecca was curious. It turned out to be some check experiments that didn't work out. According to the research vice president, the project was cancelled.'

'You think it's connected with that?'

In the driver's seat the usher shifted and said: 'I'm becoming uncomfortable about the confidentiality restrictions of this.'

Jackson said: 'You're bound by a specific court order – the judge is going to be told.' To Parnell he said: 'In court you leave everything to me, understood?'

'With as much difficulty as I'm having understanding anything,' said Parnell.

Suddenly alert to where they were, Parnell said: 'Hey, you took the wrong turn – we're going back into Washington!'

'Stop to make first,' said Jackson. 'We're going to Crystal City, to the Acme body shop. No need for you to come in when we get there. You just stay in the car.'

'Remember who I am?' demanded Parnell, rhetorically. 'I'm the person accused of what amounts to murder. I have the right!'

'I'm not contesting that right,' shot back Jackson. 'And I haven't forgotten who you are or what you're accused of. You stay in the car because I think it's best – the best for you. So that's what you'll do.'

'I'm a client!' protested Parnell. 'And I'm not used to being talked to like that!' and winced at his own pomposity.

'Look at it as a learning curve,' dismissed Jackson.

They went over the Potomac high, at the Arlington Bridge, to miss the traffic build-up, and as they turned along the George Washington Memorial Parkway, Parnell saw the Tidal Basin to his left and remembered boastfully rowing Rebecca upriver and unthinkingly said: 'Oh Christ!'

'What?' demanded Jackson, beside him.

'Nothing.'

'You said something.'

'It's not important.'

'Everything's important!'

'I just thought of something.'

'Everything you think about is important,' insisted the lawyer.

'This wasn't,' refused Parnell. Except that it was: it was the first proper, deeper realization – deeper than that which had registered with him in Burt Showcross's overcrowded office the previous day. *Rebecca was dead*, he thought, stepping the

106

words out in his mind. He wasn't any more going to take her rowing on the river or to a restaurant where their meal and wine was chosen for them, or to a shack on a bay that looked as big as an ocean, to glue themselves up eating crabs so small you ate everything, shells and all. Someone *had* killed her, murdered her! And tried to make him a victim – frame him as the murderer – as well. Why? What had she – they – done for anyone to do all that? Hate them so much to do all that? Parnell rejected the threadbare phrase that came automatically to mind. He'd make it make sense! What could AF209 mean except Rebecca's obsession with that damned French business? Who – where – was the runaway lover? Rebecca would have taken him to her uncle's restaurant – introduced him, given the man a name, just as she'd introduced Parnell. A place, the obvious place, to start. Bethesda! Even more obvious. There had to be a clue there, among her personal belongings: a photograph, a letter, a name in an address book, no matter how much she might have despised the man for her abandonment. Belongings he had no way, no right, to examine, he reminded himself. He had to find a way, any way. He'd do it – find it. Parnell came out of the reverie at their entry into an industrial park, conscious that Jackson was leaning forward to guide the court official at the wheel, actually gesturing directions from an earlier torn-off page from the much used legal pad. Almost at once Parnell saw the neon sign of the Acme repair facility, the lettering of its Toyota appointment almost as big as the name itself. The forecourt and a lot of what he could see behind the warehouse-sized building was a dead cars' graveyard.

'Wait!' insisted Jackson.

The usher shifted, uncertainly. 'I shouldn't leave him. I'm responsible.'

Parnell said: 'You mind not talking across me, like I don't exist?'

'Just give us a moment,' Jackson asked Parnell, no longer demanding. 'You'll understand soon enough.'

It was only a moment. Parnell straightened at the returning approach of Jackson and the court officer. Another man and a woman walked with them almost to his car before detouring to another vehicle, predictably a Toyota.

'All set,' announced Jackson, coming heavily into the back seat beside Parnell. 'They're going to follow. Manager and the gal whose job it is to pick up all the weekend messages. And did she do a hell of a good job!' He held up another cassette. 'Rebecca's voice is on it. I didn't want you to have to go through hearing it more than once, later in court.'

'I'm sorry,' said Parnell. 'And thanks.'

Parnell was by now accustomed to the waiting media scrum, to which Jackson repeated what he'd said outside the apartment. Everyone from the morning arraignment was already waiting inside. Parnell took the seat he'd previously occupied. Jackson sat the two Acme garage employees in the first row beyond the separating court rail, beside two men to whom he spoke after shaking hands. Finally he crossed for a whispered conversation with Vernon Hanson, showing the prosecuting attorney the two tape loops and indicating the four beyond the rail. They were interrupted by the court usher, returning from the judge's chambers. At once the two lawyers followed the man back through a door from which he'd just emerged. The usher continued on, gesturing to the two men whom Jackson had greeted. One, a slightly, studiously bespectacled man, pushed through the rail and followed the usher with an awkward, stiff-legged walk.

It was ten minutes before they returned, the usher with a tape replay machine under his arm. Bending close to Parnell, Jackson said: 'Judge Wilson listened to the tapes and heard who I intended to call. Hanson wanted to withdraw the charges there and then but I argued it should be done in open court and the judge agreed. It's payback time for Jacob Meadows . . . and you . . .'

Everyone rose to the judge's entry and this time the lawyer gestured for Parnell to sit immediately after the man was settled. There was a momentary uncertainty before Hanson rose, hurriedly but no longer with jack-in-the-box urgency, and announced that in the light of new evidence, of which the judge was aware, he wished to withdraw all the charges.

'I am aware of what has developed,' agreed the black-gowned judge. 'And in view of the considerable publicity this matter

108

has already aroused, I believe, in fairness to Mr Parnell, that these new facts should be entered into the public domain. I also think there are other matters that have been brought to my attention that should be discussed in open court. After that, you may withdraw your charges, Mr Hanson, but not before . . .' He turned into the court. 'I believe there is another attorney who wishes to make an application before me. I understand that neither Mr Jackson nor Mr Hanson has any objection?'

Both lawyers shook their heads as the man who had seen the judge in private pushed once more through the separating rail and walked unevenly to the stand. The man gave his name on oath as Edwin Pullinger and identified himself as a counsel for the Federal Bureau of Investigation. He had been made aware of evidence that had been produced in court concerning an Air France flight that had been the subject of an inconclusive terrorism investigation both in the United States and France. The FBI, in conjunction with the Office of Homeland Security, were responsible for investigations into terrorism, and he was making formal application for the death of Ms Rebecca Lang to be officially transferred by the court from Metro DC police to the Federal Bureau of Investigation.

'Mr Hanson?' questioned the judge.

'There is no objection from the prosecution,' immediately surrendered the lawyer.

'Mr Jackson?'

'I am anxious for it to be transferred,' said Parnell's lawyer.

'Before this court so orders, there are other matters for it to consider. Mr Jackson?'

Parnell's lawyer stood with a legal pad in his hand but did not appear to need the notes. His client had been arraigned on totally false charges as the result of an investigation that was this afternoon to be exposed as initially wrongly and too hastily conducted, incompetent and potentially criminal in intent, and which could have resulted in a serious miscarriage of justice. That was not strictly a matter within the FBI remit into the terrorist aspect that had emerged, but he hoped their enquiries extended to what had clearly been a criminal attempt to incriminate his client. He intended further to invite the court to order a separate examination into the conduct and competence of the Metro DC police department and its claimed expert witnesses.

As Jackson spoke, Parnell pointedly turned, looking first to Vernon Hanson and then, more intently, to the two Metro DC officers. All three were staring, unfocused, directly ahead. So was the forensics professor, Jacob Meadows.

Parnell was surprised, although he supposed he shouldn't have been, at Jackson recalling him to the stand formally to give evidence of his having discovered the answering-machine message from the Toyota-approved garage at his apartment that morning, which was confirmed by the court official, who followed him to the stand. Hanson shook his head, tight-lipped, at the overly courteous invitation to cross-examine. It was the usher who operated the tape machine to play back the repair-shop message, directly after which Jackson called its manager. The man testified that the voice on the tape was his and that he had been responding at eight-thirty on the previous day, Monday morning, to a message that had been left on their answering service timed at five thirty-two on the Saturday afternoon. The girl followed her manager to the stand. She described accessing the recorded messages as her first job of the day. Their machine had a time counter, which was how they could be so precise on Ms Lang's Saturday call coming at five thirty-two p.m. At Jackson's demand, she stopped, for the usher to insert into the replay machine the tape recovered that morning from the repair shop.

Rebecca's voice echoed into the hushed court, rising and falling, Rebecca obviously doing something else at the same time. '*A friend's car got hit, in his firm's car lot . . . he's very busy, will let it go if someone doesn't fix it for him . . . please call him . . .*' She dictated the apartment number. Then: '*If he asks how, why, you called, tell him a friend. It's a surprise . . .*'

The coughing, gulping emotion welled up within Parnell, who knew most people in the court were looking at him, as he'd known there would have been faces at the Dubette windows yesterday. His eyes misted in his effort to subdue the coughing, which he did, trying to wipe them at the same time as blowing his nose, which he needed to do. That's why she hadn't told him on the Sunday: she'd wanted an innocent, simple surprise for someone too work-obsessed to do anything for himself.

'This court rules in favour of the FBI application,' announced Judge Wilson. 'To prevent any future prejudice in what is now to be, at my formal request, an ongoing FBI investigation, I will not comment, beyond making clear my deep and profound disappointment at having such a case brought before me in the manner in which it was, even at a remand stage. I do, however, require for any future action I might consider, separate explanations from both the Metro DC police department and the attorney's division of this city, detailing how such a situation arose . . .' He nodded to Parnell, who hurriedly stood to Jackson's prompting. 'You, Mr Parnell, leave this court a totally innocent and vindicated man, with the apologies of this court for the experience to which you were subjected. I further order that complete and full costs be paid for your defence, irrespective of any separate action you and your legal advisors might contemplate. You also have the court's sympathy for your personal loss . . .'

Jackson bustled Parnell into the barely furnished anteroom in which they had begun the day together, pressing the door closed behind him by leaning against it as he said: 'Jesus, what a day! But we won. Boy, how we won!'

'Thanks,' said Parnell, simply.

'A lot of it fell into my lap: our laps. The tape, particularly.'

'How'd you get the FBI involved like that?'

'Started out in their counsel's department at the J. Edgar Hoover building, before going private. Kept a few friends there. Once I confirmed AF209, it was a walk in the park.'

'I want the bastards who did it!' exclaimed Parnell.

'It'll get done,' promised Jackson. 'You pick up on the judge's hint for a civil suit against the police?'

'Of course,' shrugged Parnell. 'But what's the point?'

'Don't make any decisions yet. It's all too soon.' He shouted: 'Enter,' to the hesitant knock at the door, striding forward to meet the FBI lawyer, whom he at once introduced to Parnell.

Ed Pullinger said: 'Barry tells me you've no idea at all how that flight number came to be in Ms Lang's purse.'

'None,' declared Parnell. 'What I do know – am totally sure of – is that Rebecca had no knowledge of or connection with terrorism. It's ludicrous.'

'Barry told me that, too. You're not planning to go anywhere, are you, Mr Parnell?'

'No.'

'I'll give you my personal guarantee that my client will remain in the city and be available at all times,' said Jackson, formally.

Pullinger nodded, smiling for the first time. To the other lawyer he said: 'You sure kicked ass in there!'

'They were bending over, making it easy,' said Jackson.

'I guess we'll be seeing quite a lot of each other,' said Pullinger.

'I guess,' said Jackson. To Parnell he said: 'You ready to meet the baying media?'

'I suppose so.'

'Don't gloat,' advised Jackson. 'You won but Rebecca's dead.'

'You think I need reminding?'

'And be careful as you go,' continued the lawyer, ignoring the retort. 'We just humiliated a whole police department who've now been put under investigation themselves and stand a good chance of being humiliated a lot more. The officer who catches you drunk at the wheel or even parking illegally goes straight on to the roll of honour, with extra laurel leaves.'

'I don't drive drunk but I hear what you're saying.'

They were overwhelmed by the waiting media on the court-room steps and this time Jackson shuffled back into second place. Responding to the questions he could select from the babble, Parnell said he was glad the matter was now in the hands of the FBI and looked forward to an early arrest of the people who'd murdered Rebecca and tried to incriminate him. He had no idea how the AF209 flight number came to be in Rebecca Lang's purse, but part of her job at Dubette had been to liaise with their overseas subsidiaries, and he believed that was the connection. He would, of course, cooperate in every way demanded by the FBI. He had not yet decided whether to sue Metro DC police. It had been a frightening experience, made the more horrifying by Rebecca's death. He hesitated at a repeated, once-ignored question before saying that he had hoped to marry Rebecca and that he was devastated by her killing. He was anxious to return to his job and his department as soon as possible. It was too early for them to expect that he or those working with him would have made any genetic breakthroughs. Of course they were hopeful, expectant even. He couldn't give any details of what the results might be. Parnell was grateful for Jackson's pressure at his elbow, moving forward to the lawyer's waiting car, shaking his head against any more questions.

Inside the vehicle, Jackson said: 'Where do you want to go?'

He didn't know, Parnell thought. It was a brief but unsettling moment of mental blankness. Hurriedly, recovering, he said: 'The nearest Hertz rental outlet. I've got some catching up to do.'

As he drove, Jackson said: 'You've got all my numbers. We'll obviously need to keep in touch. Don't forget what I said about watching your back.'

'I won't.' How absurd, unreal, to be seriously getting – and intending to take – a warning like that in the supposed land of freedom and law!

'Any time, day or night.'

'I've got it.'

Parnell hesitated at hiring another Toyota but irritably dismissed the hesitation. It was the car with which he was most familiar and which it therefore made sense for him to drive. On his way back to the apartment, he remembered the gaping-mouthed answering machine and stopped for a replacement recording loop. He approached Washington Circle cautiously, unwilling to face another media gauntlet, relieved that there wasn't one. Inside the apartment he reloaded the machine and remained reflectively by the telephone. It was already four thirty and it would probably take him an hour to get to McLean as the rush hour built up. There was no ongoing work he could usefully do until the following day – maybe not even then – so it was pointless contemplating the 17 mile journey. And he hadn't been talking about Dubette when he'd told the lawyer he had a lot of catching up to do.

It was Dubette he called, though, smiling at Kathy Richardson's immediate concern when she recognized his voice, before he'd said who he was. He assured her he was fine, that everything was fine, and got himself transferred to Beverley Jackson.

She said at once: 'We've been hearing a lot on the radio.'

'I'm OK. I only wish Rebecca was.'

'They're talking murder on the radio . . .'

'That's what it's being investigated as. Thanks for what you did, getting Barry. He's a hell of a lawyer. I didn't know, not when I called.'

'Anything more I can do?' asked the woman.

'Get me put over to Dwight Newton. I'll be in tomorrow morning.'

'Sure you're OK?' persisted Beverley.

No, thought Parnell, I'm not sure at all. He said: 'I told you, I'm fine. Spread the word I'll be in first thing tomorrow.'

Newton's secretary said the vice president wasn't there and wouldn't be in until the following afternoon. She'd mark his diary for Parnell to be his first appointment, and was glad things had worked out as well as she understood they had, but it was awful about Rebecca.

The urgent introductory music to Live at 5 was playing when Parnell switched on the television to be confronted by his own oddly averted face, a blown-up still photograph. When the voice-over commentary referred to murder, his picture was replaced by one of Rebecca Lang, which he guessed to be a Dubette's personnel file print. She looked startled almost, nervous of the camera. What about his appearance! Parnell hadn't been conscious of television cameras inside the court, which he thought he would have been. Judge Wilson's concluding speech was given in full, with Parnell half in shot, and he was curious at his own subdued appearance, which persisted outside with the impromptu press conference. Into his mind came the brief blankness in Jackson's car, and Parnell acknowledged that how he looked on film was how he'd felt, frightened, needing someone else's support. Which was as much a surprise as his earlier self-acknowledgement of being frightened, because Parnell had always been sure he could climb the highest mountain and swim the widest oceans all

114

by himself: he wasn't used to – and most certainly didn't like – the obvious loss of the confidence he'd always known and taken for granted. Barbara Spacey, Dubette's chain-smoking psychologist, would doubtless argue it was nothing about which to be ashamed or discomfited. But he was. The segment ended still on the courthouse steps, with a reporter restating the FBI's official confirmation that they were conducting their enquiry as a murder investigation. The reporter also recounted the official refusal of Metro DC police to respond to the judge's criticism of its competence, over shots of Peter Bellamy and Helen Montgomery hurriedly leaving the rear of their headquarters building, Bellamy holding his hat to shield his face.

'You're all over the papers. And on television. And you look awful!' said his mother.

'I was afraid I would be.'

'What the hell's . . . ?'

'It's OK,' stopped Parnell, not wanting another familiar phrase. 'I've been cleared by the court of being in any way connected with Rebecca's death. Someone tried to set me up.'

'What about terrorism?' demanded the woman, in England.

'It's an FBI investigation now.'

'Why should anyone want to set you up? *Who* would want to set you up?'

'I don't know. No one knows, not yet.'

'Who's Rebecca Lang?'

'A girl I've been seeing.'

'They're saying you were going to get married!'

'We were moving in together.'

'I think I should come out.'

'No,' refused Parnell. 'There's no need. I'm all right now. I've got a good lawyer.'

'Was this girl murdered?'

'We think so.'

'And they tried to get you accused of it?'

'Yes.'

'Get the hell out of there! Come home.'

'I certainly can't – won't – do that. The FBI want me here.'

'You sure you're not in any danger?'

115

No, thought Parnell, who hadn't been able to think what sort of situation he was in. 'Absolutely positive.'

'Keep in touch. I'll start rearranging my diary, just in case.'

'I don't want you to come over.'

'Because you think there *is* danger?'

'Because I don't want you to get caught up in the nonsense of it.'

'We'll see.'

'I'll keep in touch. I promise.'

'You'd better.'

Parnell timed his leaving the apartment to arrive in Wisconsin Avenue at the moment the restaurant opened, not thinking until he was passing the Four Seasons hotel, actually into Georgetown, that in the circumstances it might be shut. Having got that close, he continued anyway, the blackness of the restaurant the moment he turned up from M Street answering the unasked question. Parnell accepted that the lights at the rear could be part of a burglary precaution but ignored the closed sign and repeatedly sounded the bell, as well as knocking against the glass and rattling the door, encouraged by what he thought to be a sound from within. Finally a door opened at the back and an accented voice shouted that they were closed and couldn't he read, before Rebecca's uncle looked out and saw him. For the first few seconds Parnell believed Giorgio Falcone was still going to turn him away. Instead the man finally picked his way through the already-laid tables, opened the door and pulled Parnell in, arms around his shoulders, mumbling words Parnell couldn't understand. From the way he was shaking, Parnell realized the older man was crying.

Parnell was led back into the kitchen, where the chef he'd only ever known as Ciro and an assistant he'd never met, both dressed for work, were sitting at a table on which were already stacked three dirty plates next to a pot of remaining spaghetti. There was also one empty wine bottle and another half full.

Falcone wiped his eyes, unembarrassed, and said something in Italian and the two men stood, awkwardly, to offer their hands, which Parnell shook, self-consciously. Just as awkwardly, the chef said: 'We saw you on television. You cried.'

116

'Almost,' admitted Parnell, wishing as he spoke that he hadn't qualified it.

The other man pulled another chair up for Parnell. All three waited until he sat down before sitting themselves.

Falcone said: 'Who did it?'

'No one knows, not yet,' said Parnell.

'They'll get him though? Catch the pig-fucker?'

Parnell hesitated, deciding against saying he didn't know. Instead he said: 'Yes, they'll get him.'

'You know what happened?'

'Only what the police who arrested me told me.'

'Pig-fuckers too,' said Ciro. 'Have you eaten?'

He hadn't, not since the soft-shelled crabs, Parnell remembered. 'I'm not hungry.' It didn't seem right to eat – to want to eat, although he suddenly accepted that he did desperately.

Unasked, the other man poured Parnell a glass of Chianti.

'What did they tell you?' asked Falcone.

Parnell hesitated, looking at the red-eyed man. 'There's a canyon, a gorge, in Rock Creek Park. Rebecca's car was hit, forced over a protective barrier.'

Falcone's throat began to work but he swallowed against more tears. 'Would she have . . . ?'

'No,' stopped Parnell. 'No, I don't think so.' He didn't know if she would have suffered from her injuries before dying, he realized.

The chef muttered something in Italian and crossed himself.

Falcone said: 'Why did they accuse you?'

'They thought they had evidence, but they were wrong.' Parnell sipped his wine, aware of the hollowness of his echoing stomach.

'On television,' stumbled Falcone. 'They said on television that you and Rebecca were going to marry?'

And celebrate here last night, remembered Parnell. 'We only decided at the weekend.'

'You would have been good together,' decided the uncle. 'You would have had my blessing.' He straightened, finishing the wine between them and nodding to the chef's assistant to open another bottle. 'The funeral is Friday.'

That could be the needed excuse for his visit, Parnell

decided. 'When we were talking at the weekend, Rebecca told me she had a previous fiancé?'

Falcone frowned. 'A long time ago.'

'About two years, I thought she said?'

The man shrugged. 'Maybe. It broke up.'

'But they came here together?'

'I guess.'

'Do you remember his name? Where he lived?'

Falcone made an uncertain movement again. 'Washington somewhere, I guess.'

'What about a name?'

There was a further, dismissive shrug, the older man's mouth pulled down doubtfully. 'I don't remember. Alan, perhaps. I think it was Alan but I'm not sure. Why?'

'I thought it might be right to invite him to the funeral,' said Parnell.

'That's kind,' said the restaurant owner.

'But I don't have a name. Or an address.' pressed Parnell.

Falcone shook his head. 'I'm sorry.'

It had always been an outside chance, Parnell accepted. 'If you remember . . . ? Find something . . . ?'

Giorgio frowned, curious for the first time. 'Sure.'

'The FBI are investigating,' Parnell hurried on.

'They said, on television.'

'They might want to talk to you.'

'What about?'

'Rebecca. They'll want to know about Rebecca.'

'Everyone loved her,' insisted the chef.

'Why did they do it?' demanded Falcone, thick-voiced again. 'I want them caught! I want them dead!'

What did he want? Parnell wondered. To know *why*! he answered himself.

Fourteen

By Edward C. Grant's edict, this New York encounter wasn't at the corporate building but at an hotel, the Plaza on Central Park South, overlooking the park. It was booked from a reservations agency in an assumed name and paid for in advance, in cash. Dwight Newton was given the suite number by telephone, Grant's cellphone to his cellphone, not through the hotel switchboard or traceably dialled. Surprisingly there was coffee on a separating table when Newton arrived. Grant waited expectantly for the vice president to pour. As he did, Newton said: 'The FBI are investigating.'

'I saw the newscasts, read the newspapers,' said Grant, totally controlled, even-voiced.

'What are we going to do?' Grant had to be nervous to have arranged the meeting like this, like something out of a movie.

Grant frowned, concerned at the other man's nervousness, to assess which was the major reason for his summoning the stick-thin scientist yet again on the first shuttle from Washington. 'I'm not sure about that question, Dwight.' said the disconcerted, white-maned man. 'Not sure we need to do anything, are you?'

'The FBI are investigating, for Christ's sake,' repeated Newton. 'They'll almost certainly want to question us.'

'You,' corrected Grant, still even-voiced. 'They'll almost certainly want to question *you*. I don't see that I'll be able to help them very much.'

Newton sat with his cooling coffee untouched before him, looking as steadily as possible at the other man, wondering how directly he could ask the awful question to get the awful confirmation of his every doubt. Not directly at all, Newton decided. Instead he said: 'What shall I tell them?'

'What is there to tell them? Rebecca Lang worked in your overseas unit. She was very competent, did her work well.

We were very happy with her. We're devastated by what happened.'

'What if they ask about France?'

Grant lifted and dropped his shoulders. 'Here again, I don't see why they should. It's got nothing to do with what they're enquiring into, has it?'

Newton tensed himself, lips initially tight together. 'Hasn't it?'

Grant came forward from the opposing chair, elbows on his knees. 'Dwight, I really am finding it difficult to follow you here!'

'They'll most definitely talk to security. Learn about the telephone monitor.'

'So?'

'Her name's on the list, talking to Paris.'

'She was in the overseas liaison unit! We'd be disappointed if she hadn't spoken to Paris and a lot of other places abroad! The monitor wasn't exclusively on her telephone, was it?'

'No,' conceded Newton, expectantly.

'And her name isn't the only one on the list?'

'No,' further conceded the other man, again. Fuck you, he thought. And then he thought, I wish I could – I wish so very much I could escape from the entanglement in which I am enmeshed . . . in which you are enmeshed.

'She wasn't being specifically targeted?'

'Security came up with a lot of names,' agreed Newton.

'But none proved to be the suspected outside informant? Certainly not from any of the research-division telephones.'

It was all so easily, so satisfactorily explainable, Newton accepted. 'No,' he said. 'We didn't find an outside informant from the checks we initiated.'

'But we've every right to be vigilant?'

'Yes.' Newton had the irrational impression of being stuck in a sucking morass, mud too thick to get out of, with the rising water creeping up to engulf him.

'Could you get me another coffee, Dwight?'

The vice president poured, ignoring his own almost full cup. 'They could come across the French things.'

'Along with every other research experiment we're conducting!' exclaimed the Dubette president, genuinely incredulous. 'But let's stay with that, for a moment. Tell me about *rifofludine*. Does it have a preserving quality, in hot climactic conditions?'

'To a degree,' allowed Newton, reluctantly.

Grant sighed, theatrically. 'Does it have a preserving quality, in hot climatic conditions!'

'Yes.'

'And the colouring additives make dosage administration and recognition easier in Third World countries?'

'Yes.'

'Which means we're providing a necessary service – improving our products – for a specific market?'

'Yes.'

'I really thought we'd already talked all this through, Dwight?'

'I suppose we had.'

'We got anything more to talk through?'

'I don't think so.'

'You really sure about that, Dwight?'

'Yes, I'm really sure.'

'I'm glad about that. Really glad we're understanding each other. Now tell me about Parnell.'

'I haven't seen him yet. He rejected our attorney, Gerry Fletcher. But Baldwin kept Fletcher in court to represent Dubette's interests.'

'Why didn't Parnell want our guy?'

'Fletcher thought the only way was to enter a plea.'

Grant nodded, but didn't immediately comment. 'Parnell's an ornery son of a bitch and isn't that the truth?'

'I guess.' How much further – how much more – was he expected to capitulate?

Grant said: 'That was a good move, keeping Fletcher in court to watch our backs. Important to keep ourselves up to speed on anything and everything that might adversely affect the company. There's too much publicity: I'm worried about it affecting the stock. Let's get the legal department to ensure a legal heavyweight better than Fletcher, in case we need him.'

'Need him for what?' risked Newton.

'Unchallenged situations, getting out of hand. We've got

nothing to hide, everything to protect. You understand what I'm saying?'

'I think so.'

'Get public affairs working. Give the media full access to what Rebecca Lang did: I don't want Dubette fouled up in any mystery theories that her death had anything to do with what she was working on, OK?'

For a brief moment it was difficult for Newton to find the words, any word, to respond. 'Don't you think that might be difficult, in the circumstances?'

'Tell public affairs full co-operation, with every media outlet. Maybe you head up a press conference. After all, we've got nothing whatsoever to hide. Remember that.'

'Nothing whatsoever,' echoed Newton, flatly. The water had to be almost up to his chin now. He wasn't sure whether he wanted to strain upwards to save himself or put his head down, to drown.

'What do we know about Rebecca Lang? Family, friends, stuff like that?' briskly demanded Grant.

Now it was Newton who frowned. 'She and Parnell were going to get married, according to the papers and what he said on television. Her mother and father are both dead. Next of kin is listed on the personnel records as an uncle. Lives locally, in the DC area.'

'Get personnel involved. Wayne Denny himself. Dubette will pick up all the bills. Whatever sort of funeral they want, they get. Reception afterwards, their choice, whatever, wherever. You attend. Showcross too, of course. Anyone else in the unit who wants to go.'

'I understand.' Oh God, do I understand! thought Newton.

'Tell Parnell to take as much time off as he wants. Get Denny, anyone else you can think of, involved here, too.'

'OK.'

'How about you, Dwight?'

'Me?'

'What's happened is horrifying. A member of Dubette staff – your staff – murdered. An attempt made, apparently, to incriminate a department head. Understandable that it would have gotten to you. It's gotten to a lot of us, one way and another.'

'I'm OK,' lied Newton. He was anxious now to get away, no longer to feel he was drowning, to be part of whatever he feared himself to be part of.

'That's good to hear,' said Grant. 'Very good indeed.' He came forward once more across their intervening table, arms on his knees, intense. 'I want you to tell me something, Dwight. Something it's very important for me to know – totally and completely believe. You don't think – don't believe – that anyone in Dubette is in any way involved or connected with whatever happened to Rebecca and almost happened to Dick Parnell, do you?'

'No,' Newton finally surrendered, as he'd known all along that he would, the nausea a physical sensation deep in his stomach. 'I don't think that at all.' What would have happened to him, he wondered, if he'd said anything otherwise?

No one seemed to know how to react to his return. Parnell had accepted during the ride to McLean that he would inevitably be the focus of everyone's attention, from the very moment of his arrival at the Dubette gatehouse, but hadn't known how it would register. It started with uncertain looks – or pointedly *no* looks in his direction at all – from other drivers as he parked the rented Toyota only four spaces from where he'd left his own car three days earlier. There were more hesitant, early-warned faces at the windows and, as he got closer to the building, he was conscious of a lot of doubtful, needing-to-be-guided faces. Very occasionally there was a half wave or gesture of encouragement from people he didn't know. In front of the elevator bank, three people – a man and two women – held back for him to get a car to himself. There were more half smiles and a few inconclusive gestures as he walked the gauntlet of the overlooked corridor into the Spider's Web.

Initially the indeterminate attitude existed even in his own pharmacogenomics department, where everyone was already assembled in greeting, which they didn't know how to make once he got there. It was Beverley Jackson who broke the impasse, coming towards him with both hands outstretched to prompt his reaching forward in response, leading the rest to follow with awkward handshakes and shoulder slaps.

'We don't quite know what to say – what to do,' Beverley unnecessarily admitted.

'I don't know that there's anything to say or do,' said Parnell. 'I seem to be causing some embarrassment.'

'Whatever you want . . . need . . . just . . .' Ted Lapidus's offer trailed away, into more awkwardness.

'I think I want to get back to work. Catch up on whatever needs to be caught up with.'

'You quite sure you're . . . ?' started Sean Sato, halted by the look on Parnell's face.

Parnell said: 'We just got a new unbreakable rule for the department. No one asks me if I'm OK, OK?'

Only Deke Pulbrow said: 'OK,' and then he said: 'Oh shit!'

The Japanese American said: 'I'm sorry. It's just that . . . just that . . .'

'Just that there's nothing else to do or to say,' Parnell finished for him. He allowed space into the discomfort, hoping to puncture it. 'Thanks, all of you. To borrow Deke's word, it's been a shit time and will probably go on being a shit time for I don't know how long. Whatever, I want things to go on here, without me if it's necessary, with me, if and whenever it's possible . . .' He looked to Kathy Richardson. 'Anything I need to do, need to know?'

'A lot of media calls yesterday and already today. I've logged them.'

His newly installed answering-machine loop at Washington Circle had been exhausted by the time he'd got back from Georgetown the previous evening. Parnell hadn't responded to any and let the tape fill up again without picking up the receiver. He shook his head in refusal and said: 'Nothing else?'

The matronly secretary looked fleetingly at Beverley Jackson. 'Your lawyer called. Said he was at the office number you have and would be, for most of the day, if you want to talk.'

'Anything from Dwight's office?'

The woman shook her head. 'You want me to check?'

'He's not due back until this afternoon,' accepted Parnell. 'Just thought his schedule might have changed.' He looked around the people still gathered around him, knowing they were expecting something from him but not able, at that precise, brief moment, to formulate anything in his mind. It was going to be difficult to force the pace, the dispassion even, but Parnell acknowledged that he had to evolve a way of conducting himself to make happen what he wanted to happen, for his life to go on at two separate, equally important levels, as unlinked and independent of each other as possible. Were the two levels equally important? Of course not. Finding Rebecca's killer – who'd tried to incriminate him, as well – was the most important, his absolute priority. The department – this department – that had once, all too recently and far far too much, consumed him and his every thought was secondary now – very secondary indeed – to avenging Rebecca. Forcing himself to be still – certainly striving for a lightness that wasn't there – Parnell said: 'So, who's made the breakthrough that's going to make us all famous?'

The heads-lowered hesitation was the criticism he didn't need of how wrongly placed the remark had been. It was Beverley who hurried in, trying to cover his difficulty, talking of three experiments she'd conducted upon mice with Dubette's products without finding an immediate way of introducing a genetically linked improvement, which gradually opened the discussion among the others. It quickly became apparent to Parnell that virtually no experimental avenues had emerged to follow, which he hadn't expected anyway, but it took away the atmosphere caused by his mistaken remark and he was grateful.

It was hard for him to concentrate as fully as he knew he should upon their individual accounts, but he managed sufficiently to ask the necessarily comprehending questions. More than once Ted Lapidus remarked that everything Parnell was being told had been fully discussed and agreed in the committee-style manner in which they had decided to operate.

Sean Sato was the last to contribute and almost from the moment the man began talking, Parnell's attention became absolute. 'Avian influenza?' he queried, interrupting the man. 'I thought you were focusing on Hepatitis C?'

'We got a visit from Russell Benn, soon after you ...' Lapidus halted. '. . . on Monday. Tokyo's heading up a project decided on by the company, the species-jumping of flu from fowls and wild animals to humans that causes epidemics that start in Asia virtually every year. The World Health Organization are warning that if a human being already suffering influenza becomes infected with bird flu, the two viruses could integrate and mutate into an unknown – and currently untreatable – strain transmitting from human to human very easily, to become a global pandemic like the one that killed more than twenty million people after the First World War.'

'What direction is the project taking?' asked Parnell. He wasn't letting his mind drift now – properly, committedly, back at work. It felt good.

'A vaccine,' said Sato.

'For humans? Or birds?' asked Parnell.

'Both, if possible,' said Lapidus.

'H5N1, the avian virus that emerged in early 1997, is too lethal to be grown in chicken eggs, even to hope to create a vaccine,' Parnell pointed out.

'That's why Benn's been tasked with producing something a different way,' said Lapidus.

'And why he wants us on board,' finished Sato. 'Everything Tokyo's tried should be arriving later today or tomorrow.'

'We'd better prepare the sterile laboratory,' said Parnell.

'Already done,' said Lapidus.

'I know none of you need to be told, but have you warned Kathy it'll be out of bounds?' asked Parnell, indicating her office, to which the secretary had already returned.

'Very clearly,' said the balding, pebble-bespectacled Peter Battey.

'I like the way you've worked, while I wasn't here,' thanked Parnell, sincerely.

'I . . .' started Lapidus but at once corrected himself again. 'We talked about it and decided hepatitis could wait. This is our first chance to get involved in a current priority programme.'

And he hadn't been here when it was formulated, thought Parnell. But he was now. 'Do we know if the competition are trying to do the same as us?'

'Not at this level,' said Mark Easton, the former Johns Hopkins geneticist. 'But it's an easy guess that they are. We're

126

talking megabucks on a global scale. Thailand – just one of seven or eight Asian countries farming chicken – exports one and a half billion dollars worth of poultry every year. Europe imports a third of the chicken Thailand produces.'

'It's good to be involved, even if it's because our traditional colleagues across the corridor recognize that they need all the help they can get,' said Parnell. 'But from the rundown you've just given me, Sean's working on it alone. If it's a priority, with red lights flashing, shouldn't we make up our own definition of a task force?'

'Thought about that, too,' assured Lapidus. 'As I said, we don't yet have the specimens to *begin* work, which we should be able to do tomorrow. Sean's doing the groundwork. Now you're back, it's obviously your decision, but I was intending to join him, along with Beverley.'

The Greek had very definitely adopted the role of deputy leader, Parnell recognized. Which was good, providing it didn't arouse any jealousy or resentment among the others. And that didn't seem to have happened so far. 'Sounds a good plan to me,' agreed Parnell. 'I'll go across the corridor sometime to see how Benn and his people are working . . .'

'I really don't know how you've got the resilience to consider working yourself,' said Beverley.

'I'm not sure I have,' admitted Parnell.

Harry Johnson was Grant's second visitor of the day to the discreet Plaza Hotel suite, the bell summons repeated impatiently before Grant opened the door. The Dubette security chief was dressed for what he imagined the occasion to be, in a suit and tie but with the permanently shined, plasticized Dubette uniform shoes. The suit was baggy and stained, the shirt crumpled from previous wear.

'Nobody saw me arrive,' assured Johnson. 'What's going down here?' His visit had been arranged in the same cellphone-to-cellphone way.

'That's what I want to talk about,' said Grant. The hotel security needed overhauling, not to have questioned Johnson's dishevelled presence. Grant hoped the man wouldn't be remembered if any hotel staff were called upon to do so.

Johnson collapsed, uninvited, into an encompassing armchair, looked around the suite and said: 'Nice place. Class. That's what I like, class.'

When, wondered Grant, had the man sitting opposite ever experienced it? But then he sometimes frequented places that would have surprised anyone who knew him. 'How the fuck did AF209 get into the frame?'

'You wanted to discredit Parnell. Create a situation where you could dispense with him in such a way as to make him unemployable,' reminded Johnson. 'I didn't know Rebecca Lang was dead – how she'd died. I didn't stir this shit, like you did once before. Don't forget that.'

'Will I ever be allowed to?'

'We're a long way from the cliff edge,' said Johnson, helping himself to the now virtually cold coffee.

'You've involved the FBI, for fuck's sake!'

'I didn't know Rebecca Lang was going to die! Didn't know until I got the call from the Metro DC police guys. At which time I didn't have the opportunity to talk to you. I had to improvise – use my own judgement.'

'This isn't good,' insisted Grant. 'It could all unravel.'

'How'd she die? How – why – did Rebecca die?'

'I don't know.'

'Sir, a lot of unusual things – strangely coincidental things – happened that Sunday. Things I didn't expect to happen. Rebecca Lang's death the most unexpected of all. Can you help me with that?'

'I told you, I don't know.'

'We gotta smelly bunch of shit to pick our way through,' judged Johnson. 'You wanna point out the path we're going to take together, to make the stories chime?'

Edward C. Grant's recitation was practically a repeat of his earlier conversation with Dwight Newton. At the end of it, Johnson said: 'Could hold, if everyone in turn holds their nerve.'

'What about the two Metro DC shitheads?' demanded Grant.

'They're looking at the drop, if they start to flake. Know they're looking at steak and cake if they stay cool. But they didn't know it was murder, when we did the deal. If I've got

128

to keep a handle on this, I need to know the facts . . .' He
sniggered. 'Remember that, what they used to say in *Dragnet*.
"Just the facts; just give me the facts." I used to love that
show.'

'It's too long ago to remember,' sighed Grant, who considered Harry Johnson to be the one unavoidable, forever
inescapable, mistake he had ever allowed to happen. 'Don't
forget your drop, Harry.'

'Or yours,' came back the security chief, at once.
'Everything's superglued: nothing's going to fall apart.'

'You absolutely sure about that?'

'I'm absolutely sure about that,' echoed the fat-bellied man.
'That's what I'm employed to be, isn't it – to be absolutely
sure about everything?'

'That's what you're employed for,' agreed Grant, softly. 'I
won't forget that. Nor should you, ever.' But Johnson had
forgotten, Grant thought. He'd become complacent, not properly – fully – thinking things through to their logical conclusion. Which made him a liability. Grant didn't like liabilities,
his own most of all.

'So, we don't have a problem,' said Johnson.

'You ensure that we don't,' insisted Grant.

'You gotta drink anywhere here?'

'Find a bar downtown,' ordered Grant. 'A long way downtown.'

The greeting was even more effusive than it had initially been
on the day of Parnell's threatened resignation. Dwight Newton
was already around his desk, leg hitched upon its front. At
Parnell's entry he thrust forward and enclosed the Englishman's
hand in both of his, changing the grip as he was pumping up
and down to slap Parnell on the shoulder. The gesture was
timed to the second, abruptly ending for Parnell to be ushered
into the already prepared chair, the grave look already in place
when the head of research regained his own side of the desk.

'Good to see you back, Dick. Damned good. A tragedy, an
absolute tragedy, about Rebecca. You got my sympathy. The
sympathy of the entire upper management of Dubette.'

'Thank you,' said Parnell. Illogically he felt the sort of

embarrassment he guessed everyone had been feeling at encountering him, earlier.

'I've got some things to tell you,' announced Newton, carefully listing every assistance proposed by Edward C. Grant earlier that day in New York. 'That's from the president himself. And I'm to tell you you're to take off as much time as you want. None of us can imagine what it was like – *is* like – for you. Just can't imagine.'

'What I'd like is to get back to work, as quickly and as uninterrupted as possible,' said Parnell, repeating what he'd told his own team. 'I'm not sure how Rebecca's uncle will take the offer of help. I get the feeling he's a pretty proud and independent old guy.'

'Nothing for you to worry about. That's for Wayne Denny and personnel. I want you to know something, on a personal level. I never believed for a moment that you could be in any way involved.'

'Why not?' The question blurted from Parnell, unthinkingly, and his surprise at uttering it was increased at Newton's obvious and immediate confusion.

'It was unthinkable . . . inconceivable. You were a couple. In love. Everybody knew that. You don't murder the woman you love!'

Did everyone know it? Parnell supposed they did. 'Someone murdered her and tried to frame me.' Someone who certainly knew them both – knew their cars and their movements. Certainly Rebecca's, when she'd left Washington Circle. But whoever it was couldn't have known she wasn't staying over. So, he and Rebecca would have had to have been watched, all the time. The killer would have had to follow her from Bethesda on Sunday morning, seen them leave the apartment in Rebecca's car – both tightly, safely, seat-belted – been at an adjoining bench at Chesapeake Bay maybe, and driven behind them all the way back again. And then sat and waited and watched some more, as long as they had to, until Rebecca got into a position to be ambushed. Whoever had done that couldn't have known Rebecca wouldn't be staying overnight. So, the surveillance had to have been absolute, around the clock. It was obvious but Parnell hadn't thought the sequence through. It would be more than obvious to the trained investigators from the FBI, too, but he'd still mention it, set it out to illustrate how meticulously it had all been planned.

'What's that flight number all about?'

'I don't know,' insisted Parnell.

'You didn't know it was in Rebecca's purse?'

'No.'

'She didn't talk to you about it?'

'No.' The switch – and the interrogation – was intriguing, thought Parnell.

'I can't believe it, any of it!' protested the head-shaking vice president. 'It's monstrous. The work of a monster.' How many? wondered Newton. And led – or ordered – by the head monster? He was glad he'd changed into the white laboratory coat, sure the sweat that was gluing his body at the effort he was having to make would have soaked through his shirt to become visible.

'I hear there's a big project underway?' said Parnell, anxious to move the conversation on, accepting that this interview was a required courtesy – sympathy offered, help extended – but there seemed little point or purpose.

'I told you it didn't work . . .' started Newton, but then, quickly, said: 'The flu research, sure. We're really under the gun on this one. You think you're going to be able to help?'

'Flu – animal and human – is viral, that's how it's medically feasible for those viruses to mutate into one killer strain,' said Parnell. 'And viruses have genes we can isolate and experiment with. Which isn't a promise for any sort of discovery, just my agreeing with you and Russell Benn that it's well within the pharmacogenomics discipline.'

'You work closely with Russ,' urged Newton.

'I plan to.'

'Remember everything I said,' insisted Newton. 'Don't forget Dubette's family orientation.'

'I won't,' undertook Parnell.

Kathy Richardson was waiting for his return, jotting pad in hand, to tell him Barbara Spacey wanted to see him.

He said: 'Call her back and say thanks but I don't want – or need – to see her.'

'She said you'd say that.'

'Makes her good at her job,' said Parnell. 'Call her.'

It wasn't until he recovered the papers that he'd abandoned on the Monday morning that Parnell properly recalled what he had been working on, the compilation of their separate cancer file, which he'd been in the process of subdividing, eventually to establish a working routine when it became a project for the entire department. Now there was another more urgent project, one it was important they devoted as much of their undivided attention to as possible, which meant the cancer undertaking would have to be further postponed. But then it always had been one for the future, when they had exhausted all the immediate examination of possible Dubette updates. He'd attach himself to the flu research, Parnell decided. It was the first specific demand that had been directed at them, so it was right – would be expected – that he should lead it, as head of the department. Parnell felt a flicker of anticipation: it would, in many ways, be getting back to the pure research he'd known on the genome project in England.

Parnell was reassembling the cancer folder, to give to Kathy Richardson to file, when there was a sharp rap at the door just ahead of the secretary's warning, and the shawled and long-skirted figure of Barbara Spacey surged into his office like a ship under full sail.

The psychologist said: 'You didn't want to see me but I wanted to see you.'

'And Dwight Newton can see us both if he bothers to look, so you can't smoke.'

'See the sacrifice I'm making!'

'You needn't. I've banned the remark from the department but for just one last time I'm OK and I don't need coun-selling.'

'How do you know?'

'Because I do.' Child-talk, he recognized.

'Your fiancée just got killed and you got charged with it and there's an FBI terrorism investigation linked to an obvious murder, and you're telling me you feel fine and just want to get on with the job?'

'No. I'm telling you I feel anything but fine, because how could I feel fine after what's happened, and I want the bastards who did it caught. But that I'm not suffering any psychological problem. But if I begin to think that I am, I'll come back to you, OK?' How often, too often, that word, those two letters, entered every conversation!

Barbara Spacey pulled a chair forward, to be closer to Parnell, as she had been at their previous session, and slumped into it. The voluminous clothes concealed her like an enveloping curtain, but beneath the folds Parnell knew she would be overlapping the seat.

She said: 'Sorry buddy. Company instructions. Every care for someone in distress. They want another assessment.'

'I'm not in . . .' started Parnell and stopped, his mind focused, far ahead of this conversation. 'Two assessments?'

The you-know-how-it-is movement ruffled Barbara Spacey's layers of clothes like feathers. 'You really want to discuss – to *try* to discuss – the circumstances? Let's give everyone a break here! How do families look after families?'

'Most of the time by not smothering each other.'

'No, that's a cop-out. You realize how much support Dubette are offering?'

'I won't be smothered! The way it's going, you'll know – Dubette will know – more about me than I know about myself.'

'Isn't that what families do?' persisted the woman. Her hands were twitching over her handbag, which Parnell guessed contained her cigarettes.

'No, that's smothering, as I already told you.'

'I've got to do what I've got to do,' said the woman. 'Give *me* a break, OK?'

To co-operate would be the quickest way to get rid of the psychologist, Parnell realized. 'OK.'

'Tell me how you feel?'

'I already told you.'

'Tell me again.'

'Confused.'

'Frightened?'

133

Parnell examined the question. 'No, I don't feel frightened. I suppose I should, but at this moment I don't.'

'Why not? You're right, you should.'

'I don't know.'

'You think you can solve it, all by yourself?'

Parnell hesitated again. 'No, of course I don't think that! I'm a scientist, not a detective.'

'But you've thought about it, solving it by yourself, exacting your own justice maybe?'

Barbara Spacey's prescience was unnerving. 'Sure I've thought about it! Wouldn't anyone?'

'I'm glad you're being honest.'

'How can you tell?'

'We did this before, remember?'

Parnell didn't. 'Is that it?'

'I think so.' Her hands were actually moving, scratching at her handbag.

'Do I get a copy, like before?'

'It's the law,' she reminded him.

'Like not smoking?'

'What's your point?'

'What's your verdict?'

Barbara Spacey smiled. 'That confirms it.'

'What the hell's that mean?'

'What I was deciding.'

'You ducking my question?'

The psychologist shook her head. 'You're not so much of the asshole that you were before.'

For several moments Parnell stared at her across the desk, stunned. At last he said: 'So, what's that make me now?'

'That's the mystery,' admitted Barbara Spacey. 'I don't know.'

From behind the dividing glass between the two offices, Kathy Richardson was gesturing towards the telephone. To the psychologist, Parnell said: 'Maybe you'll never know. I analyse mysteries. I don't want to have it happen to me.'

Barbara Spacey smiled. 'I've got to go. I'm dying for a cigarette.'

Kathy Richardson was at the door, waiting to enter, as the psychologist left. The secretary said: 'The FBI want a meet with you tomorrow, wherever you want. They're suggesting ten o'clock.'

'Tell them ten o'clock's fine. At the Washington field office, to save him coming all the way out here.'

Fifteen

But for the fact that there was no facial resemblance – which didn't alter Parnell's immediate impression – the two men confronting him in the FBI's Washington field office could have been twins. They were both of the same indeterminate height and build and wore their mousy hair short and neatly parted to the left. The spectacles were rimless, the style minimal, their faces unlined by apparent worry or concentration. They didn't smile, either. The suits were grey, the faint check difficult to detect, the ties matching but subdued red. Parnell guessed the identical pins in their lapels represented a college fraternity. Howard Dingley, his seniority marked by his being behind the uncluttered desk, wore a signet ring on the little finger of his left hand. His partner, David Benton, didn't. Instead a copper rheumatism-preventing bracelet protruded slightly from beneath the left arm of his double-cuffed shirt.

Dingley said: 'We've got ourselves a very high-profile investigation here, Mr Parnell – high-profile because of what was attempted against you after Ms Lang's murder. You any idea how lucky you were that Ms Lang made that call?'

'No, I don't suppose I have, not fully,' admitted Parnell. 'I'm still trying to understand what the hell's going on.' There was the familiar buzz-saw sound to *Ms*.

'That's what we're trying to do. *Have* to do,' said Benton.

'And why you're the key to everything,' said Dingley.

Predictably the accents matched, clipped, in-a-hurry East Coast, which Parnell believed he could already isolate – guess at least – from the more leisurely Midwest or West Coast. 'That's why I'm here, to do all – everything – I can do to help.'

135

'That's what we wanted to hear,' said Benton. 'Tell us about AF209.'

'There's nothing to tell,' said Parnell. 'I don't know what it was doing in Rebecca's bag. Her job was to liaise with Dubette's overseas subsidiaries. There are a lot. It has to be something to do with that: a flight on which a shipment came in.'

'A particular flight which both your GCHQ and our National Security Agency picked up while listening to suspected terrorist chatter,' said Dingley. 'As well as French security. Which was why it was cancelled four times.'

'I know. I can't help you,' said Parnell.

'How do you know?' seized Benton.

'It was stated in court, when I was released.'

'What's your take on it?' demanded Benton. 'Your arrest – the way Metro DC police behaved?'

'You mean, what do I think?'

Dingley nodded.

'I don't know,' stumbled Parnell, awkwardly. 'I mean, I know what happened, but I don't know how or why.'

'Tell us about Ms Lang,' said Benton.

It came as a shock to Parnell to realize how very little he actually did know about Rebecca. 'We met at Dubette. Started seeing each other. A relationship began. Her father was American, her mother Italian. Both dead now . . .' He stopped, in full recollection. 'In a car crash. As far as I know, her only relation is an uncle, who owns Giorgio's Pizzeria on Wisconsin. It's called Giorgio's. His name is Giorgio Falcone. She was a graduate of Georgetown University, here in DC. Worked at Johns Hopkins before joining Dubette. She was attached to the division co-ordinating their overseas subsidiary's laboratories.'

The two FBI agents looked at him, waiting.

'Yes?' prompted Dingley.

'That's about it,' said Parnell.

Benton frowned. 'I thought you were getting married?'

'We'd decided to live together. I guess with the eventual intention of getting married.'

'But you hadn't learned a lot about each other?' said Dingley.

'That's what people live together for, isn't it? To learn about

136

each other,' said Parnell. He wasn't sounding very intelligent, Parnell realized – forthcoming even. Before there could be any further questions, Parnell said: 'I have thought about things . . . about that Sunday.'

'We'd like to hear about it,' urged Benton.

It began in a disorganized rush but Parnell stopped, correcting his chronology and his calculation of how he and Rebecca must have been under surveillance throughout their visit to Chesapeake. Towards the end of the account, Dingley began nodding in agreement.

Benton said: 'That's how we've got it figured. And why you're the key.'

They weren't making notes, so Parnell assumed the conversation was being recorded, although there was no obvious apparatus.

'What about Ms Lang's friends?' asked Dingley.

'I never met any.'

'Not a one?' demanded Benton, disbelievingly.

'No,' said Parnell, knowing how empty it sounded. 'She didn't . . . I don't know . . . it never came up.'

'You're telling us that Ms Lang didn't have a single friend, apart from you?'

'I'm telling you that she never introduced me to anyone. It was a new relationship.'

'Old enough for you to decide to move in together,' challenged Dingley.

'There hadn't been a chance to meet any of her friends. I work a lot. We were down to about one day a week, mostly a Sunday.'

'You have dangerous chemicals out at Dubette?' asked Benton.

'I'm not attached to the chemical division, but yes, I'd expect there to be dangerous chemicals on the premises.'

'Ricin? Sarin? Stuff like that?' pressed Dingley.

'They're chemical-weapons agents, with no therapeutic value. I doubt anything like that would be there.'

'Let me tell you how my mind's working,' invited Dingley. 'A terrorist group discover there's an aeroplane shipping route, between Paris and Washington. They make a contact, get tipped off in advance when there's a shipment of something toxic –

something that could have the same effect as a chemical weapon if it got loose. They put a bomb on the plane, timed to go off just before landing here in Washington DC. Bang! We got another nine-eleven, but this time we got a chemical fallout, as well as maybe four hundred people blown out the sky. How's that sound?'

'It sounds horrifying. It also sounds like you're suggesting that Rebecca was the source, which is absolute and utter nonsense. She never had any terrorist associations.'

'How do you know?' said Benton. 'You never met a single one of her friends, according to what you've told us.'

'What I've told you is the truth. I'm also telling you you're going about things the wrong way to try to link Rebecca into any sort of terrorist association.'

'Ms Lang gets rammed into a gorge and is killed. You come pretty damned close to getting charged with it. What had you, the two of you, done to make someone want to fit you up like that?' asked Benton.

'Nothing!' insisted Parnell. 'I know it sounds ridiculous but I can't think of anything sufficient for someone to want to kill Rebecca and get me accused of doing it.'

'You're right, Mr Parnell,' agreed Dingley. 'It does sound ridiculous.'

They didn't believe him: thought he was holding something back, decided Parnell. Less hurriedly than he'd recounted his realization of how they must have been watched, Parnell told the two doubting agents about Rebecca's Sunday confession of her previous relationship and the pregnancy termination, almost without pause continuing with her persistent curiosity at being bypassed with something involving Dubette's French ancillaries, with Dwight Newton's odd misunderstanding in mind as he talked.

The two men facing him remained expressionless. Benton said: 'You think there's a significance there somewhere?'

'I don't *know*,' said Parnell, regretting the exasperation the moment he spoke. 'You asked me to tell you anything that might help, and that's what I'm trying to do. I know how empty, how unhelpful, it all sounds.'

'We know you're under a lot of strain, Mr Parnell,' said

Dingley. 'And that you've lost someone very close. We're just trying to build a picture.'

'And I know I'm not doing a lot to help,' apologized Parnell.

'You got any lead to the man with whom Ms Lang had the previous relationship?' asked Dingley.

Parnell shook his head. 'Her uncle thinks his name was Alan and that he lived in the DC area. It was about two years ago.' He hesitated. 'I wouldn't imagine her uncle knows anything about the termination.'

'We know how to be discreet,' said Benton.

'I'm sorry.'

'You asked the uncle about this man then?'

'Yes.'

'When?'

'After the court discharged me.'

'Why?'

'I'm trying to find out what's going on, just as you are!'

'It's our job to find out what's going on: that's what we're trained for,' said Benton. 'We don't want you playing amateur detective, Mr Parnell. Apart from that being dangerous, you might foul things up for us, which would mean no one will ever find out what's going on.'

'Dangerous?' isolated Parnell.

'Someone's already been killed!' said Dingley, letting his exasperation show now. 'Hasn't it occurred to you that, having failed to put you in the frame for it, whoever murdered Ms Lang might make a move on you?'

'No. No, it hadn't,' admitted Parnell, incredulously. 'My lawyer . . . no, it doesn't matter . . .'

'Everything matters,' said Benton. 'What about your lawyer?'

'He told me to be careful not to give the Metro police any excuse to come at me again . . . driving, stuff like that. But I never thought beyond that, to there being some physical danger from anywhere else.'

'Think about it now. And take your lawyer's advice,' said Benton.

'But most of all take ours,' added Dingley. 'Let us do the investigating.'

139

'That's all I did, tried to find out about the other man.'

'Which we'll now do,' said Dingley.

'If someone did make a move against me, it could help, couldn't it? If they made mistakes, I mean.'

The silence seemed to last a long time before Dingley said: 'And if they didn't make a mistake and managed to kill you, it maybe wouldn't help us at all and certainly wouldn't help you.'

'You weren't thinking like a bad movie script, setting yourself up as an intentional target, were you, Mr Parnell?' said the other FBI man.

'No!' denied the scientist, honestly. 'I was thinking that if something happened . . . if I *thought* something happened . . . something occurred I thought was odd . . . I could tell you.'

'You do that,' pressed Dingley. 'You tell *us*, don't go off on your own.'

'I've already given that undertaking,' insisted Parnell. 'So, I need numbers where I can reach you?'

It was Dingley who offered the cards, Benton's as well as his own. Parnell saw there were cellphone listings as well as the field office land lines. 'Day or night,' said Benton.

'I'd like to keep in touch, hear how things are going,' said Parnell.

'You got the numbers,' said Dingley. 'We'll probably need to get back to you when things come up we haven't covered.'

'What's come up so far?' demanded Parnell.

The two agents exchanged looks. Dingley said: 'Anything we tell you, we're telling *you*. Only you. If it turns up in a newspaper or on television it could wreck the investigation, you understand?'

'Of course I understand.'

'We're concentrating on forensics at the moment,' said Dingley.

'And you found what?' pressed Parnell.

There was a further hesitation from the two men. Parnell said: 'I told you I understood!'

'There are some marks, dents, on the rear fender of Ms Lang's car that our people don't think were caused by it going over the edge of the gorge,' disclosed Benton. 'They think she was hit, shunted, in the back several times . . .'

140

'Being chased, hit and hit again, not knowing who or what it was . . .' imagined Parnell.

'Something like that,' agreed Benton.

'Seat belts!' broke in Parnell. 'The police officers told me Rebecca was outside the car when she was found – that she hadn't been wearing a seat belt. But seat belts were a thing with her. She always wore one: that's how her parents died, not fastening theirs. Was Rebecca's broken?'

'We haven't been told it was,' said Dingley. 'Our forensics guys aren't helped by everything being moved and collected from the scene . . .' He paused before saying: 'There's going to be another autopsy, too. By our pathologists.'

'The seat belt's another mystery, to add to all the rest,' said Benton.

'Could it be significant?' asked Parnell.

'It's something to flag,' accepted Benton.

'I interrupted you,' apologized the scientist.

'They're not happy about the damage to your car, either,' continued Benton. 'They don't think the dents and the paint loss was caused by your car being hit by another vehicle. The damage is too regular. They think it was more likely caused by being hit and scratched by some sort of implement or tool. If another car had been involved, it's almost inevitable that some of its paint would have been left on yours. There's absolutely no trace.'

'Something else,' remembered Parnell. 'I got the impression that the police already knew about the damage to my car, before they questioned me. But I hadn't reported it to Dubette security. During the day, there must be what, three, four hundred cars in the lot. Maybe more. How come they knew about my car, among all the rest?'

'How indeed?' echoed Dingley.

'You discovered the damage on the Thursday?' queried Benton.

'Yes.'

'In the lot?'

'Yes. When I went to get into the car, to go home.'

'What time was that?' took up Dingley.

Parnell shrugged. 'I can't be precise. Late. Seven thirty, eight o'clock.'

'Half-light?'

'Getting that way. The lot's lighted, of course.'

'What about paint on the ground? Anything at all?'

Parnell shook his head, recalling the courtroom examination. 'I don't remember seeing any. Looking even. I just thought it was a car-park knock. One of those things.'

'It was certainly that,' said Benton. 'You go through this with the deputies?'

'Maybe not in quite so much detail,' said Parnell. 'You going to talk to them?'

Benton smiled at the question. 'We're going to talk to just about as many people as we can. And maybe it was worthwhile letting you in on the preliminary forensic findings after all.'

'You are going to find out who did it, aren't you?' said Parnell.

'We're going to try our damnedest,' promised Dingley.

Parnell felt self-conscious, embarrassed, concentrating upon everyone around him as he left the FBI field office and went into the multi-storey car park to retrieve his car, checking the mirrors before and after driving out, trying to establish whether he was being followed, which he couldn't. Remembering what one of the Bureau agents had said, Parnell decided it was just like being in a B movie, but tried to convince himself that it was the sort of precaution they were advising, but couldn't do that either. How long would it have to go on? Until the unknown *they* were caught, he supposed. What if they weren't? Howard Dingley's parting remark hadn't sounded particularly hopeful. Parnell didn't think he could maintain the vigilance forever – wasn't sure he could maintain it even over days or weeks. It was a frightening conclusion, frightening enough for it to stop being embarrassing and become unsettling reality. Parnell tried to check his mirrors all the way to McLean and, with the Dubette building in sight, came close to hitting a suddenly braking car in front because he was studying the reflection of vehicles behind.

He reached the pharmacogenomics division – still an object of attention as he walked the windowed corridors – disorientated, knowing it would be difficult to keep his mind undividedly upon the priority work in which he'd decided to involve

142

himself. Initially, however, he didn't try. He shook his head against Kathy Richardson's gesture that she had some messages, and securely closed against interruption the office door he recalled telling the staff would always remain open. He dialled Barry Jackson's office number. Parnell was connected immediately.

'I just got back from an FBI interview. I don't think I did very well.'

'Why didn't you tell me you were going? Ask me to come along?'

'It didn't occur to me. Didn't think it was necessary.'

'Why don't you think it went very well?'

'I couldn't tell them anything!'

'Of course you couldn't.'

'It sounded like . . . oh, I don't know what it sounded like, as if I could even have been hiding something.'

'I should have come with you.'

'You're probably right. But wouldn't it have appeared that I *did* have something to hide, needing my lawyer beside me?'

'Representation's your legal right. We've already proved in a court that you're not involved.'

'In murder. They're concentrating on terrorism! They said they'll probably need to speak to me again.'

'Next time I'll come along.'

'They said something else, too. That I might be in physical danger. Not from the Metro DC police, although they agreed with your warning. From whoever killed Rebecca. They told me to be careful.'

'Sounds like good advice.'

'You agree with them, that it's a possibility.'

'Of course it's a possibility. I would have thought that was obvious.'

'It hasn't been, until now. It's not a very comforting thought.'

'It's not intended to be. It's intended to be advice you should take.'

'I'm trying.'

'Don't stop. And don't try going alone any more. Talk to me. That's what eventually you're going to pay a lot of money for.'

Parnell was conscious of Kathy Richardson through the

glassed separation, intently watching for him to replace the telephone, so he turned the movement into a welcoming gesture, opening his closed door to admit her.

The woman said at once: 'Dwight Newton wanted to see you, the moment you got back . . .' She offered a strong, sealed manila envelope. 'And this came from Dr Spacey.'

Parnell weighed the choices as well as physically testing the envelope, and decided upon the vice president first. On his way further into the Spider's Web, he thought he should have telephoned ahead but continued on anyway. He was admitted immediately, to a reception in distinct contrast to the previous day. The white-coated man remained hunched forward over his desk and said at once: 'You didn't tell me you were going to the FBI!'

'When we spoke, I didn't know I was.'

'I should have known! Been told! Dubette are being dissected in the media, in connection with it all. I should have known.'

'It was my oversight. I'm sorry.'

'What was it all about?'

'They wanted to interview me, obviously.'

'Someone from Dubette should have been with you.'

'I don't think so, Dwight, do you?'

'Yes, I do.'

'The lawyer you chose for me would have railroaded me into God knows what sort of situation if I'd let him represent me. If I'm accompanied for any further meetings, it'll be by the man who got me freed, on the spot.'

'Rebecca Lang's tape would have been found,' insisted the other man.

'Not by me. Or a court official.'

Newton coloured. 'So, how was it? The interview, I mean.'

'Still very preliminary. There wasn't a lot I could tell them.'

'What was said about Dubette?'

'Nothing, specifically. As I said, everything was preliminary.'

'They got any leads?'

Parnell looked steadily at the other man for several moments. 'Preliminary,' he repeated, for the third time. 'No leads, no nothing. Just mystery.' The greatest of all was when and how

– and by whom – will an attempt be made to kill me, he thought, and wished he hadn't, because he was back into a B-movie mindset.

'Your people working on the flu request?' abruptly switched Newton.

'The current samples were only due today. I haven't yet had time to check if they've arrived. I'm going to head it up, with three others.'

'I want everyone involved,' insisted Newton. 'And I want to be kept in the closest touch. About everything.'

'I hear the message,' said Parnell. It would be difficult not to, so often had it been repeated.

Back in his office, the door secured again, Parnell sat for several moments gazing down at Barbara Spacey's sealed report, wondering if the man he had just left had read it before their confrontation, confused by Newton's pendulum mood swings. Impatiently Parnell tore open the envelope, not expecting the brevity of the woman's assessment. In Barbara Spacey's opinion the events to which he had been subjected had profoundly affected him psychologically. He was making every effort, much of it subconsciously, to suppress any obvious reaction, but would be overly worried by the reaction of others towards him. She was unsure of the true depths of his feelings towards Rebecca Lang and believed Parnell felt, although he might be unable to identify the reason, a deep sense of guilt. There was a marked absence of the overconfidence that she had commented upon in her first report. She wanted another interview in the near future.

She might, thought Parnell. He didn't.

Sixteen

There appeared to be no resentment at Parnell's announcement that he was joining the expanded flu research team and it was automatically accepted that he would be its leader.

From Tokyo there were frozen specimens of the current bird flu virus, as well as quite separate – and unexpected – samples of SARS from the masked palm civet cat, the wild animal species considered a culinary delicacy in China, and suspected of being the source of a renewed but so far limited outbreak of the disease that became an epidemic in the Far East in 2003. There were also cultures from two human victims of the new SARS outbreak in China's Guangzhou city. The inconclusive research notes on both from Dubette's Japanese subsidiary ran to forty pages and included warnings from the World Health Organization of a potential pandemic from both respiratory illnesses.

'We didn't know we were getting the additional severe acute respiratory syndrome material?' queried Parnell.

Ted Lapidus shook his head. 'Maybe Tokyo is treating them as allied conditions to examine in conjunction.'

Parnell said: 'And if the viral composition is different, we could confuse ourselves.'

'It could be something Russell Benn and his merry men want to work on at the same time,' suggested Beverley Jackson.

'I'll find out,' said Parnell. 'And if it is, then let them. Here, for the moment, we'll leave the WHO worrying about SARS pandemics. We'll concentrate on avian flu and come back to SARS as a separate project.' A part of his mind was still preoccupied, which he guessed it would be for a long time to come, but Parnell believed the majority of his concentration to be back upon the work at hand and it pleased him. It made him feel in charge of himself, which he'd always been supremely sure of but hadn't felt for the last few days, needing to be reliant on – or at the mercy of – others. Which, he acknowledged, had been Barbara Spacey's psychological assessment.

'We could have a boost for our flu experiments,' said Sean Sato. 'Did a Web surf yesterday while I was waiting for the Tokyo stuff to arrive. The Scripps Research Institute in San Diego, working with the National Institute for Medical Research in England, have found how the 1918 influenza transferred from birds to humans. The importance of the discovery, from our point of view, is that it's genetic.'

'Take us through it,' said Parnell.

'They worked with genes from the 1918 virus recovered from an Inuit woman whose body was preserved in a frozen Alaskan tundra grave, and from kept samples from US soldiers who died in the pandemic,' recounted Sato, enjoying the audience. 'And isolated the bird-flu viral protein, haemagglutinin. It's got spikes, like darts. It's the darts that locked it on to human cells, like spears, and by which it gained entry to cause the infection . . .'

'Which no one would have understood at the time, because the human flu virus wasn't isolated until 1933,' intruded Lapidus.

'We know that of the fifteen different strains of bird influenza that have been identified, only three until now have ever mutated to infect humans, in 1918, 1957 and 1968,' said Sato. 'What they haven't been able to discover is why, having made the species jump from bird to human, it becomes so pathogenic from human to human.' He hesitated again, to make a point. 'I've pieced together some other already published data. We've got Tokyo's material to confirm the opinions, but one analysis suggests the current avian flu is similar to the human virus that caused the 1968 pandemic. There's another theory that it possibly has a haemagglutinin-type protein like that of 1918.'

No one, not even Lapidus, spoke for several moments, digesting what the Japanese-American had just suggested. It was Parnell who said: 'You just outlined a double-barrelled, global pandemic that would make a death toll of twenty million in 1918 little more than a starting figure.'

'I know,' said Sato, quietly. 'It frightens the shit out of me.'

'This information's public?' questioned Beverley.

'On the Internet for everyone to read,' said Sato, gesturing towards the dead-eyed computer at his station. 'Who knows how many people have put it together?'

'Why hasn't there been some WHO warning?' demanded Lapidus.

'Against what?' demanded Parnell, in return, surprised at the question. 'There's no vaccine or prevention – that's what we're supposed to be trying to find. To issue dire predictions and make the connections that Sean has just done would simply cause panic.'

147

'Scripps – and London – synthesized haemagglutinin?' queried Beverley.

'That's my understanding,' agreed Sato. 'I've downloaded individual copies of everything I've found for all of us.'

'If it's synthesized, we've got something positive to begin with,' judged Beverley.

'I'm frightened as shitless as Sean by his doomsday scenario,' said Parnell. 'Let's start by making the most obvious comparison open to us, the synthesized haemagglutinin against what's come in from Tokyo, looking for matching spikes . . . matching *anything*. And then against the 1968 Hong Kong flu, to see if there's a possible fit.'

'Which way are you thinking of going?' asked Lapidus.

'The only way,' answered Parnell. 'One step after the other. You got any thoughts?'

The Greek scientist shook his head. 'Don't like the idea we can't culture in chicken eggs.'

'At the moment that's the least of our problems. Let's get reading and get started.'

Despite Lapidus's assurance Parnell crossed to Kathy Richardson's office, forbidding her from going anywhere near the specialized laboratory in which the potentially virulent Asian samples were being stored, but asked her to prepare files in which they could record and cross-reference their experiments. The woman said she had already been told and appreciated the dangers, reminding him with a hint of stiffness that she had long experience as a medical secretary. Parnell also asked her to obtain a map of the flu-affected countries in Asia upon which the incidence of outbreaks could be charted. He dictated a lengthy email to Tokyo, asking why they had included the SARS material in their shipment, and requested daily reports on the increase or otherwise of flu outbreaks in the region, to update his intended map, and advised in advance that he might ask for more physical samples.

Parnell entered Russell Benn's laboratory complex at the end of what had obviously been a similar conference to the one he'd just held, and was ushered at once into the man's side office with the permanently percolating coffee and the Dubette-logo mugs. The black professor described what he'd just conducted as a jam session, as yet without any formulated approach apart from chemically reanalysing what Tokyo had already done. He didn't know why the SARS stuff had been included either, and looked forward to Tokyo's reply to Parnell's query. He listened intently to an account of the geneticists' discussion and, when Parnell finished, said: 'Jesus H. Christ!'

'It's theory at this stage,' cautioned Parnell.

'With a basis,' argued Benn. 'You told Dwight?'

'Nothing to tell him, until we've satisfied ourselves. We know the cause – it's the way to the cure or prevention we're looking for.'

'I haven't said how sorry I am, about Rebecca,' declared the other man, suddenly. 'Which I am, truly sorry. And for what it almost caused you, personally. With terrorism in the mix, it's one big crock of shit.'

'Let's hope the FBI can sort it out.' Parnell regretted Benn's reminder. For a brief while it had actually gone out of his mind but now it was back.

'They any idea what it's all about?'

'None.'

'I guess they'll be spending time here?'

'I guess,' said Parnell, guardedly. He didn't want to say or do anything to anyone that might stop the exchange of information between himself and the FBI investigators.

'It must be distracting.'

'I'll cope.' How well, Parnell wondered, remembering the difficult drive from Washington and Barbara Spacey's analysis.

'Look forward to our working properly together.'

'So do I,' said Parnell. He hesitated, on the point of trying to draw the man on the French experimentation that Dwight Newton had dismissed as a failure, but decided against it. It was hopefully something he could learn – or at least get a guide to – from the FBI. After itemizing it as he had that morning, it was inevitable the two Bureau agents would ask about it.

At Giorgio Falcone's insistence Parnell travelled in the lead funeral car. Apart from the restaurateur, there were two occasionally weeping aunts and a niece. What whispered conversation there was between them was in Italian. In English, to Parnell, Falcone said: 'Dubette offered to pay for everything. I told them I didn't want their charity.'

'I thought you might,' said Parnell. He'd been surprised by the Dubette contingent in the following cars. Personnel director Wayne Denny was with Dwight Newton, Russell Benn and Burt Showcross and two other men whom Parnell didn't know but assumed to be from Rebecca's division. He hadn't expected Barry Jackson or the two FBI men, either.

'The undertakers told me they've sent four wreaths, one from the president himself.'

'Rebecca was very popular. They valued her work.'

'That's what the man said who came to see me about paying for the funeral. The FBI came, too, yesterday. Asked me about the previous boyfriend, like you did. I wasn't able to help them beyond what I told you. Do they think he did it?'

'No,' said Parnell. 'They need to talk to everyone who knew Rebecca.'

'And they've searched Rebecca's house. They wanted a key. They asked for photographs of her, too.'

What had they found at the house? wondered Parnell. He felt exhausted, straining to keep any coherence in his specu-lation. He'd worked until nine on the day of his return to Dubette and wished he hadn't when he'd finally left the complex, because the car lot was almost deserted. And now, almost two days later, he ached physically from what he imag-ined he had to do to remain alert to everything and everybody around him. He'd scarcely slept on the night of the return, and the following day actually jumped, only just stopping short of crying out, at a lorry's backfire. And after that stared so hard at whom he judged to be two different suspiciously behaving men on two separate occasions that they'd frowned back with equal suspicion, one, Parnell guessed, on the point of confronting him to ask what the hell he was doing. Although he knew it was an irrational expectation and was impatient with himself for it, he'd still wanted something positive from their experiments and had been tetchy with everyone when there wasn't. He'd hardly slept the previous night, either. And he'd eaten nothing since he couldn't remember when but crackers and cheese and now there was none left of either in the apartment. All the wine had gone, too.

'You'll let me know, if you hear anything?' pressed Rebecca's uncle.

Parnell brought himself back to the older man beside him. 'If I hear anything.'

The service was in a Catholic church in Bethesda and there was an already waiting cordon of television and stills cameras, which jostled into action as the mourners formed up behind the flower-draped coffin to file into the church behind it. The priest was young and bearded, which Parnell considered odd until accepting it to be yet another irrational reaction. Parnell allowed his mind to wander during the service, believing it a brief and welcome opportunity to release the self-imposed, exhausting tension. He caught snatches, though, disjointed references to violence and tragedy and young life savagely cut short, intermingled with insistences upon God's infinite wisdom and mysterious ways. He stood and sat in time with everyone around him who stood and sat, and matched with them the opening and closing of his blurred hymn book, from which he didn't try to sing. There was more filming when the procession moved towards the grave, which Parnell, bringing his mind to bear once more, realized was that in which Rebecca's mother and father were interred. The aunts and the niece wept on during the dust to dust, ashes to ashes ritual. So did Giorgio Falcone. There were probably others whom Parnell didn't see. They all threw individual flowers into the gaping hole. Falcone plucked a lily from a waiting wreath and offered it, and Parnell dropped it into the grave, without looking down into where Rebecca's body lay. As he turned back towards the grieving family with whom he had been standing, Parnell saw that his commemorative flower had come from one of the Dubette wreaths. His spray of white lilies and his handwritten card – *Goodbye, my love to be* – had been relegated to the second row of the banked floral tributes, behind Dubette's elaborate creations. Determinedly Parnell reached forward, bringing his into the front, unconcerned at the flurry it caused among the hovering media.

There was an uncertain hiatus around the graveside, which

151

Parnell finally stirred himself to resolve, leading the immediate family back towards the waiting cars. As they walked, Falcone said: 'I wonder how many will come back?'

'Come back?' echoed Parnell.

'I've closed the restaurant for the reception. You didn't hear the priest invite everybody?'

'No,' said Parnell. It was already difficult for him to remember what he had or had not heard. The moment he relaxed he had the impression of his awareness ebbing and flowing.

'He did. It's expected.'

'Of course.' Parnell discovered, almost with a jolt, that he was back in the funeral car and assumed they were heading into Washington. He clenched his hands as tightly as he could to achieve a physical sensation, something on to which he could lock his mind to stop him drifting from what was happening around him, and he contorted his face, squeezing his eyes shut, for the same reason. It helped, just, but Parnell wasn't sure how long it would last. A touch on his arm brought him around to one of the no longer crying aunts, who said in a heavily accented voice that she thought it had been a wonderful service, and dutifully Parnell said he thought so, too. She added that she was sorry for his loss and that he and Rebecca would have made a wonderful life together, and Parnell nodded but didn't reply.

The Wisconsin Avenue restaurant had a *Closed* notice at the window and the blinds were drawn. A black-suited Ciro, whom Parnell hadn't seen at the funeral, unlocked the door, shepherding the staff in ahead of everyone and turning on the interior lights. It was not until he saw Falcone assembling the rest of the family mourners that Parnell appreciated that there was going to be a receiving line. He held back until the Italian beckoned him forward at the arrival of the others. As Parnell joined the line, the man said: 'You count as family.'

The handshaking, unheard commiseration ritual seemed to last forever and Parnell was embarrassed by it, glad when it ended. He moved away at once, taking from Ciro the offered glass of red wine, so full he needed to sip before carrying it more safely further into the room, tightening his self-control

152

to face – and understand – the impending ordeal. At once he was conscious of Barry Jackson's supporting presence at his elbow.

The lawyer said: 'You look rough.'

'So you keep telling me.'

'So you keep looking. Specific problem or just everything?'

'Constantly watching my back, I suppose. And not sleeping.'

'You could get something to sleep.'

Parnell snorted a laugh. 'I work for a drugs company and I don't take drugs. How's that for irony?'

'Stupid,' said Jackson. 'If you're not sleeping properly you can't work properly. Or be as self-aware and careful as you've got to be. Take a pill.'

Across the room, Howard Dingley and David Benton were moving among the Dubette contingent, nodding in head-bent concentration. Both were wearing subdued blue today. Following Parnell's look, Jackson said: 'They come back to you yet?'

'Not yet.'

As if on cue Dingley detached himself and crossed to them. As he arrived he said: 'Making plans to come out to Dubette.'

Jackson said: 'You're going to need to talk to my client again, of course.'

'I'd think so,' agreed the frowning FBI man.

'I'd like to be there.'

'Why's that, Mr Jackson?'

'To represent him.'

Dingley smiled, fleetingly. 'I'll have to remember to appoint you as my lawyer if ever I get into trouble.'

'My client's not in any trouble, but call me any time.'

No trouble apart from being a potential murder victim, thought Parnell. He said: 'Anything come up since we talked?'

'Nothing that helps join the dots together,' dismissed the agent.

'What about Rebecca's house? You've been through the house. Her uncle told me.'

'You're not next of kin, Mr Parnell.'

'I'm the person who was going to marry her and got wrongly arraigned for her murder and whom your partner a couple of

153

days ago agreed it was worthwhile to talk things through with.'

Dingley sighed. 'We picked up an address book and found a listing in Arlington for an Alan Smeldon. He left there about a year ago. The couple who took over his apartment think he went to California. He didn't leave a forwarding address.'

'Nothing else?' persisted Parnell.

'Like I said, nothing that takes us forward,' refused Dingley. 'Everything kept very neat and tidy. That's what Ms Lang was, very neat and tidy. You thought of anything that might help us, Mr Parnell? A friend of Ms Lang's, maybe.'

Parnell shook his head, unsure when he'd last had a comprehensible thought. But then, abruptly, the clouds cleared in his head, to a moment of crystal clarity. 'The key!' he exclaimed. 'You asked Giorgio Falcone for the key to get into Rebecca's house. But she had one, in her purse. Would have had to have had one, when she left me, to get back into her house!'

'There wasn't one among the property Metro DC police surrendered to us,' said Dingley.

'Did you and your partner do the search?' asked Jackson, entering the conversation at last.

'Yes,' said Dingley.

'You find any evidence of someone having been there before you?' persisted the lawyer.

'We didn't,' said Dingley. 'But we've got forensics there now. They're better at finding out the little things than we are.'

Seventeen

Richard Parnell thought one of his better successes – maybe even his only success so far at Dubette – was perhaps his refusal to be distracted by the fame-or-fear procession up and down the open-plan, glassed corridor to Dwight Newton's lair. He would have ignored the bustle that day, too, if Beverley

Jackson's remark hadn't included an FBI reference. Parnell looked up in time to see company lawyer Peter Baldwin hurrying towards the vice president's innermost office, leading two briefcase-carrying, dark-suited men.

He said: 'How do you figure it's a Bureau thing?'

'They're lawyers and I know lawyers, remember? They're cloned in a lawyer factory, somewhere hidden in Ohio.' Beverley had the bench space next to him for the avian-flu investigation.

'Barry doesn't look like that.'

'He was a prototype that didn't work – they abandoned the model.'

'He sure as hell worked for me,' said Parnell, uncaring at the American phraseology. He felt better. Not totally better, convinced as he once had been that he could climb mountains and swim oceans, but the cotton-wool feeling had gone from his head, and every moving part of his body didn't ache at the slightest motion. The previous night had again been more of an exhausted collapse than sleep, but it had been rest of sorts, and that morning, alert as he now had to be, there hadn't any longer been the confused disorientation of making monsters out of shadows.

'Pity he didn't work so well for me.'

It was more a throwaway line than an inviting complaint – an invitation Parnell wouldn't anyway have accepted – but he thought it confirmed that Beverley Jackson was someone who always demanded the last word in any one-to-one conversation. He decided to allow it to her, because he wasn't interested in trying to out-talk the woman.

What he was far more interested in was configuring something from the earlier influenza pandemics with the current outbreak, which yet again he accepted to be an illogical expectation but for which he'd hoped after Sean Sato's initial, seemingly encouraging discoveries. Tokyo's response to Parnell's SARS query was as Lapidus had predicted, that their research was predicated on a connecting transmission link between that and avian flu, and that they had anticipated the exploration would be duplicated in America. Parnell copied the email to Russell Benn, together with his reply that the pharmacogenomics unit were treating the two respiratory conditions separately. As an afterthought he made a separate copy to the vice president, towards whose office he'd just seen the legal procession head.

By then he, Beverley Jackson, Ted Lapidus and Sato had exhausted every microscope comparison with the limited Tokyo samples without finding anything approaching a visual match to the spiked 1918 haemagglutinin gene or the structure of the 1968 Hong Kong virus. It was because there was a momentary hiatus in their work that Beverley had been looking out into the corridor, and it was the woman who said again: 'And then there were more!'

Parnell looked up in time to see Howard Dingley and David Benton passing. Parnell almost expected them to be walking in step, but they weren't. As he went by, Dingley looked into the unit and gestured. Parnell said: 'They're FBI.'

'So I was right,' insisted Beverley.

Definitely a last-word syndrome, thought Parnell. He said: 'It was set up at the funeral.'

'What's our next step forward?' impatiently broke in Sean Sato.

There was something proprietorial in the way the Japanese-American spoke, as if his earlier findings qualified him above the other two under Parnell's supervision. Parnell said: 'The obvious one, animals. We'll try to synthesize, in mice to begin with. See if we can bring about a mutation and then monitor it, to find the bridge the virus crosses.'

'All of us?' queried Lapidus.

'We don't need to be involved, all of us, this early,' acknowledged Parnell. 'You three kick it off. I want to go back on that research Sean found, see if we can take it further and open up a separate path. We're going to need more samples from Tokyo, too. We'll jointly discuss each day's progress.'

'You're second-checking?' seized Lapidus.

Parnell was surprised at the interjection. 'Of course. Nothing's going to leave this department unless it's been second and third and fourth time checked. And that's before it goes into the statutory three-phase licensing process.'

'We going to manage that in our lifetime?' asked Lapidus.

'It's somebody else's lifetime we're concerned with,' reminded Parnell.

'I didn't mean . . .' started Lapidus, disconcerted.

'I'm talking about what emerges from this unit, not anything else,' Parnell halted him, sparing the man. 'We all clear on what we're doing?'

The two other men nodded. Beverley said: 'Perfectly.'

Kathy Richardson looked up at Parnell's emergence from the restricted laboratory, shaking her head at his enquiring look as he approached, to let him know there were no messages. Inside her office the woman was enclosed behind the battlement of file boxes, some already filled, many more waiting to be filled with the raw data she was in the process of sorting.

He said: 'It'll get better.'

'You promise?'

'I promise. And I'll send my own emails.'

'You needn't.'

'Democracy rules in the Dubette pharmacogenomics unit.'

'I'll get the T-shirts and the fender stickers printed.'

Parnell laughed openly at the gradually emerging independent irony, convinced he'd made the right choice in Kathy Richardson, as he had with everyone else. His email to Tokyo was brief, a simple request for more samples. Parnell experienced a nostalgic déjà vu of his open-minded, free-exchange period in pure research when he began communicating with the Scripps Research Institute in San Diego and the National Institute for Medical Research in London. Literally within an hour, there were enthusiastic acknowledgements from the directors of both, each promising the raw experimental data of their respective findings that had not appeared either on the Internet or in the scientific journals. From each it was flatteringly obvious the quickness of their responses came from their recognition of his name and reputation on the genome project. Parnell wondered, and quickly wished he hadn't, whether the notoriety of the past week might also have contributed.

So immersed was he that Parnell had forgotten the presence of the FBI investigators further along the corridor until Kathy Richardson's warning arrival, Dingley and Benton hovering close behind. She said: 'They're asking for a minute or two.'

Parnell waved them in.

'That's all, just a minute or two,' promised Dingley.

Benton said: 'How's it going?'

'Better than it was,' said Parnell. 'But only just.'

'How's that?' said Dingley.

'Trying to adjust. Getting used to things,' said Parnell.

Both men nodded, as if they understood.

'You wanted a minute or two,' prompted Parnell.

'Trying to fit in, to everyone's convenience, is all,' said Dingley.

'Any progress?' asked Parnell, offering seats.

'A lot of people still to see. Nothing clear yet.'

'When's there going to be anything that's clear?' pressed Parnell.

Benton made an open-handed gesture of uncertainty. 'A lot of people still to see,' he echoed his partner.

'How'd it go with the vice president?' asked Parnell, directly.

There was another hands-spread movement from Benton. 'He had counsel with him. That's why we stopped by. We're certainly going to need to speak to you again, in the next little while. Your lawyer told us he wants to come along.'

Parnell reminded himself, as he had at the moment of his premature arrest, that America was the land of litigation and that he didn't know anything whatsoever about the law. 'I'll warn him to be ready.'

'That'll be helpful,' thanked Dingley.

'What about the forensic examination of Rebecca's house?' demanded Parnell. 'Was there any evidence of it having been searched, before you?'

'Still being gone over,' avoided Dingley.

'*Still?*' queried Parnell, disbelievingly.

'They're very thorough guys,' said Benton. 'That's what their job is, being very thorough.'

'What about the flight listing?' persisted Parnell.

'You should wait until you're with your counsel,' said Dingley.

'What the hell for?' demanded Parnell, loud-voiced.

'It means you should wait until you're with your counsel,' said Benton, in another of his irritating echo responses. 'And tell him there's going to be a fingerprint request.'

'What?' asked Parnell.

'Elimination,' said Dingley. 'It's routine.'

'Will you have something, when we meet?' said Parnell.

'Maybe. Who knows?' avoided Dingley, again.

From the other side of the glass partition, Kathy Richardson was gesturing with one hand, the other holding the internal telephone.

Benton said: 'We're in the way.'

Dingley said: 'What's a good time for you?'

'That depends on Barry. I'll call him, with the choices, and get back to you.' It made sense, he knew, to have the lawyer with him, but he wasn't totally convinced of the need. He said: 'Why don't we get on with it now?'

Dingley shook his head. 'Your lawyer was very clear, Mr Parnell.' There was a close-to-imperceptible head movement back in the direction of Newton's suite. 'We get the rule book dictated to us, like we just have, we've got to go with the rule book. We make one mistake, it's all over.'

'What mistake? What's all over?' said Parnell

'Taking the wrong step in the investigation,' said Dingley.

'You still think I might be someway involved!' demanded Parnell, indignantly.

'We collect evidence, Mr Parnell,' said Benton. 'We leave other people to decide what to do with it. You'll get back to us, right?'

'Right,' said Parnell. 'As soon as I've talked to my lawyer.'

'We're obliged,' said Benton.

Parnell delayed responding to Dwight Newton's summons while he tried to reach Barry Jackson, leaving Kathy Richardson to make the contact after thirty minutes. From his side office, Parnell hadn't seen the lawyers' departure, but the research division vice president was alone when Parnell reached the man's suite. The greeting pendulum had swung again. Newton was hunch-shouldered behind his desk, glowering up from a lowered head.

'You talked about confidential work under progress here!' Newton accused at once.

'What?' exclaimed Parnell, surprised.

'You heard what I said!'

'I heard what you said. I didn't *understand* what you said.'

'I've just been officially interviewed,' protested the other man. 'Asked about work we were doing here on something that emanated from France.'

'Yes?' said Parnell. He was content for Newton to lead.

'Which you told them about,' the research vice president continued to accuse him. 'That's information governed by the confidentiality contract you signed.'

'I don't recall any clause in that contract covering a murder investigation.'

'They're talking terrorism, for Christ's sake!'

'You knew about the Air France flight listings. It came up in court.'

'Those guys are treating it as sinister – trying to make a connection to Dubette. Because of what you told them.'

'I didn't disclose any secrets, Dwight. I don't have any secrets, so I can't have breached any confidentiality contract. They wanted to know about anything – and I mean that, *anything* – that Rebecca might have regarded as out of the ordinary in the last few weeks. She was curious why she and her department had been bypassed, about France. That's what I told them. That it was out of the ordinary and she hadn't understood why. Simple as that. Simple as that and *only* that, because there was nothing more *to* tell them, was there?'

The other man gave the impression of relaxing, although only slightly. 'What did Rebecca say about France?'

'Only that she couldn't understand why things weren't normal. And that Burt Showcross told her to leave it. Which is what I told her, particularly after you told me the French idea hadn't worked out.'

Newton examined Parnell steadily for several moments. 'They spoke to Showcross. And Russell Benn.'

Parnell wasn't sure what he was supposed to say. 'With the lawyers present?'

Newton nodded. 'Do you think they will want to see you again?'

'They do,' confirmed Parnell. 'Barry Jackson will be with me.'

'He's representing you, personally. I'd like our people there, as well.'

'Why?'

'Dubette have got to be protected, from all this terror rubbish. You've seen the papers. And the television.'

'All this terror rubbish?' queried Parnell.

'Misleading accusations,' specified Newton.

'Dwight! I'm not up with you on this!'

'I know the case they're trying to build: that Dubette, with its access to drugs and chemicals, has some connection with terrorism. That's why the FBI are involved in the first place.'

'I really don't believe this! There's a perfectly understandable and acceptable explanation for why Rebecca had that flight number in her bag: her job was to deal with samples coming in by air from overseas. And Dingley and Benton *have* accepted it, as far as I am aware.'

'That's not my impression.'

'Impression?' questioned Parnell, pointedly. 'A second ago you told me they were building a definite case.'

'We're talking about company lawyers being with you for the next FBI interview,' said Newton.

'You were talking about company lawyers,' contradicted Parnell. 'I wasn't. I'm going to see the Bureau guys again, with just my lawyer. And if I get the slightest indication of Dubette being compromised, I'll stop the interview and tell you, immediately.'

'I'm not sure that's the attitude we welcome,' said Newton.

'It's not an attitude,' contradicted Parnell again. 'It's common-sense refusal to be panicked when there's no reason nor cause to be panicked.'

'I've got to see the board, up in New York.'

'I'm sure you have,' said Parnell, unsure why he was being told.

'Which will have to include your refusal to co-operate.'

'Dwight, don't you think the FBI might imagine that I – and Dubette – have something to hide if I arrive next time surrounded by attorneys? I'm not refusing to co-operate. I'm refusing to let there be any wrongful suspicion . . . wrongful suspicion about me and wrongful suspicion about Dubette. Make sure you tell the board that, in those words.'

'I'll definitely make sure of that,' said Newton, in an attempted threat that failed.

'There's nothing to hide,' insisted Parnell once more. I haven't, he thought. He increasingly wasn't sure about Dwight Newton or Russell Benn.

When Parnell got back to his department, Kathy Richardson said Jackson had suggested ten the following morning. When he told Dingley, the FBI agent said: 'You told him about fingerprints?'

'He wants to know why.'

Eighteen

Richard Parnell was at Jackson's office by eight thirty – and had to wait fifteen minutes for the lawyer's arrival – wanting advice not so much for the meeting that was to come but for the uncertainties that appeared to be arising from those that had already taken place.

When Parnell finished, Jackson said: 'What do you think you're telling me?'

'Let's not go this route,' protested Parnell. 'From the moment we first met, in the middle of the night in a detention cell, I don't know how many days or weeks ago, I've not known what the fuck I'm telling you or anyone else! It's feelings, nuances, uncertainties: square things that don't go into round holes. It's all wrong. Rebecca's dead, murdered, and something's wrong and I'm not talking about her being killed or my getting accused of it.'

Jackson tried silently to pick his way through the jumbled declaration. 'You think there is something to link Dubette with terrorism?'

'Absolutely not. But there's something.'

'Something big enough – important enough – to have got Rebecca killed?'

'Maybe. But this is another route we've travelled before!'

'You got the slightest whisper – the slightest feeling, nuance, square uncertainty that won't fit into a round hole – of proof?'

'You mocking me?'

'No,' denied the lawyer, at once. 'I'm trying to balance what you're saying – suggesting – against what precious little else makes sense.'

'And?'

'And nothing,' said the scar-faced man. 'Maybe that's the cleverness of the whole thing.'

'I don't understand,' said Parnell, exasperated by the too familiar protest.

'It's too clever *to* understand.'

'I'll accept that philosophy in experimental science. But not having stood at the graveside of someone who's been murdered. Murder can't be too clever to understand or solve!'

'Sometimes it is,' said Jackson, flatly.

'This isn't going to be one of those times.'

The lawyer shook his head. 'Didn't you tell me the FBI guys warned you against the way you're thinking?'

'Whoever set this whole thing up, did what they did, killed Rebecca like they did, has got to be punished . . . found, exposed and punished.'

'Which is why we're going where we are now, to try to achieve that,' reminded Jackson. 'Mine's the legally protective presence. You're the guy they're going to be talking to. You don't wander on about amorphous conspiracy theories without a single jot of evidence to substantiate them. You listen to the questions and you answer them as honestly – but most importantly, as succinctly – as you can. I don't want you talking yourself into a different dead end from the one I've already got you out of.'

'I'm not going to talk myself into anything,' insisted Parnell.

'That's what I'm coming along to stop you doing. Why it's essential that I do come along. And even more essential that you don't, ever, think you can do things by yourself.'

'I've already had that lecture!'

'Have it again. Listen – really listen – to it again. You're right about nuances and uncertainties. Don't entangle yourself in them. Remember what I said about not representing losers.'

'I'm not a loser,' insisted Parnell. 'Nor will I be. Ever.' He'd probably come close, he acknowledged. But suddenly, now, he felt he could climb the mountains and swim the oceans again. It was a feeling he welcomed back.

It was a different, larger, room at the FBI field office, with easy chairs and plants with polished leaves instead of desk and stiff-backed-seat formality. Parnell thought he recognized the third waiting FBI man, but it wasn't until Jackson made the reintroduction that he remembered Edwin Pullinger as the Bureau counsel from the court hearing and later, brief, anteroom hearing.

Parnell said at once: 'How can I help you further? I didn't get the impression I contributed much last time.'

'No, you didn't,' agreed Benton.

'You had any more thoughts about that airline flight number?' asked Dingley.

It was a clever, almost hypnotic double act, Parnell finally recognized, each man so finely attuned that one could pick up upon the other to weave the loose ends that Jackson had warned about into a snare. 'I thought we'd covered that?'

'So did we,' agreed Dingley. 'But you know what? We can't find any Dubette-destined way-bill on that flight out of Paris's Charles de Gaulle for the last three months.'

'Which leaves us with a problem,' took up Benton. 'What was Ms Lang doing with a number of a Paris to Washington DC flight that wasn't carrying anything for Dubette? But was, it turns out, a flight that got cancelled four times in a row on the advice of anti-terrorist electronic intercepts?'

'I don't know,' conceded Parnell, dry-throated, seeing the mountains grow higher, the oceans wider. 'What I do know, and what I've already told you, is that Rebecca Lang was totally apolitical, had no connection, interest or association whatsoever with terrorism and that the only possible expla-

164

nation is that it was planted in her bag, like paint from my car was used to make it look as if I was the one who forced her over the canyon edge.' The FBI lawyer wasn't taking part in the interrogation, Parnell realized.

'That's not quite my recollection,' said Dingley. 'My recollection is that the last time we talked you said it would have been a flight carrying a Dubette shipment from its Paris subsidiary.'

'The last time we talked I said I *thought* it would have been carrying something for Dubette,' rejected Parnell. 'You've just told me it wasn't. So, the next possible explanation is that it was planted.'

'What about your political views, Mr Parnell?' asked Benton, abruptly.

Parnell laughed, genuinely amused. 'I don't have the right to vote in this country, which I'm sure you know. In England I voted for the Liberal Democrats, the smallest of the three English political parties. I have never been a member of any radical political movement or organization, am not a Muslim nor do I subscribe to any fanatical Islamic movement or jihads or suicide bombings . . .' He looked at Jackson. 'Anything I've left out?'

'I don't think so,' frowned the lawyer, uncomfortably.

Benton said: 'That wasn't a question to be treated lightly.'

'I wasn't treating it lightly. I was treating it with the contempt it deserved.' Parnell felt his lawyer's warning pressure against his arm and recognized his returning confidence was tipping over into arrogance.

'Did you have a key to the Bethesda house?' asked Dingley, in one of his sudden directional changes.

'No,' said Parnell.

'Did Ms Lang have a key to your apartment?' asked Benton. 'No.'

'You moved back and forth, between the two?' queried Dingley, rhetorically. 'You were going to set up home together. Yet you didn't have keys to each other's homes?'

'It never came up, as a problem. We'd have got around to it, when we started to live together – arriving and leaving at different times.' He was making another bad impression,

Parnell accepted. He had to correct it – correct it and try to discover what, if anything, they had learned. Find out why they were so obviously treating him with the suspicion that they were. Before either agent could speak, he said: 'What about Bethesda?'

'Sir?' questioned Benton, in return.

'Had it been entered, before you got there with Giorgio Falcone's key?'

There was the familiar exchange of looks between the two men.

'We think so,' said Dingley.

'Was it or wasn't it?' insisted Parnell, impatiently.

'Looks that way,' admitted Benton.

'*How* does it look that way?' persisted Parnell.

'Like I think I told you before, everything was very neat. Too neat,' said Dingley.

'Which brings us to our request,' picked up Benton. 'We need fingerprints . . . for elimination. Yours will be about the place, won't they?'

'My client's not required to provide them, unless he agrees,' intruded Jackson, at last.

'Of course I agree,' said Parnell, before the FBI group had a chance to reply. 'Why shouldn't I?' Addressing the two agents, he said: 'You think something was taken from Rebecca's house?'

Benton gave another of his open-palmed gestures. 'We've got no way of telling. We don't know what was there in the first place.'

'You've got more to be suspicious about than the fact that the house was too tidy,' challenged Jackson. 'That's not even forensic. That's soap-opera bullshit.'

Dingley smiled, bleakly. 'Not quite, sir. There wasn't an item of furniture, an article anywhere, that hadn't been lifted, looked at, and replaced. But not exactly put back in the right place where it had been before it was shifted: just off-centre marks in the carpeting, that carpeting not properly re-secured where it had been lifted, to look beneath. Off-centre again where kitchen appliances had been replaced. Like I said, too neat – always too neat.'

'Was Ms Lang particularly neat?' asked Benton.

166

'Not particularly,' remembered Parnell. 'She didn't live in a mess but the house *was* lived in.'

'Magazines, newspapers, wouldn't have been carefully stacked and aligned? Books always in the shelves for the titles to be read, none with dust-cover flaps used as bookmarks?' said Dingley.

Parnell shook his head. 'I don't think so.'

'And?' persisted Jackson.

This time Dingley looked back at the FBI lawyer, who nodded and said: 'OK.'

Dingley said: 'There wasn't any personal mail. Forensics *are* thorough. Suggested we check the mail drop, for the Monday Ms Lang was found murdered. Mailman remembers three, one package bigger than the other two, which were ordinary letter size. There wasn't any mail when we got there. Or any that our forensics guys could find.'

'And?' repeated Jackson.

Benton said to Parnell, 'You ever write to Ms Lang? A note, a proper letter maybe?'

Parnell didn't respond at once, thinking. 'No,' he said, almost surprised. 'I never did – never had to, because we worked in the same place – not even a note. But why?'

'There wasn't a single personal letter in the house,' said Dingley. 'Utility bills, credit card receipts, all carefully filed. But not a single personal note, from anyone listed in the address book we found . . .' He looked back again to Edwin Pullinger, for another permissive nod. 'And the telephone answering equipment in Ms Lang's machine was brand new. Hadn't been utilized before, on any call.'

'What's the significance of that?' demanded Parnell.

'Answering-machine loops are used and rewound to be wiped and rewound and wiped again and again and again,' said Dingley. 'Our forensics guys can recover things from loops that are supposed to have been wiped, like they can with computer hard disks. Ms Lang's loop had been taken, a new one put in its place.'

'It was her call on my machine that saved me,' remembered Parnell, softly.

'Which brings us to another request,' chimed in Benton.

Parnell stared at the man, refusing the ventriloquist's-dummy role.

Finally Benton said: 'Would you come to Bethesda, to the house, with us – look for anything you think might be wrong, anything that makes you curious . . . anything out of place . . . ?'

Jackson said: 'That's a hell of an unusual request.'

'This is a hell of an unusual case,' said Pullinger, coming into the discussion for the first time. 'You can refuse, of course.'

'No!' said Parnell, hurriedly. 'Of course I'll come: try to do whatever you want me to do. But I didn't – don't – know the house well – know where Rebecca kept things. What might be missing or what might not. Sure I stayed there, but it wasn't my place, not with my things in it. I've told you, it was all too new. We hadn't . . . we hadn't got that far . . .'

'We'd appreciate it,' said Dingley.

'Unannounced!' insisted Jackson. 'My client will not go to Ms Lang's house as a media exhibit.'

'The investigation is out of the hands of the DC Metro police,' reminded Pullinger pointedly.

'I've got to have your guarantee, Ed,' insisted Jackson. 'We pitch up to a media reception and blinding lights, we ain't stopping the car. I'm not having my client publicly exposed or compromised in any way.'

'We've no intention of publicly exposing or compromising your client in any way,' retorted the other lawyer, stiffly.

'That's good to hear,' said Jackson, unrepentant. 'When we pull up, I still want to see the surroundings to Rebecca Lang's house emptier than a Kansas prairie in December.'

It was going too fast and in the wrong direction, Parnell decided, with things still unresolved in his mind irrespective of everyone else's uncertainties. 'I still don't understand the Air France flight number.'

'As I told you, that's our biggest problem, too,' said Benton.

'How'd you check that flight didn't carry anything for Dubette in the last six months?'

'Air France dispatch, here and in Paris,' said Dingley. 'We're as thorough as our forensics people, in our own way.'

'I'm sure you are,' said Parnell, unconcerned at getting

under the other man's skin. 'You double-check, with Dubette
. . . with their security division, I guess?'

'That's who are responsible for the Dulles airport collec-
tion, security,' agreed Benton.

'That isn't the answer to my question,' said Parnell.

'Dubette security have no record of any Dubette-addressed
consignment on AF209 in the last six months,' recited Dingley.

'There is another inconsistency, here, Mr Parnell,' said
Benton. 'One we were coming to. You told us that Ms Lang
didn't understand why she was being bypassed by something
from Paris? But that, whatever it was, it hadn't worked out
in the laboratories at McLean, anyway?'

'Yes,' said Parnell, glad he had not needed to be more
direct.

'That's not the impression we've got from the people we've
spoken to at Dubette so far,' said Benton.

'How not, specifically?'

'Seems the French research wasn't a failure after all.
According to Mr Newton, it's being incorporated into some
of your existing products.'

'I didn't know that.' But now he did, Parnell accepted.

'You must have been mistaken.' suggested Dingley.

'Obviously,' said Parnell, who knew he hadn't been. 'I hope
that didn't mislead you.'

'It made us curious, along with everything else.'

'I can understand that. I'm sorry. It's been a difficult time
. . .' He let the apology trail.

'We understand that,' said Benton, in what sounded to
Parnell like mockery.

It created something else for him to understand, too, decided
Parnell. 'What about Dubette security? And the Metro DC
officers? You talked to them yet about knowing my car was
damaged, before we went out into the lot?'

'Only to the security chief, Harry Johnson, so far,' said
Dingley. 'He told us he didn't know anything about your car
until you all got to it that morning. That he hadn't had any
conversation with the Metro DC guys about it. Wasn't even
sure what your car was.'

'Looks like another mistaken impression,' said Benton.

Parnell curbed the instinctive reply. Instead he said: 'I guess it does.'

'Why don't we clear a few things up?' unexpectedly suggested Barry Jackson. 'We're happy to provide finger-prints and come out to Bethesda. Why don't we do both right away?'

'I told you no media leak would come from here,' said Dingley.

'Is there any reason why we can't do it right now?' persisted Jackson.

'No,' said Dingley.

'So?' said the lawyer.

'Let's do it now,' agreed Benton.

They'd driven to the FBI field office in Barry Jackson's car, so they went in convoy to Rebecca Lang's Bethesda clap-board, the most direct route to which was through Rock Creek Park past the gorge into which Rebecca's car had plunged. When he realized the way the FBI agents were going, Jackson said: 'You all right with this? I could use different roads.'

'I'll be all right,' said Parnell. Despite washing his hands after being fingerprinted, his fingers still retained some of the blackness of the ink.

'You could do better,' said the lawyer.

'What?'

'An investigative technique – a courtroom technique – to catch people out is to make them lose their temper – speak without thinking. Which I've warned you about. You lost your temper back there.'

'Why are they trying to catch me out – trick me!' exploded Parnell.

'You're doing it again.'

'Barry! Help me!' How many times had he made that plea?

'That's what I'm trying to do. You heard what they said – a lot of things aren't making up any sort of picture. Until it does, they've got to poke sticks into every bee's nest. You're not doing yourself any favours, snapping back. So stop it. Don't take every question as a personal attack or accusation.'

'That's what it sounds like,' said Parnell, petulantly.

'That's what it's supposed to sound like. I just told you that, for Christ's sake!' The lawyer's voice softened. 'We're getting close now. You sure you're all right?'

Parnell did not immediately respond, recognizing the twisting, narrow roads, realizing – shocked – that he hadn't properly until now fixed in his mind the precise location of the crash. He knew now, before they got to the fatal turn, what lay beyond. Suddenly there it was – the crumpled, supposedly protective barrier over which she'd been forced, the impact marks running almost its entire length, the final collapsed edge where the vehicle had mounted and then gone over the end, oil marks as black as death. And then they were past.

'Oh fuck!' said Parnell, in a breathless rush, not aware until that moment that he had actually been holding his breath, not knowing what he was going to confront.

'OK?'

'I think we should have gone the other way. Can you imagine . . . ?'

'No!' stopped Jackson. 'I don't want you trying to imagine it, either. Leave it. Leave it if you can. You've got things to do – things to concentrate upon.'

'You think they did it purposely, brought us this way?'

'Maybe. Don't let it get to you.'

'How the fuck can I avoid that?'

'By not letting it get to you.'

'Don't you start double-talking, like everyone else!'

'That's not double-talking. That's straight-talking. You ready? We're almost at the house.'

'I hope I'm ready.'

'So do I.'

The Bethesda cottage was secured by yellow police tape and there was an obvious police black and white parked outside, the driver and observer competing for boredom-of-the-year awards.

As they assembled from the two cars, Parnell said: 'I thought Metro DC were off limits?'

'They are,' said Dingley. 'They're just here, by court order, to stop anyone who isn't authorized going near the place.'

'That's going to piss them off.'

'It can't piss them off any more than they already are.'

'So, how do you know they're doing their job?' demanded Jackson.

'We got temporary – but inconspicuous – CCTV in every room. And external, in every direction. And a tap on the telephone.'

'You didn't tell us that,' complained Jackson.

'I've got all the court orders,' said Pullinger.

'We should have been told!' insisted the other lawyer.

'The house isn't your jurisdiction,' said Pullinger.

'Ed, it's our co-operation you're asking for. You're not doing a lot to encourage it,' warned Jackson.

The three FBI men began to move off towards the house but Jackson didn't move, keeping Parnell with him. Softly he said: 'You want to go through with it?'

'Don't you think I should?'

'I don't think we should look as if we're accepting it.'

'Your call,' said Parnell.

The others had stopped, about ten yards away. Pullinger shouted: 'Is there a problem?'

'We can't hear you,' Jackson yelled back.

There was a hesitation before the three men walked back. Pullinger said: 'I asked if there was a problem?'

'Yes,' said Jackson. 'We going to operate on level ground or we going to fuck about?'

'You want me to say sorry?' asked Pullinger.

'I want you to do it right, like we're doing it right.'

'You've made your point. I've taken it,' said Pullinger. 'Shall we go on inside?'

Jackson held them for another moment or two before moving towards the house, bringing the rest with him. It was Dingley who opened the door, standing back for Parnell to go in first. The last time – when? he thought, unable to remember – had been with Rebecca, hurrying in ahead of him, carrying the lightest of the grocery shopping, him the packhorse behind, she talking as she always talked, butterflying from point to point, never properly, fully, finishing what she was saying before fluttering to something else, queen of her own castle, self-proclaimed queen of his, dropping the bags, gesturing where she wanted him to drop his, turning on lights, music,

172

opening windows, hurrying him back to the car for what they hadn't been able to bring in the first time. No, he thought suddenly, moving through the living room into the kitchen. Rebecca hadn't been neat and tidy. Organized, certainly, written-out shopping lists for stores and markets listed in convenient order, but not like this, not as if the house had been made ready, prepared, for a prospective buyer. In quick recollection he looked into the double sink, then the empty dishwasher and finally to the coffee pot, opening it to confirm the filter chamber was clean.

'What?' asked Benton.

'On the Sunday morning, when Rebecca came to pick me up,' remembered Parnell. 'I asked her if she wanted coffee, because I was just making some. She said she'd already had some. And juice. There's no cups or glasses . . .'

'And the coffee pot's empty and clean,' Dingley accepted.

Parnell led the way into the den, dominated by the television and music system and saw the regimented books and the orderly magazine arrangement and then up to the bedrooms – the bedroom he and Rebecca had occupied and loved in and partially discovered each other in first – and made himself look around it and open and close drawers, although he didn't know now what for, and then he looked around the other two bedrooms, knowing even less what he was supposed to find out of place – or, rather, wrongly in place, before he retreated downstairs.

'Well?' demanded Dingley.

'It's an impression,' said Parnell. 'That's all it can be.'

'That's all we're asking for.'

'No,' said Parnell. 'It's not right. Doesn't feel right. That's all I can say. This doesn't look, feel, like the house that Rebecca left that Sunday morning to pick me up . . .' He stopped, at another recollection. 'That's why the coffee pot's wrong . . . no cup in the washer. She was late, said we had a drive to get where we were going – she wouldn't tell me where we were going – in time. It was in time to get a table, for lunch, although she wouldn't tell me that, either. If she was late, in a hurry, she wouldn't have cleared away, would she?'

'Not unless she was particularly fastidious,' said Benton.

'Rebecca wasn't particularly fastidious,' said Parnell.

'Then no, she wouldn't.' agreed Dingley.

'Where's this all got us?' demanded Jackson.

'We don't know, not yet,' said Pullinger. 'We're looking forward to something we can understand that does get us somewhere.'

Once more it was pointlessly too late for Parnell to drive out to McLean. He telephoned from the apartment that he would be in the following morning before going out again to shop uninterestedly for essentials, bread and milk and packaged meals he could heat in seconds in the microwave. He also, just as uninterestedly, bought three litre-sized bottles of screw-topped red wine, which he thought was as much as he could carry. On his way back to the apartment he saw one man whom he thought might be watching him, but there wasn't any longer a stomach lurch. Before he reached him the downtown bus arrived and the man got on it.

Back in the apartment Parnell unpacked and opened one of the bottles of wine, slumping with the glass between his cupped hands, reviewing the day. He hadn't done well – he had, in fact, been stupid, losing his temper. Too late now, for self-recrimination. He'd got it wrong, again, and deserved Jackson's rebuke, and next time he'd try to remember and behave better. He had little doubt there would be a next time: maybe even a time after that. Bethesda had disorientated him, although not in the way Jackson suggested the FBI agents had expected him to be disorientated. He hadn't suddenly collapsed, said anything or done anything, on being somewhere where he'd been with Rebecca, to indicate any guilt or awareness of something he hadn't told the investigators. The disorientation had actually been far deeper than any of them had imagined. On the near-wordless return to Washington, Parnell had confronted a truth he hadn't wanted to admit to himself, let alone to anyone else. He didn't think he'd loved Rebecca. He had feelings, of course – maybe, in time, he would even have come to love her, although that was the most scourging of uncertainties. But not that Sunday when he'd unthinkingly talked of their living together. And not now, not ever. So, he had a lie to live, pitied by the few who

174

knew him here, as someone who'd lost a woman whom he'd planned to marry. How difficult, he wondered, would that be to live with? Something else he didn't know, like so much else.

He jumped, startled, at the telephone, recognizing his mother's voice as soon as he'd answered. 'What's going on?' she demanded at once.

'You know. I told you. It's all right.'

'It's not all right! I've been questioned. So have people at Cambridge.'

'What!' Some of Parnell's wine spilled, with the urgency with which he came up out of his chair.

'Two Americans. FBI, from the London embassy. They wanted to know if you were political. If you belonged to any organizations. That's what they asked the people at Cambridge. I've had two calls, one from Alex Bell, your old tutor. Everyone here is worried about you.'

'There's nothing to worry about. It's an unusual investigation.'

'I want to come out.'

'No,' refused Parnell. 'It's not necessary and I don't want you to.' If he were a target, so would she be, he supposed.

'Who's looking after you?'

'I'm looking after myself, very well.'

'Why not come back? Quit and come back?'

'That isn't a question I thought I'd hear you ask. At this stage of the enquiry I doubt I'd be allowed to leave the country anyway. And I don't want – or intend – to leave the country.'

'There was an attempt to frame you once. How do you know it won't happen again? Succeed this time?'

'Because it won't. I've got a good lawyer and I'm not going to be framed.'

'I didn't like being questioned as I was, as if you were still a suspect or in some way involved in terrorism.'

'Is that what they talked about, terrorism?'

'Of course it was! Asked about foreign countries you'd visited, how long you'd stayed there. That's what they asked everyone else here, the same questions.'

'I'm sorry. Call me back, with the names of everyone who was bothered. I'll call them and apologize. And I'm sorry to you, too. I didn't imagine it would come to that.'

'They're hysterical, about terrorism.'

'Everybody is.'

'Not everybody,' she contradicted. 'You want anything? Money?'

'No, thank you.'

'You'll tell me if you do.'

'Yes,' lied Parnell.

'Call me. I want you to call me every day.'

'Not every day, Mother. Often.'

'I want your lawyer's name and contact numbers. Just in case.'

'Just in case of what?'

'Just in case.'

Nineteen

It was a welcome change for Dwight Newton to enter the Dubette corporate building on Wall Street at the same time as everyone else and take a public elevator to the executive floor. He'd been able to catch a later shuttle, too, but he'd still allowed himself time for waffles and maple syrup, unsure if the emergency meeting of the parent board and its subsidiaries would run over lunch time. He entered Edward C. Grant's office through the secretarial cordon, to smiles and insistences it was good to see him again. The moment Newton was inside, without any greeting from behind his enormous desk, Grant demanded: 'Bring me up to date. I need to know everything!'

The other man was frightened, Newton guessed, enjoying the thought. Prepared, having even made himself prompt notes to read on the plane from Washington, the research vice president recounted his encounter with the FBI agents, for once without any interruption from Grant.

'The lawyers have to intervene to prevent any awkward questions?'

176

'No,' said Newton. He'd have to disclose the problem, but not this early.

'That's good. Right they should have been there but we don't want to give the impression of having anything to hide.'

'I thought we'd decided, you and I, that we didn't have anything *to* hide?' Newton actually felt superior to Grant and he enjoyed that, too.

'What about that godamned flight number?' Grant ignored him.

'They didn't ask.'

'That's good, as well,' nodded Grant. 'How did it go with the others?'

The upset wasn't far away, accepted Newton. 'We got a bit out of synch there.'

'What do you mean, out of synch?' The concern was immediate.

'The way they set out their interview request was to see me first, then Russell Benn and after him Harry Johnson. That's how I arranged it, to have the lawyers with me, waiting, before going on to Russell's interview and after that to Harry's. But they saw Harry first.'

'Alone!'

'Yes.'

'Shit!'

'I think it's all right.'

'It'd sure as hell better be! I want it – all of it – in every little detail!'

'Harry's a former Metro DC officer.'

'I know that. Do they?'

'They didn't ask. He didn't tell them.'

'What did they ask?'

'If AF209 ever carried anything *addressed* to Dubette. Which it didn't, did it?'

Grant stared across his desk, momentarily unspeaking. Then: 'Baldwin think that's OK?'

'I haven't talked it through with him.' Because I don't want to be complicit, Newton thought.

'No, perhaps not. What do you think?'

'I'm a scientist, not a lawyer,' refused Newton.

Grant stirred, irritably. 'What's Johnson say, from his police experience?'

'That he answered all their questions completely honestly – that that's how it could be argued in court, if it ever got to a court – that he was asked a specific question to which he provided a specific answer,' said Newton.

Grant remained unmoving, his face fixed. With witch-doctor clairvoyance, he said: 'What else?'

'He didn't tell them anything about the phone-tapping.'

'Why not?'

'They didn't ask, so he didn't offer. His interpretation of the law, you answer the questions you're asked, not those that you're not asked.'

'He shouldn't have been left by himself.'

'It wasn't intended he should be left by himself! I told you how it happened!'

'He's not to be alone if the FBI come back to him.'

'I know that! He won't be. If there's another approach, he's to tell me before it happens and we'll get the attorneys back, with Baldwin.'

'Did Johnson set the tap up by himself?'

'He says so – says he learned to do it when he was with the police, and that he didn't need help, from any electronics guys.'

'The switchboard must have known something!'

'It's automated. Just a few supervisory staff and Johnson says it was easy to use his security authority to get by them and work unobserved.'

'It still in place?'

'I wanted your views, today.'

'Take it off. Get rid of it. Today, as soon as you get back.'

'I will.'

'We got some frayed edges,' decided the president. 'Too *many* frayed edges. You seen the *Journal*?'

He should have bought the *Wall Street Journal* at the airport, Newton immediately realized. A bad mistake. 'I didn't have time.'

'They've picked up on today's meeting. We've dropped three points already.'

Your problem, not mine, thought Newton. 'We had to be affected, in the circumstances.'

'We've got to lose this terrorism tag. I don't want this to become a mess.'

'I don't see why it should. Dubette hasn't done anything wrong – doesn't have any skeletons in any closets, does it?'

'You know what I mean,' said Grant, carelessly.

'No, I'm not sure that I do.' Newton thought he'd made that refusal before. He wondered how many more times he was going to have to say it again. He became aware how creased, unkempt, Grant's suit appeared to be. Newton was glad he'd had his pressed.

The boardroom, normally over-large, was today inadequate for its intended function of reassuring unsettled boards. The cause was the electronic paraphernalia needed to link every other subsidiary board by satellite on to a wall-dominating screen, in many cases in what was the middle of their nights or early mornings. Each location was served by three cameras, the primary to provide a single, encompassing view of each and every board composition, the others to enable split-screen close-ups, against that general view, of individual speakers. To make that visually possible, none was able to sit, in the normal way, around a complete table, but had to be in a horseshoe, each chief executive at its middle, Edwin C. Grant heading the assembly – and the global gathering – from New York. Irrationally – but even more unfittingly – Dwight Newton had a mental image of the Last Supper, even before noticing that, including himself in New York, there were a total of thirteen men. He refused to extend the Judas reflection.

The worldwide gathering began, oddly, with the unnecessary introductions of individual boards and each member from each country. That done, the master camera came back upon Grant. They were, said the president, caught up in a situation beyond their control. The tragic death of a valued member of their headquarters staff was upsetting enough – the repercussions of her having in her possession the number of an Air France flight which had been the subject of a terrorist alert

179

was severely affecting the company. Already, that morning, the stock was down three points on the Dow Jones after this conference had been publicized, which brought to a twelve-point drop the total loss since Rebecca Lang's killing and the discovery of the flight details. Certain people at McLean were co-operating fully with the FBI investigation. The parent board hoped for an early and successful conclusion of that investigation, until which time they had reluctantly to expect Dubette to be the subject of unsubstantiated speculation. To restrict that as much as possible – and by so doing limit any further stock-market uncertainty – the parent board's lawyers were retaining additional attorneys to initiate immediate action against publication of any material judged malicious or likely adversely to affect the reputation of the company. There was going to be a full media release at the end of today's meeting, in which this precaution was going to feature prominently, as a warning to the media. The parent board wanted that release simultaneously issued by each subsidiary. Additionally, legal teams were to be established by each overseas board he was addressing, to take similar action against any confidence-damaging publication in their respective countries.

One by one the chief executives of the subsidiaries recounted the individual effects upon them of what publicity there had already been. There had been stock-slippage in England, Germany, France and Japan. There had been no drop so far in Italy, Spain or Australia. Anti-terrorist police or agencies had examined company laboratories in England, Germany and France. It was chief executive Henri Saby who spoke from Paris. Newton only just stopped himself physically coming forward, and thought he detected a similar held-back shift from Grant. The thinning-haired, urbane Saby appeared quite relaxed on the satellite link, the superbly cut grey suit a sharp contrast to that of the president. In addition to scientifically examining everything in their laboratory, French anti-terrorism officers had personally questioned him about the AF209 flight listing being in Rebecca Lang's possession. Like everyone at Dubette headquarters, he had been unable to explain it but had assured the investigators of his full co-operation on any future developments.

Edward C. Grant picked up on that, insisting that all

180

subsidiaries offer every assistance to official enquiries and investigators. The promised media release had been prepared well in advance by Dubette's public affairs division and faxed to every overseas branch. The president invited improvements, additions or corrections from every link-up. There was no challenge from any foreign division.

'This has the utmost priority,' concluded Grant. 'I want daily input from all of you. We must know, here in New York, of everything that happens in your countries. Nothing – nothing whatsoever – is too small or inconsequential . . .' He hesitated and then, as if they'd had a choice, said: 'Thank you for participating, particularly those of you for whom your local timing is inconvenient.'

The parent board remained in session after the closedown of the satellite connection, but the discussion was a pointless repetition of what had been debated before and after the global conference. They adjourned both for the electronic equipment to be removed and to watch the midday television news in an outer office. All three major networks carried the press release threatening legal action against malicious publication, tacked at the end of stories about the global conference. To groans from almost everyone – and the outburst of 'shit' from Grant – all three described it as an emergency session and listed the current stock-market loss.

To Dwight Newton's surprise, lunch was provided, in the restored boardroom. By the time they emerged, Dubette's stock was down a total of ten points on the day.

'Sorry I couldn't see you yesterday,' apologized Newton. 'I was up in New York.'

'I saw the stories on television. And read about it in this morning's *Post*,' said Parnell.

'You got something on the flu research that's going to lift our spirits and maybe our stock ratings?' said Newton.

'Not exactly,' said Parnell.

The vice president frowned. 'What is it then?'

'There seems to have been a misunderstanding,' said Parnell.

Newton's frown remained and he felt a twitch of apprehension. 'About what?'

'When we spoke about that business from France, I understood you to say it was something that hadn't worked.'

'I don't recall, exactly,' said Newton, warily. 'Why?'

Liar, thought Parnell. 'That's not what I understood from the FBI guys. They thought it was something ongoing. Something that's being adopted?'

It wasn't a problem, Newton decided. 'Maybe I gave the wrong impression. Like I said, I don't really remember. It's some changes being made to the routine formulas coming out of France on proprietary stuff: cough mixtures, linctuses, decongestants, that sort of thing.'

'What type of changes?'

'Colourings, mostly. For better recognition. All placebos, but we had to check them out chemically, of course. That's what it was, safety checks.' Newton was sweating now under the regulation white coat, again glad he was wearing it.

'At the seminar I thought the president referred to it as a way of preventing piracy of our products?' persisted Parnell.

There was nothing dangerous in the truth, Newton thought. 'That too. It's a winner, every which way. If the formula is pirated, it makes it more expensive than our competitors. If the products are bought genuinely, it makes them easier to recognize by people who can't read too well.'

'I looked on my list – everything made available to check out genetically,' pressed Parnell. 'I couldn't find anything as up to date as that.'

Newton smiled. 'Wasn't that list provided *before* we checked out the French stuff?'

'Only for our French subsidiary? Nowhere else?'

'No.'

'Why not across the board?'

'I told you, specifically targeted. It's in the Third World where the piracy is greatest and where the literacy and comprehension is the lowest.'

'I'll ask Russell for some samples, shall I?'

Newton's frown return. 'What the hell for?'

'I thought I was getting everything? That's the arrangement, isn't it?'

'And I thought your unit had been very specifically tasked.'

182

'It has. And we're working on it in every way that's open to us. I'm not for a moment suggesting we break away, certainly not on something like placebo infusion you've already cleared to be totally safe. I just want to stick with the working arrangement we agreed when we set my unit up, to get everything and look at everything over the course of time.'

There was no danger, Newton told himself again. He shrugged. 'Sure, get samples from Russ. Just don't take your eye off the main ball, OK?'

'I won't take my eye off the main ball,' promised Parnell, an assurance more for his satisfaction than Dwight Newton's.

Twenty

Parnell tried to seize the moment and see Russell Benn that afternoon, talking generally of comparing their separate progress – not disclosing his lack of it – but the chemical research director pleaded pressure of work and postponed a meeting until the following day, which Parnell guessed to be a delay to consult with Dwight Newton, and which lost him his hoped-for advantage. Benn was waiting when Parnell arrived, his desk cleared, the coffee prepared. Once again Parnell had gone into Benn's territory, and he continued the concession, providing his empty account first. Benn declared himself impressed by what he called the generosity of the Scripps Research Institute and the National Institute for Medical Research in sharing their research material more or less in its entirety, disclosing in return his division's equal failure even to know where to start upon a commercial vaccine after Parnell further conceded his department hadn't yet succeeded in synthesizing a gene from the Tokyo samples, nor produced anything worthwhile from their animal testing.

'What about the complete mapping of the poultry genome?' asked the black scientist, displaying his medical-publication awareness.

Once more, fleetingly, Parnell had the impression of being tested. 'It gives us – and every other researcher and group trying to do what we're attempting – three thousand million bases, to compare against three thousand million human genetic bases, to find one, just one, that might provide a mutating-inviting host cell.'

'Which you're doing?'

'Of course we're doing it,' said Parnell, although refusing to rise to the other man's challenge. 'But there are at least six different strains of domestic chicken farmed in China, quite apart from all the other global test species. But let's just stay with China. Which, alone, gives us a multiplication of eighteen thousand million.'

'I can work out the mathematics for myself,' patronized Benn.

'But not, chemically, a quicker way towards a treatment!'

'Maybe neither of us will be the lucky ones,' Benn said, with forced philosophy.

'I didn't believe we were allowed to think like that here at Dubette.'

'We're not,' smiled the other man. 'Don't tell anyone I ever said it.'

'I spoke with Dwight yesterday, about the work you both did on the French stuff,' announced Parnell, impatient with the sparring.

'It was just placebo additions to existing formulae,' dismissed Benn, the confidence confirming Parnell's belief of prior consultation with Dwight Newton.

'Dwight explained. He agreed the improvements should be added to everything else I've been given, to be looked at genetically some time.'

'Not sure we've got any batch samples left,' said Benn. 'Once we established the safety, I think they were all destroyed.'

'Could you check?'

'Sure.'

'And if you don't have made-up samples, you'd have the old and new formulae? And I could get shipped from Paris the old against the new, couldn't I?' insisted Parnell.

'Sure,' said Benn again. 'Like I said, I'll check.'

By noon the following day, Parnell received fifteen differently name-marked phials, with the comparable number of Dubette commercially packaged and identified bottles previously produced in France. Using that comparison he quickly discovered the major differences between the old and new formulae were liulousine and beneuflous, which the pharmacological register described as expectorants, and a flavouring agent called rifofludine, which in hot climates had a limited function as a preservative when refrigeration was unavailable. There were also six colouring agents, all of which were listed as simply that, non-medically-active colourants.

Also that day, the raw research material, each with its research notes, arrived from San Diego and London, both far more extensive and detailed than Parnell had anticipated. Parnell stored everything from Russell Benn's division under refrigeration, separating the rifofludine for later temperature match. The whole operation took him less than an hour and was completed long before Russell Benn unexpectedly came into the pharmacogenomics unit.

'Get everything you wanted?' greeted the man.

'If fifteen samples are everything I wanted, then yes, I have. Thanks.' Parnell saw Benn looking at the just-opened packages occupying virtually all of his desk. 'And it took all of this to discover the haemagglutinin protein of the 1918 flu epidemic.'

'What are you going to do with it?'

'Study it. Hope to get an idea – a possible path to follow at least. Somewhere among all this is the specific attempt by the Scripps Institute and the London School of Medicine to match the chicken genome. If they'd done it already, it would have been announced. I'm hoping we'll get a lead from everything they've done, from which we might find a different approach for our particular needs.'

'And if you don't?'

'We go on stumbling about in the dark.'

'You get a lead I could follow as well, I'd appreciate your telling me . . .'

'If I get any sort of direction, I'm not going to keep it to myself,' assured Parnell.

There was an overwhelming temptation to start on the material at once, but Parnell remained strictly professional, actually helping Kathy Richardson make duplicates not just for the four seconded to the specific influenza team, but for Mark Easton and Peter Battey as well. He included the two men in the regular end-of-day general discussion, offering each their full dossier cases and suggesting their spare-time input.

'What spare time?' mocked the pebble-spectacled Battey.

'Coffee breaks, lunch periods, those sort of times,' Parnell partially mocked back. 'I don't know if we're ever going to get anywhere, but if we don't it won't be for want of trying.'

'I'd certainly like to get out of the cul-de-sac I'm in at the moment,' complained Sato, whose Internet find the 1918 genetic discoveries had been. 'All I'm doing is killing mice.'

'What are you cutting your genetic strings down to, for ease of working?' asked Lapidus.

'Ten thousand at a time,' said Sato. 'You?'

'Five.'

'This way we'll still be comparing when we're old and grey,' said Beverley Jackson.

'Maybe we take a break from routine practical application and instead go through this stuff looking for a new approach,' proposed Parnell. 'The source notes alone might lead us somewhere. One, or both, will have already covered a lot of the ground that we're duplicating.'

'Is that an order?' asked Beverley.

'Let's give it a shot, stop our eyes glazing over,' said Parnell.

They all worked on late that night, with Parnell the last to leave, taking more files with him to continue working on at home. It had become a no-longer-unsettling habit to check his surroundings crossing the now sparsely occupied car park and constantly to check his mirrors once he began moving. He drove with his mind hedge-hopping between what he'd been studying – none of which had given him any new ideas – and stray, unconnected thoughts. Enquiring when he could have his own car back would give him an excuse to speak to the FBI agents in the hope of learning of any progress. There hadn't been any mention of the second autopsy at their last meeting, but the funeral wouldn't have been allowed unless it had been completed. He had no doubt that Russell Benn had been fore-warned of his approach about France, which made nonsense of the man's prevarication about there not being any surviving samples when there blatantly had been. How – why – had Rebecca had the Air France flight number? It had to be signif-icant. But how? Why hadn't she done as she'd promised and stopped probing? Had those headlights now in his rear-view mirror been there as long as he imagined? He slowed, eyes constantly flickering to the mirror, the more so when the lights grew bigger, brighter, but abruptly the following car pulled out and past with an impatient blast on the horn. No hurry to get home. No one waiting for him. He supposed he should eat, although he wasn't hungry. He couldn't remember what pre-packed meals he had in the refrigerator. He'd choose some-thing he could cut one-handed, with just a fork, so he could eat and read at the same time. He was still less than halfway through the San Diego material. He had to avoid the growing tempta-tion to go out of sequence and read all the source notes instead of waiting for their numbered listing in the developing research narrative. Had Dwight Newton and Russell Benn told him the truth? He'd look further than the pharmacological register to find out more about liulousine, beneuflous and rifofludine. And the supposed harmless flavourings. But carefully. Unsuspected – unseen – by anyone. Rebecca's murder was unquestionably connected to Dubette. And despite every FBI and lawyer's warning, Parnell remained determined to discover that connec-tion. Until he did, he was going to have his eyes a lot on the rear-view mirror, watching for headlights closing behind.

Parnell had always intended to stop when he'd reached that part of the San Diego material in which the attempts had been made to connect – and then intrude – the spike-shaped haemag-glutinin protein into a receptive human host cell, and awoke at two a.m., startled, cold and disorientated, to discover he'd sprawled across the table, too close to the remains of a now near-sickening, pre-cooked lasagne. The last litre bottle of wine, now empty like the glass, was on the table beside it. Parnell ached, from how he'd slumped for however long it had been, and his stomach churned from the smell of the abandoned food. His eyes felt as if there was grit or sand in them every time he blinked, and blurred when he initially tried to focus upon the papers to see what section he'd reached. Parnell forced himself to clear the table and dispose of the debris of the meal, leaving his clothes where they fell, almost literally to crawl into bed, his last conscious thought that he'd reached that part of the research from which he most hoped to find a way forward – everything he remembered reading before epitomized the purity of research science, but hadn't taken his mind any further forward in any direction.

Parnell awoke again, later than he had intended, still gritty-eyed but glad he'd cleared away and didn't have to leave the previous night's litter festering in his urgency to get back to McLean. He was still the first to arrive, deeply into what he'd expectantly decided to be the genesis for their specific interest, before Beverley came into the unit, closely followed, almost in procession, by everyone else.

Parnell waited until they were at their benches before emerging from his office. 'I know I'm going against our established schedule but anyone had any startling revelations overnight from what you might have read?'

There was no immediate response. Then Deke Pulbrow said: 'We're not big enough, don't have sufficient resources, to do what we're trying to do. You count how many *countries* contributed to decode the domestic chicken genome? Six countries, with all the resources of six leading scientifically advanced institutions. Competing against which there's just six of us – six ordinary people, not six countries – you making up the seventh, Dick. What chance do you think we've genuinely, practicably, got?'

'It comes down to fractions,' admitted Parnell. 'You saying, because it's fractions, we shouldn't try?'

'No,' denied Pulbrow, at once. 'What I'm saying is that we're pissing into the wind to imagine we've a chance in hell of finding anything, no matter how hard we try. And I can't imagine anyone trying any harder than us guys are trying.'

There was another brief silence. Parnell said: 'Deke's point is taken. Anyone else?'

'I'm not proposing I break away from the new regime, reading all that there is here for us to read, but I'd like to run another string through the synthesizer,' said Sato.

'Go ahead,' agreed Parnell at once. 'Anyone else?'

This time there was no response. Parnell said: 'OK, let's keep reading. Anyone get any brilliant ideas, let's hear them right away.'

As he read, with growing acceptance that he wasn't going to get a lead, Parnell felt the disappointment of the others at San Diego's unsuccessful efforts to find link between their 1918 flu discovery and the genome map they'd chosen from one of the most commonly eaten Chinese chickens, although conceding immediately that the connection was not the direct focus of their investigation but a naturally ongoing – and maybe ultimately successful – progression of it. Initially the only movement in the outside laboratory had been Sean Sato moving around his equipment, but that soon ended. No one bothered to leave for a coffee break, all accepting Kathy Richardson's offer to bring it in. Lunch was more to rest wearily fogged eyes than to eat. No one took more than half an hour away from their desks or benches.

Without any conscious decision, six o'clock had evolved into the time for their end-of-day review, and that Friday night Parnell stuck rigidly to it, coming out of his side office precisely on time and bringing everyone up with the cry of: 'OK, guys. Day's over, as well as the week. Make it a full weekend. I know you're going to take stuff home, like I am, but keep it light. The way we're working we're going all of us to end up brain-dead, and brain-dead we're no use to anyone, certainly not to wives or partners or loved ones . . .' He was instantly aware of the abrupt attention from everyone at the remark, not sure himself why he'd said it. It had just come naturally and there hadn't been any clog of emotion when he'd said it. He hadn't even been thinking of Rebecca. 'Let's clear our minds and our heads and start again on Monday,' he concluded.

Parnell didn't intend waiting until Monday, of course. And he had other work in mind, as well.

Parnell arrived at McLean just after seven on the Saturday morning, his reading until midnight bringing him two thirds of the way through the Scripps material. He put what remained of the American documentation beside that from San Diego on his desk, everything temporarily suspended, sure what he intended would only take up the morning, possibly even less. He accepted that there would have to be an explanation for the rest of the unit when they saw the obvious evidence of an experiment, but was unconcerned about it. He was, after all, working in his spare time, and by Monday he would have completed all the necessary reading, so he'd be further ahead than anyone else. On all their benches and desks there were sections of both dossiers obediently left for the following week. Parnell concentrated his experiment upon the medicines to which the additional expectorants and the rifofludine partial-preservative had been added, recording the dosages of each to his carefully separated test mice, from each of which he first took a blood sample to provide a comparative DNA string to measure the effect, if any, of the new formulae against the old. He was almost at the end of his preparation when the other idea came to him and he physically stopped what he was doing, considering it. With the exception of the three new constituents, every drug had gone through the required three-phase licensing process, and those three ingredients could not, in themselves, be humanly harmful. He wasn't, anyway, considering human testing as such, just a shortcut to extend the experiments beyond mice.

He prepared each petrie dish with a measured sample of every brand product containing liulousine, beneuflous and rifofludine. It was difficult extruding the vein in his left arm and he inserted the hypodermic awkwardly, hurting himself, but he managed to withdraw sufficient blood identically to match the drug measures already in the culture dishes.

He was concentrating so totally upon storing them that he didn't hear Beverley Jackson come into the laboratory. The first he knew of her presence was when she said: 'What the hell are you doing?' And so startled was he that he came close to dropping the culture dish in his hand.

He turned to face her at the door, aware that the shirt sleeve of his left arm was still rolled up and that the hypodermic, with some blood remaining in the chamber, was lying very obviously on the bench alongside Russell Benn's samples.

190

'I'm just working my way through something,' Parnell said, inadequately.

Beverley came further into the room, absorbing everything as she did so. 'For Christ's sake, Dick, you're experimenting on yourself! What is it? What have you injected? Tell me you haven't done anything stupid! Holy Christ!'

'Stop it,' he said, hoping his calmness would calm her. 'I haven't injected myself *with* anything. I just needed human blood and I was the only donor.'

'What for?' she persisted, looking more intently at the neatly stacked bottles and phials. Before Parnell could answer she said: 'They came from the chemical division a couple of days back, right?'

'Yes,' he said. 'I'm just carrying out a few tests, that's all.'

'Why? Why on these specific samples when we've got hundreds of others we haven't even looked at yet? And when we're supposed to be working exclusively on the flu research, which, incidentally, is what I've come in here today to go on doing.'

It could only be his suspicion that there was some connection with Rebecca's killing, but he couldn't compromise Beverley in any way. 'I want you to trust me. Trust me and not talk to anyone about what I'm doing. Which is what I am going to ask everyone else on Monday, when they see the mice and the cultures.'

'It's personal?'

There was only one inference if he answered that. 'Trust me.'

Beverley regarded him steadily for several moments. 'Am I going to regret coming in here today?'

'You could go.'

'I'm logged in, at the security gatehouse. As you are.'

Shit, thought Parnell. 'You don't know anything. You're not part of anything. There's probably nothing to know or be part of.'

There was another silence. 'Were you and Rebecca doing something you shouldn't have been?'

Beverley was too clever, too prescient, Parnell conceded. 'Neither Rebecca nor I were betraying Dubette in any way. Nor were – or have – either of us done anything illegal or against the company.'

'I've got to trust you on that?'

'I'm *asking* you to trust me on that,' qualified Parnell.

'Do I get to know sometime?'

'I can't answer that. Like I said, maybe there's nothing to know.'

'It would have been a good day to stay at home, wouldn't it?'

'It would have avoided a lot of complications.'

Beverley Jackson didn't reply and Parnell accepted, surprised, that he'd had the last word.

They read – Parnell retreating into his private office – for the rest of the morning. He was surprised, although not as much as he had been earlier, by her sudden arrival at his office door. 'What are you doing about lunch?'

'I hadn't thought about it. Probably won't bother.'

'You know what you look like . . . ?'

'Don't!' stopped Parnell, realizing he hadn't even bothered to shave that morning. 'And yes, I know. Everyone keeps telling me.'

'Shit,' completed the woman, refusing the interruption.

'That's it. That's what everyone keeps telling me.'

'Did you make breakfast?'

'I didn't have time.'

'What was dinner last night?'

'That really was shit. A prepared lasagne: I didn't get all the plastic covering off, before the microwave. It didn't add to the flavour. But then I don't think anything could have done.'

'You lectured us last night, about the danger of being brain-dead?'

'Yes?'

'You're a mess. And getting messier. For a lot of reasons I know and for a lot more that I don't. What I do know is that a messed-up – fucked-up – head of department is even more of a danger than being brain-dead.'

'I'll do better – eat better, get better – tonight.'

'I know you will,' said the woman. 'I'm personally going to see that you do. But also that you shave first. Christ, you really are a fucked-up mess!'

Twenty-One

Parnell managed to finish all there was to read by two a.m. on the Monday without finding a direction from either the English or American flu discoveries, to pursue his unit's particular search. There was always the possibility, he told himself, that someone else in the pharmacogenomics section had spotted something he'd missed – it was at least a slender straw at which to clutch. He was at McLean by seven, determined to be the first there, although still without an explanation for the experiment Beverley had caught him conducting on the Saturday, trying to convince himself that, as head of the department, he didn't necessarily have to provide one. He'd expected Beverley to press him further during dinner but she hadn't, not in fact referring to it once, which he didn't fully understand. Most of the time the talk had been light, although they'd obviously discussed the influenza project, but not in any depth, Parnell warning that neither of them at that stage had completed their reading, creating the need to avoid one misguiding the other with half-formed or ill-formed impressions. And although there'd been no indication of it, Parnell tried to overcome any difficulty Beverley might have by openly referring to Rebecca. That had been the moment he'd expected Beverley to challenge him about that morning's experiment. They hadn't talked at all about her ex-husband. He'd enjoyed the evening – positively, physically, relaxing. Beverley chose the restaurant, in a part of midtown he hadn't been to before, and met him there. It was traditional home-town American cooking, which dictated portions sufficient to relieve an African famine, even though he tried to order minimally. He decided the only thing missing from the rib-eye steak were hooves and tail. As he had anticipated, Beverley initially led the conversation, but gave way to him as the evening progressed, and by its end he'd realized, surprised, that he was dominating the exchanges and Beverley

193

appeared content to let him, not once trying for the last word. He refused her demand that they split the bill, which she accepted without continuing argument, and they'd parted quite comfortably outside the restaurant, without any awkwardness about nightcaps at another bar or either's apartment. In the cab on his way back to Washington Circle, Parnell found himself wondering what possibly could have gone wrong between Beverley and her husband. That reflection prompted the half thought that he'd found the first evening with Beverley easier than he had with Rebecca, but that was where he'd halted it, as a half thought not to be completed. It left him feeling guilty, which was worsened throughout the following day by his failure to pick up something from the San Diego or London research. Richard Parnell wasn't a man upon whom the rarity of professional disappointment rested easily.

None of the mice he'd injected with the French-suggested drug modifications showed any obvious ill effects after the forty-eighty-hour period, and he was halfway through extracting blood comparisons when Beverley Jackson arrived.

She said at once: 'We going to learn all today?'

'You finished the flu-identification papers?' avoided Parnell.

'Almost.'

'I didn't get a lead.'

'I haven't either, not yet.'

'Let's hope you do before you finish. Or one of the others might come up with something.'

'You didn't answer my question,' she said.

'No,' Parnell agreed, turning back to his sampling.

He was conscious of other arrivals behind him but didn't respond to them until he had the tests from all the experimental mice on to slides. He turned back into the main laboratory unsurprised to find himself the focus of everyone's attention. He said: 'This has nothing to do with what we're looking for. It's something I set up over the weekend. Anyone come up with anything, anything at all, from what you've read so far?'

There were various head-shakes. Deke Pulbrow said: 'Not a godamned thing.'

Sean Sato said: 'It's great research but there's nothing here that's going to help us.'

'I haven't found anything either,' conceded Parnell, again. 'Let's talk about it when we're all through.' He'd tell them as much of the truth as he felt able, Parnell finally determined. Not about his suspicion that Rebecca's death was somehow connected with the French material, but that he had become curious at the apparent secrecy in which it had been chemically tested, and had decided to put it through the most basic of genetic programmes without interfering in any way at all with what they were concentrating upon.

Parnell worked with total concentration, able as he always had been to isolate himself from all or any surrounding distraction, bow-backed over his microscope to contrast his before-and-after slides, anxious for a variation he didn't find. Reluctant to accept yet another disappointment – at the same time objectively warning himself that there should not be any change after Russell Benn and Dwight Newton's medical clearances – he repeated every examination under stronger magnification. And once more found nothing.

With growing, unwelcome resignation, Parnell eventually turned to his own before-and-after blood specimens, starting at the lower magnification, and for the briefest of seconds not fully absorbing what he was seeing. Parnell was too consummate a professional to accept a single illustration. Patiently, although with increasing satisfaction, he checked every single treated and untreated slide, one against the other, and obtained the same result in every case. It was only when he pushed his stool away from his bench, stretching against the aching tension in his back and shoulders, that Parnell became properly aware of how tightly and how long he had been hunched over his microscope. It was a fleeting discomfort, virtually at once compensated by a surge of excitement. Which, in turn, was tempered by further inherent professionalism. He had positive findings from a lot of separate, uncontaminated tests. Which in his own opinion was unequivocal. But which, by the standards of research – and certainly the challenge he would have to face – was insufficient. There had to be separate, independent experiments, with no prior, alerting indication of what the expected result might be. And he needed to duplicate everything himself – on himself – against the remote possibility that this initial analysis had inadvertently *been* contaminated to produce a faulty result.

Only Ted Lapidus was still reading when Parnell emerged into the main laboratory, surprised to find it was already noon. The rest of the unit looked up at him in solemn expectation. He said: 'Any bright, shining pathways?'

There was a further series of head-shaking. Mark Easton said: 'In the words of the prophet, back to the drawing board.'

'I want everything temporarily suspended, at least for the rest of today,' announced Parnell. 'I'm asking all of you to conduct blind blood-sampling, using your own blood, involving something Dubette is making available on a limited market.'

'What are we looking for?' asked Lapidus, coming up from his final paper.

'Blind tests, like I said,' refused Parnell. 'No prior indication. I don't want us challenged on this.'

'We're bypassing phase-one animal assessment?' queried Battey.

'Yes,' acknowledged Parnell.

'Why the mystery?' demanded Beverley.

'There isn't one. I want independent, corroborative findings, that's all.' Or was it all, he asked himself.

Parnell refined – and extended – the confirming experiments, testing upon the altered Dubette medicines before individually duplicating the experiments by separately adding liulousine, beneuflous and rifofludine. Having already established the research once, Parnell completed the repetition ahead of everyone else. He withdrew briefly to his side office, to avoid the appearance of hovering over them, but used the vantage point to watch them at work. Once again he was impressed at how quickly – and expertly – they had unquestioningly adjusted to his limited briefing.

Beverley was the first to finish of the rest of the group. As Parnell came out into the main laboratory, she said: 'I expected to sweat blood, not give it!'

'This is a one-off situation,' said Parnell.

'I hope it is,' said Lapidus. 'I've never gone along with this scientist-test-yourself mumbo-jumbo.'

'Neither have I,' assured Parnell. 'As I said, it's a one-off.'

'When do we know what it's all about?'

He didn't know, Parnell acknowledged. The mutation on his own initial self-experiment had shown after forty-eight hours, but it could have occurred far quicker than that. He should have monitored it during the Saturday, and most certainly have checked on the Sunday. Not having a time sequence risked his first findings being dismissed as flawed research. 'Let's give it an hour.'

'What were you doing when we arrived?' pressed Sato.

'I've duplicated everything, for a comparison.'

'You expect us to do that too?' demanded Battey.

'No,' assured Parnell. 'If your findings match mine – and my second tests corroborate – that'll be enough.' Should he set up a meeting with Dwight Newton in advance? There was every reason to move as quickly as possible if his findings were confirmed and the French subsidiary were already in production. But his findings *weren't* yet confirmed. And until they were he couldn't risk setting off alarm bells and challenging a company vice president and the director of chemical research.

There was another familiar hiatus throughout the unit. Sean Sato and Deke Pulbrow returned to their earlier contrasting of chicken and human DNA strings. Parnell told Kathy Richardson how he wanted the San Diego and London research filed, and dictated letters to both institutions congratulating them upon their exploratory work but regretting it hadn't led them anywhere.

Parnell adhered strictly to his hourly check. There was no mutation on any of his carefully prepared petrie dishes. One by one, unasked, the rest of the unit ran their own checks on their own experiments. There was no response from anyone.

Impatiently Lapidus said: ' I really don't see why we can't be told what we're looking for!'

Neither did he now, conceded Parnell. It was overly cautious, imposing blind comparisons as he had: he deservedly risked the ridicule of the rest of the unit – whose respect he believed he'd had until now – if his cultures were inconclusive. 'You'll see it soon enough.'

197

'How long do you want us to stay here?' questioned Sean Sato. 'I'm not complaining but I actually have something fixed for tonight I need to rearrange if this is going to go on.'

He needed at least one independent observer, accepted Parnell. 'Let's give it another hour. We'll decide what to do in another hour.' He sounded weak, ineffectual, he realized. He hadn't thought it through, prepared properly.

Beverley said: 'I'm not doing anything – in no hurry to get away.'

'Neither am I,' said Peter Battey. He led the afternoon coffee break. Parnell declined. So did Beverley.

When the two of them were alone Beverley said: 'This is looking a little strange.'

'It's looking fucking ridiculous!' corrected Parnell.

'That's what I meant.'

'I didn't want to influence anyone, as I didn't want us to influence each other on Saturday when we were halfway through reading the flu research.'

'You can't influence a genetic reaction by telling someone in advance what it might possibly be! It'll either happen or it won't. And if it doesn't, you're not going to look good.'

'I've already realized that.'

'You ought to talk to people more.'

'Maybe I should.'

Everyone was back fifteen minutes before the next scheduled culture-dish examination. Again Parnell was the first, the focus of every eye. He was even aware of Kathy Richardson watching from her separate office.

It was a warm, positively physical feeling, deep within him, as if he'd ingested something – a quick-reacting drug, even, which was an analogy that irritated him, although only for a passing second, because there was no irritation or disappointment at what he was looking at through the microscope lens. The mutation wasn't as extensive as it had been when he'd first looked that morning – so far only three out of a total of fifteen of the newly prepared petrie dishes – but it was sufficient confirmation to substantiate his every fear. And there was every reason to be frightened, he realized, still bent over his apparatus but no longer concentrating solely on what

198

was happening on the slide in front of him. He couldn't remember an experiment – either one he'd conducted himself or one he'd read about, in any scientific research paper – in which a mutation occurred as quickly as this appeared to be doing.

He turned to face them, all personal satisfaction – euphoria even – gone, his attitude and mind coldly analytical. 'I didn't do this right, asking you to work as I did. I'm sorry. If it ever arises again, which I hope it doesn't, it'll be different. Give your cultures a little longer than the hour we decided upon. I'm going to analyse mine later, but particularly try to isolate if any of the three drugs that have been introduced appear to be causing the greatest damage.'

'What sort of damage?' asked Pulbrow.

'France may be producing a range of Dubette-brand medicines that are going to kill people,' declared Parnell, already on his way to the door.

As he walked further into the Spider's Web, Parnell tried to calculate the fall-out from what he was about to do – what he had no alternative but to do – but very quickly gave up. There could only be one consideration, the ethical, diagnostic requirement; any personal repercussions were secondary, less than secondary even. Dubette should actually be eternally grateful, although he doubted that they would be; he certainly doubted if Dwight Newton and Russell Benn would be. Parnell hesitated at the door into the chemical research division, wondering whether to alert Benn first, but hurried on. The alarm, however it was sounded, had to come with the authority of Newton. To discuss it first, explain it first, to Benn would be a waste of time, and from the speed of the mutation Parnell didn't believe there was any time whatsoever to waste. Any production of the new products had to be stopped immediately, any distribution not just halted but withdrawn, every single last bottle or pill, no matter how difficult to trace. And if that distribution were in Africa, that was going to be very difficult indeed to find.

There were still three women in Newton's outer secretariat, all of whom looked up in surprise as Parnell burst in.

'What . . . ?' trailed Newton's personal assistant.

'I need to see Dwight.'

The woman shook her head. 'He's chairing an audit meeting. And I know he wants to get away early.'

'Tell him . . . !' began Parnell but stopped, abruptly guessing there would be a damage-limitation operation. Less urgently he said: 'Tell him that something extremely important has come up. Something that can't wait until tomorrow: something he's got to hear about and act upon tonight. I'll be waiting in my office. Will you tell him that?'

'What on earth is it?' asked the woman.

'Very important, like I just told you.'

Parnell did stop at Russell Benn's unit on his way back. The research director was in his side office, notebook calculations and reference books side by side on the cluttered desk before him. Benn said: 'You're whipping up quite a wind, the speed you're moving around.'

'Hope you're not planning to leave early tonight,' said Parnell.

'Why shouldn't I?' demanded the man.

'I've told Dwight I need to see him right away. *Now!* You need to be included.'

'In what?' frowned Benn.

'Stopping Dubette killing people,' declared Parnell, shortly.

'*What!*' exclaimed Benn.

Parnell nodded at the shelves of textbooks behind the other man. 'Look up hypoxanthine guanine phosphoribosyl transferase. And get a message through to Dwight that you want to be there when he and I speak.'

Everyone had completed their initial analysis by the time Parnell got back to his own department. Lapidus said: 'How did you know?'

'I didn't,' admitted Parnell.

'What's causing it to happen?' asked Beverley.

'I don't know that, either. I just know it is happening, that in humans, at this rate of mutation, it's potentially fatal. And that it's got to be withdrawn.'

'You mean it's already in production?' said Pulbrow.

'I think it might be.'

200

'Why? How?' said Beverley.
'I guess it comes down to money,' said Parnell.

Twenty-Two

Parnell had anticipated that Russell Benn would already be in Dwight Newton's office when he arrived, seated oddly at the side of the vice president's desk, which gave the impression of a two-against-one confrontation. He'd expected it to be that, too, an initially belligerent confrontation, but it didn't begin that way.

Quietly, without hectoring, Newton said: 'What's this about Dubette killing people?'

'You told me everything added to the French formulae were placebos? That you and Russell had run all the checks and cleared them as safe.' Parnell decided as much as possible against it appearing a challenge, although he guessed it wouldn't be easy.

'They are,' insisted Benn, at once, more forceful than the vice president.

Benn at least considered himself to be challenged, Parnell accepted. 'What animals did you test on in your clinical trials?'

'Mice,' said Benn. 'They're the most compatible.'

Parnell nodded. 'You look up hypoxanthine guanine phosphoribosyl transferase, as I suggested?'

'A growth enzyme,' identified Benn.

The man had not looked beyond the dictionary definition, Parnell guessed. 'Present in mice and humans. And essential. People born without it rarely reach maturity. Over-production of it can lead to all sorts of genetic imbalances – can even cause tumours or leukaemia. And the human body has no HPRT control mechanism . . .'

'I told you we tested on mice,' insisted Benn. 'There was no harmful effect whatsoever.'

'Mice *have* a control mechanism. Why or how hasn't been

201

isolated . . .' He looked directly at the black scientist. 'I've tested everything you gave me, made up from the new French formulae, on human blood. Everyone else in my department has done the same today, independent blind tests. All with the same unequivocal results. In about two hours there is a rapid increase in the production of HPRT . . . an increase a human body couldn't control. Administration, quite obviously, will be fatal. Production in France has got to be stopped, immediately. I hope to God distribution hasn't already begun . . .'

'There must be more . . . different . . . independent experiments,' blustered Benn, all truculence gone.

'Production, distribution, has got to be stopped right away,' insisted Parnell. 'I extended my tests, separately upon liuloutsine, beneuflous and rifofludine. By themselves they don't cause any HPRT increase. There has to be some chemical effect when they're combined in the cocktail, or maybe with the colouring agents, although I doubt the colorants contributed.' Parnell hesitated, unsure if he'd left anything unsaid. Quickly he added: 'I've obviously kept all the tests, all the cultures, for you both to examine.'

'Why did you do this?' asked the virtually silent Newton, still quiet-voiced. 'You – your unit – had been given a specific assignment.'

Parnell felt the rising anger but suppressed it, having hoped the absurd demand wouldn't be made but, deep within himself, believing himself adjusted now to Dubette thinking and Dubette rationalizing, he was not truly surprised that Newton had asked it. Tightly, careless of their inferring contempt or disgust in his tone, Parnell said: 'Which we have been working upon, uninterrupted, except for two or three hours today. And that interruption was upon my very definite instructions, to confirm my initial personal findings. I worked here on Saturday. Russell had made the samples available to me after our conversation, Dwight, about France. I did the tests on impulse, because the samples were there, right in front of me. You really want to talk about why I did it – my having just told you there was no positive reason – when I've just also told you what Dubette are manufacturing in France? And what

202

the result of that manufacture will be?' He didn't feel like the explaining schoolboy any longer. Instead he very much felt himself the castigating schoolmaster addressing careless, culpably inattentive students. They even looked like caught-out, culpable, inattentive students, no longer unchangeable senior pharmaceutical executives. It didn't give Parnell any satisfaction.

Newton said: 'It's late in France. Gone midnight.'

'Wake people up,' insisted Parnell.

'I think . . .' began Newton, but stopped.

'What?' demanded Parnell.

'I should talk to New York,' finished the skeletally thin research vice president.

'You do whatever needs to be done. If the French production isn't stopped it will destroy Dubette as an international pharmaceutical conglomerate.'

'Yes,' accepted Newton, dully.

Just as dully, practically to himself, Benn said: 'We cleared everything as safe.'

Caught by a sudden uncertainty, Parnell said: 'Did I have everything? Or was there more?'

'More,' admitted Benn, unhesitatingly. 'Some children's decongestants. Some linctuses.'

'It's all got to be stopped. Withdrawn,' demanded Parnell, frustrated by their apparent failure to understand the urgency.

'Yes,' said Newton again.

The other two men were virtually shell-shocked, Parnell decided. Careless now of patronizing or challenging or even demanding, he said: 'It will be done, won't it? You will speak to New York or Paris or whoever you need to warn? Tonight?'

Newton made a physical effort to recover, straightening in his chair, although yet again all he managed to say was, 'Yes.'

'Do you want me to be part of any link-up, technically to explain what's happened – and the effect of it?' asked Parnell.

'No,' refused Newton, recovering further. 'It's scarcely technical.'

'I think my unit should examine all that we haven't so far tested of what France was going to distribute,' persisted Parnell, a tiny, irritating sand grit of doubt settling in his mind. He looked once more directly at Russell Benn. 'And that you should start again, from the beginning.'

'You've made your point well enough,' bristled the man, emerging from his lethargy. 'You want me to tell you we fucked up? OK, we fucked up! Satisfied?'

'I will be when I'm sure nothing's being distributed throughout Africa. Or that anything that has is being withdrawn and destroyed,' said Parnell. 'I'm not scoring points, looking for admissions of mistakes. I'm trying to stop a potential disaster.'

'I accept that. And thank you,' said Newton.

'What about the cultures?' asked Parnell. 'Do you want to examine them now?'

'I'm prepared to take your word for the moment,' said the vice president. 'The calls I've got to make are more important.'

Only Beverley Jackson was in the pharmacogenomics unit when Parnell returned. She said: 'By yourself?'

'Dwight has calls to make.'

'We thought they'd want to see for themselves – that it would be more discreet if as few as possible were around.'

'It is eight o'clock,' Parnell pointed out. He calculated that it would be two a.m. in Paris.

'From the way you talked on Saturday, you're an authority on the bars of Georgetown. You fancy buying a girl a drink on her way home?'

'Sure,' accepted Parnell, surprised as well as pleased.

'I'll follow you.'

It meant he didn't have to worry about lights in his rear-view mirror, Parnell supposed, as he led the way back into the city. One thought prompted another. Apart from the first two or three days after having his lawyer's warning confirmed by the FBI, Parnell had increasingly found it difficult completely to believe he was in any physical danger, the more so as the days passed, although he still did what he considered to be taking care. But the FBI *had* been serious. So, too, had Beverley's ex-husband. From which it was logical that anyone was exposed by association with him. He took his normal route home, crossing at the Key Bridge, but didn't find any convenient parking in Georgetown itself, so he continued on to his reserved slot at Washington Square. There was a second space for Beverley practically outside the apartment.

He held her door open for her and said: 'I hope you don't mind the walk.'

'It hardly counts as a walk.'

She took his arm almost automatically as they went back into Georgetown. He chose the bar he'd found on his first few days in the city. The student he'd got to know wasn't there any longer. Beverley asked for beer and he had the same.

She said at once: 'I didn't wait on at work accidentally. I'm the elected spokesperson.'

'To say what?'

'To ask what,' she corrected. 'Why'd you test that particular batch of stuff, rather than anything else?'

The question brought Parnell's mind back to his thoughts about inherent danger on the way in from McLean. 'I was thinking, on the way here. Rebecca was murdered. The Bureau and Barry both think I could be targeted, too.'

'Why?'

Parnell humped his shoulders. 'No one's worked out yet why Rebecca was killed. Or why anyone would want to kill me. But if I'm at risk, then so must be anyone who's with me.'

'Me, you mean!' She sounded surprised.

'You're with me.'

She sniggered an uncertain laugh and actually looked around the crowded bar. 'It's not easy to take that on board.'

Parnell said: 'That's what I did, the first time I was warned – actually looked around me as if expecting to see someone coming at me.'

'Has anyone? Come at you, I mean?'

'No.'

'Maybe there was something . . . ?' Beverley stopped, looking awkwardly into her drink.

'I think that's a big part of the investigation, trying to find out if there was anything in Rebecca's past,' guessed Parnell. He definitely had to use the excuse of getting his own car back to talk to Howard Dingley or David Benton.

'I'm sorry . . . I wasn't . . .' Beverley stumbled.

'It's OK.'

'It seems unreal . . . talking about murder and the possibility of someone trying to murder you. Talking of *terrorism*! All unreal. I don't think I ever believed it . . . properly took it in . . . when Barry used to talk about cases . . . killings.'

'I thought it was right I should tell you.'

'Thank you.' She sniggered again. 'This seems unreal as well, doesn't it – you warning me I might get hit by a bullet meant for you?'

'They go in for car accidents,' corrected Parnell.

'You didn't answer my question, about testing those French formulae improvements. It was something to do with Rebecca, wasn't it?'

'She was curious about it, that's all.'

'With good reason.'

Parnell shook his head. 'Not because she thought there was anything wrong with them. They went outwith the normal delivery system.'

'Hardly sufficient to become curious.'

'It doesn't seem to be, not now,' accepted Parnell. 'It did to her.'

'What did you mean about everything coming down to money?'

That had been a stupid, unthinking remark, acknowledged Parnell. 'I don't want you – any of you – to get mixed up in this, any more than you already have been. I'm sorry now that I asked you all in the first place. It had to be done in a hurry, for the confirmation I needed to get it stopped.'

'To get what stopped?'

'The production and distribution.'

'Distribution where?'

'Stop it, Beverley.'

'We – the unit – *are* involved.'

'No more.'

'Did Dwight Newton and Russell Benn sign it all off as being safe?'

Parnell refused to reply. She was back in her last-word mode, he decided.

'You know what I find strange?' she continued, undeterred.

206

'If I was head of an entire division, a vice president, or the research director, and a guy told me that something I'd cleared as safe could – would – kill people for whom it was prescribed, the first thing I'd do would be to demand it be proven to me under proper laboratory conditions.'

'It was more important to put a stop on it – on the production and marketing.'

'I'd have still wanted proof before I did anything.'

'I offered them the opportunity. They didn't take it. My priority was getting it halted.'

'The other guys were uneasy about what happened today.'

'I gave them – and you – my word it won't ever be that way again. And it won't.'

She sipped her beer in silence for several moments. 'It's a pretty impressive success for the department, isn't it?'

'I suppose it is.' It was the first time he'd thought of it being that.

'What did Newton say?'

'They were both numbed. But he did thank me.'

'They weren't professional – cut corners,' declared the woman. 'They should be called to account for that.'

'Not everything was made available to us. I've asked that it should be.'

'You going to go over their heads, complain to New York?'

'I hadn't thought of doing that,' admitted Parnell. 'That's what Newton said he had to do, talk to New York.'

'Let's hope he does it.'

'He can't avoid it!' exclaimed Parnell.

'You'd be surprised what someone will do to keep five hundred thousand a year and stock options.'

'He can't avoid it,' insisted Parnell, although another sand speck of doubt settled in his mind.

'It's late,' Beverley suddenly announced.

'We should eat,' accepted Parnell. Giorgio's restaurant was less than a hundred yards up Wisconsin Avenue. It was unthinkable that he should go there with another woman, totally innocent and uninvolved though they were.

'I've got something ready at home,' said Beverley.

Parnell later decided that it was probably the thought of

207

Giorgio's trattoria and the celebration he'd planned with Rebecca there that prompted his response. 'You mind if I drive home with you? In your car, I mean?'

Beverley looked steadily at him, understanding immediately. 'You are taking it seriously, aren't you?'

'If I'd been with Rebecca that night, she would probably still be alive.'

'Or you'd both be dead.'

'I prefer it my way.'

Beverley took his arm again on their way back to Washington Square but Parnell could feel a stiffness. Beverley's apartment was off Dupont and they drove there in silence. As she parked she said: 'I didn't like that.'

'I'm sorry. I'm being overreactive.' He made no attempt to get out of the car.

'There's enough for two,' said Beverley. 'I was going to butterfly it anyway.'

It was, coincidentally, rib-eye steak, large enough easily to be shared between the two of them. There was salad and a Napa Valley red but not a lot of conversation.

As he helped her clear away, Parnell said: 'I'm sorry if I frightened you.'

'It's OK,' said Beverley, in a voice indicating that it wasn't.

'We've only been out together twice,' said Parnell, trying to lift the mood. 'Maybe we should avoid each other from now on.'

Beverley held him for several moments with one of her direct looks. 'Maybe,' she said, in the same voice as before.

'I'm at dinner, with guests,' complained Edward C. Grant.

'This can't wait,' insisted Dwight Newton. He could hear people in the background.

'What?'

Newton told him. Unsettled by the length of the silence from the other end, Newton said: 'You still there?'

'I'm going into the study. Wait.' The line went dead and then picked up again, without any background noise. Grant said: 'You told me it was safe, Dwight. You said you and Benn had run all the checks and that it was safe.'

'I double-checked Russell's tests,' tried Newton.

'But you didn't, did you?'

'He didn't do this test.'

'Why didn't you? You take two weeks and tell me everything's kosher, Parnell takes two days and discovers it's fucking fatal!'

'It's a genetic discipline.'

'This ... whatever it's called ... is known not to affect mice, upon which Benn *did* test, but it does affect humans, right? That's what you said.'

'I know what I said.' Newton wished he hadn't sounded so uncertain.

'So, it would have been obvious to do the comparison.'

'It wasn't done,' capitulated Newton.

'You know I should fire you? And Benn?'

'Yes.' But you wouldn't, Newton thought.

'But that I can't, because of the attention it would attract.'

'You want us to resign?' That wasn't possible either.

'Still too much risk of publicity. You're hanging on by a thread, both of you. Hanging on by default. You hear what I'm saying?'

'Yes.'

'Benn with you?'

'No.'

'You tell him what I'm telling you.'

'You pressed me on this ... wanted the decision you got,' said Newton, clumsily.

The line went silent again for what seemed longer than before. Finally Grant said: 'If that was a threat, the thread by which you're hanging just started to fray, Dwight.'

'It wasn't any sort of threat,' retreated the vice president, weakly. 'Have France gone into production ... started to distribute?'

'I don't know.'

'It's got to be stopped ... all of it.'

'Of course it's got to be stopped!' said Grant, irritably. 'You call them, right now. Wake Saby up.'

'I thought you'd want to do that,' said Newton. He was soaked in perspiration, bowed forward over his desk with his free hand supporting his forehead.

'It's your responsibility, Dwight. Everything's your responsibility. You've got the authority. Exercise it.'

'You going to tell the board?'

'Of course I'm going to have to tell the board. And you're going to be here when I do, explaining it.'

Newton felt physically sick, swallowing against the bile at the back of his throat. 'What about Parnell?'

'What about Parnell?' echoed the other man from New York.

'Hopefully he's prevented a potential catastrophe. Shouldn't he be thanked . . . congratulated?'

There was yet another hesitation, although shorter this time. 'Did you thank him?'

'Yes.'

'That'll do, for the moment.'

Until you've worked out your escape from every danger and pitfall, you bastard, thought Newton. 'OK.'

'Talk to me about Parnell,' demanded Grant. 'Is he a whistle-blower?'

Newton at once saw the chance to unsettle the other man. 'He's certainly got a lot of principles. All he kept on about today was stopping everything.'

'You ask him why he made the check that he did?'

'Of course. He worked the weekend, in his own time. Said he did it because the stuff was just there, in his laboratory. That there was no positive reason.'

'You believe that?' asked Grant, his voice betraying that he clearly didn't.

'I'm telling you what he said,' insisted Newton, uncaring about the petulance. He felt drained, too exhausted to keep his thoughts in order.

'What else did he say?' persisted the president.

Newton weighed the questioning. 'He wanted to run his tests of *everything* from France when he learned that there was some stuff he hadn't been shown.'

'Let him,' instructed Grant. 'I don't want him thinking anything's being kept away from him.'

'I was obviously going to anyway,' said Newton.

'They were in it together, weren't they?' abruptly demanded Grant. 'Parnell and that damned girl, probing together. And

210

now he's discovered this! If he tells the FBI, the FBI will tell the Food and Drug Administration, who'll tell whoever's responsible for licensing in France. And we're dangling from a high branch.'

Newton felt a surge of satisfaction at the fear that was coming clearly down the line. Unusually emboldened in his own desperation – sure there was nothing left for him to lose – Newton said: 'We'd better hope he doesn't suffer an accident to make the FBI – and the media – even more curious than they already are, hadn't we?'

The line went dead from the other end.

Twenty-Three

David Benton described Parnell's call as coincidence, because they'd intended contacting him to arrange another meeting.

'You got something?' demanded Parnell, at once.

'Just touching bases,' side-stepped the FBI man. 'Guess you'll need to liaise with your attorney. Get back to us asap.'

Barry Jackson's secretary didn't know when he would be out of court. Parnell asked for the lawyer to call back, juggling in his mind all the things he had to do, smiling to himself as Benton's phrase intruded into his mind – trying to remember all the bases he had to cover. It was a bitty, fragmented schedule. He supposed he should add to it the promised phone call to his mother. That morning there had been two replies from England to his apology letters – one, from someone he'd worked with on the genome project in Cambridge, asked why he didn't come back. There was a position available. All he had to do was officially apply and it was his. Sublime academia awaited. Parnell thought it truly sounded sublime, as well as knowing he wouldn't make the application.

First on Parnell's list of things to do was to reassure his unit after what Beverley had told him. He waited for everyone to arrive, Beverley being the last, before going out into the communal laboratory, conscious of their waiting expectantly.

'I told you yesterday that what happened then won't happen again,' reiterated Parnell. 'Now I'm telling you one more time, because I know there's some concern. You all know now that it was necessary. And why it was necessary. But I've made it clear to the vice president how and why it had to be done. He's grateful. Now we get back to the assignment we've been given.'

'Has everything been stopped in France?' said Lapidus.

'The vice president was talking to New York overnight,' said Parnell.

'So, what's the answer?' demanded Lapidus. 'I – none of us – want to get caught up in a licensing situation.'

It was career concern, which was understandable, accepted Parnell. Positively, he said: 'That's not going to happen either.'

'It surely had to go before the licensing authorities in France?' said Sato.

'These are things I'm going to find out,' promised Parnell. 'I have to . . .'

'Find out today?' broke in Peter Battey. 'We none of us know what the hell's going on. Which isn't any way to work. How we came here to work.'

Another base to cover, thought Parnell. 'If I can. I'm waiting to hear from the vice president. We didn't get the whole range of French products made up from the new formulae. When we do – something else I'm hopefully arranging today – I'll personally do the testing, no one else. After all, we scarcely need confirmation.'

'Everything requires confirmation,' contradicted Beverley.

'Which Dwight and Russell can provide, after my initial examination,' suggested Parnell.

'You involved us,' said Lapidus, close to an accusation. 'We found the bad science, we're caught up now in bad science. Your professional reputation's established. Ours isn't.'

'What is it you want?' asked Parnell.

'Written acknowledgement that this unit – each of us named – found and exposed the bad science,' declared Lapidus.

There couldn't have been more than one smoky-bar-room

or wine-and-cheese session to have reached that decision, decided Parnell.

Beverley said: 'Get real, for Christ's sake, Ted! You think you're going to get something like that on paper from Dubette!'

Beverley hadn't been in a smoky bar room or had cheese and wine, Parnell knew. 'I'll try to get it, in the form of an official letter of thanks, which is the best I imagine I can hope for. If I can't even get that . . .' He hesitated, embarrassed at what he intended to say. 'If I can't get that, taking into account my professional reputation, will you all accept individually written letters from me to each of you?' From the uncertainty that went through the group before him, Parnell guessed none of them had anticipated such an offer.

Lapidus, clearly once more the dominant figure, said: 'I think we need to consider that.'

'I don't,' said Beverley. 'I don't think I need any sort of letter. I think this is fucking ridiculous!'

'I'd be happy with something from you,' Sean Sato told Parnell.

'So would I,' agreed Mark Easton.

Parnell shook his head. 'Do what Ted suggests, think on it. While you're thinking on it, keep always in mind that I'll do everything possible, everything in my power, to avoid your careers being affected by this. I don't, in fact, see why your careers should in any way be affected, apart from being bettered, but obviously it's something worrying you . . .'

'Some of us!' qualified Beverley.

'However, I'm looking beyond this,' picked up Parnell. 'I could not be happier, more satisfied, with the way this unit's worked out. We've considered what's worrying . . . some of you . . . Now hear what's worrying me. What's worrying me is that this is going to fuck up what we've had going, thus far. I don't want it to. And I hope you don't want it to – won't let it – happen either.' He looked at Beverley. 'What we've done for Dubette should establish us, not knock us off balance, damaging what we're building between us. Have I made myself clear?'

'I hope we both have,' said Lapidus.

*   *   *

213

Parnell decided a further hour without contact from Dwight Newton was sufficient. Refusing to wait any longer – or risk being fobbed off on the telephone by one of the man's protective secretariat – Parnell made another unannounced approach into the centre of the Spider's Web. This time he did stop off at the chemical research unit and wasn't surprised to be told Russell Benn was with the vice president. At Newton's outer office, the man's personal assistant, an indeterminately aged woman with crimped hair, not wearing a wedding band, said the vice president was in conference and could not be disturbed, under any circumstances. Parnell said he would wait but asked that the woman tell Newton that he was doing just that, waiting in the outer office.

'He told me he wasn't to be disturbed under any circumstances,' repeated the woman, making no move towards Newton's office.

'And you told me,' said Parnell.

'I've no idea how long it'll be.'

'As long as it takes,' said Parnell, settling himself in an easy chair in direct line with Newton's office door. He ignored the magazines on a side table, near a tall plant with polished leaves, reminiscent of the FBI field office, inwardly unsettled by the doubt of the previous evening's conversation with Beverley. Surely Newton had called New York – spoken to Edward C. Grant! It was inconceivable that Newton wouldn't have made the call. Salaries and stock options didn't come into the consideration – any consideration. For Newton to have hesitated, looked for an excuse or an escape, would be criminal. Literally criminal, opening him – and Dubette – up to both criminal and civil prosecution. But what if Newton hadn't telephoned New York? Had looked – was still looking – for a way out? Should he go over the vice president's head, as Beverley had asked if he would? He'd have to, Parnell accepted. He'd have no alternative. Another recollection from the previous night swirled into his mind, his now embarrassing insistence upon travelling home with the woman in her car. About which he shouldn't be embarrassed, he told himself. The danger did exist. Without any reason, any evidence, for the speculation, he asked himself if it would increase, become

214

any clearer, if he did go directly to New York? He didn't have to, he realized. There was an intended meeting with the FBI team. He wasn't sure – didn't care – if it came within their jurisdiction. They'd have to take some action if he told them. It would, after all, amount to possible mass murder.

'Would you do me a favour?' he called to the obstructive personal assistant. 'Would you just slip a message to Dwight and tell him I'm waiting out here. That the FBI are waiting on me to fix a meeting?'

'He doesn't want to be interrupted.'

'Just tell him that,' insisted Parnell.

'He doesn't want to be interrupted,' the woman repeated.

'He'll want to be, about this.'

She hesitated, looked for guidance to the other secretaries, each of whom shrugged, refusing advice or involvement, and finally got to her feet. She reappeared almost immediately at Newton's office door, smiling with relief. 'He says to come in.'

'What meeting with the FBI?' demanded Newton, virtually as Parnell crossed the threshold.

'They want to see me again.'

'What about?'

Russell Benn was beside the desk again and Parnell thought they looked like two boys exchanging secrets. 'They didn't say. I was told you were in conference. I thought I might have been invited.'

'You were just about to be.'

'Fortunate I came by, then. Have Paris been stopped?'

'Yes.'

Parnell was unsure whether to believe the man. There was a possible way of finding out, he thought. 'Had any been distributed?'

'They're checking.'

'They don't know?' queried Parnell, disbelievingly.

'It was the middle of the night!' said Benn.

'Now it's getting towards the middle of their day!' insisted Parnell.

'They're checking,' repeated the vice president.

'You haven't yet seen the cultures.' The overnight HPRT production was enormous.

'I'd like to go over them in my laboratory,' said Benn, unable to meet Parnell's look as he spoke.

To avoid an accusing audience, thought Parnell, at once. The cultures weren't sterile, so there was no reason why they shouldn't be transferred. No reason, either, why Newton or Benn should be humiliated further. 'Sure. Did you tell Paris we want everything that hasn't been tested?'

Newton said: 'I'm going to speak to Saby again, later. I haven't forgotten.'

'I've already prepared a schedule of what's to come,' added Benn, supportively, offering the single sheet of paper from which Parnell quickly saw that there were still six missing items. All were for child treatments.

'They need to be withdrawn, ahead of any examination.' said Parnell.

'That's what I've told Paris, that everything's got to be stopped,' assured Newton.

Parnell paused, mentally rehearsing his promised approach. 'I think it would be appropriate for my unit to be thanked officially, by letter, for their contribution yesterday.'

'You're the unit director,' said Newton, sharply. 'Haven't you thanked them?'

'Of course.'

'Then it's done,' insisted Newton. 'Just as I thanked you, last night.'

'I'll tell them Dubette is grateful.' But not tell you I'm doing it by the official letter you're frightened will lock you into a scandal, Parnell decided. He'd known in advance what Newton's response would be, and had only asked the question because he'd promised the unit he'd do so. Newton's rejection was still . . . What? Indicative, he supposed.

'When's the meeting with the FBI?' asked Newton, abruptly.

'Not fixed yet,' said Parnell.

'But it's about Rebecca . . . ? Her death . . . ?'

They were shit-scared about France, Parnell guessed at once. With every cause and reason. 'They didn't tell me what it was about. But it has to be connected with Rebecca, doesn't it?'

'There's . . . I'm sure you're aware . . .' stumbled the vice president.

'You got something to say, why don't you say it, Dwight?' demanded Parnell.

'After Rebecca's murder, your discovery could totally destroy Dubette if it ever became public,' blurted the thin man.

'Dwight! That's what I told you, in as many words, remember? I'm not going to talk to anyone about it. Neither is anyone in my unit. Your only risk – Dubette's only risk – is if some of this stuff has already been shipped, for sale or use. And people start dying.'

'I know. And thank you, again. For the assurance, I mean.'

'That's what we need, not my positive assurance, but far more importantly the positive *guarantee* from Paris that everything's recovered. Destroyed. We're agreed on that, aren't we! We can't be anything else but agreed on that!' challenged Parnell, abandoning all his previous reservations about what he said at this encounter. Abandoning, too, any reliance upon Newton to achieve anything. Into Parnell's mind drifted Beverley's cynicism: Y*ou'd be surprised what someone will do to keep five hundred thousand a year and stock options.* The vice president and Benn were still shell-shocked, their ears ringing – deafened – from the reverberations of an explosion they hadn't ever imagined.

'That's what we're getting,' promised Benn.

Parnell wasn't at all sure that *was* what they were getting – or would get. He still needed to be convinced, even, that Dwight Newton had done everything he should to contain the situation. Fleetingly doubting it was something he should do as head of department – but very much aware of his undertaking to distance everyone else in his unit from any further involvement – Parnell personally transferred all the exploding HPRT cultures to Russell Benn's section – to which Benn had still not returned – pedantically insisting that he got, while he waited, an individually itemized receipt from Benn's impatiently sighing secretary for every sample. He missed Barry Jackson's returned call while he waited, but reached the lawyer at his second attempt, glad of the further delay because it had given him time to think and decide upon something else, something he initially dismissed as paranoid, until forcing himself to confront Rebecca Lang's murder, and his insisting upon driving home the previous night with Beverley, and the fear of blazing headlights in his rear-view mirror. Jackson said the following morning, before eleven, was good for him, and Benton promised they'd be expecting him at the FBI's Washington field office any time after nine.

When he went back to Jackson to confirm the FBI encounter, Parnell said: 'There's something else I think I need to do, before tomorrow. You free at lunchtime?'

'I don't often eat lunch.'

'I wasn't inviting you to lunch anyway.'

Russell Benn said: 'Parnell's got us by the balls. And he knows it.'

'You think I need to be told that?' said Newton, impatiently. The conversational carousel had gone around and around since Parnell left, always arriving back at the point at which it began.

'You've got to call Saby.'

'I don't need to be told that, either!' retorted Newton.

'Why hasn't he come back to you?'

'I don't know.'

'It's been despatched, hasn't it? Some of the stuff's already gone into distribution.'

'We've got to give him time!'

'Are New York giving you time?'

'I've got another couple of hours.'

'We're going to stay together on this, aren't we, Dwight? You and I? I mean . . .'

'I know what you mean,' cut off Newton. 'Of course we're together on this. What else can we be?' He fervently wished he knew – that there was some escape he could make, abandoning the other man.

'I don't like my balls being in a vice,' said Benn.

'I'm in there with you.'

'You think you can trust the son of a bitch?'

'How the fuck do I know – does anyone know?' erupted Newton. 'He came to me – didn't blow any whistles to any authorities.'

'As far as you know,' cautioned Benn. 'That reassure you? It sure as hell doesn't reassure me.'

'Just making a point,' said Newton, wearily. He didn't think he'd slept at all the previous night and he was having problems now concentrating upon every point being made to him.

'What did Grant say?'

'He didn't believe it was like Parnell said, that it was a spur of the moment decision to analyse the samples, just because they were there.'

'What are you going to tell the board?'

'What the hell can I tell them? We screwed up. Parnell might – just might – have saved us. Saved the company.'

'*We* screwed up,' echoed Benn, although with emphasis.

'I'm not going to dump on you, Russ. How can I?' repeated Newton.

'You really sure we're all right? I got commitments, Dwight. More commitments than I know what to do with – know how to handle.'

'We're going to be all right.'

'Providing Parnell stays all right. You should call Paris.'

'Let's give Saby another couple of hours.'

'Another couple of hours, that's all,' conceded Benn. 'I think whatever Parnell does – or might do – depends on whether or not France has started distributing.'

Barry Jackson went line by line through Parnell's sworn affidavit and still didn't speak after several moments. Finally he said: 'Sometimes lawyer-client confidentiality is a burden.'

'One we're both having to bear,' said Parnell.

'You did the right thing, swearing this statement,' reassured Jackson. 'You think Dubette killed Rebecca?'

'I think someone in Dubette knows who did. And why.'

'You going to tell the FBI that tomorrow?'

'Without an iota of proof?' challenged Parnell, in return.

'You going to tell them this?' asked the lawyer, fluttering the affidavit.

'Does what was almost allowed to happen in France constitute a crime in this country?'

Jackson gave an empty laugh. 'You're making a point I should have made!'

'You think I should tell them?'

'I think we first need to know what's happened in France. One way, it could be as serious as negligent homicide. The other way, it's a responsible double-check by a responsible international pharmaceutical company that prevented a catastrophe.'

'What personal protection is that?' asked Parnell, nodding to the statement on the table between them.

'None whatsoever if Dubette's into murder and they know you've sworn it.'

'You know what a maze is?' demanded Parnell, rhetorically. 'A lot of dead ends with only one way out.'

'I know what a maze is,' said Jackson. 'I do my best not to get into any.'

'I wish I could get out of this one,' said Parnell. He hadn't told the lawyer about the two occasions with Beverley, and decided now against doing so: neither were important – dangerous – and last night he'd decided there wouldn't be a third.

By the time he got back to McLean, Parnell calculated it was just after six in the evening in Paris and hoped he was not too late, annoyed for not saving the travelling time by making the intended call from his more conveniently close apartment. He risked a further few minutes confirming with Kathy Richardson that there'd been no contact from the vice president, although Russell Benn had called to thank him for the cultures, and wondered where he was and seemed surprised when she'd said she didn't know.

Parnell got the Paris number from the Dubette directory and dialled it himself, his no-longer-always-open door securely closed against intrusion. There was an uncertain moment before a woman answered from Henri Saby's office, and a further worrying, echoing gap after he'd identified himself, before a man's voice came on the line.

The English scarcely accented, Saby said at once: 'It seems we have a lot to thank you for.'

Parnell hadn't realized how tensed he'd been at the fear of

calling too late in the day, until he felt it easing away. His excuse for making the call carefully prepared, Parnell said: 'There's still some we need to look at. I thought I'd just run through the list I've been given.'

'I've already done that with Dwight.'

'It was a double-check that picked up the problem.' Parnell hadn't expected the advantage of the Frenchman knowing his name or how the danger had been isolated.

'Sure,' accepted Saby. He reverted to French and verbally ticked off with a curt 'oui' each of the outstanding items Parnell recited from Russell Benn's list.

'That's all there is, nothing more?' asked Parnell. He'd let the conversation run to gain the other man's confidence.

'That's everything,' confirmed Saby.

'And all the production has been stopped?'

'When was the last time you talked with Dwight?'

'Not since this morning,' replied Parnell, honestly. 'He hadn't spoken to you then.'

'I told him everything had been halted.'

Saby's English was so good that Parnell detected the doubt in the man's voice. 'What about distribution?'

There was a hesitation from the other end. 'It's being recalled. I told Dwight that, too.'

Parnell forced himself on, not wanting his immediate alarm to be obvious. 'How difficult is that going to be?'

'Not easy. But possible.'

'I'm a research scientist,' Parnell seemingly apologized. 'I don't know anything about marketing. Is there batch numbering . . . some way you can be sure you've got everything back?'

'There are batch numbers,' allowed Saby, questioningly.

Not a complete enough answer to the question, Parnell decided. 'From which you can be sure of getting it all back?'

'I've discussed all this with Dwight. Why not talk to him?'

'I will,' said Parnell, knowing that he didn't have to: Paris couldn't guarantee recovering medicine that could result in people – children – dying.

'The additional stuff you want?' Saby unexpectedly asked.

'You want to use the box number rather than the normal delivery, like before?'

What the hell did that question mean? 'Yes,' risked Parnell. Remembering the word from Rebecca's conversations, he added: 'You'll let me know the waybill number? Tell me direct, I mean.'

'What about Harry Johnson?'

What about the head of security? wondered Parnell. 'In view of the sensitivity, I think it's best if you tell me. I can involve Harry from this end.' And he would, Parnell decided, if he could find a way.

Twenty-Four

There was a familiarity about being collected from Washington Circle by Barry Jackson and logging in at the FBI field office, and not needing the stipulated escort to find his way to the two waiting agents with their oddly cloned dress code. Today's was muted brown check. The waiting coffee was an innovation.

'So, how's it going?' asked Jackson.

'That's our problem,' admitted Dingley. 'It's not. We've interviewed everybody – even Alan Smeldon, the guy Rebecca had the previous relationship with – and so far we've got diddly squat.'

'We've even started to wonder if Ms Lang wasn't the victim of a crazy, just picked at random.'

'She wasn't picked at random,' insisted Parnell, irritably. 'Her keys were taken, her house searched.'

'I said we even *started* to wonder, not that we're going that route,' placated Dingley.

'Which is why we wanted to talk to you again,' said Benton. 'You thought about anything more that might help us along?'

'Absolutely nothing. I was expecting you to tell me of some progress,' said Parnell. Virtually the only subject of his conversation with Jackson on their way to the field office had been France. Parnell had told the lawyer of his doubts about the tainted medicines being recovered, although he had not told him about the box number or secret delivery, or Saby's reference to the Dubette security chief, because he couldn't see a connecting relevance. Jackson had advised against prematurely disclosing Dubette's drug mistake, arguing it could confuse rather than assist the investigation.

'I told you we were just touching bases,' reminded Benton.

'Like I said,' offered Dingley. 'We've gone back through Ms Lang's life since before grade school. We couldn't find a single person with whom she'd ever had what you'd call an argument.'

'Which keeps bringing us back to Dubette,' picked up Benton. 'And where we hoped you might help us further, Mr Parnell. We've got this feeling – a feeling, nothing else – that there has to be some connection to Ms Lang's workplace.'

'Let me ask you something,' said Dingley. 'You familiar with anyone out at McLean who carries a knife? Maybe one of those little itty bitty clasp things that people sometimes use to pare their nails?'

'*What?*' exclaimed Jackson, seconds ahead of Parnell saying the same thing.

'Something sharp like a knife,' repeated Benton. 'A chisel, even.'

'I don't understand this questioning,' said Jackson.

'You mind if Mr Parnell answers us first?' said Benton.

Jackson moved to speak, but before he could Parnell said: 'I suppose a knife might be the sort of thing a security guard or officer might carry. Something sharp might be part of a police car's equipment.'

'That's what we thought, about security guards,' said Dingley. 'Harry Johnson told us he never carries a knife. Nor do any of his people, as far as he's aware.'

'What about police-car equipment?' asked Parnell.

'We asked the two who took you into custody,' said Benton. 'They said no, too.'

'You talking about my car? How the paint was chipped off?'

'We told you what our forensics people thought,' said Benton.

'And there was Ms Lang's seat belt, the seat belt you were always so sure she would fasten,' said Benson.

'What about it?'

'It was cut,' disclosed Dingley. 'Forensic's first impression was that it had snapped, but after the second autopsy they looked again and changed their minds. They're saying now it was cut.'

'What about the second autopsy?' asked Jackson. He was looking intently between the two FBI men.

'The medical examiner isn't sure Ms Lang sustained . . .' Benton stopped, coughed and resumed with what he thought better-chosen words. '. . . suffered all her injuries when the car went over the edge.'

'You mean her broken neck?' demanded Parnell, bluntly. 'We know someone went down after her, into the canyon: they had to, to get the keys to her house. Are you saying she was still alive? But that she was cut out and murdered?'

'That's the way the technical guys are putting it to us.'

'That's planned murder . . . assassination . . . a professional,' said Jackson, still intent.

'Which brings us back, God knows how, to the flight number and terrorism,' said Dingley. 'Terrorists are professional assassins.'

'And you've traced Rebecca's life back to before grade school,' reminded Parnell. 'You know she's never had the slightest connection whatsoever with or to terrorism. And from your questioning of my mother and friends in England, you know I don't either.'

'See our problem?' invited Dingley.

'You're forcing into the jigsaw pieces that don't fit,' said Jackson.

'We're coming around to thinking that,' agreed Benton. 'Which is the wrong piece?'

'It's got to be the AF209 flight number,' insisted Parnell.

'That's the reason we're here – you're here,' said Dingley. 'Until we discover the relevance of that, to everything else, Ms Lang's undoubted murder is a federal enquiry. And people along the road at the J. Edgar Hoover building are getting impatient as well as pissed off being told by the media what an inefficient, jerk-off organization the Bureau is.'

'There was something wrong about my arrest,' insisted Parnell.

'Metro DC – uniforms particularly – couldn't find an egg in a hen house,' said Benton. 'You were a victim of bad policing.'

'They'd made their minds up!' persisted Parnell.

'They thought they had something being served up to them on a plate, commendations and headlines all round,' sneered Benton.

'You had a lot of trouble – obstruction?' guessed Jackson, smiling expectantly.

'Let's say they weren't overly co-operative.'

'What about fingerprints?' Jackson demanded unexpectedly. 'Did they go along with the elimination?'

'We didn't get a match,' said Benton, to his partner's sharp look.

'Match to what?' pressed Jackson.

Dingley shrugged. 'We got a half thumb print – a right thumb – from the flight number scrap of paper. It wasn't Ms Lang's. Didn't match the two Metro DC guys, either. Or you, Mr Parnell. We want it kept under wraps, obviously.'

'You think it could be the person who killed her?' asked Parnell.

'We won't know what to think until we match it,' said Benton.

'Judge Wilson made some court orders,' reminded Jackson.

'Sir?' queried Dingley.

'About civil suits and claims, for wrongful arrest,' said the lawyer.

'Which you haven't pursued?' said Benton.

'Not yet. If Mr Parnell chose to sue, there'd legally have to be full disclosure.'

'Yes, there would,' acknowledged Dingley, smiling now.

'I think my client and I should talk about that, don't you?'

'Full, legally required disclosure might be interesting,' said Benton.

'Anything, beyond what we've got, would be interesting,'

said Dingley. 'Mr Parnell's in a kind of limbo until we get somewhere with this, wouldn't you say?'

Parnell hadn't considered himself to be in any sort of limbo, but supposed he was. He'd definitely have to speak to his mother tonight. And reply to the letters. There'd been two more that morning, one enclosing cuttings of the English media coverage of the case. The extent had surprised him. One article had, quite wrongly, identified him as the leading British research scientist in the genome-mapping breakthrough. He said: 'If you all think this might break the logjam, let's do it.'

'We'll discuss it,' cautioned Jackson.

Jackson began that discussion directly upon leaving the FBI field office building. 'They're good.'

'What?' frowned Parnell.

'Those guys back there, they're good. They got exactly what they wanted.'

'I'm needing some help,' said Parnell. As usual, he thought.

'Ed Pullinger, the FBI counsel, was in court, remember? He heard the judge's orders. The Bureau are getting the closed door. A civil suit might be the way to open it, just a little. It would certainly tighten the media screw on Metro DC police department.'

'You mean that was a set-up back there! The whole meeting?'

'I think so. Even to the disclosure about the thumb print.'

'Jesus!'

'From their point of view, it's a good move.'

Beverley abruptly came into Parnell's mind. He said: 'You warned me to be careful of police harassment, as well as being a target for whoever killed Beverley. Won't the risk of harassment increase if we sue?'

Jackson shook his head, positively. 'Not even Metro DC would dare. It'll act more as a protection. I should have thought of it earlier.'

'But is it really likely to get the investigation any further forward?'

'We shan't know that until we serve the writs and start demanding disclosure,' said Jackson.

*   *   *

226

Dwight Newton had expected an inquisition but not that it would be led by Grant, nor that it would be so scathing. With virtually no defence, he tried to hide behind jargon – talking of hypoxanthine guanine phosphoribosyl transferase instead of HPRT, and mutations and the unpredictability of drug cocktails – but there was sufficient knowledge among some of the board members not to be deflected, and at one stage the white-haired president told him to cut the scientific crap and explain the problem in words they would all understand. Newton tried, too, to shift the primary responsibility onto Russell Benn, minimizing his function to that of a secondary check, but was refused that escape by having to concede – as he had earlier had to admit to Edward C. Grant at one of their private encounters – that if that had been his role, then he'd singularly failed to perform it.

The accusations and recriminations logically gave way to a slightly less hostile – but even more commercially based – debate upon the damage to public confidence – as well as that to be expected from the regulatory authority – that Dubette would suffer from any leaks, publicity or exposure, which brought into the exchanges a renewed use of words like catastrophe and disaster and meltdown. And kept the concentration upon Newton. He tried, in a desperate snatch for recovery, to stress Parnell's assurance of discretion, to be confronted by two separate challenges from directors, about the loyalty of the rest of the pharmacogenomics unit, who'd demonstrated his blatant scientific inefficiency. Which were the precise words that were used, blatant scientific inefficiency.

It was not so much the final straw that broke the camel's back, but the final, unendurable bruise from the misdirectedly wielded stick. More loudly than he had intended, Newton said: 'OK! Let's take a few things into consideration here. I am—'

'You're not,' Grant stopped him, positively, refusing any awkward defensive outburst. 'A mistake was made. Mistakes *do* get made. It's the nature – the sometimes inevitable result – of the business we're in. It's been isolated – dealt with. I do not recommend – would argue as strongly as possible against – any reprimand or censure . . .' He paused, a man with the fifth ace in his hand. 'This is, in fact, an unrecorded composition of the board, and therefore restricted by regulations, of which I am sure we're all aware. I repeat, a mistake was made – a series of mistakes. We're all of us fallible. Those mistakes have been corrected. We are, I'm sure I don't have to remind you, meeting in unrecorded session, to which all of us agreed earlier. One of the regulatory restrictions is that decisions made during such discussions legally need to be confirmed by a recorded meeting of the board, the records made available to an annual meeting, or by a specially convened meeting of shareholders . . .' The pause was as timed as the words were rehearsed.

'But that means . . .' said a voice.

'Each of you know the terms of reference of the board's composition – the company restrictions I have just outlined. My concern – which I anticipated to be the concern of us all to preserve the company – is to limit within corporate legality the sort of public exposure we've agreed during this discussion would lead to the total destruction of Dubette . . .'

Newton was never to be sure that, however briefly, his mouth didn't visibly fall open in his incredulity at the piratical manoeuvre. Certainly the expression on at least three of the men around the table was of astonishment. Another began scrabbling through a document case, Newton presumed in a search for the company formation regulations.

'I don't agree with this . . . it can't possibly be legal . . .' said the man who had first protested.

'Everyone has a copy of our formation and incorporation documents,' said Grant, looking at the man still rummaging through his briefcase. 'For those who haven't, I'll specify the section I'm referring to – it's paragraphs four through seven – but I'd draw your attention to paragraph nine. Those preceding sections, four to seven, can be superseded by a majority vote, here and now, for us to go on record. Or for a special shareholders' meeting to be convened.'

'To commit commercial suicide, like lemmings jumping off a cliff!' said the outspoken objector.

'Each of us around this table agreed the terms, presumably upon the advice of our individual investment lawyers,' said Grant. 'I certainly did.'

The searching man found what he was looking for, consulted it and sat back in his chair, shaking his head.

Grant said: 'I am not coercing this board into anything illegal, merely reminding it of its operational parameters. Our research vice president, Dwight Newton, has acknowledged and apologized for his oversight and his error. I propose that is how it remains, a rectified matter restricted to a very limited number of people. The alternative is in your hands, as I have already set out.'

'How is this board going to look if it does become public knowledge?' demanded the man with the regulations still in his hand.

'Like a responsible body of responsible men operating as it is legally empowered to do, to protect its shareholders' interests and investments, as well as reacting promptly to prevent any harmful effects from a mistaken batch issue,' said Grant. 'I invite a vote on the course I am proposing.'

It was unanimous.

A buffet lunch was arranged to follow. At least half the board left without eating anything. Those who remained picked and sampled, the most token of token gestures. What conversation there was was mumbled, serious-faced, with a lot of head-shaking. Newton ate nothing and drank club soda. At his shoulder, as the room thinned with tight, perfunctory farewells, Grant told Newton: 'Don't go, not until we've talked.'

'Where can I go?' asked Newton.

'Nowhere,' said Grant, refusing the self-pity.

It was a further hour before they got yet again into the president's office. As soon as the door closed behind them, Newton said: 'You hung me out to dry back there.'

'You deserved to be hung out to dry. You fucked up. There wasn't a member of the board, me included, who didn't want to sacrifice you. What I did instead was save your ass.'

'Yours with it,' fought back Newton. 'I didn't say anything about other meetings like this.'

'Because there was nothing *to* say. I told you all along everything had to be safe. You didn't ensure that it was. You still got a job. Be grateful.'

What right had this manipulative, never-guilty-of-anything motherfucker to treat him with contempt, Newton asked himself. 'What did you want me to stay on for?'

'Parnell called Saby direct. Asked about getting everything back. Saby thought Parnell was on the inside. Somehow Parnell knows about the box-number route – he obviously got that from that damned woman.'

'You heard from Saby direct?'

'How the hell else would I know?'

'What did you tell Saby to do?'

'Send the stuff, as they discussed. I couldn't do otherwise.'

'What else did Saby tell him?'

'That it could be got back – that's what Saby told me. With the taps lifted, we don't know exactly what was said, not any more. We got too many loose ends, Parnell the loosest.'

It never appeared to have occurred to anyone at the board meeting to thank Parnell for what he'd possibly prevented, Newton suddenly realized. But then, he accepted, officially it had been an *un*official, unrecorded meeting, which he supposed meant any corporate gratitude was impossible. 'You going to see Parnell? There's enough reason.'

'Arrogant son of a bitch,' said Grant.

Not an arrogant son of a bitch, mentally corrected Newton – someone who wasn't afraid of Edward C. Grant and who hadn't been sucked into the imploding black hole of Dubette Inc. 'Are you?' he repeated.

'Have Johnson set up some surveillance on him again. Let's find a weak spot.'

Grant's modus operandi, thought Newton. 'What if he hasn't got one?'

'Everyone's got a weak spot,' insisted the president.

Newton wondered what Edward C. Grant's weak spot was. Then he thought it was time – long after time – that he tried to evolve some personal protection for himself. But what?

'Talk time again!' announced Barbara Spacey, sailing into Parnell's office on a gust of nicotine.

'I'm busy.'

'That's good. A lot of psychologists deny it, but work is often a good stress reliever. Would you believe that?'

'I'll believe anything you tell me.'

'I'm not asking you to go that far. So, how are you?'

'As I was when we met last time, I'm fine.'

'How are you sleeping?'

'Like a baby.'

'How do you occupy your spare time?'

'With the stress-relief of work.'

'You miss Rebecca?'

'That's an offensive question. Of course I miss Rebecca.'

The woman appeared unperturbed. 'The police getting anywhere?'

'It's not a police investigation. It's the FBI.'

'The FBI getting anywhere?' There was no reaction to the correction.

'They don't take me into their confidence,' lied Parnell, suddenly attentive to the questioning. Before she could ask something else, he said: 'This is the third time we've talked. You normally interview staff this many times?'

'You're the first staff member to be involved in a murder. A hell of an unusual murder, at that.'

'I think you misdiagnosed my other assessments,' he goaded.

'You're allowed to lodge an objection. Seek a secondary opinion, even,' reminded the woman. 'Don't forget the Freedom of Information Act. No one can sneak any more!'

'Didn't think it important enough. You get many objections?'

'A few.'

'How'd you score?'

'Pretty good. I've still got a job.'

'What happens to these assessments?'

'They go on your personnel file.'

'So, who has access to that file?'

'Personnel. Senior executives,' Barbara Spacey gestured towards the outside laboratory. 'You've got the authority to see your guys' assessments.'

'I didn't know you'd made any.'

'I haven't, not yet. About to start.'

'Who else has access?' persisted Parnell.

'Legal department . . . Security.'

'Seems a lot of people.' suggested Parnell.

'Dubette's a caring company.'

'I think you told me that already. Some people would say it was an inquisitive company.'

'Is that what you think?'

'It wouldn't be difficult for me to think just that.'

'Which I might judge to be paranoia.'

'Do,' invited Parnell. 'Are you familiar with a very famous book by an English author named George Orwell, about a control State? It's called . . .'

'Nineteen Eighty-Four,' she finished for him. 'Yeah, I've read it.'

'How'd you diagnose that?'

'How about paranoia?'

'I thought it was about the danger of a control State.'

'I don't remember Winston Smith, who tried to fight the system, coming out of it all that well,' said the woman.

Twenty-Five

Richard Parnell didn't set out upon a warned-against personal investigation, although there was something about the last meeting with Barbara Spacey that stayed in his mind, like a distracting noise for which he couldn't locate a source. But there suddenly seemed to be a lot he found distracting. Although he fully understood his mother's concern, her insistence upon such regular contact was intrusive and he found it irksome having to respond to letters from former vague acquaintances in England who'd obviously got his Washington address from closer, genuinely concerned colleagues, and written as if it were a members'-club obligation. The most positive, persistent distraction of all, of course, remained the discontinuity within his unit. The lack of a single, feasible experimental idea to further the influenza research had made the previous night's end-of-day discussion virtually pointless, although he'd thought Sean Sato's suggestion of a combined discussion with Russell Benn's unit worth pursuing, until being told by Benn that morning that his scientists didn't have anything to contribute either. Parnell was increasingly accepting Ted Lapidus's view that they weren't ever going to find a treatment as objective logic rather than impatient defeatism, although he hadn't yet openly admitted it.

It was the persistent nag of uncertainty from his meeting with the psychologist that prompted Parnell to go to the personnel department, in a part of the complex so remote he had to use the wall guides. As he moved through connecting corridors, he supposed it would have been a courtesy to tell Wayne Denny that he was coming, but accessing his own personnel file – without any positive reason for doing so – scarcely justified bothering the department director.

He was greeted at the enquiry section, quite separate from an open-plan, glassed-off office beyond, by a blonde, milk-fed girl who clearly recognized him without needing to read his ID tag. Hers identified her as Sally Kline. Adopting the American informality, he called her Sally. She called him professor. With 'have a good day' glibness she assured him retrieving his file wouldn't be a problem, which it obviously wasn't, because she returned from a side room with a manila folder in minutes. Directing him to one of the several reading tables, she asked if he wanted coffee. Parnell thanked her but refused.

The folder was thicker than he'd expected. And far more detailed. All his references had been taken up and there were copies of every scientific publication paper he could remember submitting. Surprisingly – the beginning of what became intense, even unsettling, curiosity – there were confirming copies of all his academic testimonials – school as well as college – duplicating every one he'd disclosed on his original application. A substantial reason for the file's thickness were cuttings of what Parnell judged to be every newspaper account he could remember – and some he couldn't – of his work on the international genome project, including all the interviews he'd given after his participation became public. There was also at least a quarter of an inch taken up by media accounts of Rebecca Lang's murder, the inexplicable terrorism connection, his initial arrest and subsequent release. Several, he saw, were even from British newspapers, from which he was able to see how widespread the coverage had been in England and better appreciate his mother's concern. Beyond the printed text were a selection of photographs of him at the time of his arrest, and afterwards, on the court steps. They were on top of an assortment of other prints, two of him gowned and mortarboarded at graduation ceremonies, and three showing him in rowing strip at college events. Barbara Spacey's first and second assessments, her third yet to come, were attached to his itemized personal records, the second so specific that it ran to two single spaced A4 pages.

Parnell's surprise had grown into astonishment by the time he finished the dossier. It contained, he calculated, more information than he knew about himself – certainly things he had totally forgotten about himself. And more, much more, than he believed any employer, no matter how caring, to use Barbara Spacey's justifying word, would or should need. His remark to Barbara Spacey about Nineteen Eighty-Four was very apposite. Parnell's mind jumped. The FBI had traced Rebecca back to grade school, according to Howard Dingley. Had they had access to her Dubette file? The answer should be obvious, but so very little of what he knew about Rebecca's murder investigation seemed obvious that it was definitely worth mentioning to the two agents.

He ached from the concentration with which he'd read all about himself, realizing for the first time that he'd been hunched over the table for forty minutes. Sally Kline responded at once to the summons bell. Through the glass behind her, Parnell saw several obviously alerted people looking at him in the smaller office.

'Everything OK?' she asked.

'Fine.'

'I filled out all that's necessary for you,' she said. 'All you need to do is sign your access.'

'I'm sorry?' frowned Parnell.

'The log,' explained the girl. 'Every file has an individual log, recording the date and the arrival and departure times of anyone reading it. I filled in everything for you. All you need to do is add your signature, to agree my figures.'

The document was upside down on the counter before him, but he could see there were three entries above his own name. 'That's who's read it before me?'

'Yes,' confirmed the girl.

Parnell accepted the offered pen, tensed for the users' log to be reversed towards him. He instantly registered the names Barbara Spacey, Harry Johnson and Dwight Newton. Each was timed and dated. The security chief was listed, ahead of the vice president, as having spent fifty minutes with the dossier, starting at ten past five in the evening, four days before Rebecca's death. 'I'm sorry,' he said. 'I've just remembered something. Could I just quickly check what I've forgotten? It won't take a minute.'

'If it's only a minute,' said Sally. 'I've already written down your hand-back time.'

'A minute,' pledged Parnell. Which was all it needed to find his itemized personal records and confirm that the number of his Toyota was dutifully recorded.

Three days before the Sunday when Rebecca was killed would have been the Thursday he'd found his car damage – the car whose make and number Johnson had told the FBI he hadn't known.

When he got back to his unit, there was a message from Henri Saby in Paris that the missing samples had been despatched, as arranged, with the waybill number. Parnell telephoned Harry Johnson first on the internal system, and immediately afterwards Barry Jackson on an external line. The lawyer said clients always had to pay for lunch.

'I should have been told Parnell knew about the box-number facility,' complained Harry Johnson.

'I didn't know myself until yesterday,' said Newton, determined to get as much as he could from the abruptly demanded meeting with the security chief.

'How much does he know?'

'The president isn't sure,' said Newton, taking the first step to distance himself as much as possible from Edward C. Grant.

Johnson shook his head. 'I don't understand this. I've just had a call from Parnell asking me to collect some outstanding samples from Paris "that would be arriving the box-number route". Those were his exact words, the box-number route. How does he know there is such a system? It's supposed to be restricted!'

'You're going to have to ask him, I guess,' said Newton.

Johnson looked at him suspiciously. 'You've specifically spoken to the president about this?'

'In New York, yesterday,' confirmed Newton.

'So, what did he say?' insisted the security chief, impatiently.

'You normally deal direct with Grant, don't you?' challenged Newton.

'I wanted guidance this time, before I did.'

'That might be a good idea in the future, you and I talking to each other,' suggested Newton. Could he make an ally – an informant – of this man?

'Why?' asked Johnson, the tone openly suspicious now.

'It was me he spoke to, about Parnell's call to Paris. And he told me that it should be handled as it normally is. I don't know why he didn't bother to call you, as well.'

'Saby didn't call me, which was the arrangement I understood,' agreed Johnson.

'We'd both avoid being left out of decisions if we talked to each other. Things are too uncertain to be left out.'

'Maybe you're right,' accepted Johnson. 'So, I'm to collect it, as Parnell's asked me to?'

'Yes.'

'Who do I give it to?'

'Parnell.'

'Not you? Or Russell Benn?'

'Parnell,' repeated the research director. 'And you're to reimpose the surveillance on Parnell.'

'New York tell you that, too?'

'Yes.'

Johnson stared challengingly at Newton. 'Do Dubette think they can afford to cut me out of the loop?'

'I don't know what that means, Harry.' He'd sown more doubt than he'd imagined possible, decided Newton.

'I'll talk to New York,' said the security chief, intending it to sound like a threat.

'I don't know what your direct contact is all about,' said Newton. 'But I definitely think you should get on to New York. But it'll still be an idea for us to talk about it, too. And for you to let me know what happens when you deliver the French stuff to Parnell.' How much was he protectively going to learn from this man, wondered Newton.

Parnell was disappointed at Barry Jackson's calm reaction. The lawyer continued to pick at his Caesar salad and sip at the mineral water he'd chosen in preference to Parnell's wine, and when Parnell finished recounting his morning discoveries in Dubette's personnel department, said: 'Have you spoken with Beverley?'

'Beverley? What's she got to do with what I've just told you?'

'Nothing. My misunderstanding. Forget it.'

'Barry, haven't you heard anything I've said?'

'Every word.'

'So, why are you asking about Beverley?'

'Professional indiscretion. I said forget it.'

Parnell didn't respond for several moments, totally confused. 'So, what have I just told you?'

'Something intriguing.'

'Intriguing enough to tell Dingley and Benton?'

'Definitely,' decided the lawyer. 'But not yet. Not before we serve the wrongful-arrest writs upon Bellamy and Montgomery, which we'll do within the next twenty-four hours. As well, now, as summoning Johnson as a material witness, locking him into the frame. Incidentally, I'm setting the claim against Metro DC police department at ten million dollars.'

'What?' demanded Parnell, not immediately understanding.

'It's a civil case. We're claiming damages for loss of reputation and character. You're a publicly known guy, with a reputation and character to protect. We won't get anything like that, of course, but it'll concentrate their minds. And stop any intimidation move against you. You OK with that figure?'

'I'm not interested in any figure,' said Parnell, still curious at Jackson's reference to Beverley.

Jackson grinned at him. 'You might be when you get my final bill.'

Parnell didn't smile back. 'What I've told you fits in with what Dingley and Benton said, about Rebecca's death having something to do with her workplace, doesn't it?'

'No,' refused Jackson, at once. 'It gives them a very good reason to talk to Harry Johnson again, that's all.'

'He lied, about not knowing what car I drove. The fucking number's in a file he read the very same night my car was vandalized in the car park!'

'There's proof he read your personnel file. Not that he noted your car make and number.'

'That's playing with words.'

'That's what the law is, playing with words. You've got to make those words work in your favour.'

'What about Johnson's involvement – knowledge – of the French situation – the sideways route that made Rebecca so damned curious?'

'Exactly what it is, damned curious,' agreed Jackson. 'Which is what I'll get him to explain in a lot more detail in a court, on oath. That's where we can have him twisting in the wind.'

Parnell pushed aside his pastrami sandwich, half of it uneaten. 'It'll make public what the French division, with Washington's approval, were preparing to do – *did* do, if it's not all recalled – won't it? Conceivably destroy the company?'

Now Jackson finished eating. 'Don't get faint-hearted, after what almost happened to you – after what happened to Rebecca. And could have happened to God knows how many people, kids, in Africa, if you hadn't picked up on it.'

'I'm not getting faint-hearted,' denied Parnell.

'What, then?'

'It's difficult sometimes, like now, fully to accept what the outcome of it all could be . . . to believe that it's real and that I'm part of it.'

'Not part of it,' corrected Jackson. 'Central to it.'

'I don't understand why you asked about Beverley.'

'I told you, I misunderstood.'

'What did you misunderstand?'

'What would you say if I told you it was covered by client confidentiality?'

'I'd say bullshit.' Should he tell the lawyer about the two utterly meaningless occasions?

'It's covered by client confidentiality,' recited Jackson.

'Bullshit,' said Parnell. But nothing more.

Barry Jackson had compromised, driving part of the way out to McLean, so Parnell was back at the Dubette complex by two o'clock. Only Deke Pulbrow and Mark Easton were in the department.

Pulbrow said: 'Everyone else is at lunch except Ted. He's got a dental appointment. Getting to be like a regular work-place, nothing to do, lots of time in which to do it.'

There was a note on his desk from Kathy Richardson, who also wasn't in her office, that Harry Johnson wanted to see him. The security chief answered his own phone and said he'd collected the French shipment and did Parnell want him to bring it over. Parnell said he'd appreciate it, his mind at that moment more occupied by a further distraction, as well as disappointment at the quickness with which antipathy appeared to have permeated the unit.

Harry Johnson came into the laboratory with a package about the size of a twelve-bottle wine case easily under one arm, encompassing the inactivity of the office with the look to locate Parnell's office.

'Your guys go in for long lunches,' Johnson commented, as he entered the smaller room.

'And long mornings and even longer afternoons, right into the evening,' said Parnell.

'Here's your stuff, safe and sound,' announced Johnson. 'All right here on the desk?'

'Fine,' said Parnell. 'The waybill number attached to it?' The box number, which he still didn't know, should show on it.

'I signed, in your name,' said Johnson.

'That's irregular, isn't it?'

'Thought it was easier – more convenient.'

'I'm a foreigner here, working by permission. I'm sure as hell not going to contravene postal regulations. Give it to me to countersign.'

Johnson hesitated before taking the folded document from his uniform breast pocket. The box number was 322 at McLean's main post office. 'Your signature's not on the top copy. That's the record of delivery.'

'I'll keep this one, as proof that it was delivered to me.'

Johnson shook his head in immediate, bureaucratic refusal. 'It's got to go in with all the other proper records. It's regulations.'

At that moment Parnell saw Kathy Richardson returning to her office and gestured before she had time to sit down. When she entered he asked: 'Make me a copy of that, will you?' To Johnson he said: 'There! That'll satisfy everyone, won't it?'

'I guess,' said the security head, tightly.

The man was red-faced from what Parnell guessed he saw as – and Parnell himself regarded as – the stupidity of the exchange, but the delay allowed the idea to form. The French parcel was heavily bound in protective adhesive tape, every open edge covered. Parnell said: 'All we've got to do now is get into it. You got a knife, Harry?'

'Sure,' said the security man, taking the switchblade familiarly from his right rear pocket and snapping it open in the same movement.

Parnell's first impulse was immediately to call Jackson with the disclosure of the security head's further lie to the FBI investigators about never carrying a knife, but he held back, cautioned by his earlier conversation about proof and assumptions. Instead he personally unpacked the cut-open box, sorted the French samples and assembled the new and old formulae on his personal work space. It put his back to the doors and he was unaware of Beverley Jackson's arrival until she spoke, startling him.

'I'd like to talk to you, alone,' she declared.

He ushered her back into his office, following, concerned

the approach had something to do with the atmosphere in the department. 'What's the problem?'

'I've been told I have to take a psychological test. I consider it an intrusion into my civil rights – that it even contravenes the constitution. Barry says it's an argument that could be made. I'm going to refuse but I wanted you to know first. I don't want to upset anything here. Do you object to my refusing?'

'Of course I don't.'

'Why are you smiling?'

'You talked to Barry today?'

'I just told you I had.'

'I had lunch with him. He obviously thought it was about this. When he realized it wasn't he talked of client confidentiality. I thought you'd told him about the couple of times we'd been together and was worried you might be at risk, by association.'

Beverley smiled back. 'I did tell him about it. He said he hoped I'd enjoyed it and to be careful, and I told him I would be. And I don't give a damn about any risk by association.'

Twenty-Six

The hoped-against but expected HPRT mutations had begun in the newly delivered French products within the predicted two-hour timeframe in which it had registered in all Parnell's earlier experiments, and by the following early morning, when Parnell arrived back at McLean, had become as overwhelming as before. He isolated all the cultures to be doubly verified by Dwight Newton and Russell Benn, and because Kathy Richardson wasn't due for another two hours, he once more wrote his own emailed memoranda to both, inviting their comparison. He sent a separate email warning the vice president of the impending writs upon the two arresting Metro DC policemen, although saying nothing about involving Harry Johnson in the suit as a material witness.

241

Parnell worked knowing in a put-aside part of his mind that he was filling the time – as he'd tried to occupy the previous evening by going, long overdue, to Giorgio's trattoria in Georgetown – to avoid trying to acknowledge the all-too-obvious inference from Beverley Jackson's remark. She'd immediately retreated, discomfited, after saying it, and he'd tried to help by ignoring it, but it had hung between them like a reflecting, two-sided mirror, and for the first time since the creation of the unit, she'd left early, long before five. The one telephone call the previous night had been from his mother – providing the opportunity to warn her of the inevitable and renewed publicity of the civil writs – but not from Beverley, which he'd expected. Throughout the entire evening, even at Giorgio's on what, he supposed, was a guilt-inspired visit, he'd mentally wrestled with the idea of calling Beverley, but hadn't, not knowing what to say. Which he still didn't.

There were already too many mazes and cul-de-sacs and dead ends to contemplate this further complication. More – altogether too much more – than a complication. It had only been weeks, recollectable days, since Rebecca had been murdered. It was inconceivable that he respond – which, most guiltily of all, he *wanted* to do – to Beverley's clear innuendo, if not open invitation.

With the time difference between the United States and Europe to his advantage – and still wanting to fill that time – Parnell called Henri Saby before eight a.m. American time to tell the French chief executive of the complete and conclusive findings, which were initially received in silence.

At last the Frenchman said: 'Are you going to experiment to isolate the rogue drug in the cocktail?'

'No,' said Parnell, at once. 'If I'm asked, which I haven't yet been, I am going to recommend the abandonment of the entire idea. It's too unstable to be safe ...' He paused. 'In fact I'm not going to wait to be asked. I am going to recommend it anyway.'

'A lot of thought and effort was put into this ... thought and effort that the president and parent board appreciated.'

'Until it turned out as it did,' rejected Parnell. 'I've told you what my recommendation is going to be. Whether it's accepted or not isn't up to me.' He'd make sure to find out if it was, though.

'No,' agreed Saby, heavily. 'It's not up to you.'

'What about the recall?' demanded Parnell. 'Has every single thing been traced and recovered?'

'Yes,' said the Frenchman.

Too quick, decided Parnell: the man had been waiting, tensed, for the question. 'Every single thing?'

'I just told you it has been.'

'People – children – will die if it hasn't been.'

'I've just told you it has,' insisted Saby.

'Then Dubette – and your subsidiary – has nothing to worry about,' said Parnell. 'You must be relieved?'

'Thank you, for what you've done,' said Saby.

'Let's hope it's enough,' said Parnell, unconvinced. 'I'd appreciate our keeping in touch, in case anything comes up.'

'If anything comes up – and I must admit I don't quite understand what that phrase means, precisely – I'll keep in touch through Mr Newton, your superior,' said the other man, officiously.

'You do that,' encouraged Parnell, refusing the condescension. 'I'll memo him today that you've positively guaranteed that everything has successfully been recovered, that there is no danger whatsoever to Dubette, but to expect immediately to hear from you if there are any further problems you haven't anticipated. That should cover it, shouldn't it?'

'Your success has made you extremely confident, Mr Parnell.'

'On the contrary, Monsieur Saby, what I discovered made me extremely concerned. As I imagine it did you and your research staff.'

Parnell sent his third email of the morning to Newton, setting out the conversation with Henri Saby and his recommendation that the proposal be abandoned and not pursued to eliminate the mutation-causing element in the cocktail. Parnell paused, in mid-composition, unsure whether to include his suspicion that Paris hadn't recovered everything, but decided against what amounted to calling the French chief executive a liar.

Beverley Jackson was the last to arrive that morning, frowning at the already assembled group, but directly and without embarrassment meeting Parnell's look, not childishly trying to avoid it. There were going to be some operating changes, Parnell announced, anxious to correct the drift he'd detected within the unit. He told them he considered it point-less involving everyone in a stalled research programme. He wanted to concentrate the influenza search with Lapidus, Pulbrow and Beverley, freeing up the others for work upon which they had been engaged before being given the specific assignment. If Lapidus's team made any promising advances – or there was progress from Russell Benn's division – it could revert to being a full-unit project.

'You should know, too, that the additional French stuff mutated like all the rest. I've recommended to Newton that the entire development be abandoned.'

'If it ever should have been tried in the first place,' said Lapidus.

'If it ever should have been tried in the first place,' echoed Parnell, in agreement. 'Anyone got any problems with the new routine?'

'Fine by me,' said Sato. 'Be good to get back to something practical.'

'Do you want to be the liaison with Benn's people?' asked Lapidus.

'Makes more sense for you to do it, as team leader, doesn't it?' suggested Parnell.

'I think so,' accepted Lapidus. 'I'll make a call and get myself known. Which group do you plan to be part of?'

'Something else you should know,' offered Parnell, still anxious to re-establish the earlier cohesion between them. 'Writs for my wrongful arrest are being served today on the DC police who arrested me. There'll be publicity, how much I don't know. But I'll be occupied elsewhere from time to time.'

It was a remark that would return to mock him.

'What the hell do you think you're doing?' demanded Dwight Newton, his voice barely controlled.

'I've sent you three emails this morning, Dwight,' reminded

244

Parnell. 'Which – what – are you asking me about?' The similarly high-pitched summons had come within thirty minutes of his return to his office from what he hoped to have been a restoration of the near-camaraderie of their early days.

'You know damned well what I'm asking you!' insisted Newton, striving to recover although the words were still strained. 'Suing Metro DC police! That's what I'm talking about – stirring it all up again!'

'The judge allowed me that course of action.' He had expected internal reaction but not this initial level of something close to hysteria. Something else which might be indicative, although he wasn't sure of what.

'You know what's going to happen! Just when things were calming down!'

'Dwight, it hasn't anything to do with Dubette. It's to do with me and a Washington DC police department . . . my civil right. I was wrongfully arrested and charged, without any proper investigation, and I've every justification – and legal invitation – for doing what I'm doing.'

'And every justification and legal invitation to do this?' demanded the thin man, waving a sheaf of lengthy legal papers, the discarded envelope for which was teetering on the edge of the man's desk.

'I don't know what that is,' said Parnell.

'A witness summons, that's what it is. I'm being legally required to appear in court for your damned action!'

Which meant, Parnell reckoned, that Harry Johnson would have received the same warning notice. He hadn't expected it to be like this. 'I didn't know that you were going to be called. But I did tell you about the writs, earlier, in one of this morning's emails. And you were there, at my arrest. Saw how it all happened,' reminded Parnell.

'What about the other email you sent?' continued Newton, spider's leg fingers drumming on the table in front of him. 'Dubette could be destroyed if anything else leaks out!'

'Why should it? How can it?' demanded Parnell, wishing there was a recording being made of this exchange. 'France hasn't got anything to do with my arrest or Rebecca's murder or suspicions of terrorism, has it, Dwight?'

'What sort of question is that?'

'One you prompted me to ask, by what you said.' Jackson's cliché wormed into Parnell's mind. How quickly – for what reason – would Newton twist in the wind of cross-examination in a witness box? 'You've seen from my email that I spoke to Saby?'

'You tell him about the continuing mutation?'

'Of course. And I've kept everything for you to examine.'

'I'll have Russell Benn duplicate, as well,' said Newton.

'I've recommended that everything be abandoned,' said Parnell.

'I read your email,' insisted Newton, stiffly.

'Will it be scrapped?' persisted Parnell.

'I've got to talk to people,' avoided Newton. Suddenly, the words bursting from him as they came into his mind, the man said: 'This is a total mess – a mess of your causing.'

'Dwight, I don't properly understand why you're so over-wrought. Of course Dubette will come into focus again, because of the circumstances. But the case is between me and a police department. Dubette are on the periphery.'

'I'm being called!' protested Newton, again.

'As a formality,' improvised Parnell. 'I guess everyone who was in Showcross's office that morning will be summoned. They'll have to be.'

'You talked this through with Jackson, Beverley's ex-husband?'

'Of course I talked it through with Barry Jackson, my attorney,' qualified Parnell. It was obvious Newton would know of the former husband-and-wife relationship, but Parnell hadn't liked the phrasing of the question.

'You should have talked it through with me . . . with Peter Baldwin . . . as well.'

Too many immediate responses crowded in upon Parnell. 'Have you told Baldwin?' Would Jackson have enjoined the company counsel, along with everyone else?

'I wanted to talk to you first. Understand what's happening.'

'Why should I have talked to you and Baldwin?'

'Courtesy,' said Newton, shortly.

'It was courteous that I told you this morning, before the

issuing of the writs and before you received the witness summons.'

'Your association with Dubette hasn't been a good one, has it?' suddenly demanded the vice president.

'No,' agreed Parnell. 'Although I would have thought there was one particular association of which Dubette would be profoundly and commercially grateful. And I'm disgusted by the other inference possible from that question.'

Newton flushed. 'I'm sorry ... I'm ... I'm sorry ...'

'You got something else ... something you haven't said yet ... that you want to talk to me about, Dwight?'

'No!' said the other man, sharply. 'What do you mean?'

'I don't know what I mean,' admitted Parnell. 'There's been a lot of this conversation that I'm not sure I've understood what you've meant, either.'

'Dubette can't withstand being this constant focus of attention!' protested the research vice president.

'I couldn't withstand the prospect of wrongly being accused and maybe even jailed for murder,' said Parnell. 'I guess that gives us something in common.'

His required copy of Barbara Spacey's third psychological assessment was waiting for Parnell when he got back to his office. The overconfidence, verging upon aggression, that she'd noted in her first examination had been evident, which she interpreted to be his recovering from the trauma of his recent experiences. He had been more questioning about the need for such assessments than during either of their two previous encounters, referring to a well-known English novel involving police-state control and even brainwashing. She'd assessed that as a restoration of his earlier self-confidence. She hadn't used the word paranoia, which Parnell wouldn't have protested at if she had, unwilling to draw any attention to the personnel files that he intended disclosing to the FBI investigators.

It was mid-morning when Barry Jackson came on the line. 'Everything's served,' the lawyer announced.

'I know. I've already had a complaint session with Newton.'

'He should have taken counsel's advice. It could be argued he shouldn't have done that.'

'You should have warned me.'

'Too late now.'

'There's something I want to talk to you about.'

'There's a lot I want to talk to you about. I've scheduled a press conference for this afternoon.'

'You should have warned me about that too, for Christ's sake!'

'That's what I'm doing now! You can make it, can't you? Dubette can't stop you. You've got the legal justification. And a judge's virtual guidance.'

'It would still have been polite to have told Newton that there was going to be a press conference.'

'You tell him!' said Jackson, with a hint of exasperation. 'He's got all the time in the world to round up as many lawyers as he wants to attend, if they think there's a need.'

'They'll think there's a need,' predicted Parnell.

'I'll break the inviolable rule and buy lunch, but on one condition.'

'What's the condition?'

'Today you drink water, not wine.'

'Very biblical.'

'You didn't know I could walk on water?'

'I'd hoped you could.'

Twenty-Seven

B arry Jackson arranged the conference in a midtown hotel, and chose the restaurant to which Beverley had taken him on their first outing, which tightened Parnell's discomfort. It increased further when Jackson remarked that it was one of Beverley's favourites, and Parnell decided to confront his difficulty.

He said: 'I know.'

Jackson smiled, nodding. 'So do I. She told me you'd been out together, although not that she brought you here.'

'The first time,' quickly admitted Parnell. 'It's only been twice. And I want . . .'

The lawyer's hands came up like forbidding shutters. 'I don't want any explanations for why you and Beverley saw each other. I told you, we're good friends with separate lives, to pursue as we want . . . as we choose. You and I will never have a personal problem about you and Beverley . . .' Jackson let a heavy moment settle. 'But there's a reality to talk through. Your fiancée was murdered. You almost got railroaded. You've got the sympathy vote, Joe Ordinary – except that you're not that ordinary – who got caught up in a situation beyond his control. But today we might, just might . . .' Jackson narrowed his forefinger against his thumb. '. . . manage to shake a few trees eventually to bring down a few forbidden apples. We got the FBI waiting, with their baskets outstretched. You and Beverley are grown-up, consenting adults, responsible for everything you choose to do. And whatever you guys choose to do is entirely your business. I'm the last one to sit in judgement. But others would and are being invited to be judges and juries. And there's the media, before whom a feast is being laid out, with you with the apple in your mouth. If there is the faintest whisper that so very soon after the death of your young fiancée you're involved with another woman, you lose your sympathy vote so fast there'll be scorch marks on the ground. And quite irrespective of however much convincing law I can argue – and I can argue a hell of a lot – I need totally innocent, railroaded Joe Ordinary next to me in every court and in every witness box . . . you in step with me and with what I'm saying?'

'It's a pretty effective and convincing speech,' said Parnell, sipping the insisted-upon mineral water but wishing it were wine.

'It's meant to be. I spent almost as much time rehearsing it as I did preparing for this afternoon's conference.'

'There's nothing between Beverley and me!' insisted Parnell.

'You missed the point,' accused Jackson. 'It's nothing to do with whether or not you and Beverley are into a relationship, which I know you're not, because Beverley told me you weren't, and she and I only ever lied to each other once and haven't done since. It's public perception.'

'I do know – do hear – what you're saying,' assured Parnell. 'It isn't a problem, because it isn't a problem – a situation that exists.' What had Jackson meant about he and Beverley only ever having lied to each other once?

'I'm glad that's cleared,' said Jackson.

'So am I,' said Parnell, meaning it.

'How's your steak? I only ordered a salad when it was your treat, remember?'

'The steak's great and there's still your bill to come.'

'With other things,' said Jackson seriously, the brief respite over. 'I told Beverley to talk to you about refusing a psychological assessment.'

'She did. I told her I'd back her.' A flicker of doubt bubbled up in his mind.

'Why did you take the assessment?' asked the lawyer, directly.

'It didn't seem important enough to refuse,' said Parnell. 'Being asked to undergo it was written into my contract.'

'You still feel that it's unimportant now?'

Parnell shrugged. 'I'm English, not American, so I'm not protected by your constitution. It's difficult now to know what's important and what isn't. But I think I've discovered something that is.'

'What?' demanded the lawyer, at once.

Parnell recounted the arrival of the remaining French samples and Harry Johnson's easy production of the flick knife and said: 'Which he lied about, to Dingley and Benton.'

'Doesn't make him guilty of anything *but* that,' qualified Jackson, once more.

'I think it's interesting. And that Dingley will find it interesting, too.'

'Let's keep it until we get this over with,' cautioned Jackson. 'You ready for this afternoon?'

'How the hell do I know?'

'I'll take all the questions,' insisted Jackson. 'Decide those you can answer and those you can't. We don't want to risk a contempt of court.'

'Why hold a press conference at all, then?'

'To impose pressure. That's the object of this exercise, remember? Did you tell Newton?'

'Of course. By email.'

'And?'

'When I did see him, he was only just holding on. There were times when he was practically hysterical, particularly about France becoming public.'

'It's enough to become hysterical about.'

'It shouldn't come out publicly through what we're doing, should it?' asked Parnell.

'I don't see how it impacts,' said Jackson, shrugging again. 'But who the hell knows?'

'You're talking of destroying Dubette.'

'And you're talking like a terrified, piss-pants employee frightened of losing his job. You forgotten being promised the joys of communal buggery and oral sex, English boy?'

'You're confusing the two,' protested Parnell. 'And that's what I don't want to do, confuse the two.'

'Why not!' demanded Jackson, aggressively. 'You got any good reason to be concerned about Dubette and its stock-market valuation, a company prepared to put a product on to a market where, but for the fluke of your involving yourself, it would have killed God knows how many people, probably without it ever becoming known? If what they tried to market through France becomes public – which I'm not intending it to, unless it simply happens that way – then tough shit for Dubette. You got some convoluted conscience about it, with the money I'm going to get you awarded, build a hospital in Africa where the kids who would have died can be properly treated with proper drugs.'

'I thought the money you were going to get me was to pay your bill?' said Parnell, with attempted cynicism that didn't work.

'Depending on how successful I am, there might be a little left over,' said the lawyer. 'Get hardass, Dick. Everyone else is, and there are more of them than there are of you.'

They entered the hotel through a side entrance, avoiding the initial camera ambush, but it was duplicated inside, lights and lenses directly in front of the dais and all around the edges of the cavernous room. A hedge of microphones had already been built on the waiting table. Every seat in the room was occupied. Parnell immediately isolated Peter Baldwin. Gerry Fletcher, the initially engaged trial lawyer, was beside him. Two other men Parnell didn't know were clearly part of the Dubette group, all in the front row. Also in the front row, although quite separate from the lawyers, was Edwin Pullinger, the Bureau attorney, with Howard Dingley and David Benton. The room was extremely noisy and questions began to be shouted the moment they entered, adding to the din. The sudden flood of television lights and camera flashes made it difficult at first to see beyond the first four or five rows.

Jackson flapped his hands up and down in a quietening gesture and eventually the row subsided, although not completely. He had convened the conference to announce a civil suit against Metro DC police department and two of its officers, Jackson announced. A claim was being made for ten million dollars for the inconvenience, humiliation and damage to the professional reputation of his client, Richard Parnell, a renowned international scientist employed by Dubette Inc. Mr Parnell had been wrongfully and very publicly arrested on insufficient and inadequate evidence following what subsequently proved to be the murder of his fiancée, Rebecca Lang. Because of some unusual circumstances, that murder was currently being investigated by the Federal Bureau of Investigation. His client would take questions but respond under advisement.

It was initially impossible to distinguish one question from another, and again Jackson had to wave for quiet, changing the gesture when the noise lessened, to indicate a woman near the front.

'What's your explanation for Ms Lang having a terrorist-associated flight number in her possession?' asked the woman.

Jackson nodded his agreement to an answer and Parnell said: 'I don't have one. Rebecca was not a political person, nor associated or connected in any way with terrorism or

252

terrorist organizations. I understand that to be the findings of the FBI after exhaustive enquiries.'

'What about you?' called someone deeper into the hall.

Jackson shook his head but Parnell said: 'I am completely apolitical. I have never had any links with any radical organization, let alone one that could be described as terrorist. That's also been established by the FBI.'

'Did Metro DC police know of the terrorist flight number when they arrested you?' called someone else.

The room was quiet now and this time Jackson took the question, before Parnell could speak. The lawyer said: 'What the Metro DC officers did or did not know at the time of my client's arrest will obviously form a substantial part of the claim my client is making against the department. Just as obviously, I am not able to disclose any part of that at this stage, although I can say that it will be a most rigorously pursued aspect of the eventual hearing.'

As his lawyer talked, Parnell saw that three men and a woman separating the Dubette group from the FBI officers were making notes on yellow legal pads, and wondered if they were police-department attorneys. Jackson intervened on several more occasions, refusing to let Parnell answer whether he had been subjected to any physical or verbal abuse, whether he had resisted arrest or if his position at Dubette had been affected by his detention. Parnell listened intently, aware that, with every response, Jackson was conveying the impression that there were a lot of accusations to be levelled against Peter Bellamy and Helen Montgomery.

Hammering the threat home in a reply to a further question, Jackson said: 'It has not been confirmed to me that the two officers who are named in this action have been suspended, as you suggest. But I would have been surprised had they not been. The evidence I already possess and intend producing during the case will bring Metro DC police into considerable disrepute. There are others not directly named on the writs whose conduct will also be shown to be highly questionable, if not verging on criminal collusion.'

That reply produced a flurry of demands for explanation,

all of which Jackson refused, choosing an intervening question from a woman journalist about Parnell and Rebecca's relationship in order to hand over to Parnell. Parnell did so haltingly, badly unprepared. It was inexplicable that he'd allowed Rebecca to drive home alone to Bethesda. It was a mistake he'd regret for the rest of his life. No definite date had been decided upon for the wedding. There was evidence – Parnell's reply brought a twitch from Jackson, the lawyer tensed to intervene, although he didn't – against Rebecca being a chosen-by-chance victim of a random attack. He was appalled at Rebecca's killer or killers escaping, because of Metro DC's incompetence – Jackson leaned forward again, ready – but that was something to be explored at the impending civil court hearing. He had every confidence in the FBI bringing a successful criminal prosecution.

Jackson rejected every request for one-to-one television interviews – including those from the three major American networks, as well as six from England, France, and Germany – and from eight American and foreign radio stations. Jackson had taken a suite, as well as reserving the conference room. There was wine and alcohol as well as coffee waiting for them when they got there.

'Now you can have a glass of wine,' Jackson announced.

'Who's this for?' asked Parnell.

'You did well. Damned well,' praised the lawyer, familiarly avoiding the question.

'I'm not sure what we achieved.'

'I think we achieved everything, and more, we set out to,' contradicted Jackson. 'We had to make some cracks into the wall facing the FBI. Which we did and then some. There's guys out there thinking hard about personal survival or escape. Or both.'

Which Edwin Pullinger virtually repeated minutes later when he arrived – with Dingley and Benton – answering Parnell's earlier unanswered question about the reason for the suite.

'Thank you,' added the FBI attorney. 'We made some worried people a lot more worried.'

'And there's no reason to stop,' Jackson said to Parnell.

'*Now* tell them the other intriguing things you've come across.'

Parnell channel-hopped, watching prime-time coverage of the conference, surprised at the memory blank he had over quite a number of the questions. His general recollection was of uncertainty – nervousness even – but it wasn't evident on the screen and he was grateful. He decided against eating again that day, but considered walking along to Giorgio's – or maybe another Georgetown bar – for a drink, but decided against that, too. He was depressed that nothing had been produced by his division. He paraded all the balancing arguments in his mind – that it had only been months, not years, and that research took years, not months – but it didn't lift the disappointment. He'd become accustomed to success, too expectant perhaps, after his involvement in the genome project. But that had taken years, he reminded himself – engaged dozens, hundreds even, of scientists on an international level, his involvement coming luckily at the end, when so much mapping had already been achieved, and not at the beginning, with every twist of the double helix to unravel. But everything was overshadowed, totally overwhelmed in fact, by Rebecca's murder, the unexplained terrorist-flight alert and now this civil claim that he abruptly realized had been virtually thrust upon him, and which he wouldn't have considered but for the hope of it moving on the FBI investigation. What if it didn't? What if the murder enquiry remained stalled, months running into years like research ran from months into years? Would it anchor him to Dubette? There *was* an insidious Big Brother ambience about everything at McLean, with its spider's-web imagery and inches-thick personal files, and intrusive psychology and silent, empty faces at watchful windows.

The entry bell jarred into the apartment, startling him, and sounded again before he reached the receiver.

'It's me,' announced Beverley Jackson, from the entrance lobby.

'You didn't phone?'

'No. Spur of the moment detour, on my way home.'

255

'Something come up?'

'I'd like to,' she said, twisting his question. 'Or are we going to have a conversation like this?'

Parnell pressed the downstairs release and opened his own front door for the arrival of the elevator. When Beverley emerged, she was carrying her briefcase, from which Parnell knew that she really had been on her way home.

He said: 'I didn't expect you.'

'No,' she said, tossing her coat and case on to a chair, slumping into another.

'There's wine.'

'Maybe a small one.'

'Something come up?' he repeated, as he poured for both of them.

Beverley said: 'Your health,' and raised her glass.

Parnell raised his in return. There wasn't the difficulty he'd expected from their next being alone together. He didn't believe he should feel as glad as he was that they *were* together alone again.

'I told personnel I wouldn't undergo the psychological assessment,' declared Beverley. 'Wayne Denny wants to talk to me about it. Deke Pulbrow doesn't want to take an assessment, either.'

Parnell shrugged. 'You know how I feel about it.'

'You'll support Deke, too?'

'It's hardly likely I'd back you and not Deke, is it?'

'I think Deke's worried a refusal might go against him, at Dubette.'

'I thought Barry told you there was a legal right to refuse?'

'It was a knee-jerk. He needs to check to be sure,' said the lawyer's former wife. 'I'm going to ask him to make sure.'

Would the extent and intrusiveness he'd discovered in the personnel files help their objections? wondered Parnell. He wouldn't say anything now, but he'd remind Jackson if it became a problem for either of them. 'You sure it's just Deke who's worried?'

'I told you my only concern.'

'And I told you I wasn't worried about it.'

A separation of silence came down between them. Hurrying

to fill it, Beverley said: 'You're becoming quite the star television performer.'

'Not from choice,' said Parnell.

'What are you going to do with ten million dollars?'

'Pay your ex-husband's bill,' said Parnell, glad of the well-rehearsed joke. 'We had lunch at your favourite midtown restaurant today. I told him we'd eaten there.'

'Who paid?'

'He did.'

'It'll go on your bill. I told you he knew – not about the restaurant but that we'd been out a couple of times.'

It was best they confront it, Parnell supposed. 'He said you'd only ever lied to each other once.'

'That's off-limits,' she refused, instantly.

'OK,' accepted Parnell, just as quickly. 'We talked about it, you and I being seen together. He said it wouldn't play well if it became public – talked about losing the sympathy vote.'

Beverley let more silence build up, but with a purpose. Looking very directly at him, she said: 'Are we going to risk being seen together?'

'I feel a total shit,' Parnell confessed, needing to purge himself, raising his hand to just beneath his chin. 'I've got guilt up to here.'

'You and me both,' she said. 'What are we going to do about it?'

'I don't know,' said Parnell, another admission he didn't like making.

'I don't want to jeopardize anything. Cause any embarrassment. Or disrespect to Rebecca.'

'You and me both,' echoed Parnell. 'Although I don't actually give a damn about any ten-million-dollar court case.'

'You tell me you don't care about ten million bucks, I'll try to believe you, but it won't be easy.'

She was trying hard, Parnell acknowledged. He said: 'We're avoiding the question.'

'Let's take everything very slowly,' suggested Beverley. 'We're talking like people with a secret, and there's nothing to be secretive about! At the moment it's no more than we like being with each other and seem to understand each other's jokes, although we could possibly do with more of those.'

'If there was more to laugh about,' said Parnell.

'You like big band, Glen Miller music?'

'I could find out.'

'There's a concert at the Kennedy Centre at the weekend.'

'I'll get tickets.'

'I already got them.'

'You always this forthright?' So much for excuses about spur-of-the-moment detours. And his undertaking – and understanding – with Barry Jackson.

'Not always. I figured you already had a lot to do.'

'You want more wine?'

Beverley shook her head, rising from the chair. 'I'm driving. And I'm going now. Like I said, everything nice and slow.'

The duty private investigator from the agency – hired cash in advance, under a false name and using an equally anonymous cut-out procedure – let two cars come comfortably between him and Beverley Jackson for the short ride to Dupont Circle. The light had been bad but the man was sure he'd managed at least two identifiable photographs of her leaving Parnell's apartment building.

When Parnell got to McLean the following day, there was a waiting memorandum that the half-yearly seminar had, without any given reason, been postponed until after the forthcoming annual stockholders' meeting. It was to be the first of several memos he received that day.

Twenty-Eight

Overnight the pendulum swung and Parnell's day began with the mountains seeming higher and the oceans wider. Richard Parnell's unsettling disappointment in himself was compounded by what he'd so easily agreed with Beverley the previous evening, which scarcely made sense because he wasn't in any way disappointed or depressed by the thought of being with her the coming weekend. He wanted very much to be with her, and that wish outweighed all the rest of the conflicting doubts, like guilt and concern at their being seen together or at his being accused of hypocrisy, or whatever the accusation might be, if the outing – or any that hopefully followed – became public. In fact, the biggest contradiction of all, for someone with so many conflicting emotional confusions, was that, for the first time for a very long time, he felt remarkably happy by the time he arrived at McLean. And that had everything to do with the idea that had come to him after Beverley left, a thought that had so excited him he'd even considered calling her, needing someone with whom to talk about it. He hadn't, though, because it would have appeared too much like an excuse, and by then he hadn't rationalized his uncertainties as he believed he had, finally, on his way to North Virginia the following day.

Ted Lapidus was the first to arrive after Parnell, and told him at once that the previous day's meeting with Russell Benn hadn't shown any chemical research progress, adding that his impression had been that Benn's unit were expecting a lead from pharmacogenomics.

'Which, from the way it's going so far, they'll be lucky to get,' remarked the dolefully moustached Greek scientist.

'Let's talk, when everyone else arrives,' suggested Parnell. 'I've had a thought.'

Beverley was once more the last, although it was still only just past eight. She smiled and said, 'Hi!' when the Greek geneticist led his group into Parnell's instantly overcrowded office.

Parnell said: 'I've been thinking about approaches. So far we've been trying to follow how the flu virus attaches itself and enters a host cell, like the spiky little bastard of 1918, right?'

'That's the A, B, C, D system,' confirmed Lapidus.

'Why don't we try D, C, B, A?' proposed Parnell. 'Offer up a host target molecule, coloured so we'll be able to trace which, if any, get hit.'

'You get the idea from the colorants the French introduced?' seized Pulbrow, at once.

'As a matter of fact, I did,' admitted Parnell. 'This time the mutation, if it occurs, will be beneficial, not the other way around. I can't understand why the method didn't occur to me earlier.'

'Or any of us,' accepted Lapidus, doubtfully. 'It's worth trying.'

'If going backwards gets us forwards, then let's try it,' said Beverley. 'It's the only idea in town.'

'It'll be a slow process of elimination,' warned Deke Pulbrow.

'It was always going to be that,' Parnell pointed out. 'But it doesn't necessarily have to be that slow. Influenza is basic-ally respiratory – that narrows our genetic field.'

'By a few thousand,' said Beverley.

'We'll need more samples. And a lot more mice,' said Lapidus.

'Get as many samples as you need from Tokyo,' said Parnell.

'We've got enough to start already,' said Beverley, enthu-siastically. 'Kathy's the mouse mother.'

'Then start,' urged Parnell.

Pulbrow hesitated, as they began filing out, and Parnell said: 'Beverley told me. Why not close the door?'

Pulbrow did so, but stayed by it. 'I don't want to cause trouble.'

'As far as I'm concerned, it's entirely down to you whether you undergo the assessment or not. I'm certainly not going to put any pressure on you. I don't see how I could. Or why I should.'

'You think I should have it?'

The man wanted someone to make the decision for him, guessed Parnell. He said: 'I think you should decide yourself what you want to do. And then do it.'

'I've talked around. This seems to be a pretty structured, authoritative organization.'

'The organization might be. This unit certainly isn't,' said Parnell. 'No one's holding a gun to your head, Deke.'

'You took it?'

'I thought it was a waste of time. Still do, for that matter. I couldn't then be bothered to refuse.'

'Then?' questioned the other man.

'I think I might tell her to forget it next time, if indeed there is a next time.'

'Her?'

'The psychologist is a woman. Kind of an earth mother.'

'I'll think some more about it,' said Pulbrow, uncertainly.

'You do that,' encouraged Parnell, looking up at Kathy Richardson's entry.

'You're high on Dwight's demand list,' said the secretary. 'Written confirmation after the telephone call.'

Why the duplication? wondered Parnell.

The truckers' stop, about ten miles into New Jersey beyond the Hudson tunnel, had been designated by Edward C. Grant, who had been waiting when Harry Johnson arrived, the untasted coffee like a totem before him, the menu pushed to one side. Johnson chose the Big Breakfast, with an extra side order of hash browns and a double orange juice, his necessary and already marked serviette tucked tightly into his collar in a forlorn attempt to protect his shirt.

Johnson said: 'You should have ordered this. Breakfast is the most important meal of the day – sets you up.'

'I'm not hungry,' said the white-haired man. He sat strangely in their window booth, overlooking the interstate car park of dinosaur-sized trucks, as if he feared contamination by contact with the table or the red plastic seat or even the mug.

'You haven't touched your coffee, either. It's good coffee.'

'I'm not thirsty.'

'I'm glad we could meet like this,' said the Dubette security chief, who'd made the demand.

'So am I.'

'How'd you know about this place? Know how to dress to fit in, like you belong?'

Grant was wearing jeans and a work shirt, although neither had ever been worked in. Johnson's better fitted the surroundings, more stains being added by what the inadequate serviette wasn't catching.

Grant said: 'That's not what we're here to talk about. What do you want?'

261

'You're right about that,' said Johnson. 'I'd say there's a lot for us to talk about, one way and another, wouldn't you?'

'What's your problem, Harry?'

'That's *exactly* what my problem is!' said Johnson. 'It's not knowing what my problem is.'

'You watch a lot of television, Harry?'

'Crime stuff, mostly. The old life, before Dubette, I guess. You know how it is?'

'No,' denied Grant. 'I don't know how it is. I'm waiting for you to tell me.'

'Which is what I thought the arrangement was between us, you telling me, me telling you. But always direct, not through any intermediary . . . like Dwight Newton.'

Grant sighed. 'There was a directors' meeting in New York. It was easier, more convenient, to pass the message on through him.'

'It was never easier, more convenient, before. I don't like the way everything's falling down. I particularly don't like the idea of being cut out of the chain of communication. I wouldn't have thought you would, either.'

'The problem's that fucking flight number!'

'You told me there was a problem: that something had gone wrong and that the girl was dead and Parnell had to be incriminated. I thought the flight number, which the Paris office used a lot in the past, would make it look as if they were stealing secrets. I forgot the earlier terrorist alerts. If Parnell hadn't dismissed Fletcher, there would have been a plea, imprisonment, and Parnell would have been disgraced, imprisoned and unemployable anywhere else. Which was what you also told me to fix . . .' Johnson looked again around the truck stop packed with drivers. 'And if you'd had me fix the accident, the driver wouldn't have killed Rebecca, just created the accident in a police district where I could have handled everything.'

'What can the FBI find out?'

'Nothing!' insisted the man. 'It'll run into the ground.'

'Like Dubette's stock value!'

'Your problem, largely of your making,' insisted Johnson. 'I'm more interested in personal things – you and I, for instance. As I think you should be.'

262

'You're not being cut out of anything!' insisted Grant. This was wrong, all wrong – his worst nightmare. He wasn't sure what the feeling was, but didn't want it to be fear, because Johnson was the sort of man who could smell fear, like the animal he was.

'That's good to hear. That's very good indeed. I really wouldn't like that,' said Johnson. He mopped up the egg and grease with a piece of bread, ate it, and immediately belched. He said: 'See how good it was.'

'You got anything else to say?'

'I got this witness summons.'

'You've been in enough courts.'

'You see the fucking press conference? Hear the threats?'

'What can they threaten you with?'

'I don't know. The lawyer talked about a lot of evidence.'

'It's got to be exchanged. You'll know what you're facing, before you're called to the stand.'

'I want a good attorney.'

'You're going to get the best. You know how Dubette looks after its people.'

'I think I got particular reason to be looked after.'

'Don't worry.'

'I do worry when I think I'm being cut out of things.'

'We've gone through that.'

'I'm not sure about the Metro DC guys. I think they're flaky.'

'They drop you, they drop too.'

'I told them I knew where Parnell's car was. I think I told the FBI I didn't know.'

'So what? You forgot, then you remembered. That's how it happens.'

A saggy-breasted waitress came by with coffee refills, freshened Johnson's mug and took away the congealed plate. As she left, Johnson ordered toast, peanut butter and jelly.

He said: 'You didn't tell me how a guy like you knows about a place like this!'

'Stop it, Harry. I'm not amused.'

'What happened to the girl, Ed? What happened to Rebecca?'

It was the first time ever that Johnson had felt bold enough to address Grant like that, and a shudder visibly went through the older man. It was several moments before Grant could reply. 'I don't understand your question.'

'I organized the detective-agency stakeout, like you told me to when we were dealing direct. Alerted you to their Sunday day out to Chesapeake. Called my people off, like you told me. Then . . .' He clicked his fingers. '. . . POW, poor kid's dead at the bottom of a ravine. You know what I think? I think Rebecca Lang might just still be alive if I'd kept agency guys on the job . . . I wouldn't be at all surprised if they're more than a little concerned, the way things happened . . .'

'They don't know you or your connection with Dubette, do they?'

Johnson's laugh was more of a sneer. 'Of course not! I'm a professional, remember?'

'And you're using another agency now?'

'Just as anonymously.'

'So, there's no problem.'

'You can't guarantee that, Ed. For the first time for a very, very long time, we're into things you can't control or guarantee, which I'm sure you don't like any more than I do.'

'You know I was concerned at the possibility of a commercial leak. Putting in place the precautions that we did was perfectly justifiable. As was my taking them off, as I did, when I did.'

'It's the coincidence that worries me, Ed. Deciding on a Sunday of all days that Rebecca Lang wasn't a snitch, and lifting the surveillance from her and lover boy a couple of hours before she's shunted over the edge of a canyon . . .' He sat back for his new order to be placed on the table between them.

The waitress said: 'You sure believe in keeping your strength up, don't you?'

'Gotta lot of grateful gels to keep happy,' smirked Johnson.

'Surprised you can manage it, the size of that gut,' the woman smirked back.

'. . . And then there's Parnell's car,' resumed the security chief, as if there hadn't been any interruption. 'That's another coincidence, your asking me for its make and registration on the very day it got damaged like it did. Wouldn't you say that's one hell of a double coincidence, Ed?'

Grant said: 'Stop calling me Ed! No one calls me Ed!'

'I'm sorry,' said Johnson, not sounding it. 'I didn't mean any offence. You want to try some of this toast, with a little jelly? It's terrific.'

'You're so far out of line, Harry, that you're in danger of getting lost and not being able to find your way back,' said Edward C. Grant. 'You *are* watching too many bad crime movies. You should try different channels. And try remembering who I am and who you are. I don't ever want anything like this – your imagining you can put on anything like this – again. You've got a direct line to me because I worry – because it's my job to worry – about security at Dubette. Everything I've ever had you do is provably just that, my worrying about product and marketing security. You can stuff coincidence up your fat ass, like you're probably going to have to stuff an enema up your fat ass to get rid of all that shit you've been putting down your throat. I don't take threats, Harry. I make them. There anything I've said so far that isn't clear to you?'

Harry Johnson stared back across the table, holding Grant's look, his jaws crunching slowly, rhythmically, on his toast. A lost blob of red jelly made its way down his chin, finally pitching off to miss the serviette and add another stain to his already much marked jeans.

'I asked you a question,' said Grant.

'Let me ask you one back,' said the other man. 'You think we understand each other now?'

'I sure as hell hope you understand me,' said Grant.

'And I sure as hell hope you understand me,' came back Johnson. 'And that we can go on just as we were before this misunderstanding came up between us. You think we can do that?'

Grant was white-faced, once more not able immediately to form words. When he did speak, his voice was restricted, as if his throat was blocked. 'You told me there was something to show me?'

'Show *you*,' insisted Johnson. 'Not pass on through Dwight Newton.'

Grant sat, waiting. It seemed a long time before the security head responded, not speaking either, but sliding a photograph across the table.

'It's not a good picture,' complained Grant.

'Good enough,' said Johnson.

'Who is she?'

'The ex-wife of Parnell's lawyer, Barry Jackson. She's a geneticist in Parnell's unit. The picture was taken last night, as she left Parnell's apartment, where she'd been for two hours.'

'You've ignored a specific instruction!' accused Dwight Newton.

'How's that?' asked Parnell, calmly. The mountains and rivers were back at their proper, surmountable heights.

'I told you I wanted – Dubette wanted – maximum concentration on avian flu. You've downscaled, put Lapidus in charge of a smaller group . . . ignored what I asked you to do.'

It would have been Ted Lapidus's hoped-for liaison visit across the corridor, Parnell guessed, scarcely interested and even less intimidated by the vice president. 'I downscaled first to save you and Russell Benn and Dubette. I'm still hoping both of you – and Dubette – will be saved. I won't know until I'm sure about Paris, which at the moment I'm still not . . .' Parnell stopped, scarcely interested either in the redness that suffused Newton's face. 'We weren't getting anywhere – in fact, we were getting in each other's way – all trying to work on the avian problem when there was only one path to follow and that seemed to be blocked. It made absolute research sense to reduce the number of people and occupy other people elsewhere, which is what I've done and what I want to continue to do. Which is not ignoring and certainly not minimizing the project you gave me and my unit. It's responding properly, sensibly and scientifically, to it. We are today beginning a new approach, which it is still too early even to discuss. If there's anything whatsoever to discuss, you – and through you Russell Benn – will be the first to know . . .' The pause fitted, to make his point, but Parnell also needed to take breath. 'And I really do think, Dwight, that if you're going to get anything at all worthwhile out of my unit, you should let me run it and organize it and not keep calling me in here every five minutes to explain the last thing I've done or thought about. You told me in the beginning you wanted to know what I was doing. I heard you. When there's something that makes sense to tell you and share with other people in this research area, then I'll tell you and share it, just as I hope you will tell me and share with me anything that comes up elsewhere, as happened in Paris. Doesn't that seem to you to be a sensible way for us to operate?'

Newton's face was blazing now, the long-fingered hands twitching, seeking a scuttling direction. 'We need to establish . . . recognize . . . a working relationship.'

'I thought that was what we're talking about,' said Parnell.

'Were you going to tell me about Beverley Jackson?'

'What about Beverley Jackson?' asked Parnell, guardedly.

'She's refusing to undergo a psychological assessment. She's told Wayne Denny that you know and that you've said you won't pressure her.'

'That's exactly what I have told her,' confirmed Parnell. 'And no, I wasn't going to tell you, because I think that's an administrative company matter for personnel to deal with – which is what they exist for – most certainly nothing important enough to bring before the vice president of research. Which brings us back to our problem, Dwight. Why are you worried, involved even, in whether Beverley sits some half-assed mind test?'

'Have you seen today's newspapers?' asked the man, instead of replying.

'No,' replied Parnell, who hadn't bothered to stop at a news-stand or a gas station on his way from Washington DC. 'I guess the coverage is pretty extensive?'

'Dubette stock is at a six-year low and the prediction is that it will fall lower.'

'I won't accept my action against the police is solely or even partially responsible for that,' refused Parnell. 'You think, given a choice, I'd have gone through any of this?'

'I got the impression from what you said on television, what I read in the papers, that you're in close contact with the FBI?' Newton's colour was subsiding, his voice no longer strained.

'They've needed to speak to me,' said Parnell, guardedly again.

'They got anything positive? Suspects?'

'If they have, they haven't told me,' Parnell said evasively.

'They must have said something!'

'They haven't,' insisted Parnell. 'Nothing that's given me any reason to think they're anywhere close to an arrest. Anywhere close to understanding it.' *Not understanding* it was joining the long litany of clichés, he thought. Parnell said: 'What about you, Dwight? You're engaging yourself in everything: what do you think about Rebecca's murder and French flight numbers? You managed to find a connecting thread?'

Parnell waited expectantly for Newton to say he didn't understand, but instead he said: 'Maybe I could see something if I knew all that was going on . . . if I had an overview . . .'

The remark rang like a bell in Parnell's mind. 'You spoken to the FBI yet?'

Newton answered the internal telephone at once, identified himself but contributed nothing to the exchange before putting the instrument down. He said: 'Sorry. Something's come up. Will you excuse me?'

He'd leave the office, Parnell decided. But he wouldn't excuse Newton from anything.

'Which personnel files?' demanded Newton.

'He didn't specify,' said Wayne Denny. 'His name's Pullinger. A counsel for the FBI. He said he hoped their agents would be allowed access to the personnel records without needing a court order. Baldwin says it might give a misleading impression if we insisted, but that he wants himself and myself to be present.'

'Go back and tell Pullinger that,' decided Newton. 'If he objects, then ask for a court order – that'll be them creating a problem, not us.'

Twenty-Nine

The interview was geared for psychological pressure. There'd been a considerable input from the FBI's profiling division at their Quantico training facility in Virginia, from which both Howard Dingley and David Benton were graduates, and the pressure was imposed even before the encounter began, by inviting Harry Johnson to the Bureau's Washington field office – not by their going out to McLean – and advising the security chief to be accompanied by counsel, an obvious implication that he'd need legal protection.

Johnson arrived – in a sharply pressed suit, not his Dubette security uniform – with two lawyers, the company attorney, Peter Baldwin, and William Clarkson, whom the agents recognized from Dubette's huddled legal group at the press conference. Clarkson, a quick-talking, fidgeting man, immediately challenged Dingley's request to record the questioning, which Dingley countered by insisting it was as much to protect his client as it was to establish a verbatim record. A duplicate tape, as well as a transcript, would obviously be made available.

'I don't mind,' intervened Johnson. 'Let's get it all down, hear what we've got to say to each other. Why not?'

'Thank you,' said David Benton, activating the machine.

'It's good of you to come. We appreciate it,' added Dingley, at once seizing Johnson's overconfident belief that he could handle whatever he was about to face, even on alien Bureau territory.

'Anything to help,' said Johnson.

'You've probably got more experience of this sort of thing than us,' flattered Benton.

'I don't know about that,' said Johnson, too quickly.

'You were with Metro DC police before joining Dubette, weren't you?' said Benton.

269

Johnson's face tightened, almost imperceptibly. 'Uniform, never detective. Certainly not murder or terrorism.'

'Don't remember your telling us that you were with Metro DC police department when we first spoke,' remarked Dingley. 'We didn't know that until we went through Dubette's employment files.'

'Don't remember your asking,' came back Johnson, truculently.

'Maybe we didn't,' Benton appeared to accept. 'Our oversight.'

'What's the importance of my client having been with Metro DC police?' demanded Clarkson, sharply.

Benton's frown was almost overemphasized. 'The two arresting officers were from Metro DC . . .' He looked at the security man. 'I guess you already knew them, didn't you, Mr Johnson?'

'I'm not sure,' doubted Johnson, quickly. 'I left . . .'

'. . . in '96,' finished Benton, more quickly. 'Peter Bellamy and Helen Montgomery were at that time both serving in the Metro DC police department.'

'Were they?' said Johnson and stopped. There was a wariness now, the overconfidence wavering.

'Yes,' said Dingley and stopped.

The windows were double-glazed, preventing any outside traffic noise. There was none from any inner corridors, either, just the faintest sigh from the air-conditioning.

Clarkson broke the impasse. 'Is this meeting over?'

'No,' said Benton. 'We weren't sure your client had completed his answer.'

Johnson was looking at the flickering light of the recording machine. 'I had.'

'I'm surprised, Mr Johnson, that you didn't know Officers Bellamy and Montgomery,' pressed Benton.

'I was in administration in '95 and '96.'

'Where were they?' asked Dingley.

'Outside uniform . . .' started Johnson, stopping at appearing to know. 'They must have been,' resumed the man, again. 'They'd have had to be, wouldn't they, for me not to be able to remember if I knew them or not?'

'We don't ask questions to answer them ourselves,' said

270

Benton. 'Is Metro DC police division that big? There's shared communal facilities, surely? Canteen, recreational areas, stuff like that . . . ?'

'I've told you, I didn't know every single person in Metro DC. Officers Bellamy and Montgomery I didn't call to mind when they came to Dubette. After they came to Dubette, I remembered seeing them around, in the department.'

'What's the purpose of this questioning?' asked Clarkson. 'Are you regarding my client as being criminally connected with what you are investigating? In which case . . .'

'We are not at this stage regarding or treating Mr Johnson as anything other than an essential witness in an ongoing murder and terrorist-linked investigation,' broke in Dingley, formerly and with the same interruption preventing whatever closedown threat the lawyer might have intended.

'It would be unfortunate if we strayed away from the reason for this meeting,' warned Benton. 'Things appear to be becoming confused, and that's what we're trying to avoid, things that are already confused becoming more confused.'

'I think that's an excellent precaution,' said Johnson's lawyer. 'I'm also approaching the time when I am going seriously to query the point of a lot of this questioning, if it continues in the way it has so far done.' During the exchanges, Johnson smiled and straightened in his seat, his confidence visibly returning.

'I'm very sorry it went off course,' apologized Dingley. 'Our mistake. So, we've established, Mr Johnson, that although you worked for the same police department over an overlapping period, you never knew Officers Bellamy or Montgomery?'

'Not as people I hung out with. Nineteen sixty-nine is a long time ago. We certainly weren't friends.'

'You left – retired from – Metro DC prematurely, didn't you, Mr Johnson?' asked Benton.

'Again, what's the relevance of that question?' said Clarkson.

'Establishing the reliability and credibility of witnesses in a forthcoming criminal prosecution,' said Benton. 'Our prosecutors don't like courtroom challenges that could have been anticipated . . .' He nodded towards the recording apparatus. 'Now there it is, unequivocally on tape.'

'Are you impugning my client's integrity?'

'Absolutely not!' insisted Dingley, enunciating each syllable to enforce the denial. 'At the moment – as we probably haven't sufficiently made clear or established – we look to Mr Johnson as an essential witness.'

'To what?' Clarkson continued to challenge. 'My client was briefly present at an arrest, an arrest now the subject of a quite separate civil case in no way involving or concerning the FBI. How can that brief involvement make him an essential, material witness?'

'At this stage of our enquiries, Mr Johnson is one of the *only* witnesses to anything!' said Benton. 'We're anxious we don't leave unasked any question that might give us an opening.'

'I am glad, after all, that this interview is being recorded,' said Clarkson.

'So are we,' said Benton, immediately. 'That's why we asked for it to be done.' He switched quickly to Johnson. 'You did leave Metro DC police department prematurely, didn't you, Mr Johnson?'

'I'd reached my first available retirement opportunity. I chose to take it.'

'Why was that?' asked Benton, mildly.

'A position came up at Dubette, in their security division.'

'As head of their security division?'

Johnson's wariness was back. 'Yes.'

'That was quite a jump, going straight in as head of a unit,' commented Dingley.

'I had the qualifications and experience. I was headhunted, if you like.' He smiled at his own pun.

'As I'm sure you most certainly liked,' Dingley smiled back. 'How'd that happen, Mr Johnson? How did Dubette come to think of you – find you – out of every likely candidate – out of Metro DC, where there were so many officers that you didn't even get to remember Peter Bellamy and Helen Montgomery, who were your contemporaries?'

Johnson's smile remained. 'Their previous security chief,

Joe Blanchard. He'd earlier worked for Metro DC police. Put me forward with a personal recommendation.'

'It's not what you know, it's who you know,' Benton said. 'Isn't that what they always say?'

'That's what they always say,' agreed Johnson.

'So you left Metro DC in, what was it, November 1996?'

'Something like that,' said Johnson.

'*Exactly* like that, November ten, 1996,' said Dingley. 'We got it from Metro DC records. Not a good time around then for Metro DC police. Lot of internal enquiries. Lot of people leaving the force. You remember that, Mr Johnson?'

'This has got to stop!' protested Clarkson.

'Sir!' came back Dingley. 'This is a murder and potential terrorism investigation. Two Metro DC officers arrested a man in questionable circumstances . . .' He raised his hand, against the lawyer's further interruption. 'All right! That's being challenged elsewhere, in a court with which we have no involvement or jurisdiction. But we do have a very real interest in their reliability as witnesses in our ongoing investigation. We'd hoped your client could simply give us a steer on that reliability.'

'My client has already told you he did not know Officers Bellamy or Montgomery well enough to be able to attest to that,' persisted Clarkson.

'Indeed he has,' said Benton. 'But the question wasn't about the two officers, was it? It was about an unfortunate, embarrassing time within Metro DC police department.'

'An embarrassing time in which my client was in no way involved,' said Clarkson. 'And which has no relevance whatsoever to the investigation in which you're currently engaged.'

'That wasn't the question, or the inference, either,' persisted Dingley. 'I asked if Mr Johnson remembered it.'

'Of course I remember it,' said Johnson. 'The enquiries were internal but they were widely covered in the press.'

'Evidence-tampering . . . bribery . . . stuff like that,' recalled Benton. 'Which brings us up to date with our current investigation. There's indications here of tampering with or planting forensic evidence. You think Officers Bellamy and Montgomery would be capable of doing anything like that, Mr Johnson?'

'How many more times do I have to tell you that I don't know them well enough?' protested the security chief. 'How can I judge what they're capable of?'

'What about that day?' persisted Benton. 'You're a professional. You were with them, saw how they operated. They look to you to be good, honest cops?'

'As far as I was aware – what I saw – they behaved perfectly properly and professionally,' said Johnson.

'This is getting ridiculous!' re-entered the lawyer.

For the first time, the agents ignored the interruption. Focusing solely upon Johnson, Dingley said: 'You – and the security officers you control – carry weapons, don't you? Smith and Wesson thirty-eights? Police Specials?'

'For which we are licensed,' said Johnson.

'We know. We've already checked,' assured Dingley. 'Anything else? Mace? Pepper spray? Batons?'

'My staff and I protect a pharmaceutical research facility, a very obvious target in the drug culture in which we live,' said Johnson.

'So, what else is it you carry?' persisted Dingley.

'The night staff – sometimes the day staff, too – carry Mace. And batons.'

'Ever had to use it? Or discharge your weapon?' asked Dingley.

'No,' said Johnson.

'Let's hope you never do,' said Benton.

'There's an inconsistency we'd like you to help us with,' said Dingley, in a sudden change of direction. 'Our recollection – and Dave and I have checked our notes on this – was that you told us you didn't know what car Richard Parnell drove. Or what its registration was. Is that right, Mr Johnson? Is it right you didn't know the make of the car or its registration number, until Richard Parnell took you to it on the morning of his arrest?'

The blink was of a country road animal on a dark night, transfixed in the lights of an oncoming vehicle. Johnson said: 'I don't remember . . . what I did or didn't tell you, I mean . . . don't remember your asking . . .'

'So, let's ask you again, Mr Johnson,' said Benton. 'Until

274

the day of Richard Parnell's arrest, did you know the make or registration of his vehicle?'

'I told you I don't remember!'

'No!' refused Dingley. 'What you didn't remember was what you told us when we first talked. The question now is whether, before Mr Parnell's arrest, you knew his car details.'

'Dubette have a research and administration staff at McLean close to two thousand people,' said the man.

'One thousand, eight hundred and forty-two,' supplied Benton. 'Out of that one thousand eight hundred and forty-two, did you know the details of Mr Parnell's car?'

'No!' blurted Johnson.

'You absolutely sure about that?' said Benton. 'On the evening Mr Parnell found his car damaged . . . damaged sufficiently to remove paint later found around – but not adhering to – Ms Lang's car, you logged on Dubette's personnel file access system as having examined Mr Parnell's personal records. And in those documents is listed the make and registration of Mr Parnell's car. Do you remember going through Mr Parnell's file?'

The approaching headlights were blindingly in Johnson's eyes. He shook his head, blinked a lot, and looked sideways for help to his lawyer. Clarkson said: 'This interview ceases, now! I need further time . . . instruction . . . with my client . . .'

'We can fully understand that,' accepted Dingley. 'As we made very clear from the outset, by having this interview recorded, we are extending every legally required courtesy to your client, Mr Harry Johnson. Which is why I think this is the moment formally to read him his Miranda rights . . .'

On cue, as Dingley stopped talking, Benton recited Johnson's legal protection against self-incrimination.

Continuing the double act, Dingley picked up the moment his partner finished, speaking more towards the recording apparatus than to the security chief. 'I am now showing Mr Johnson and his attorney the search warrant issued earlier today by a judge in private hearing . . .'

'I should have been informed of this before this interview began!' protested Clarkson.

'That warrant authorizes the FBI to search Mr Johnson's

home as well as his office and locker at Dubette Inc. at McLean, North Virginia,' continued Dingley. 'It effectively seals every article in every stated place under court jurisdiction until Bureau searches have been completed.'

The email had been waiting when Parnell arrived that morning, addressed to him, not Lapidus, despite the request for further avian-flu specimens coming from the Greek geneticist. More cultures were being despatched. So were preliminary papers from Shanghai University updating research on a SARS vaccine incorporating DNA from the infecting virus. Part of the paper indicated that the Chinese were also experimenting upon a similar method of immunization against the current lethal bird flu.

'It's an idea,' suggested Parnell, when Lapidus's team assembled.

'It goes along with your D, C, B, A approach,' said Sato.

'And there's the linking respiratory factor in both conditions,' Beverley pointed out.

'The gamble comes, as it always does, in finding an acceptably safe level,' said Lapidus. 'Remember, we can't try culture growth in eggs.'

'What about the mice we already tested?' asked Parnell. 'Did we isolate a specific host gene?'

'I tried, obviously,' said Sato, at once. 'The damned strain is so mephitic it's like a pump gun – everything gets shot away.'

'Maybe Ted's just shown us a path,' said Parnell. 'We minimize the strength of the virus, under controlled conditions, to the point of destruction. Every level's logged. Against each level we administer until we lose the pump-gun effect. And then go for tolerance, working through the logged levels. At an acceptable tolerance, we might locate our most likely friendly host. We get the mouse host, we look for a human match.'

'Elementary, my dear Watson,' gently mocked Lapidus.

'How long's a few thousand comparisons going to take?' Parnell mocked back.

Seriously, Lapidus said: 'How many other companies do

you think might, as our people have, pick up on Shanghai?'

'I don't even want to make a guess. I know this is a race but I don't want any of us running so fast we trip over ourselves,' cautioned Parnell. 'Dubette came far too close to that – to doing that – all too recently. We follow this research line, if it turns out to be feasible, like the scientists we are, and always will do as long as I am the director of this unit. And that's scientifically. If someone comes out ahead of us, so be it. They did better than us and they deserved to get there first . . .' Parnell came to a halt, suddenly embarrassed, at the same time as being aware of how often he seemed to need to stop talking, to draw breath. 'That didn't start as the lecture it turned out to be,' he apologized.

'I didn't think it was a lecture,' said Beverley. 'I thought it was a professional commitment.'

A three-man forensic unit led the entry into the fetid apartment, on the Anacostia side of Capitol Hill, with the investigators, Johnson and the two lawyers behind. Which was where they remained, virtually unspeaking, as the protectively suited three methodically worked through Johnson's home, room by room. Johnson insisted he had a licence for a second .38 Smith and Wesson discovered in the dishevelled bedroom, and which Benton bagged, but remained silent at the gradual accumulation of name-stamped Dubette property, which ranged from pens and notepaper to crockery, linen and towels. A switchblade, one half of the handle broken, was found in a kitchen drawer, among an assortment of tools. Benton put that into an evidence envelope, too. In the living room there were several photographs of Johnson in Metro DC police uniform, none of them featuring either Peter Bellamy or Helen Montgomery. There was also a scrapbook of newspaper cuttings of reported cases in which Johnson had featured. There were also six newspaper stories of the 1996 corruption investigation into the Metro DC force. After a momentary hesitation, Johnson felt beneath an adjoining drawer for the taped-in-place hidden key to the one locked part of a bureau, in which was found Johnson's bank deposit book, with a credit balance of $260,402.

As Dingley said they were seizing the book, Johnson started: 'I want to say . . .' before Clarkson said: 'No, you don't!' stopping the man.

'Do you carry a notebook, a message pad?' asked Dingley. 'Maybe there's one in your office . . . around somewhere?'

Johnson reached into the drawer in which the deposit book had been locked and groped a plastic-bound pocketbook from its rear.

'Why do you want that?' intruded Clarkson.

'The warrant gives us legal right to seize whatever we decide to be necessary,' said Benton.

'Necessary for what?' demanded the lawyer.

'There has to be later disclosure, but not at this stage,' reminded Dingley.

There was no conversation whatsoever during the journey out to McLean, Johnson and Clarkson in the rear of the FBI car, Peter Baldwin following in his own vehicle, ahead of the forensic scientists. The flick knife Parnell had described Johnson carrying in his trouser pocket was found in a locker drawer, as well as a set of brass knuckledusters. The forensic examiners extracted the entire drawer and sealed it for further laboratory tests upon what appeared to be small specks of grey paint among debris and dust at its corners and bottom. The holstered .38 Smith and Wesson was in another drawer, along with two spare clips of ammunition. In a top drawer of the desk in Johnson's office, the search uncovered complete photocopies of both Richard Parnell and Rebecca Lang's personnel files.

Dingley said: 'That's fortunate. Personnel told us Ms Lang's records had been destroyed before we asked for them . . .'

The field office bar was on 14th Street and it was tradition to celebrate the first potential break in any case. Benton touched glasses with Dingley and said: 'You know what I think we've got enough evidence for? Stealing a bunch of towels and serviettes from his employers.'

'Don't forget the salt and pepper shakers.'

'And a set of salt and pepper shakers,' added Benton.

'How's a bum like Johnson get over a quarter of a million bucks in the bank?' asked Dingley.

'You think he's going to tell us?' asked Benton, cynically.

Dingley looked unnecessarily at his watch. 'Ed Pullinger is making the wire-tap application about now. Maybe that's how we'll find out.'

'Let's not forget *why* we're involved,' reminded Benton. 'It's not so much the murder. It's suspected terrorism.'

'Terrorism's well funded,' said Dingley. 'It's a point Pullinger is arguing to support the tap. And he's trying for an order to get at Metro DC police records, too.'

'Towels, serviettes and salt and pepper shakers,' insisted Benton, gesturing for the bartender's attention.

'Don't you forget the paint in the locker drawer.'

Thirty

The interviews with the two suspended Metro DC police officers were, of course, conducted separately, again at the FBI field office, and from both there was immediate legal insistence upon, instead of objection to, tape recordings. Each was also individually accompanied by two demanding lawyers, one personal, the other representing the Metro DC police department. Despite their separation, each officer quickly appeared to follow a virtually identical script. Of course they knew Harry Johnson: they'd worked with him. But they hadn't been friends, acquaintances even – he was just a guy they'd seen around. No, Harry hadn't indicated that he knew Richard Parnell's car until the scientist himself led them to it. They had not recovered every item from Rebecca Lang's purse from the bottom of the gorge when they arrested him – the terrorist-alert flight number had been shown to them for the first time by a Metro DC forensic scientist, Professor Jacob Meadows, who'd produced the entire contents of the handbag after the recovery of the body and the vehicle. Neither had been present at that recovery. As far as they knew, the recovery had been carried out by police engineers who had also collected up material later handed over to Professor Meadows. Their involvement had begun, after a radio alert while they were on patrol, with the discovery, from the ID in her purse, that Rebecca Lang had worked at Dubette. At the time of their going to McLean, the death of Ms Lang had been considered a fatal traffic accident, not murder. Both believed it was Harry Johnson who had told them of the personal relationship between Ms Lang and Richard Parnell, although it might first have been suggested by Dwight Newton – neither could be absolutely sure. They had not attached any significance to the flight number when they found it among Rebecca Lang's belongings – it had been Parnell's attorney who had introduced that significance into the initial court hearing. They had believed there was bona fide justification to take Richard Parnell into custody, considering the circumstances of what they then believed to be a fatal accident and the damage to Parnell's car. Their arrest procedure had conformed to every legal regulation and guidance. There had been no intimidation, harassment or abuse, either verbal or physical – throughout they had acted fully within the legally established boundaries of suspect arrest, based upon preliminary forensic findings. Neither remembered Johnson specifically drawing their attention to the damage to Parnell's car – it had been obvious as they approached. They didn't look around the Toyota, for any paint-debris evidence of it being hit by a neighbouring car.

Helen Montgomery had been the first to be interviewed, in the morning. Towards the end of the encounter, Dingley said: 'The only reason for your detaining Richard Parnell when you did was because of the damage to his car?'

'We'd been told the dead woman's car had been in collision with a grey vehicle. The Toyota was grey.'

'You'd also been told, according to what you're now telling us, that Richard Parnell and Rebecca Lang were into a relationship,' said Benton. 'Wasn't it a very long jump to connect him to the death purely on the basis of the colour of his car?'

'Is that a question for your specific enquiry?' immediately intruded the Metro DC lawyer, Phillip Brack, a man so obese he had to sit with his legs splayed, unable to bring them together.

'It could very well be, if your client was curious about an

inexplicable Air France flight number being on the body of the dead woman,' said Dingley.

'My client has already told you that, at the moment of the arrest, she was unaware of that flight number. Or its apparent significance.'

'So, it was what?' questioned Benton. 'Taking Richard Parnell into police custody for further questioning into what was nothing more than a possible coincidence?'

'We're in danger of straying into wrong territory,' warned Brack.

'I think we're on the right side of the dividing line,' insisted Dingley.

'That's what it was,' said the woman. 'Further questioning.'

'For which he had to be manacled?' demanded Benton.

'That's it!' stopped Brack, just ahead of Helen Montgomery's personal attorney, a heavily bespectacled, Ivy-League-suited black lawyer named Donald Sinclair.

'That's too much,' said Sinclair, rewording his protest.

'It wouldn't have been, for a suspected terrorist,' said Benton.

'We've already covered that ground,' reminded Sinclair.

'I'm not sure we have, to our satisfaction – to satisfy an FBI involvement,' disputed Dingley. 'Unless you knew of the terrorist implications, I can't see why you had to take Richard Parnell into custody in chains. Take us through the conversation you had with Harry Johnson, as best you can remember it.'

For the first time, Helen Montgomery showed a hesitation. 'I've told you. We got a dispatcher's message that there'd been a fatality in Rock Creek Park, Rebecca Lang, whose ID gave Dubette as her workplace . . .'

'Do Metro DC automatically record their communications?' broke in Benton.

There was another pause. 'Yes.'

'So, there'll be a tape of that exchange?'

'I guess so. Anyway, we get to Dubette, ask to see Harry in security, who takes us up to Ms Lang's division and calls in the vice president as well as the personnel director . . .'

'Whoa!' stopped Benton. 'Let's take it all a lot slower. You knew Harry Johnson was head of Dubette security. You call him from the car? Tell him you were on your way?'

'I may have done. I'm not sure.'

'You arrive at Dubette, you tell Harry what?'

The woman shrugged. 'I can't remember, precisely. Something like someone who works for Dubette, Rebecca Lang, looks to have been killed in a motor accident . . . forced over the edge of a drop in Rock Creek Park and . . .'

'That's what the dispatcher said, was it?' intruded Benton once more. 'That it wasn't just an accident . . . that Rebecca Lang's vehicle had been forced over the edge of a drop . . . ? That's what the tape will show?'

'I'm not sure . . . I mean, I think so, but I can't recall the precise words,' stumbled the woman.

'Guess that might just have been a reason for cuffing Parnell,' offered Dingley.

'What did Harry say to that?' picked up Benton.

'Maybe "how terrible" or something like that. And that we'd better tell people in authority. Which is what we did.'

'So that's when you first heard the name Richard Parnell, when you got to someone in authority?' said Dingley.

'No, before that,' said the woman. 'As we were going through the building, I told Harry we needed to find out what Ms Lang had been doing, to be in Rock Creek Park. Harry said Parnell would be the person to tell us. That he and the girl were involved and that Parnell would be the person to know.'

'Know what? Tell you what?' asked Dingley.

'Whatever we wanted to know, I suppose.'

'Did you talk about Parnell's car?'

'Not that I remember.'

'How did Parnell take it, when you told him?' asked Benton.

'All right, I guess.'

'All right, you guess!' exclaimed Benton. 'You tell a man his fiancée's been killed in a car crash and he takes it all right!'

'No. He was shocked, I suppose. But he didn't break down or anything like that.'

'How did Parnell's car come into the conversation?' suddenly asked Dingley. 'And why? You go to Dubette to tell them an employee has died. You discover she's into a relationship with someone there, you go into the car park to find his car damaged, so you manacle him and take him into custody. Wasn't that all a bit too quick . . . too circumstantial . . . ?'

'I'm coming in here again . . . !' Brack began to object, but Dingley overrode him.

'Come in as much as you want, for the benefit of the tape and to protest later. But we're talking terrorism and it seems to me, to my partner and I, that decisions were made either prematurely . . .' The halting hand came up again. '. . . or on the basis of evidence which isn't being disclosed to us. Which is very much part of our investigation. So, we'd appreciate an answer.'

'Nothing whatsoever has been withheld,' insisted the woman.

'Why do you think Johnson couldn't remember you or Officer Bellamy?'

'My client has already answered that question,' said Sinclair. 'If you want it repeated, I'll repeat it: she has no idea.'

'Was he involved in the internal Metro DC police department enquiries into corruption and evidence-planting in 1996?' demanded Benton.

Brack said: 'Stop!' just slightly ahead of the black lawyer.

Sinclair said: 'Upon my advice, my client refuses to answer that question.'

Brack added: 'A question that is grossly improper.'

'I don't consider it is,' said Dingley, mildly. 'But there would be records of those internal enquiries, wouldn't there, Mr Brack?'

The obese lawyer shifted in his inadequate chair. 'I have no way of knowing that.'

'We hope to be able to,' said Benton.

'She wasn't spooked,' complained Benton. They'd just finished listening to the tape replay, reloading the machine for Peter Bellamy's afternoon arrival, their sandwiches still uneaten on Dingley's desk.

'She came close,' argued Dingley.

'Close wasn't close enough. We're still looking at towels and salt and pepper shakers.'

'The taps will be on Johnson's phones by now . . .' started Dingley, stopping to pick up the telephone, which was nearer to where he was by the desk. In quick succession he said: 'OK . . . good . . . shit . . . OK . . . that's what we do to restore faith in the Bureau.'

'What?' asked Benton, when his partner replaced the receiver.

'We got our access order, against Metro DC police,' said Dingley.

Looks between Dingley and Benton were sufficient within an hour of their afternoon interview unspeakingly to agree that there had been careful rehearsal between Peter Bellamy and Helen Montgomery. The waddling Phillip Brack again represented Metro DC police department. Bellamy's personal attorney was a woman, Hilda Jeffries. She wore a trouser suit, a short hair-style and no make-up.

It was within that hour that the FBI agents took Bellamy through the echoed preliminaries they'd earlier recorded with Helen Montgomery, this time with Benton leading the hard-cop/soft-cop routine, although with a sudden, hopefully confusing, twist. Bellamy was at the end of a denial of any prior conversation about damage to Parnell's Toyota when Dingley said: 'What sort of guy do you think Harry is?'

'Good. Lucky . . .' began the police officer, before being halted by Brack.

The Metro DC lawyer said: 'Where's this questioning getting us?'

'An inch at a time, because of so many interruptions,' said Benton. 'Why do you consider Harry Johnson a lucky guy?'

'That was a hell of a job he landed himself at Dubette, right out of the department,' improvised Bellamy.

'I thought it was a shoo-in,' said Dingley. 'Joe Blanchard opened the door for him.'

'It wasn't that guaranteed,' said the man, believing there was firm ground underfoot.

'How do you know that?' persisted Benton.

'What bearing has this upon your investigation?' demanded the female lawyer.

'I won't know until I hear the answer,' said Benton. To Bellamy he said: 'Why wasn't it guaranteed that Harry would get the Dubette job, with Blanchard's backing?'

'It couldn't have been, could it?' floundered Bellamy. 'There must have been other applicants.'

'What about you?' said Benton. 'You ever think you could slot into a Dubette job, knowing Harry like you did?'

'Could have been an ace in the hole.'

'We hear Dubette pay well,' invited Dingley.

'Top dollar,' smiled Bellamy.

'How much time you got, before you can leave?' queried Benton, tuned to his partner's approach.

'Coupla years . . . three maybe.'

'Is Dubette your ace in the hole?' asked Benton.

'Where's this going?' lumbered Brack.

'In a direction,' replied Benton, intentionally dismissive. 'You got it in mind that you can get a job with Dubette if you choose to leave Metro DC police, right?'

'It's always a thought,' conceded Bellamy.

'You ever get caught up in all those troubles in the Metro DC police department in 1996?' abruptly demanded Benton.

'My client declines to answer that question,' interrupted Hilda Jeffries, at once.

'I think you should know that the FBI has obtained a court order enforcing full disclosure not just of the conclusions of internal hearings of that time, but also of inconclusive investigations,' announced Benton.

'I wasn't advised of this application,' protested Brack, at once.

'We were only advised ourselves of the application by counsel at the J. Edgar Hoover building a few minutes before this interview began,' said Dingley, easily.

'This is something I need to discuss with my client,' said Hilda Jeffries. 'Something Phil and I should definitely have been told earlier.'

'This was the earliest opportunity,' insisted Dingley, unrepentantly.

285

'Before this recorded interview began was an earlier opportunity,' insisted Hilda Jeffries, in return. 'This could well become a court protest. Certainly this meeting will progress no further.'

'They're dirty,' insisted Benton, an hour later in the 14th Street bar. 'I got five bucks that says Harry and Pete Bellamy and maybe Helen Montgomery got investigated in 1996 but that there was insufficient proof to prosecute. Harry just got asked to leave. How's that sound?'

'Sounds like a very feasible local police corruption deal,' agreed Dingley. 'Which isn't an FBI problem or investigation.'

'I know we're missing our terrorism link,' conceded Benton. 'But a local police corruption deal *is* an FBI investigation if Metro DC police computers have been going beyond State borders and looking at things they shouldn't be looking at.'

'That's a wild guess that gets us nowhere,' refused Dingley.

'I think we've taken a step forward,' argued Benton.

'Half a step,' cautioned Dingley. 'All we've got in addition to lies is a lot of conjecture.'

'I'm encouraged beyond towels and salt and pepper shakers,' said Benton. 'And we shouldn't forget Dwight Newton had a look-see at Parnell's file, according to the log.'

'No reason to leave him out,' accepted Dingley. 'Let's give it the weekend for him to stop worrying – think we're not interested. We've got a lot of reading to do.'

'You know what I'd like, just once?' said Benton.

'What?'

'To have an interview without a goddamned lawyer in the way.'

'Law enforcement would be a hell of a lot easier without lawyers,' agreed Benton.

They ate at the Kennedy Centre before the concert. Inevitably they talked about Johnson's headline-grabbing arrest and previous day's bail release, and Parnell said there hadn't been an opportunity to ask the FBI agents if it was a break in the case – he'd hoped they would have called him if it were, which they hadn't. He had planned to contact them at the beginning of the following week, but as he and Beverley talked, Parnell remembered Dingley's assurance always to be reachable at the numbers they'd given him – surprised he'd forgotten – and decided to try the cellphone listings the next day. Work had started on the controlled toxicity-reduction of the newly arrived avian flu viruses but it was necessarily slow. No safe level had been established, which left nothing more to say which hadn't already been said during their customary and so far inconclusive end-of-the-day discussions. Beverley judged Ted Lapidus a good research-team leader, but thought Sean Sato would be the one most likely to make a discovery, and finished by saying: 'And now I want to know about you.'

'I'll get involved the moment we get to a controllable virus level,' promised Parnell, deciding against telling her of the most recent confrontation with Dwight Newton.

'That wasn't the question,' she said.

'I wouldn't have thought there's anything left to know about me,' said Parnell. 'Let's hear about Beverley Jackson.'

'Dull story,' she insisted. 'Dad was an industrial chemist, so I guess I inherited the interest. Found I was good at it. Got caught up in the new science of genetics and wanted to prove I could be good at that too, which is why I came after the Dubette job. Didn't think you were particularly impressed by me at the job interview, incidentally. Didn't believe I stood a chance. Not sure how I feel about the company itself – I've got to see Wayne Denny next week, by the way, about this psychology nonsense. Sean's decided to go ahead and take it. Thinks to refuse will screw him up with the company. That's about it.'

'You missed out marriage and Barry.' Would she tell him about the one time they'd lied to each other? he wondered.

'College romance, stars in our eyes,' she said. 'Didn't live together long enough to get to know each other. Turned out we were both more interested in work and our careers than we were in each other. We talked about it and decided it was a mistake for which neither of us were to blame. Just one of those things that didn't work, so instead of ending up miserable and disliking each other, we'd call it a day ...' She

287

giggled. 'Barry did the divorce for free and I abandoned any claim for alimony.'

'Just like that!' said Parnell.

'It was a good deal. We end up friends, even go out together sometimes. His folks are dead, like mine are now, and we spent last Christmas together at Aspen. Barry paid.'

'All very grown-up and civilized,' said Parnell. He wasn't going to discover the great unsaid – maybe there was nothing to learn.

'Waste of time being any other way.' She looked around her, at an obvious exodus. 'About time we made a move, don't you think?'

They didn't bother to go to the bar at the intermission, and afterwards Parnell declared himself a fan of big band. 'Do you feel like a drink now?'

'Not in a bar.'

'I guess I'm going to have to get used to this directness.'

'That's if you want to.'

'I think I do.'

They went to Beverley's apartment at Dupont Circle without discussion. They did open wine but neither finished their first glass, although when they got into the bedroom and Parnell realized his nervousness he wished he had, because it might have helped. They kissed a lot and began exploring and searching each other, which initially made it worse for him. But Beverley was very patient, relaxing, stopping, quietly caressing, and gradually his tension eased away and they joined in perfect rhythm and climaxed together to her tiny, sobbing mew.

When he was able, Parnell said: 'I didn't think . . .'

But she put her fingers gently against his lips, stopping him, and said: 'But you did and it was wonderful.'

The lighting that night was much better outside Beverley's apartment than it had been at Washington Circle, and the photographs of their entering together were much better and the prints were timed, too. They were again timed, at ten thirty-three, when Parnell and Beverley left again the following morning, and sharper still in the bright daylight.

'So, what did Dingley say?' Beverley asked as they got into her car.

'It was going slowly but he was hopeful,' replied Parnell. 'He called it a step at a time.'

Thirty-One

Criminal investigation – particularly interrogation – is surprisingly a near-science of routine: comparing one person to another, one answer against another, overlaying one human template on top of another, seeking out the misplaced word, the displaced fact, the slightest chink in the protective wall that people who see themselves in danger try to build. That is the psychological ethos inculcated at Quantico and which Howard Dingley and David Benton religiously observed with Dubette research vice president Dwight Newton, although they were never professionally to know how effective it was.

It required, as it had with the others, that Newton be brought into the FBI field office and unsettlingly accompanied by lawyers, as always Dubette's Peter Baldwin and Gerry Fletcher, whom Newton loyally elected to retain. It was Fletcher who immediately challenged the FBI demand for their being summoned into Washington – as well as the use of a tape recording – Newton having already co-operated fully at the first interview, for which the FBI agents had courteously travelled out to McLean, and beyond which neither he nor his client could imagine any further help was possible.

'We most definitely do not – did not – intend any discourtesy,' said the soft-cop rehearsed Dingley. 'There's a lot coming in at us, from every which way – we've imposed upon your good nature in asking you to come here.'

'You're getting somewhere?' quickly asked Newton. He hoped his suit jacket was as effective as his white laboratory coat in covering the sweat rings. They had to have something (what, for Christ's sake!) to bring him in like this.

'Still trying to fit pieces together,' said Benton, the placating clichés arranged in his mind like cards in a poker game. 'That's how we hope you will be able to help us.'

'How?' said Fletcher, on behalf of his client.

'That flight number's our biggest problem,' insisted Dingley. 'I know we talked about it before, Professor Newton, but have you had any thoughts – recollections – since our first meeting, how it came to be in Rebecca's purse?'

'I told you then, absolutely not.'

'You most certainly did,' agreed Benton, as if in sudden recollection. 'We didn't know then that you'd accessed Richard Parnell's personnel file the day after he was arrested. Why'd you do that?'

'Professor Newton had every right and authority to access the records, as Richard Parnell's immediate superior,' said Baldwin.

'We're not doubting that he had,' said Dingley. 'Our question is why.'

'Dick had been arrested – I'd tried to arrange his legal representation,' said Newton, itching around his back and sides from the soaking perspiration, and exaggerating the shrug in an effort to relieve it. Not feeling able to explain that it had been personally to discover from the log – not the file that had been his excuse for consulting it – whether the omnipotent Johnson had examined it prior to the encounter in Showcross's office, Newton desperately extemporized: 'I wondered if there might have been anything there that could have helped.'

Dingley and Benton went through their look-exchanging formula, as if each was inviting the other to ask the obvious question. It was Dingley who spoke. 'Mr Parnell already had independent legal representation the day after he was arrested. By noon there were newscasts indicating that the case against him might collapse. You're not registered as having taken the records out until two ten that afternoon.'

'And only looked at them for just under ten minutes,' added Benton.

'That's how long it took me to realize that it was a stupid idea – that there couldn't possibly be anything there,' said Newton. 'I was . . .' There was another irritation-relieving shoulder twitch. '. . . just trying to help. Like I said, until it was obvious how pointless it was . . . I was casting around . . . a well-respected and loved member of Dubette had died . . .'

'You were there, in Burt Showcross's office,' said Dingley. 'Tell us about the arrest.'

'I don't understand.' said Newton. He was being sucked down again, the water coming in more quickly to engulf him.

'Did you get the impression there had been a lot of discussion between Harry Johnson and the two Metro DC police officers before you all got together in Burt Showcross's office?' asked Benton.

Yes, which was why I looked at the personnel records, thought Newton. He said: 'I didn't think about it . . . I guess there was . . . what . . . ? An affinity, I guess. They were all police officers – Harry was, once. They have a way of behaving . . . talking . . .' He had to get out, stop this sort of questioning! He was going to be dragged down. Destroyed. He didn't want to be destroyed by a system and an environment and people – a person – who believed himself to be God. All he wanted – the only thing he wanted – was to escape, to run away somewhere, anywhere, and hide and never be found again.

'Think about it now,' urged Dingley. 'Parnell's arrest doesn't seem right to us – almost as if it had been decided upon in advance.'

'Is that a focus of your investigation?' demanded Fletcher. 'That's surely a matter for the separate enquiry initiated against the two officers by Mr Parnell?'

'Difficult not to cross boundary lines,' smiled Benton, in empty apology. 'We're troubled by what seem to have been assumptions, without obvious evidence to support the action that was taken.'

'I don't see how my client can possibly help you with that,' said Fletcher.

'No,' quickly said Newton, seizing the more immediate, open-door escape. 'I can't help you with any of this . . .' Honestly, he said: 'I was shocked by it all . . . by Rebecca's death . . . how she died . . .'

'How was that?' persisted Benton, at once. 'When the officers

291

told you . . . more importantly, when they told Parnell. Exactly *what* did they say had happened?'

Newton hesitated, trying to anticipate the pitfalls. 'That there'd been a traffic accident. That Rebecca had died.'

'Did they give any details of the accident?' asked Dingley.

Where was the trap? The thing he should or shouldn't say? 'I think they said there'd been a collision . . . I can't properly remember . . . that Rebecca's car had been forced into a canyon, I think . . . I'm not sure . . .'

'Forced into a canyon?' echoed Dingley.

What were the implications of those words? 'Something like that. I told you, I can't properly remember . . . can't swear to anything . . .'

'You're not being asked to swear to anything, Professor Newton . . .' said Dingley.

'Not yet,' finished Benton.

'Do you have a case to make against anyone?' demanded Baldwin, at once.

'Not yet,' said Dingley, in a tone indicating that it could be imminent.

'You sound hopeful,' pressed the Dubette lawyer.

'We're always hopeful,' said Benton. 'We got an eighty-five per cent success record, Howie and me. We work hard to stay that way, at the top of the league.'

'I hope you can with this,' said Newton, in a brief flash of belligerence.

'We will,' predicted Benton. 'So, you were happy with the way Professor Parnell was treated?'

'I didn't make a judgement!' protested Newton, further hoping to recover. 'How do you expect me to know how police are supposed to behave . . . ?'

'Just by . . .' started Dingley but was stopped by Fletcher.

'This isn't your investigation,' insisted the lawyer. 'This line of questioning belongs to the civil action.'

'For which we understand you've been served with a witness subpoena?' said Benton.

'What importance do you attach to that?' said Baldwin, overly intrusive.

'None,' said Dingley, calmly. 'Just making a comment.'

'Was Ms Lang considered a problem employee at Dubette?' suddenly asked Benton.

'My client declines to answer that inappropriate question,' refused Fletcher.

'Someone murdered Ms Lang,' reminded Dingley. 'So far, we haven't been able to discover any motive for such a murder . . . any murder.'

'My client cannot help you on that,' blocked Fletcher.

'Why can't Professor Newton answer for himself?' asked Benton. 'He is vice president in charge of the McLean installation. He was Ms Lang's ultimate boss. He's in a position to know if Ms Lang was a problem employee, surely?'

'Rebecca Lang was an exemplary employee,' said Newton.

'Thank you,' smiled Benton. 'Here's another question I hope you can help us with, as vice president of Dubette research and development. Upon Dubette's premises at McLean there are very dangerous things . . . viruses, disease samples . . . infectious agents . . . ?' generalized Benton.

'Kept, preserved and protected in conditions of total safety,' insisted Newton, comfortable for the first time on territory in which he felt safe.

'If they were released into the environment, into the atmosphere, could what is kept, preserved and protected at Dubette cause a major health risk? Infection? Contagion?' asked Benton, the question pedantically phrased.

'If some of the experimental cultures were to escape into the environment, there could potentially be public-health concern,' replied Newton, just as pedantically. 'The method and safety precautions in which such samples are housed makes such accidental release impossible. All are kept in individual chambers within chambers, each separation alarmed to trigger an immediate alert in the event of the most minuscule escape. At each level there is a shutdown procedure, doubly sealing the penetrated section. If the leakage were to continue – which is an impossibility in the event of an accident – the final section is incendiarized. It is automatically heated to two hundred degrees centigrade. No known bacillus or virus can survive such a temperature.'

Both FBI agents listened patiently through the exposition. When it was over, Dingley said: 'Dubette has a total of twelve overseas subsidiaries?'

'Yes,' agreed Newton at once, believing he could anticipate the questioning.

'How often is material of the virulence that we are discussing passed between those overseas subsidiaries and McLean?'

'Extremely rarely,' said Newton, confidently. 'Any such transfer is always contained within protective, crash-resistant outer casings tested to the destruction capability of a major explosion. Each container is equipped with a similar triggering mechanism to that at McLean, to self-destruct if the casing is breached . . .' He smiled at the two agents. 'And I'm sure you'll be reassured to know that no such shipment has moved in either direction between Dubette or any of its overseas divisions in the last eighteen months.'

'We are reassured,' agreed Dingley. 'You know that and now we know it. But a potential terrorist group able to learn when and how shipments were going back and forth wouldn't know it, would they?'

'For me to answer that question beyond its hypotheses, you'd have to define the extent of that capability,' said Newton, his stomach hollowing again. 'Dubette is highly protective of its research and development. There is no such leakage within McLean or any of Dubette's overseas subsidiaries.'

'If you suspected that there were, you'd move immediately to seal it, of course?'

'Of course,' said Newton, with insufficient thought.

'You couldn't, though, if you hadn't uncovered the source of such leakage, could you?' Benton pointed out.

'No,' admitted Newton. 'But there wasn't one!'

'Dwight!' said Baldwin, close to shouting across the car on their way back to McLean. 'I'm talking to you!'

The slumped scientist came out of his reverie. 'Sorry. What did you say?'

'I said that I thought that went very well,' repeated the company lawyer.

'I didn't. They think I'm hiding something.'

Baldwin, at the wheel, chanced a look towards the other man. 'That's ridiculous! You've got nothing *to* hide, have you?'

'No,' said Newton, hoping the doubt didn't sound in his voice.

'Then I don't know what you're talking about. It went well. Believe me.'

Even if Parnell's later-discovered HPRT effect had been known, the exchanges between McLean and Paris would not have required self-destructing packaging, Newton tried to convince himself. But the protection should have been more substantial than the standard polystyrene and cardboard wrap. How could he get out? Where was his escape, a way – a place – to hide?

There was not, in fact, a lot coming in from every which way for Howard Dingley and David Benton to examine, although they had initially expected their entire weekend to be taken up reviewing the 1996 Metro DC police internal corruption investigations. Ironically the delay was caused by the necessary police records having to be duplicated to comply with the quite separate court order obtained by Barry Jackson to pursue the false-arrest action. And by the time it was all assembled, they risked being overwhelmed by its arrival coinciding with the forensic results from the searches of Harry Johnson's Anacostia apartment and his Dubette workplace. Their resolve was roughly to divide it, Benton taking the Metro DC police material into his separate office, leaving Dingley with the forensics report. Dingley, with less than his partner, finished first but needed the time for a lengthy telephone discussion with the FBI laboratory at the J. Edgar Hoover building. He'd just finished when Benton returned.

Benton handed his partner a five dollar note and said: 'You won the bet. Johnson was investigated on suspicion of improper use of equipment – using Metro DC police computers to access records of other forces – and for accepting bribes. Everything collapsed for lack of evidence but he was invited to retire . . .'

'Didn't anyone examine the bank account?' broke in Dingley.

'Apparently not,' said Benton. 'Don't forget it was an internal enquiry, carried out by people who knew each other. According to Parnell, Johnson's the man who picks up shipments to the separate box-number address. He'd know whenever a special consignment was arriving, wouldn't he? Just the sort of terrorist information we were talking about to Newton.'

'Too circumstantial,' judged Dingley.

'I know,' accepted the other agent. 'Would you say this is?'

The photograph he handed across the desk was one of three that had been among the surrendered material. It showed Johnson, in uniform, with his arm around Helen Montgomery, also in uniform. Peter Bellamy was among a smiling group in the posed background.

'I'd say I'm surprised Johnson had so much trouble remembering Helen Montgomery and Peter Bellamy as former colleagues,' said Dingley. 'Looks to me as if he's got his hand under her left tit and she's enjoying it. What about those two?'

'One enquiry, again failed, into Bellamy. Complaint of undue and unreasonable force during an arrest. Montgomery was his partner. It was her evidence, denying everything, that got the accusation thrown out.'

'Might help Parnell's civil case. Doesn't do much for us.'

'None of it does unless Johnson tells us where he's got his quarter of a mill from. And we sure as hell know he ain't going to do that. He wouldn't shift from careful saver and lucky gambler, not if we pulled his fingernails out.'

'Lucky gamblers aren't careful savers.'

'Psychology isn't evidence,' reminded Benton. 'You any luckier?'

Dingley smiled. 'The half thumb print on the flight number is Johnson's. Perfect match for prints off the handles of both flick knives, the knuckleduster, and on the butt of the Smith and Wesson in his uniform holster.'

Benton smiled back. 'And he told us, on tape, that he didn't know anything about that piece of paper!'

'It's not all good,' cautioned Dingley. 'Forensics took both flick knives to pieces. Not a scrap of fibre in either to match Rebecca's cut seat belt. The grey paint debris from the bottom of his locker drawer isn't from Parnell's car. And the sheet of paper from his pocketbook isn't a match to that on which the flight number is written.'

'Shit!' said Benton. 'What about other fingerprints on the flight number?'

'None. Just Johnson's half print.'

'That doesn't fit!' insisted Benton at once. 'There would have had to be Rebecca's mark on it!'

'I know,' agreed Dingley. 'So do forensics. They checked every other article in Rebecca's purse. Every one had her prints on it.'

'You think it's time we had another little chat with Harry Johnson?' suggested Benton.

'Not immediately,' decided Dingley. 'Why don't we tell his lawyers we want to see him again in, say, three or four days: that something's come up during ongoing forensic examination that we don't understand? And then listen to the phone taps to hear who he calls?'

'Right!' agreed Benton, at once. 'Why don't we do that?'

'We're killing a lot of mice,' said Ted Lapidus.

'To save a lot of human lives,' said Parnell.

'Mice are genetically our closest match, right?'

'Yes?'

'What happens if they ever take over, start killing us off with their experiments to save their lives?'

'I saw the movie,' said Parnell. 'I thought it was crap.'

'The mice would have loved it.'

'I gather nothing's happening, apart from killing mice?' questioned Parnell.

'Nothing,' confirmed the Greek geneticist.

'Anything from Russell Benn?'

'A hollow echo.'

A week ago, days ago, the impatience would have welled up within him, but now Parnell didn't feel any frustration – not, that is, with his own unit's efforts. But there were outside concerns which he was increasingly coming to believe he had professionally to confront – was remiss, in fact, for not having already done so. 'You got any improved ideas, a quicker approach, I'm listening.'

'I haven't,' Lapidus at once conceded. 'We're expecting too much of ourselves.'

Parnell accepted that wasn't in any way intended as personal criticism, but just as easily recognized it could be taken as such. Although he had not intended to – couldn't remember doing so – he supposed he could have infused his own un-realistic, overambitious expectation into the rest of his team. It would have been a bad professional mistake, if he had. Scientists in a hurry missed things – sometimes the most obvious – and almost invariably made mistakes, went the wrong way. And he was, Parnell acknowledged, thoroughly pissed off with misdirections, reverses instead of progress and, overall, too many dead ends. He couldn't, though, declare a change of approach. *Sorry guys. Got it wrong. Don't go at it like a rat up a drainpipe. Relax. Take every weekend off, leaving early on Friday, start whenever you choose on Monday. Illogical to drive you, as I have been driving you. Too soon out of research science. This is my first managing position. That's my problem. Sorry, like I said.* Unthinkable, Parnell recognized. The sort of soul-baring that would once more – although worse this time – risk the cohesion he believed rebuilt from his last mistake.

He'd talk it through with Beverley. He'd become very comfortable – reliant was a word he refused to consider – in his relationship with Beverley. The guilt hadn't gone but he'd got it compartmented now, packaged and locked away, every-thing under control.

He wasn't sure – didn't in fact believe – that Paris was under control – that what should have been called back had actually been withdrawn. With no contribution he could make to any of the eliminations or tests that were being conducted in his department, he crossed the corridor for another unan-nounced visit to Russell Benn, endured the coffee ritual, and after thirty minutes got the same impression as Lapidus, that the chemical and biological division were not only blocked in a dead end like his own, but that, unlike his own, were

298

content to stay there, gazing at a blank wall until they got an exit map drawn or suggested by someone else.

'You heard from Paris?' Parnell demanded, finally.

'About what?' asked Benn.

'Their misconceived idea.'

Benn's face became fixed. 'Do you see any point in talking about that any more? I thought you'd got your acknowledgement?'

'I don't want acknowledgement. I want to be told – and convinced – that none of it got out on to the market.'

'Ask Paris. Or Dwight. I'm very definitely out of that loop and don't want to be caught up in it again.'

Which was what Parnell did the moment he returned to his own unit, curious at the strength of Benn's rejection. As on the one previous occasion, Parnell's connection to the French chief executive was immediate, although Henri Saby's response was noticeably more restrained on this occasion.

'What's the difficulty?' demanded the Frenchman, the clipped English perfectly modulated.

'I don't know that there is one,' said Parnell.

'What, then?'

'I received the missing test samples.'

'You acknowledged that. And gave me the results,' reminded Saby.

'When we talked the last time, you told me there were batch designations from which you could tell if everything had been withdrawn? If, in fact, there had been any release?' reminded Parnell, in return.

'Yes?'

'I thought by now all the checks and comparisons would have been carried out, through your marketing division and against their records?'

'Is French marketing a matter for the head of Dubette's pharmacogenomics?'

Too quick an answer – and the wrong answer, decided Parnell, feeling the first lurch of positive concern. 'Yes, when Dubette's pharmacogenomics unit discovered what could have caused human, not to say a commercial, damage to that marketing!'

'I'm sorry,' the Frenchman immediately retreated. 'I did not wish to sound discourteous. I have already been in contact with New York. And with your vice president.'

'Yes?' questioned Parnell.

'I think we're straying outside the proper channels of communication, as I believe we did when we last spoke.'

'It's a simple question,' persisted Parnell, careless of the irritation. 'Have you got it all back or haven't you?' He didn't need to be told, Parnell decided.

'Let's remain within the proper channels of communication,' refused Saby, outright.

'You're . . .' started Parnell, too loudly, but stopped.

'What were you about to say?' demanded the Frenchman.

'We're in the wrong channel of communication,' said Parnell. Certainly you are, you evasive bastard, he thought, only slightly venting his feelings by slamming down the telephone. He slammed the office door, too, startling everyone in the laboratory on his way out.

Parnell was prepared for another waiting-room sit-in, but Dwight Newton didn't keep him waiting, frowning up at the obvious anger when Parnell thrust into his office.

'It got out, didn't it?' challenged Parnell, immediately. 'Some of that French shit got distributed and hasn't all been got back? How much? Where? What's being done?' Parnell ended with his hands on Newton's desk, leaning over towards the man, who visibly pulled back in his chair.

'Sit down,' said Newton, weakly. 'Why don't you sit down?'

'I don't want to sit down! I want the answers to the questions!' Why had he left it? There'd always been the nagging doubt, but he hadn't responded to it, as he should have done. Which virtually made him as guilty as everyone else.

'Please sit down,' repeated Newton. He felt beaten, exhausted, too tired to use his authority or fight any more.

Parnell did sit but stayed forward in his chair, demandingly. 'What are the answers, Dwight. Saby's just told me you know it all.'

The research vice president shook his head. 'Not everything. People are still working on it, to get it all back. It'll get done.'

'Where?' demanded Parnell.

'Africa. Just Africa.'

'Just Africa!' echoed Parnell, incredulous. 'Africa's an entire fucking continent! Which countries in Africa, for Christ's sake?'

'I don't know, not precisely. New York does, I think. I guess it'll be East Africa. That's where the French have their colonial links, isn't it?'

Parnell forced the control, determined against overlooking anything in his fury. 'How much?'

'I'm not sure.'

'How much, Dwight?'

'I told you I'm not sure. Maybe a few thousand doses.'

'A few thousand doses of *each*? Or a few thousand in total?'

'I'm not sure,' parroted Newton. 'I've told you, it's being gotten back.'

'It's been weeks now! There's no way of knowing how much has been used – what's been started!'

He knew how to escape, Newton abruptly decided. All very simple, very easy. Why had it taken him so long? Too long. Still time. He'd just get out. Quit. Grant couldn't force him to stay. No one could. Premature retirement, like Harry Johnson from the police force. Be simple enough to get a physician's note if he needed one. Couldn't imagine that he would. Maybe something official involving his pension or severance or stock-option valuation. His lawyer could handle all that. His lawyer and his doctor – that was their job. Newton actually felt a physical relief at the jumbled thoughts, unaware that he was slightly smiling.

'What the hell's so funny?' demanded Parnell.

'I'm sorry . . . nothing . . . I wasn't smiling.'

'You're not making sense!' protested Parnell.

'I don't know it all. New York's handling it. But I know it's under control.'

'How the hell can it be under control when there are thousands of doses unaccounted for!'

'I told you, they're being gotten back.'

'There's got to be a public warning!' insisted Parnell.

301

'Everything's got to be named and warnings issued, to prescribing doctors and pharmacies. Public notices.'

Newton felt quite calm now, as if he were discussing something in which he was quite uninvolved. 'You're probably right. But I don't have that authority. Only New York could initiate a programme like that.'

'Then New York's got to do it,' insisted Parnell.

'I'll speak to them,' said Newton.

'Do I have your word on that, Dwight? We're talking urgency here!'

'I know. You've got my word. I promise I'll speak to New York. If they can't assure me everything's been recovered, I'll talk about public warnings.'

'Maybe we should both speak to New York?'

'I'll suggest that, too,' undertook Newton.

'Don't suggest it!' pleaded Parnell. 'Make it happen!'

'Or what?' picked up Newton. In a week – just days – he'd be away from all this.

'Or someone's got to,' said Parnell.

'Yes?'

'Are you alone? Able to talk?'

'Yes. What is it?'

'They want to see me again.'

'So?'

'It's something about forensics.'

'So?'

'I don't know what they've got, Mr Grant.' The tone was wheedling, subservient.

'What could they have?'

'Nothing, I don't think.'

'We've talked everything through.'

'I don't want anything to come out wrong . . . for Dubette, I mean.'

'I don't want that either, Harry. That's why we're talking like we are talking now. Why you have this number, so we can protect Dubette at all times. You got anything more to tell me?'

'I want to know you're with me.'

'When have I ever not been?'

'I just want to know.'

'You know. What about Clarkson?'

'He's OK.'

'He's top of the tree.'

'I guess.'

'When are you seeing the FBI again?'

'Coupla days. Three.'

'Let me know.'

'It'll be the flight number . . . something about the fucking flight number.'

'Remember.'

'Yes.'

'It happened. What's the problem?'

'OK.'

'Let me know, OK?'

'OK.'

'Edward C. Grant, the president of Dubette Inc. himself!' said Benton, turning off the wire-tap replay.

'I haven't been up to New York in quite a while,' said Dingley.

'Time we went again,' said Benton.

Thirty-Two

Dwight Newton had risked doubling the dose of the strongest tranquillizers Dubette made, welcoming the light-headed feeling of unreality and sure he could hold on for what he had to do. He was tempted to take a third but didn't, knowing he couldn't afford a mistake. It had been sensible as well to talk first about what he intended, with both his personal physician and his lawyer, although he was disappointed at the blood-pressure reading his doctor had insisted upon taking, despite it supporting the reason for his quitting Dubette. But because Dubette manufactured it, he knew the prescribed calcium antagonist would keep it under control. The word stayed in Newton's uneven mind. That was what he was going to do, just minutes from now: free himself of Dubette's control. Not Dubette's, Newton corrected himself immediately: the tentacle-encircling control of Edward C. Grant. He smiled emptily at people he didn't know entering the corporate building, and again in the elevator, and when Grant's personal assistant suggested it was going to be a nice day, Newton replied that he was sure it was going to be a very nice day indeed, pleased at the quickness of his reply.

Grant was at his favourite vantage point, at the penthouse window, when Newton entered, and he stayed looking out over the Manhattan skyline for several moments, even though he knew Newton was in the room. When he finally turned, there was a faint although satisfied smile on his face, and Newton thought, the supercilious son of a bitch thinks he's king of all he surveys.

The expression went at once. Grant said: 'What's so important you had to come all the way to New York when I hadn't asked you to?'

Newton was uncertain at the quickness. He hadn't rehearsed what he was going to say and wanted to get it over with as soon as possible, but at the same time he'd hoped for a slightly longer lead-up, to savour the eventual moment. 'I'm resigning, asking for premature retirement, whatever you want to call it!'

'You're what?' exclaimed Grant, smiling in disbelief.

'Quitting Dubette,' declared Newton. He took the envelope from inside his jacket and pushed it across the overly large desk towards the now seated president. 'Here's the formal letter.' Newton wished his hands and face hadn't felt so numb. Still in control, though. Knew what he was doing. Saying.

'Sit down, Dwight,' ordered Grant. 'Sit down and let's talk.'

It was practically a replay of his conversation with Parnell, remembered Newton. He didn't like it having to appear that he was obeying the man. 'There's nothing to talk about.'

'I think there's a lot to talk about,' said Grant. 'I won't have things sprung on me like this.'

Newton nodded towards the untouched envelope. 'I'm not

304

springing anything on anyone. I'm sick. Severe hypertension's the most obvious. It's all set out in there, in a supporting letter from my doctor.'

'Hypertension is easily treated,' dismissed Grant.

'It isn't my only problem.' Or yours, he thought. He'd expected more immediate anger from the man and was glad it hadn't come. All he wanted now was to get out, back to Washington. He'd take another tranquillizer on the plane.

'I got the impression that things weren't right,' said Grant.

Newton was confused by the remark, not understanding it. 'Then you can't be surprised.'

'Barbara didn't think it was this bad.'

The response silenced Newton. His last formal assessment with Barbara Spacey had been months ago, just before the last seminar. And until now he hadn't known Grant received personal copies. 'My recollection is that she had little to remark upon from our previous session.' He was sure that's what she'd written.

'Easily aroused irritability. A tendency to believe himself manipulated,' quoted Grant.

'I don't recollect that in my copy of her assessment,' protested Newton, his control faltering.

'It was in my account,' stated Grant, simply.

'You have . . . ?' started Newton, running out of words in his astonishment at the apparent disclosure that those seemingly pointless, repetitive encounters with the tent-attired psychologist were Grant's way literally to get inside selected people's minds. 'So, you're not surprised,' he managed.

'You're my vice president supervising everything that's ongoing in Dubette research and development,' said Grant. 'Is it likely that I am going to agree to your leaving, taking with you everything that you know?'

'You don't have to remind me of the confidentiality agreement. I had it all re-explained to me by my lawyer, yesterday. I'm not looking for another job, with another pharmaceutical company. I'm getting out of the business. Quitting, like I told you.'

'You've discussed it with your lawyer?' Grant's voice rose for the first time, although only slightly.

305

'And my doctor.'

'I don't want you to go, Dwight. Won't allow you to go. I want you to have a full medical at the centre at McLean, talk to Barbara again maybe, and we'll get whatever seems to be the problem out of the way.'

'I'm going,' insisted Newton, sure his voice didn't betray the nervousness an encounter with the other man always engendered. 'I've just told you I've talked with a lawyer. His advice is that you can't legally hold me.'

Grant frowned. 'I think my lawyers might disagree.'

'Do you want to put that to the test, in court?' Newton's voice still gave no hint of his inward, hollowing turmoil. It was difficult to believe he was confronting Grant like this.

'I wasn't threatening, Dwight. Why don't you tell me what you want?'

The Edward C. Grant approach to any difficulty, thought Newton: beat it into submission or buy it. 'I told you what I want. I want – intend – to leave.'

'The board have got to agree the surrender period of stock options,' said Grant. 'If we agree their immediate valuation, you'd lose a lot of money.'

'That is a threat,' recognized Newton. 'And you know what? I don't give a damn. I'm gone. And you know something else? There's nothing you can do about it . . .' He hesitated. 'This worm's turned.' And the moment he said it, he wished he hadn't. But it didn't matter. Only getting away from Grant mattered. And he was going to do it. Going to escape.

Grant sniggered. 'You sure as hell are upset, aren't you? I don't ever remember calling you a worm. But if that's what you think of yourself as . . .' He shrugged, intentionally not continuing.

'Not as upset as you might be,' said Newton, desperate to recover. 'Parnell knows we haven't got all the French stuff back. He wants a public warning . . .'

'*What!*' exclaimed Grant, the carefully controlled anger exploding at last.

'He wanted to come with me. Make the demand in person.'

'Who told him?'

He'd done it, thought Newton, triumphantly: he'd knocked Edward C. Fucking Grant off his self-satisfied, unassailable perch. 'He talked to Paris. Saby. Saby refused to say either way. Told him to talk to me. Or you.'

'And you confirmed it!'

'I told him it was being gotten back. I don't intend causing Dubette any more harm than it's already suffered.'

'How about I refuse your resignation and fire you, instead? No pension, no stock-option recovery?'

'How about I sue you for wrongful dismissal, get everything discussed in open court? Or would that make driving dangerous for me before we got there?' Brilliant! That was absolutely brilliant, and Newton knew, despite the light-headedness, that he'd stopped the other man dead in his tracks.

Grant's face didn't redden. The reverse. It whitened, almost unnaturally, making him appear ghoulish. 'I told you . . .'

'I know what you told me,' refused Newton, astonished at his own bravery and further emboldened by it. 'Just as I know there's no proof, no way even of tracing the money it must have cost, which was misspent anyway because it's cost you double in lost stock value. But Dubette – you personally – couldn't withstand the accusation, could you? Just as another fatal car accident – any fatal accident – would be too much of a coincidence. Don't worry. I'm not going to make any accusations, any more than you are going to fire me. You're going to accept my resignation, on grounds of ill health. And you know what I think I'd like, in addition? I'd like a reference to it, at the stockholders' meeting. Some official regret, at my departure. And an acknowledgement, appreciation for everything I've done. After all, I have done a lot, haven't I?'

'You're right,' said Grant, hoarse-voiced. 'The worm has turned, hasn't it?'

More than knocked him off his perch, Newton thought, euphorically. He'd done something he'd never believed possible, and emerged superior in a confrontation with Edward C. Grant. 'What you're looking at now is its ass.'

'I'll tie you up in so many legal restrictions and restraints, you'll think you're a Christmas turkey!'

'You force me, I'll contest them in court,' Newton threatened back. He had to get out soon. He didn't think he could hold on much longer.

'Get out!'

'Don't forget Parnell wants an answer. Or what a problem he can be.'

'Get out!'

'I'll tell him to speak to you direct, shall I? And don't forget my official acknowledgement at the stockholders' meeting.'

Grant sat unspeaking, spectre-like, behind his overpowering desk.

Newton rose but didn't immediately turn. 'This has almost made up for all the hell I've gone through working for you, Ed. Almost. But not enough. I don't think there'd ever be enough.'

'Get out!' yelled Grant, yet again.

Newton thought there was a falter in the hoarseness of the other man's voice, but wasn't sure. Perhaps he was hoping too much. He had, after all, achieved more than he'd ever imagined possible. There was a water cooler in the vestibule and Newton knew he couldn't wait until he got on the plane. Hurrying to it, he gulped the third tranquillizer, grateful there was a cab immediately outside on Wall Street, because his eyes suddenly began to fog and his vision to ebb and flow.

Richard Parnell had been surprised – and encouraged – to learn from another attempt to talk to the man that Newton was in New York less than forty-eight hours after their confrontation. But within three hours of his arriving at McLean that morning, there was a deflection from his most immediate concern, with the smiling presence of Ted Lapidus at the now open office door.

'We haven't stopped killing mice, but we're slowing it down,' announced the Greek. 'I'm trying not to get excited.'

Parnell was greeted in the main laboratory by the rest of the dedicated research team, all smiling as well.

Lapidus said: 'It's Sean's show. He should tell you.'

The Japanese-American said: 'This could be premature, a fluke. I'm not ringing any bells and don't think we should for a long time yet. But I've prolonged the life of six SARS-infected mice, so far for seven days. Two weeks ago I had same-day mortality.'

'Vaccination?' asked Parnell, immediately.

Sato nodded. 'There was no way – or proper reason – to imagine we could reduce the virulence. It was far too fierce. Because of that, I concentrated on killing the virus completely . . .'

'The rest of us tried the Jenner approach to smallpox, infecting with something closely allied but not fatal,' broke in Lapidus, predictably. 'Nothing worked.'

'I boiled a selection of samples of the SARS virus in variously concentrated acids,' resumed Sato. 'The mice I've got still alive this morning were vaccinated by the virus sample killed by an acid ratio of twenty per cent.'

'What's their condition?' asked Parnell.

'They're sick,' conceded Sato, at once. 'They're going to die. But I think we're going in the right direction.'

'How are you following it?' It could lead to a vaccine, accepted Parnell. Why, he wondered, hadn't Beverley told him of the progress? And immediately answered himself. She was part of a team – which he wasn't, yet – and hadn't allowed their personal involvement to influence her professionally. Which was the same rule that he and Rebecca had so briefly tried to follow, he reminded himself, uncomfortably.

'Further minimal dilution,' said Sato.

'Which I think some of us should switch over to,' said Lapidus.

'I agree,' decided Parnell, at once. 'You tried DNA colour-tagging?'

'Far too soon,' frowned Sato. 'This is the first time we've kept our mice alive for more than a day.'

'Too impatient,' apologized Parnell, at once. 'As Ted said, it's exciting. We're taking blood samples, though, for DNA mutations? And matching, for eventual colouring?'

'We will be, from now on, from our six survivors,' said Lapidus.

'We're talking SARS,' isolated Parnell. 'What about avian flu?'

'Bev and I have been trying the same route,' said Deke Pulbrow. 'The avian virus is a big bastard with muscles. We're not getting anywhere.'

'Edward Jenner virtually invented vaccination by preventing smallpox with the injection of the far less virulent cowpox, over two hundred and fifty years ago,' said Parnell, speaking the thought aloud as it came to him. 'We've been concentrating on the 1918 virus because the haemagglutinin has been discovered. There's a lot of samples from the other two pandemics, in 1957 and 1968. Why don't we spend a little time following Jenner, obviously reducing toxicity, but seeing what happens when we vaccinate with one of the previous outbreak viruses and then infecting with this latest one?'

'We haven't tried it so far,' said Beverley. 'So why not?'

'We're behind, on SARS, according to the published papers,' reminded Lapidus.

'I thought we'd decided we're not in a race?' said Parnell. 'There'd be more than enough room in the marketplace for two products if we came in second. Third, even.' He was thinking like a commercially orientated scientist, Parnell realized, surprised. Newton would be pleased. What he was being told *was* exciting, but it would be premature to talk about it to the research director this early.

'At last we've got a focus, for each set of experiments,' declared Lapidus.

'We *hope* it's a focus,' qualified Parnell. 'I think it's good. Well done. Let's see where it takes us.'

Parnell waited until mid-afternoon before approaching Newton's office again. The secretary told him the vice president had called to say he was sick and wouldn't be returning to the office that day. He wasn't sure he would be in the following day, either.

Dingley and Benton separately compared the transcript of the automatically recorded conversation between the Metro DC control-room dispatcher and the arresting squad car with their previous interview statements from Harry Johnson, Helen Montgomery and Peter Bellamy.

Benton looked up first and said: 'The dispatcher didn't say anything about Rebecca's car being forced over the edge of any gorge.'

'Bellamy and the woman only said they *thought* it had been mentioned,' reminded Dingley. 'That they weren't sure.'

'Johnson was more definite,' argued Benton.

'It's not a smoking gun,' insisted Dingley.

'Something that might unsettle them, along with Johnson's thumb print and the internal investigation,' said Benton.

'We do them first or pay a visit to Edward C. Grant?' wondered Dingley.

'Them first,' proposed Benton. 'We might prompt another call from Johnson to New York. 'I'd like a damned sight more than that first conversation.'

'I'd like a damned sight more about anything,' complained Dingley. 'We're not looking good on this, old buddy. In fact, we're looking downright fucking bad, and I am no longer as glad as I was that we got a case this high-profile.'

'Me neither,' agreed Benton. 'Our problem is what to do with it now that we've got it.'

'I wish I knew,' said Dingley. 'I wish that very much indeed.'

Thirty-Three

It was David Benton's idea to change the previous routine and arrange the interviews with Harry Johnson and the two Metro DC officers to a tightly controlled schedule preventing any intervening exchange between the three. The FBI agents ensured that each of the personal lawyers, as well as the attorneys for Dubette and Metro DC police, knew not just of the agenda but also its sequence, in the hope of unsettling the security chief and the two police officers more successfully than they had previously.

Johnson was first. He wore the same crisply pressed suit as before, but this time there was none of the bravado swagger.

He sat in the field-office interview room between William Clarkson and Peter Baldwin, pointedly avoiding eye contact with either FBI agent, deferring to Clarkson to acknowledge the reminder that he had already been read his Miranda rights against self-incrimination, and also during the discussion about formal recording. Clarkson agreed to the tape procedure and waited until it started before stating that he was aware of the formal warning of a later court challenge from Peter Bellamy's representative, and placing on record the possibility of his entering a matching inadmissibility objection in the event of any charges being proffered against his client.

'I also wish recorded that my client has fully co-operated whenever called upon to do so,' continued Clarkson.

'A co-operation which is noted and which is appreciated,' said Dingley.

'Fact is,' continued Benton. 'We've come up with a few more things that puzzle us. That photograph, of you and Helen and Bellamy, for instance.'

'I declined to allow my client to answer that question,' said Clarkson. 'I continue with that advice.'

'Why is that?' said Dingley.

'It has no bearing on this enquiry whatsoever.'

'It has a very direct bearing on whether Mr Johnson knew or did not know Officers Montgomery and Bellamy before they arrived at Dubette Inc. on the day they arrested Richard Parnell,' said Benton.

'Why?' demanded the lawyer.

'The inconsistency, between what Officers Montgomery and Bellamy have told us – that they knew your client – and his assertion that he didn't know them.'

'I forgot,' burst in Johnson, shrugging off Clarkson's restraining hand. 'It's as simple as that. I think that photograph was taken at my farewell party, a whole bunch of Metro DC police guys having a good time, having a few drinks. Now I've seen the pictures, of course I can remember them, but only as people I saw around. And I didn't recognize them the day they arrived at McLean to ask about Rebecca Lang.'

'Tell us about Edward Grant?' suddenly asked Dingley.

Instantly there was the caught-in-headlights blink of the previous encounter. Clarkson looked enquiringly sideways, but Johnson didn't respond. Peter Baldwin said: 'As the attorney representing Dubette, I'd like an explanation of that question.'

Both agents ignored him. Still talking to the security chief, Dingley repeated: 'Tell us about Edward Grant.'

'What about him?' said Johnson.

'That's what we're asking you,' said Benton.

'I'd like this explained,' Baldwin continued to protest.

'You friendly with him, Harry? Know him socially maybe?'

'This is ridiculous!' said Baldwin.

'Sir!' said Dingley, turning to the company lawyer at last. 'I think we could be very close to a criminal investigation being impeded . . .' He switched back to Johnson. 'What's the answer, Harry? How well do you know the president of Dubette Inc.?'

'Of course I know of him,' said the bulging man. '*Because* he is the president of the company.'

'You know him when you joined Dubette, way back in 1996?'

'No!'

'Even before you joined Dubette, when you were in Metro DC police administration, surrounded with all those computers and records and files?'

'This transcript will be challenged,' declared Clarkson.

'Absolutely,' said Baldwin, supportively.

'We got the court release, Harry. Of all those '96 internal investigations,' said Benton. 'Interesting reading.'

'You got a special relationship with the president, Harry?' picked up Dingley.

'I want . . .' started Baldwin, but Johnson spoke over him. 'I am the head of a division. Of course I know Mr Grant. And he knows me. It's that sort of company.'

'Somebody told us about that, one big happy family,' remarked Benton. 'So, how soon did you get to know Edward Grant, after you joined Dubette.'

'I don't remember, not exactly. A few months, maybe.'

'Even though he spends most of his time in New York?' said Dingley.

'He comes down often enough.'

'That's the only time you see him, the only times you speak?' seized Benton. 'On the occasions when he comes down from New York?'

The blinking had subsided, replaced by the wariness which both agents recognized. Johnson said: 'There've been occasions when we've talked.'

'In New York?' pressed Dingley.

The guardedness stayed, but Johnson shifted in his chair, as if preparing himself. 'I told you before that my section has to be alert for people – drug dependants – trying to enter the premises – gain access in some way. There's another sort of burglary, nothing to do with addiction. Commercial stealing, by competitors. That, in fact, is far more serious than losing a few phials of tranquillizers or stimulants. If a competitor got an informant inside McLean, it could cost the company millions – millions in wasted research expenditure and millions more if someone else got the product on to the market first. That's how – and why – Mr Grant and I talk sometimes.'

'How, you going to New York?' asked Dingley. 'Or when he comes down to Washington?'

'I don't go to New York. When he comes down to Washington. Sometimes by phone.'

'Where is this taking us?' demanded Baldwin.

Once more the agents ignored the intervention. Benton said to Baldwin: 'Mr Grant obviously knows about your involvement in this case. Have you and he spoken about it?'

'I have been keeping New York informed of every aspect of the enquiry, to the extent to which I know about it,' said Baldwin.

'Has Mr Grant spoken to you about it?' asked Dingley.

'Through Dwight Newton I know that he was – and continues to be – extremely distressed, as does the rest of the board,' said the company lawyer. 'Mr Grant ordered that every assistance be given, to everyone involved. He even offered to pay for Rebecca's funeral and the reception afterwards. The family declined.'

The switch back to Harry Johnson was like a whip snap. Dingley said: 'How'd you think part of your left thumb print

314

came to be on the flight number you said you didn't know anything about? The only print, in fact, on that piece of paper found in Rebecca's purse?'

'How . . . ?' began Clarkson, but this time it was Johnson who put his arm sideways, silencing the lawyer.

'I think I know . . .' said Johnson. 'I didn't remember it . . . still don't, not in the way that helps . . . but some time back a shipment from Paris got lost. I got involved looking for it. So did Rebecca: co-ordinating shipments was a part of her job. The actual flight number, as being the one that got involved and cancelled in a terrorist alert, didn't register with me. But I think it was the one that the shipment was supposed to have been on.'

'How long was that before her death?' asked Benton.

'I don't know,' shrugged Johnson. 'Weeks, I guess.'

'Was the shipment found?'

'Yes,' said Johnson, at once. 'It was a customs mix-up, at the French end.'

'So, why did Rebecca keep the number in her purse?' said Benton.

Johnson shrugged again. 'I haven't any idea. I didn't even know it was there until you told me. And even then couldn't account for it.'

'As you have now?' said Dingley, not trying to hide the disbelief.

'It's the best, the only, explanation I can give you,' said Johnson, no longer unsettled. 'I realize my not being able to account for it until now might have caused some confusion, misled you even. I'm really very sorry about that.'

'It seems perfectly understandable to me,' said Clarkson. 'I see it as yet another example of my client doing every-thing he can to co-operate and help an ongoing criminal investigation.'

Once again the similarity between the answers of Helen Montgomery and Peter Bellamy indicated close rehearsal. And once again the interviews were cluttered with inter-ventions and objections by their respective lawyers. There was no contradiction between the two officers as to who

315

listed the contents of Rebecca Lang's handbag: the woman said she itemized everything, for Bellamy to create the inventory.

'How, exactly, did you do that?' Dingley asked Helen Montgomery. 'Did you take things out individually, one at a time? Or what?'

'I think I tipped everything out on the table and separated them, piece by piece, for Pete to write down.'

'Separated them how?' asked Benton.

The woman frowned. 'I don't understand.'

'By hand?' prompted Dingley.

'Maybe. Maybe with a pencil, so that they wouldn't be marked. And I kinda think I kept my driving gloves on.'

'You didn't get given that handbag until you got back to the station, right?' said Dingley.

'Right,' she agreed.

'After you'd left Harry Johnson back at McLean?' said Benton.

'Yes.'

'How'd you explain the piece of paper with the AF209 flight number that you told us you found in Rebecca Lang's purse having Harry Johnson's thumb print on it?' said Dingley.

Helen Montgomery showed no uncertainty or surprise. Neither her personal lawyer, Donald Sinclair, nor the Metro DC police attorney intervened.

'Ms Montgomery?' pressed Benton.

'I can't,' said the woman, calmly. 'Haven't you asked Harry?'

Instead of answering, Benton said: 'Did Harry Johnson give that flight number to you at McLean, to put among Rebecca Lang's belongings?'

'That . . .' started Phillip Brack, the police attorney.

'. . . is not an improper or inappropriate question,' refused Benton. 'Please answer it, Ms Montgomery.'

'Absolutely not!' the woman refused, the indignation sounding genuine. 'The first time I saw that piece of paper was when I emptied the purse on to the table. I didn't even know, guess, it was a flight number until I opened it out.'

'So, you did touch it?' demanded Dingley. 'Handled it?'

'Like I said, I think I had my uniform gloves on.'

'And you didn't find it difficult, clumsy, to open a scrap of paper wearing thick leather gloves?'

'I guess not.'

'The Metro DC dispatcher didn't say anything about Ms Lang's car being forced over into a gorge, when you got sent to McLean,' said Benton. 'We got the transcript.'

'I must have got that wrong,' said Helen Montgomery, without any hesitation. 'I think I told you before that I wasn't sure. I must have been told when we got back to the station and got it mixed up in my mind.'

'As a police officer, do you often get things mixed up in your mind?' asked Benton.

'Officer Montgomery declines to answer that question,' said Brack.

'On the instructions of us both,' added her lawyer.

Peter Bellamy was only slightly less assured than his partner, most obviously when Dingley disclosed Johnson's thumb print, and let his lawyer, Hilda Jeffries, reply for him that there was no way he could answer such a question, which should be put to Johnson. She did not let him respond to the accusation that either he or Helen Montgomery had planted the paper after being handed it by Johnson when they first arrived at McLean, protesting that the suggestion was preposterous.

'We got a chink to prise open,' insisted Dingley. It was a sandwich lunch again, both men anxious to review the morning's work, neither of them with any thought of celebrations on 14th Street.

'That big,' objected Benton, narrowing his thumb against his forefinger so closely that there was no visible gap.

'It's something,' insisted Dingley. 'And we've still got Grant.'

'Who'll meet us fully briefed by the company lawyer,' predicted Benton.

'He doesn't know about the telephone tap.'

'Which hasn't produced anything worthwhile to put before a court,' refused Benton. 'So far we haven't learned much

317

more than that Johnson likes telephone sex to jerk off to, and pepperoni and chilli home-delivered pizza.'

'In Italy pepperoni and chilli pizza is probably a crime.'

'Pity it isn't a federal offence here.'

'They're good, all three of them,' reluctantly conceded Dingley, seriously. 'Too damned good.'

'Which is how they got away with everything in 1996.'

'You really think Johnson was on Dubette's payroll, before he left the force?'

'I'd bet my pension on it.'

'If we can't prove that Johnson is lying, about the flight number . . . if all we've got is his explanation . . . then there's no terrorism link, and if there's no terrorism link there's no grounds for FBI involvement,' said Dingley.

'If Grant is in some way involved, it's conspiracy across State lines. And that's us, whether terrorism is in the mix or not,' contradicted Benton.

'According to Ed Pullinger, the gods at the J. Edgar Hoover Building are pissed off up to here with the heat they're getting from the Department of Homeland Security and every media outlet as far away as Outer Mongolia, wherever the hell that is,' said Dingley. 'And you and I ain't got Teflon asses.'

'You don't need to tell me that, either,' said Benton.

'I'm not looking forward to New York as much as I was.'

'Neither am I.'

Richard Parnell had only ever been to Manhattan twice, both times before taking up the Dubette genetics directorship, tourist map in hand, exhausted walking towards skyscraper land-marks he could see but which never appeared to get any closer, like retreating mirages in a high-rise desert. Beverley had promised to take him to the real parts he'd never seen, which served things other than hamburgers and hot dogs, and as the shuttle turned over the bay into Le Guardia, Parnell resolved to take up the promise, uncomfortably yet again remembering Rebecca's mockery of his not knowing America beyond a 17-mile-long traffic lane into north Virginia and a mile walk into Georgetown. Parnell was surprised at the summons to Dubette headquarters, as he was by the continued absence from McLean of Dwight Newton, whose personal assistant was now saying she had no idea when the research vice president would be medically allowed to return.

Which concentrated Parnell's mind on why he was in New York, no longer the tourist. He was glad he was here in person, not trusting Newton as the warning intermediary. How much – how far – could he trust Edward C. Grant, the Big Brother lookalike? Not an immediate consideration. The immediate – absolutely essential – consideration was getting the assurance from the man in authority that every available warning was circulated as widely as possible throughout the African countries they distributed to, about an unknown quantity of potentially fatal medicines. And if he didn't get that assurance, he needed to decide what he personally was going to do. There was nothing really to decide, he thought at once. He supposed he should talk first to Barry Jackson, although ethically the confidentiality restrictions didn't apply and it would be too late for Dubette to invoke them anyway. He had to find his own way to sound the alarm, and as his taxi crossed the Triboro Bridge, he looked down the East River to the United Nations skyscraper and decided that would be a convenient start.

It was a magic-carpet ascent to the penthouse level when Parnell identified himself at the ground-floor reception, the door to Edward Grant's panoramic-view office already open in readiness for his arrival, the smiling, white-haired man slightly back from the doorway to prevent his shortness being too obviously framed in the doorway. Grant only allowed the briefest of handshaking greetings before retreating behind his protective desk.

'This meeting's long overdue,' announced the company president. 'And mine's the fault, for which I apologize. What you did about France was outstanding and I should have personally thanked you long before now. I told you at the seminar, I was expecting great things. I never imagined the proof would be so immediate . . .' The man allowed the break. 'And I also want you to know how very, very sorry I was about Ms Lang and what happened to you.'

'Thank you,' said Parnell.

'I know you refused our legal representation. Your choice. But the offer that was passed on to you remains. Anything Dubette can do . . .'

'That's very generous and I appreciate it,' said Parnell. 'It's France I want to talk about.'

'You spoken to Dwight?'

Parnell shook his head. 'Not since he came here. His office say he's ill.'

'On the very edge of a complete nervous breakdown, according to his doctor. And Dubette's – Barbara Spacey as well – whom I've had see him.'

'I had no idea,' said Parnell.

'None of us did,' said Grant. 'He'll get every treatment, of course.'

'Treatment?' queried Parnell.

'Hospitalization,' said Grant. 'Dwight's seriously unwell. It's going to take a long time. No one can predict how successful the recovery will be. He collapsed, apparently, when he got back from seeing me. A highway patrol found him talking to himself, on a lay-by, the car still running. They thought at first he was drunk.'

The mood switchbacks had always been unpredictable, but Parnell had never suspected Newton to be seriously mentally unwell. 'There's been nothing said . . . no indication . . . at McLean?' Why, Parnell wondered, had Grant asked if he'd spoken to Newton if the man were as ill as this?

'There'd been warnings, from his doctor. That's what he came up to tell me. And to resign as research vice president.'

'Resign?' said Parnell.

'He'd been with Dubette for more than twenty years. His contribution to the company is incalculable . . .' There was another hesitation. 'Can you believe, as sick as he was, coming up here to resign, he still managed to tell me of your concern?'

'Yes I can,' said Parnell, bringing himself back to the purpose – and the determination – of his being in New York. 'I think it should be your concern, too. I'm not convinced the French mistakes have been cleared up. I tried to find out when I spoke to Henri Saby. He told me to talk to Dwight or to you. Dwight said it was still being recovered. Obviously there's

320

a lot still in circulation: thousands of doses, according to Dwight. There's got to be a public statement, a warning. If there's not and there are provable deaths, Dubette could be destroyed . . .' Parnell checked himself, hearing what he was saying. 'The deaths don't have to be provable. People, children, will die if they take the medicines Dubette's French subsidiary has put out on the market.'

'I know,' said Grant.

The simplicity of the answer – and the admission – deflated Parnell's carefully prepared argument. 'What's being done?'

'Newton said everything you've told me, although perhaps not as well,' said Grant. 'As I told you, I'm surprised that, as ill as he was, he managed to tell me anything. I've already spoken to France. They're checking distribution. In any country from which there's not been full recovery, a warning has been issued, through national governments to health authorities and quite separately, through national and local media outlets. Nothing's going to be allowed to remain unaccounted for.'

'You really mean that . . . promise that?' said Parnell.

'Do you have the presumption to question me?' demanded Grant, affronted.

'It's not presumption,' said Parnell, unintimidated. 'It's a very real and genuine concern.'

'Which is precisely what's motivating me. And why I've authorized the action that I have.'

'I . . .' said Parnell, seeking words 'Thank you. For the assurance and for doing . . . Thank you . . .'

'Is it conceivable that I wouldn't?'

'No. I'm still glad to know it's been done.'

'You've proved yourself, Richard. Not in the way I expected, but in a way for which Dubette will be forever grateful.'

'I see it as one of the functions for which I am employed.'

'Dwight won't be coming back,' said Grant. 'He's resigned, as I told you. He'll hopefully recover – he's going to get every care and treatment to ensure that he does – but he'll never be able to resume the responsibility of research director.'

'That's . . . unfortunate. Sad,' said Parnell, at once aware of his own hypocrisy. Practically from his first day at Dubette he'd lost any respect for Newton.

'I want you to take the position,' announced the president. 'You've more than proved your ability. And your integrity, here today.'

'I couldn't be more surprised,' Parnell managed.

'There'll be a salary increase, obviously. And stock options. The lawyers will have to work it out, like they have to work everything out. I'm thinking in the region of six hundred thousand dollars. There'll be travel opportunities, too. I don't want another debacle like Paris. Part of your increased responsibilities will be to visit the overseas subsidiaries – make sure none of them ever come up with such a half-assed idea ever again.'

Parnell shook his head. 'As I've said, I'm totally surprised. Astonished. I need time to think . . .'

'I don't know why, but of course,' said the Dubette president. 'At the stockholders' meeting I'm going to announce Dwight's prematurely enforced retirement. I want to announce your succession at the same time. I don't want any vacuums.'

'You said to call.'

'What was it?' demanded Grant.

'Forensics, like I said. My thumb print was on the flight number.'

'What did you tell them?'

'About the lost shipment.'

'Not a problem, then?'

'Clarkson doesn't think so.'

'What about the other two?'

'Clarkson won't let me speak to them direct. He's spoken to their attorneys. He says they're standing up fine.'

'The FBI want to talk to me.'

'They asked me about you.'

'What did you tell them?'

'That we talked from time to time. About security.'

'Which we do.'

'Yes.'

'Newton's sick. Collapsed. He's leaving the company.'

'What do you want me to do?'

'Nothing. Barbara's seen him. Thinks the treatment will wipe his mind clean. I'm giving the job to Parnell.'

There was a pause from Washington. 'That going to mean any changes?'

'We keep dealing direct, you and I.'

'What about the surveillance?'

'Lift it.'

'Maybe we should talk, after you've seen the FBI?'

'Maybe.'

As before, the line went dead without any farewell.

Thirty-Four

The review preparation was for its later submission to FBI lawyers for their decision, but it enabled Dingley and Benton to fly up to New York fully rehearsed for the meeting with Edward C. Grant. Both men were subdued, no more encouraged by the second intercepted conversation between Grant and Harry Johnson than they were by the first.

Trying to lift the despondency on their way in to Manhattan from the airport, Dingley said: 'We still haven't heard back from Paris. Or Dulles airfreight.'

'You know how high my hopes are for either?' said Benton, once again narrowing his thumb and forefinger too closely for any chink of light.

'I suppose we should call in on the guys at the Broadway field office?' suggested Dingley.

'Let's see how we feel after we've talked with Grant,' said Benton. 'Wakes depress me.'

'Nothing's dead yet.'

'Dying by the minute,' insisted Benton.

Peter Baldwin was the only person with the Dubette president when they were shown into the penthouse office suite. It was the company lawyer who made the introductions but Grant who solicitously led them away from desk-focused

323

formality to the flickering, genuine fireplace around which were arranged leather-upholstered easy chairs and couches. Both agents refused Grant's offer of coffee.

Accustomed to the legal assembly of the previous interviews, Dingley said: 'Are we waiting for others?'

'Who?' frowned Grant.

'I thought . . .' said Dingley, discomfited.

'You're surely not implying Mr Grant requires a criminal attorney?' said Baldwin.

'They seem to have featured a lot during the enquiry,' said Benton, trying to help his partner. 'But no, of course we're not suggesting that. It would have been Mr Grant's right, that's all.'

'I don't think there's any risk to my rights, do you?' smiled the white-haired man.

'We appreciate your agreeing to help us,' said Dingley, their customary opening.

'I'm not quite sure how I can, but let's get on with it, shall we?' said Grant, a busy man with a busy schedule.

'There are some inconsistencies in what Mr Johnson's told us, things we can't quite fit into the puzzle,' said Benton. 'You spoken directly to Mr Johnson since Ms Lang's death?'

'Yes,' said Grant, at once. 'I think he believed it was his job to do so. I agreed.'

'How many times?' asked Dingley.

'Twice,' frowned Grant, as if he had difficulty in recalling. 'Yes, twice.'

'Did you speak about the flight number in Ms Lang's purse, which is the reason for FBI involvement?'

There was another frown. 'There was some mention, I think. I can't remember precisely what the context was.'

'His thumb print was on it,' said Benton. 'He'd earlier told us he didn't know anything about a number or why it should have been in Ms Lang's bag.'

'Really?' remarked Grant. And stopped.

'Did you and Harry Johnson specifically discuss the flight number?' asked Benton.

'We might have done, after it emerged in court. I really can't remember.'

'We're surprised at the direct communication between you and your security chief,' declared Dingley.

'Why?' demanded the man.

'You're the head of an international conglomerate. Harry Johnson is head of security at McLean,' said Dingley. 'That seems quite a divide.'

'You a snob, Mr Dingley?'

'I don't believe myself to be, sir,' said the FBI man.

'Sounds like it to me,' said Grant. 'I run a different sort of organization than a lot of people – than perhaps the FBI. I *want* my chief executives and division heads to talk to me. That way problems get solved before they become problems.'

'So, it's not unusual for you and Harry to speak?' persisted Dingley.

'Not at all.'

'How often would you say?'

'Whenever it's necessary,' shrugged Grant.

'How? He come up here to report to you direct? When you're in Washington? Telephone?'

'Whichever's convenient,' shrugged the president, again. 'I always make a point of speaking to every division head in Dubette whenever I'm down there. And there's the telephone.'

'Did you know Harry Johnson before he joined Dubette from Metro DC police department?' asked Benton.

'*Before?*'

'That was my question, sir.'

'How could I have known him before?'

'We thought you might have done,' said Dingley.

'What reason do you have for thinking that?' came in Baldwin.

'Just an impression,' said Benton.

'I thought the FBI worked on the basis of evidence and facts,' said Grant. 'I did not know Harry Johnson before he joined Dubette.'

'How did that come about, his joining Dubette?' asked Dingley.

'The previous security chief was retiring. Recommended Harry. He seemed to fit the bill.'

'Who employed him? You personally? Or your personnel division?' pressed Benton.

'It would have been personnel, obviously,' said Grant.

'Eighty thousand dollars a year is a substantial salary.'

'He heads what is considered an important division. Dubette is noted throughout the industry as a substantial payer.'

'You seem well informed about how Harry Johnson came to be employed,' said Benton.

'I'm well informed about every senior employee at Dubette,' said Grant. 'Perhaps security more than most. Security is very important for a company like mine.'

'Because of stealing and commercial theft and piracy,' anticipated Benton.

'Precisely,' agreed Grant.

'You suffer a lot of it?'

'We take every precaution to ensure that we don't.'

'When was the last time?' asked Dingley, building up to what he and his partner hoped to be the puncturing question.

There was the now familiar shrug. 'There was some warehouse pilfering about three months ago.'

'Did you get the guys?' asked Benton.

'It was a delivery driver, supplying pills to kids. He drew a year. I'd have liked it to have been more. I know the danger of drugs as well as their benefits.'

'What about commercially?' said Dingley.

'Last attempt was three years ago. A competitor got an informant into McLean. Harry got him before there was any serious damage.'

'I can't imagine Richard Parnell would steal pills from a Dubette warehouse,' said Benton.

'*What?*' exclaimed Grant, astonished.

'We can't imagine Richard Parnell stealing pills from a warehouse,' echoed Dingley. 'Why was he under surveillance, Mr Grant?'

Grant looked first to Baldwin, then to the huge desk with its orderly bank of variously coloured telephones.

Baldwin said: 'We'd like an explanation for that question.'

'We'd like an answer to it,' said Dingley. 'We know of Richard Parnell being under surveillance. And of Harry

326

Johnson being aware of it. It's extremely relevant to our terrorism and murder enquiries and we need to know why.'

'Are you bugging my telephones?' demanded Grant, looking back to his desk.

'No,' replied Benton, honestly.

'So, it's Harry's,' said Grant, answering his own question.

'For which I hope you have a court order,' said Baldwin.

'Of course we do,' said Dingley, impatiently.

'Harry Johnson has explained to you how his thumb print came to be on the flight number,' said the lawyer.

'Which you've doubtless told Mr Grant in detail,' anticipated Benton. 'What no one's explained to us yet is why Parnell was under surveillance, with Harry Johnson's knowledge. And yours, Mr Grant.'

'I would have thought that would have been obvious,' said the man.

'Not to us it isn't,' said Dingley.

Grant sighed, all the condescending affability gone. 'A valued member of my company was murdered. An elaborate effort was made to frame a senior executive for that murder, for which, as I understand it, you have no suspects. I believed that Parnell might remain in danger. I felt it justified the setting up of some protective security – having photographs taken, even, to see if Parnell might be being watched by a person or a group of people. It's been pointless . . .' The man paused, looking to the telephone bank again. 'And, as you obviously know, I've spoken to Harry about it – told him to lift everything.'

'So, you no longer fear Richard Parnell is in danger?' said Dingley.

'I think it would have happened, some attempt would have been made, by now,' said the Dubette president. 'I was being overprotective.'

'Having Parnell under surveillance wouldn't have actually prevented anything happening to him, would it?' said Benton.

'It would if it had established he was being stalked.'

'These photographs,' said Benton, 'who's been taking them?'

'A private detective agency,' said Grant.

'We'd like its name,' said Dingley.

'Get it from Harry,' snapped Grant. 'I don't know it.'

'I'm surprised that you don't, as closely as you and Harry liaise,' said Dingley.

Grant sighed again but didn't speak, looking pointedly at the lawyer.

Baldwin said: 'Is there anything else with which we can help you?'

'During your conversation with Harry Johnson, you asked, and I quote, "What about the other two?" What other two would that be, Mr Grant?' said Benton.

'The two suspended Metro DC police officers, obviously,' said the man.

'Why were you curious about them?' pressed Benton.

'The suggestion is that they mistreated . . . wrongly arrested . . . a senior Dubette executive, isn't it?'

'And part of Johnson's reply to your question, and again I quote, is, "He . . ." – he being Clarkson, Harry Johnson's lawyer – ". . . says they're standing up fine." What did you understand from that reply, Mr Grant?'

'I'm not sure that I understood anything from it.'

'You asked about them, Johnson gives you a reply you don't understand, and you don't ask him to explain it?' pressed Dingley.

'No, I didn't,' said Grant.

'Do you still find it difficult to understand, now that we're talking about it? Now that you've had time to think about it?' said Benton.

'Yes,' said Grant.

'Before Johnson says that the two Metro DC officers are standing up well, he says, and again I quote, "Clarkson won't let me speak to them direct,"' persisted Benton. 'We've got two police officers who are alleged to have mistreated – wrongly arrested – a senior member of Dubette's staff, and Harry Johnson wants to talk to them. But then tells you they're standing up fine. You know how that looks, to my partner and I, Mr Grant? It looks like there was collusion between the three. Wouldn't you say that's an interpretation?'

'I don't think Mr Grant can usefully speculate, as you are

speculating,' said the lawyer. 'What I do think is that there is an obvious inference that, if it is pursued, could result in consideration of the sort of court action in which a quite separate claim has already been mounted, which could seriously embarrass you two gentlemen personally, and your already seriously embarrassed, ineffective employer, the FBI, to a far greater degree.'

'The question was put to Mr Grant, who has not answered,' said the unintimidated Benton.

'I think Mr Baldwin has already adequately answered on my behalf,' refused Grant. 'What I would say is that I think it is very fortunate for you both that I did not bother to include criminal lawyers in this interview.'

'Which is concluded at this time,' declared Baldwin. 'If the Federal Bureau of Investigation seeks to resume it, it will be conducted in the different sort of circumstances that Mr Grant has indicated.'

Outside the Dubette building, on Wall Street, Dingley said: 'You fancy calling in on the guys? Broadway's only just up the road.'

'Why don't we just get on back?' said Benton.

'Yeah, why don't we?' agreed Dingley.

Beverley Jackson was the only one in the pharmacogenomics division to know of Parnell's visit to New York, and then not in detail, because he maintained his decision not to involve her – or anyone else – any further in the French near-disaster. And there was in any case something far more immediate when he arrived back at McLean.

'Why are they dying again so quickly when they're vaccinated by lesser-strength preparations?' Parnell rhetorically asked Sean Sato. 'It doesn't make sense!' The disappointment was palpable throughout the laboratory.

'I said the six we kept alive could have been a fluke,' reminded Sato. 'I've gone back to the twenty per cent ratio.'

'What about blood from those that survived longer?' demanded Parnell. 'Any specific molecular assault?'

'None,' said Lapidus. 'We can't attempt to colour match the new tests, because we don't have a suspect DNA host.'

'What about those that died subsequently?'

'Nothing,' said Deke Pulbrow.

'What about the brief survivors?' persisted Parnell. 'Anything different about them from the others who subsequently died? Anything about their strain, breed suppliers, diet, anything at all like that?' He was conscious of the anxiety in his own voice.

'Everything checked, even their comparable weights and ages,' said Beverley. 'Nothing.'

'We started yet, with the twenty per cent ratio?'

Sato shook his head. 'We waited, to talk it through with you.'

'Let's follow blood,' suggested Parnell. 'Isolate the mice, individually. No urine or faeces contamination between any. Strictly measured and itemized food. Blood tests from all, before infecting with SARS. And daily – no, half-daily – sampling after infecting, for DNA comparison between those treated and those untreated.'

'Which assumes there will be a survival over a period of days,' commented Lapidus.

'We'll have an additional test,' Parnell pointed out. 'We've got the blood of the first survival group. If we don't get a DNA profile somewhere out of that, life's not fair.'

'My mother always told me that it wasn't,' said Pulbrow. 'And my mother was always right.'

It was not until two nights later, when they were eating once more at Beverley's favourite midtown restaurant, that Parnell told her of Dwight Newton's breakdown and Edward Grant's offer.

'Poor Dwight,' was Beverley's first reaction. 'I hardly knew him, and what I did know I didn't particularly like, but to be too ill to work again is a rough call.'

'It's not going to be announced until after the stockholders' meeting,' warned Parnell.

'I'm not likely to tell anyone,' promised the woman. 'What about you? You going to take it?'

'I haven't decided, not yet.'

'Vice president responsible for research and development

in just under a year!' she said, with faint mockery. 'The upward rise of Richard Parnell continues!'

'If I take it.'

'Of course you'll take it!'

'We'll see. You coming back tonight?'

'I thought you'd never ask! I was beginning to wonder if it was all over.'

When they entered Parnell's apartment, Beverley went at once to the lidded laptop on the bureau and said: 'Hey, what's this! Dubette's new vice president has got himself a new toy!'

'It's convenient,' said Parnell. 'I can access anything I want at McLean and download it here if I want. I should have thought of it before.'

'You know what they say about all work and no play.'

'It's turned off, isn't it?' said Parnell, uncomfortably reminded yet again of Rebecca's similar remark.

'If it wasn't, I'd turn it off,' said Beverley. 'I want to play.'

'So, it's a no-no?' demanded Dingley, when Ed Pullinger finished telling them the legal opinion.

'On what you've got so far,' confirmed the lawyer. 'After the shit we got following nine–eleven we're not going to move on anything we can't come out of with haloes and marching music. Everything here would be challenged, discredited or ruled inadmissible, and we'd lose. Lose, that is, if the Attorney General would even consider a Grand Jury, let alone any court hearing. You know what you've got here? You've got a hell of a lot that could help Barry Jackson in his civil action, diddly squat for a criminal prosecution. And that's disappointing everyone at the J. Edgar Hoover building, because this is high-profile and all we're getting is more shit.'

'You thought of talking to Barry Jackson? Parnell maybe?' asked Benton.

'And risk my pension?' smiled the lawyer.

'Who would ever know?' asked Dingley.

Barry Jackson called Parnell at McLean just before lunch the following day. The lawyer said: 'Just got a call from the FBI. Might be an idea for you to come along.'

Thirty-Five

'So, what *have* you got?' demanded Barry Jackson, exasperated, when the FBI lawyer finally stopped talking. They had been, for more than thirty minutes, in Barry Jackson's office, all the calls held. Neither Jackson nor Parnell had spoken throughout, until now.

'A conspiracy, of some sort,' said Ed Pullinger. 'It's what sort – to achieve what result – that we don't know. And don't at the moment think we can find out.'

'Are you saying that Johnson, the two police officers, and Edward Grant conspired to kill Rebecca?' demanded Parnell, as incredulous as his lawyer.

'No,' denied Pullinger, at once. 'I've just told you we don't know ... haven't got sufficient to prove anything against anyone. But there's something there to prove ... very definitely something that isn't right.'

'The fingerprint, on the flight number,' seized Jackson. 'Johnson says he'd given it to Rebecca but forgotten about it, some time ago. Forensically it's possible to distinguish between old and new fingerprints.'

'We know that. We also know that it's new, not something given to Rebecca weeks ago ...'

'So, he's lying!' broke in Parnell.

'Yes, he's lying,' agreed the FBI attorney. 'But why? A consignment scheduled on that flight did go missing: Charles de Gaulle airport confirm it and Dulles airport confirm it and Paris customs admit it was their fault.'

'There was a foul-up over a shipment,' remembered Parnell, dull-voiced. 'Rebecca used it as an excuse to call Paris direct, to try to find out what the mystery was.'

'And it got found,' said Pullinger. 'If we had a case to bring – if there'd been a fibre match from the flick knife or if the paint in Johnson's locker had matched your car – the lie about the flight number being old would be something to introduce. As it is, it's nothing except another question we can't answer.'

'Rebecca never dealt with Johnson, as far as 1 know. The only shipments he worried about were those addressed to the box number.'

'As far as you know,' echoed Pullinger. 'A lost consignment is the sort of thing a security man would get involved in.'

'A security *man*,' Parnell echoed back. 'Not the *head* of security.'

'Not according to Grant,' refused Pullinger. 'He told our guys security is one of the most important divisions in a business like Dubette's. It would be an easy argument to make, that Johnson was involved without Rebecca's knowledge.'

'How'd Johnson get over two hundred and fifty thousand dollars in his account?' demanded Jackson.

'He gets eighty thousand a year and says he's a lucky gambler. He's quoted us winning horses and Las Vegas visits when we've challenged him on substantial cash deposits. The horses *did* win. And hotel reservations match the dates against the name Harry Johnson. As well as the credit-card charges with his provable signature.'

'So Johnson never loses?' said Parnell in desperate cynicism.

'And it doesn't look as if he's going to this time,' said Pullinger.

'Grant's explanation about surveillance is total bullshit,' decided the other lawyer. 'What did the detective agency say?'

'They didn't know they were being engaged by Dubette. They identified Johnson from a photograph Dingley and Benton showed them . . .' Pullinger looked directly at Parnell. 'Their brief was to watch your apartment and photograph anyone you left or entered with. If anyone entered, they had to time their departure, discover who the person was and where they lived.'

'Who'd the photographs go to?'

'They had a cellphone number, listed under a phoney name. They called it and Johnson came immediately to pick up what they had.'

'You got copies?' asked Jackson.

Pullinger looked at Parnell again. 'Yes.'

'What – who – do they show?'

'It's a little . . .' started Pullinger, awkwardly.

'Beverley,' anticipated Parnell. 'There would have been some photographs of Beverley.'

'It's not a secret, Ed,' dismissed Jackson. 'What about others?'

'There aren't any others,' said Pullinger. 'And surveillance has been pulled off.'

'They were supposed to be looking for people stalking Richard, not Richard himself. Or who went into his apartment,' said Jackson. 'Grant lied, like Johnson lied.'

'Yes,' agreed Pullinger, as immediately as before. 'But about what? Lying to the FBI isn't a crime in itself. If it was, the entire state of Texas would be concreted over, for one great big federal penitentiary.'

'I can't believe this!' protested Parnell. 'I can't believe you can do nothing, about all that's happened . . . a murder, for Christ's sake! Barry only saved me by . . . by . . .'

'A good memory, not a fluke,' completed the lawyer, unoffended. To Pullinger he said: 'If you've got to accept Johnson's explanation about the flight number, there's no cause any more for FBI involvement.'

'No, not unless there's any evidence of conspiracy across State borders.'

'Which you haven't got,' said Jackson. 'Who takes over the murder enquiry? It can't be Metro DC. I'm suing the two arresting officers. The entire department could come under investigation again, just like in 1996.'

'I can't work it out, and I'm glad it's the Attorney General's headache, not mine,' said Pullinger.

'Wait a minute!' demanded Parnell. 'The Bureau, with all its facilities and expertise, are at a dead end, and it could easily be ruled it's no longer an FBI investigation anyway. The police department who would normally be responsible are disqualified. You can't guess – and the Attorney General hasn't decided – who should take over. Is that it?'

'That's it,' accepted Pullinger. 'But we haven't been ruled out yet.'

'You going to disclose the flight-number explanation to the Department of Homeland Security and the Attorney General?' asked Jackson.

'We're mandated to do so,' said Pullinger. 'Can you imagine what the Bureau would be hit with if it was announced it was withdrawing from an investigation that's got as much media attention as this has, in which it had no need to be in the first place? We'd be ankle-deep in blood.'

'No one's going to be caught, for Rebecca's murder, are they?' said Parnell, weak-voiced in acceptance at what he was being told. 'No one's ever going to know why Rebecca was murdered . . . by whom . . . they're going to get away with it. Whoever killed Rebecca and tried to get me convicted of it are going to get away, Scot free.'

'I said we hadn't been taken off the enquiry yet. The thinking at the Hoover building at the moment is that it's better to take the heat we are getting for not making any progress than use Johnson's flight-number explanation as a way of getting out.'

'What are you more worried about – concerned with! Justice? Or saving the fucking FBI any more embarrassment?' exploded Parnell.

'Both, equally,' said Pullinger, calmly. 'If we could get the first, we'd achieve the second. I've just tried to explain the difficulties.'

'We appreciate it,' thanked the more controlled Jackson.

'You got any hearing date? Preliminaries, even?' asked Pullinger.

Jackson didn't immediately reply, looking steadily at the other lawyer, before saying: 'We're getting close to disclosures.'

'Obviously nothing that I've told you today can be included,' said Pullinger.

'Obviously,' acknowledged Jackson. 'Have you ever heard of investigating FBI officers being called as supplementary witnesses, after the emergence of evidence unknown at the time of disclosure?'

'Don't think I ever have,' admitted Pullinger.

'Anything in the FBI charter that would preclude it?'

'I'd need to check, but nothing comes immediately to mind.'

'It was good of you to come, Ed – fill us in on a few things,' thanked Jackson again. 'I'd welcome your letting us know if your guys get officially withdrawn.'

'You'll know the moment I know,' promised the FBI attorney. To Parnell he said: 'I'm sorry it's worked out like this.'

'Not as sorry as I am,' said Parnell.

'You sure there's no way the FBI could have intercepted the call?' demanded Edward Grant.

Johnson smiled, enjoying the other man's rarely betrayed worry. 'I gave Clarkson the call-box number in an envelope sealed in a way that could be recognized if you knew how. Which he didn't. He gave it to Pete Bellamy's dyke lawyer, to pass on unopened. When I rang Pete from my call box, I told him how to recognize the seal. It hadn't been broken.'

'What if one of the lawyers tells the Bureau?'

'Lawyer-client confidentiality,' replied Johnson, easily.

Grant smiled, relieved. 'That's good. You're good.'

'That's what you employ me – and pay me – to be.'

'You'll find out how grateful I am when this is all over.'

'Which it will be,' promised Johnson. 'Baldwin filled me in on your meeting and Pete says he and Helen haven't given anything away – nothing that helps any case against us, anyway . . .' The hesitation was for effect. 'There's still the civil case against them, of course. If they lose that, it could cost them their jobs.'

'You got another call-box to call-box arrangement?'

'In a couple of days. I told Pete I was coming up to see you.'

'Tell him – and get him to tell the woman – they'll be well looked after.'

'They'll appreciate that,' said Johnson.

'You don't think there could be a problem with your coming up here?'

'What problem? I'm your head of security. The Bureau know we talk – that I come here sometimes. I flew up using my own name, came in the front door and used the public elevator. The curiosity would have been if I *hadn't* come up, after they came here.'

'I didn't like that, the FBI coming here . . . questioning me like they did.' The small man flicked at his deep-brown suit, as if dislodging some unwelcome speck.

And it's showing all over your sweaty face, thought the security chief. 'This hasn't been good. Too much was done with insufficient thought and insufficient discussion.'

'Baldwin told you what I said to them, about putting Parnell under surveillance?'

Johnson nodded. 'They haven't come back to me, to check it out . . .' Enjoying himself unsettling a man who so much enjoyed unsettling others, he added: 'Something else that didn't have sufficient thought or discussion.'

'They sprang it on me, for Christ's sake! You should have guessed they'd tap your phones!'

He should, Johnson supposed. 'I didn't think they'd go that far – believe they had enough to apply for the order. In the end there was no damage.'

'If they had enough for the order, perhaps they've got enough to charge you!' suggested Grant, in fresh alarm.

'With what, forgetfulness?' jeered Johnson. 'I've been through it every which way with Clarkson. They've got nothing.'

'What do we do now?'

'Just that. Nothing. We carry on doing our jobs and let their investigation run into the ground.' And from now on I'm king of the castle and you're a dirty old rascal, he thought. 'So stop worrying, Ed, OK?'

'OK,' said Grant, without objecting to the familiarity.

The love-making over, Parnell and Beverley lay side by side in the darkness of her apartment bedroom, hand in hand.

'You know what's creepy?' she said. 'It's learning that we were being watched – photographed – without knowing it. It's like being . . . being violated.'

'And I was supposed to be taking extra care, watching my own back all the time!'

'I'm sick to my stomach at the possibility of there being no prosecution for Rebecca's murder!'

'I'm even sicker.'

'What are you going to do, if there isn't a prosecution?'

'I haven't decided.'

'What about immediately? The vice-president offer? I thought you had to decide before the stockholders' meeting?'

'I told Grant today that I'll take it.'

Beverley was silent for several moments. 'I'm surprised.'

'I'm sure we're going the right way with a SARS vaccine. And I don't want to give up on avian flu, either.'

'I'm still surprised.'

'For surprised should I read disappointed?'

'Yes, after what the FBI lawyer told you,' she said, bluntly.

'We don't definitely know that there isn't going to be a prosecution. If there is, I have to be here. If I'm definitely told nothing's going to happen, I'll think some more about it.'

Beverley took her hand from his and turned away from him in the darkness.

Thirty-Six

'I knew you'd accept,' said Edward Grant.

'I needed to think,' said Parnell.

'Of course you did,' patronized Grant, at the penthouse window looking out over the financial heart of the world. 'And you came to the right decision.'

'I bought some shares, to qualify for the stockholders' meeting, before you invited me.'

'Then you bought in cheap. Got a good deal.'

'I hope it turns out that way.'

'The board have agreed the terms I offered you.' said Grant, turning back to a package on his desk. 'There's your new contract, setting out the salary and the stock options for your lawyer to look over. Ours already have. All you've got to do, if your guy agrees, is to sign it.'

'It's all happened very quickly.'

'We've only got one priority now – restoring confidence. Your name – your publicly being here – is important in beginning that process. And maintaining it.'

'You know I'll do what I can.'

'There's going to be a media release, to coincide with my announcement of your appointment. Not just here, world-wide.'

'I spoke to Wayne Denny, about Dwight,' said Parnell. 'Thought I might go out to see him. Wayne said he didn't think he was well enough.'

'He isn't,' said Grant, at once. 'Won't be, for a long time. I've got a lot to say about Dwight later.'

'That's good.'

'You've been through a hell of a time too, Dick. And come out well.'

'It's dragging on.'

'You really sure, about suing those two sons of bitches?'

'My lawyer thinks I've got a good case. I'm doing it on his advice.'

'I'm thinking about Dubette. All the publicity it'll stir up again.'

'I hadn't thought about it from that point of view.'

'Think about it over the next little while,' urged the president. 'You know what I'd like, for us all? I'd like an out-of-court settlement offer, a public apology from the Metro force, and for that to be the end of it, all forgotten in a week. It would go a long way towards the healing process, restoring the confidence I was talking about.'

Parnell shrugged. 'The offer would have to come from the other side.'

'Your attorney could suggest it to theirs. That's how these things are done. I'd really appreciate it – Dubette would really appreciate it.'

'I'll talk it through with him.'

'Tell him that's how you want it to be. He's working for you, remember.'

'OK.'

'Let me know how it goes.'

'OK.'

'That's how it'll be, from now on. You and I talking together. Direct.'

'I've got a lot to learn.'

'I wouldn't have offered you the position if I hadn't thought you could hack it.'

'I hope it doesn't cause any resentment at McLean.'

'You're the man there now. Complete control, my complete confidence. Whatever you need to do to establish yourself, do it. You want some words of real wisdom?'

'Please.'

'No one likes the man in charge, *because* he's the man in charge and everyone else thinks they can do his job better. Never worry about not being loved. Enjoy being disliked and proving them all wrong.'

'I'll remember that.'

'I thought about bringing you on stage, when I make the announcement. But I don't think that would be right.'

'I don't think so either,' agreed Parnell. 'Particularly not in the circumstances . . . Dwight, I mean.'

'But I've had a place kept, near the front. When I announce the appointment, I'd like you to stand up . . . be recognized. There'll be some media there.'

'Good job I'm not wearing the yellow sweater.' Parnell was, in fact, in a conservative blue, Ivy-League suit, the first he'd bought at Brooks Bros.

Grant's face clouded, then cleared as the recollection came. 'That's a long time ago. A misunderstanding. You're part of the family now.'

'Part of the family,' echoed Parnell.

'There's an invitation-only reception after the meeting. You're on the list, of course.'

'I'll see you there.'

'There are some people I'm looking forward to introducing you to.'

'I'm looking forward to meeting them,' said Parnell.

It was a stop-start journey up a traffic-clogged Sixth Avenue from Wall Street, but Parnell was still among the first to arrive. The acceptance had been enormous, because of the publicity and its effect upon the stock valuation of the company, and the ballroom had been taken over. Parnell shuffled forward in the queue, the formal admission ticket his stockholding allowed him in hand. As soon as his name was recognized he was escorted to a reserved aisle seat in the fourth row from the front. The noise increased as the room gradually filled behind him. Once, Parnell swivelled, trying to estimate how many people there would be, but gave up trying. There was a central aisle, against which he was sitting, with two passages on either side of the seated area. In each were already established men with cordless microphones for when the meeting was thrown open to questioning from the floor. One was directly in front of the temporary stage, beneath a podium. Parnell ignored the prepared reports awaiting him on his chair. He considered opening his contract package but decided against that, too. Three tiered rows of seats were set out on the stage and he guessed the rear two were for the members of the overseas subsidiary boards, almost immediately confirmed when the raised area began to be occupied and he recognized Henri Saby from the Washington seminar.

Edward C. Grant led the parent board on to the dais, looking expectantly out into the slowly silencing hall. He did not sit but strode at once to the podium-mounted microphone, his prepared speech – which was not among the already distributed papers – in hand. There was an abrupt blaze of camera and television lights and Parnell was instantly reminded of his court appearance and the midtown press conference.

Grant arranged his papers in front of him on the angled stand, but made no attempt to start, staring out into the room until it became totally quiet. When it did, he smiled and said: 'Good morning and thank you all for coming.'

He did not look down to his speech, appearing not to need it. Dubette had endured a turbulent year, due to circumstances beyond anyone's control. A respected and admired member of staff had been savagely murdered, another briefly wrongly accused, about neither of which he could comment, because of ongoing investigations and possibly impending court actions. The adverse publicity had severely affected stock value, which he understood to be the concern of everyone in the room. There was no need for that concern. Dubette, as an international pharmaceutical conglomerate, remained as strong as it had ever been, and he was confident it would recover its value in the coming year. As an indication of that confidence the dividend this year would be an increase of five per cent upon the last, the funds coming from their more than adequate reserves. There were to be important changes within Dubette. It was with great personal as well as professional regret that he had to announce the premature retirement, on health grounds, of Dwight Newton, who, as vice president responsible for research and development, had made an incalculable contribution to the commercial success of Dubette Inc. over the past twenty years. He was sure the meeting would join him in wishing Newton a speedy recovery and contented retirement.

Grant had spoken looking towards the rear of the room. Now he looked down directly to where he knew Parnell was sitting. 'At our annual meeting last year, I announced the intention of establishing a pharmacogenomics division. From media releases since that time, you will all be aware that Dubette were successful in recruiting the world-renowned English geneticist Professor Richard Parnell to head that division. It is with great pleasure, personal pride and expectation of an enormous contribution to the continuing success of Dubette that I today announce that Dwight Newton's position as head of research and development has been offered to Professor Parnell . . .' Grant stepped to the side of the podium, gesturing for Parnell to stand. '. . . whom I am introducing to you today . . .'

There was another glare of camera lights as Parnell dutifully stood but moved immediately to the waiting man with the cordless microphone standing directly beneath Grant. Turning back into the packed hall as he snatched the microphone from the startled man, Parnell said: 'Offered as a bribe for my not making public the fact that Dubette is knowingly inflicting harm, in some cases killing, hundreds of people by not recalling badly manufactured medicines . . .'

'Stop him . . . get the microphone . . . !' said Grant, from behind, not realizing that he was still away from his own sound equipment and that the shout only reached the first few rows.

Parnell was conscious of someone running from behind, and thrust instinctively backwards, pushing away the man

342

whose microphone he'd snatched, retreating deeper into the room as he did so, the live mike clutched in his other hand.

'Stop him . . . get the microphone . . .' said Grant again, back at the podium, his now hysterical voice amplified.

'Do you want me stopped or do you want the truth?' demanded Parnell, warding off the scrabbling attendant again.

There was a moment of silence and then a groundswell of noise began, inaudible at first but forming into a recognizable chant of, 'Let him speak, let him speak.'

And Parnell did.

Thirty-Seven

Richard Parnell did not return to Washington DC for a further three days, because of the immediate and unpredicted effect – which the *New York Post* awarded the macabre headline, Fall Out – of his denunciation and the aftermath of a continuing, back-to-back series of meetings and interviews with US Food and Drug Administration officials and their French counterparts, specially flown-in French intelligence officers, officials from five West African countries at the United Nations, World Health Organization executives, the familiar FBI duo and Barry Jackson. Jackson demanded to know why the fuck Parnell hadn't told him what he intended to do, to which Parnell replied that the lawyer would have tried to prevent it on grounds of libel, commercial slander and breach of confidentiality, which Jackson at once agreed was exactly what he would have done, an admission that ended the argument. Parnell maintained telephone contact with the executive vice president administering Dubette's affairs from New York, and briefly with Beverley – and even more briefly with his mother in England – but it was a full two weeks before he and Beverley were alone together, at her insistence, at her Dupont Circle apartment.

When he arrived she gestured him away from her and

said: 'I want to make sure you're the same guy I used to know.'

'I'm not sure I'm the same guy that I used to know.'

'"Hero's" been used a lot. Then there's "brave" and "courageous" and "whistle-blower extraordinary" – and I've even cut out "genius" from *Newsweek*. Take your choice.'

'I think I'll pass on the lot. Christ, I've missed you.'

'I've missed you, too. And been as worried as hell.'

'It'll take time, for things to settle. But they are settling.'

'Why didn't you tell me? Why did you let me think you were a lily-livered shit who'd sold himself out?'

'I wasn't sure I could do it. Didn't know until I actually got into the room that there was going to be a microphone I could grab. I was going to try to get on the stage. Grant could have stopped me then, prevented it all coming out.'

'How did you know he hadn't kept his word about issuing the health warning about the French shit?'

'With what you called my toy. From home, on the laptop, I accessed the United Nations and the World Health Organization and the public websites of every West African country on the map. There wasn't a warning on one of them. And if there had been, it would have been a media sensation anyway. And there wasn't one. The son of a bitch – and all the other smaller sons of bitches – thought they were God and little people didn't matter. Me included among the little people.'

'The papers and television said he ran.'

'There was incredible confusion. He didn't actually run but he got out of the room before I finished talking. Couldn't be found in the hotel. No one expected him to commit suicide, of course. Me least of all.'

'Would you have still done it, if you had?'

'I've had meetings with government people from Guinea-Bissau, Monrovia, Sierra Leone, Ghana and Niger. With more scheduled. There's never going to be an established figure, but a conservative estimate is that over a thousand people have died. It'll be even harder to put a number on those who've been permanently harmed. Of course, I would have done it. Pushed the bastard out of his penthouse window, from which he jumped, if I could have done.'

'It was his favourite view, according to what I've read. Stood there all the time.'

'When he wasn't fucking up people's lives. Prying into people's lives.'

'Do you know the full extent of what he had, on so many people?' asked Beverley.

Parnell shook his head, in disbelief. 'There was actually an entire room, linked to his office, to hold it all. The FBI are still going through it. They've already found most of the computer-accessed stuff Johnson supplied when he was in Metro DC police. Seems he used police authority to get into every competitor system, particularly any police records on any of its executives. And there's the entire stolen evidence of Edward Grant being caught in a parked car getting a blow job from a hooker. Johnson's plea bargaining, says he's got a lot to tell the Bureau. Bellamy and Montgomery are trying for a deal, too. And Metro DC want an out of court settlement for wrongful arrest – seems the idea was to discredit me, get me thrown out of the country. Barry actually warned me it could have happened, if I'd been convicted.'

'I need to ask it,' declared the woman.

'You don't,' anticipated Parnell. 'All three deny knowing anything about Rebecca's murder. Or who did it. Johnson's got some story about a truck stop in New Jersey that the Bureau are trying to check out.'

'So, we'll never know?'

'Whatever, whoever, Grant organized it. And he's dead.'

'Is that enough?'

'It's got to be.'

'What about you?'

'Would you believe the emergency board have asked me still to be vice president in charge of research and development! The stock is trading at little more than pennies and obviously they want to use the appointment for all its publicity value. But, having caused so much damage, I figure I should try to repair some of it. And I meant what I said about believing we're close, with SARS. And not wanting to give up on the flu research.'

'I was frightened Dubette might have invoked the confidentiality clause.'

'And get even worse publicity? They wouldn't have dared, once I'd got it all out.'

'Seems like some of the media descriptions fit.'

'There are some changes I want to make. I don't see any reason to keep Barbara Spacey. Or Russell Benn.'

'There's some coverage of the woman's special assessments, for Grant.'

'He had what amounted to a manual for a blackmailer. Or a control freak. I guess he was a combination of both. You know what Barbara Spacey's real psychological assessment was of me? I was supremely arrogant, unlikely ever to adjust to the Dubette management and work system and someone likely to be a continuing unsettling influence at McLean.'

'Ain't that the truth!' said Beverley.

'When the FBI are through with all of it, I'm going to have every single assessment destroyed.'

'If you're going to take the job, you'll be staying?'

'If you'll have me.'

'That wasn't quite my question,' said Beverley.

'Answer mine.'

'If you'll have me.'

'You ever going to tell me what went wrong between you and Barry?'

'No. That's his business – his problem – not yours.'

'How do you know it won't happen with us?'

'We make love, don't we?'